HEARTLESS BOYS NEVER KISS

SJ SYLVIS

AUTHOR'S NOTE

Heartless Boys Never Kiss is a **complete standalone** in the St. Mary's series but it is recommended you read the rest of the series first to avoid any spoilers! Heartless Boys Never Kiss is a DARK boarding school romance intended for MATURE (18+) readers. This book is labeled as dark due to the dark themes (strong language, sexual scenes, and situations) throughout. Be aware that it contains TRIGGERS that some readers may find bothersome. Reader Discretion is advised.

For anyone who needs to heal.

HEARTLESS BOYS NEVER KISS

S.J. SYLVIS

PROLOGUE

4 YEARS ago

SLOANE

Rain trickled down the gutter, landing on top of the lush green bushes that I contemplated jumping into. I was stuck on the balcony of our sitting room, cursing the fact that my parents decided to come home early from their function. I brushed away the stray hair that had fallen from my low bun and continued rubbing the wing of the bird that had flown straight into the window, pulling me onto the balcony in the first place.

I pulled my phone out of my back pocket and quickly sent my best friend, Willow, a text.

Me: My parents came back as I was sneaking out, so I went onto the balcony. I'll be a minute, unless they stay. In that case, I'll have to jump and probably break my neck.

That wasn't completely true. I was technically already on the balcony because I had heard the bird fly into the door, but if there was anything genuine about me, it was my love for animals.

The faint breaking of a twig stole my attention away from my phone, and I went back to caring for the little bird. I sighed as it hobbled over to the iron rods, preparing itself to fly again. I hoped my parents wouldn't open the door and see me crouched down, encouraging a little bird to fly with a half-broken wing while wearing my tight-as-sin jeans and shirt that would make my dead grandmother rise from the grave.

Not only did my parents expect me to be the dutiful young woman that was plastered on the news and in newspapers, proclaiming me to be the sweet, loyal daughter of Mayor McCann, but so did the rest of the state. I was patted on the head so many times at galas and fundraising events that I half-expected to wake up barking like a dog one day.

"Beatrice, why don't you get us all some drinks?"

I shot my gaze to the balcony door, my brows furrowing with confusion. *My mother is fetching drinks? Where is Angelica?* My parents never gave the maid the night off, not even when they were out for the evening. The clacking of my mother's heels across the tiled floor pulled me away, and I looked back down to my phone, seeing Willow's name pop up.

Willow: I will speak at your funeral, don't worry.

I let out a light laugh, making sure to stay quiet. Willow and I had been inseparable since we were in grade school— our parents running in the same circles of politics. We'd been put in the same elite private school since fourth grade and had done all the same activities growing up. Although, Willow was better at tennis than me, we still stuck it out together, and when I decided to quit, she did, too. It was always Willow and me running off together when our parents had meetings and such. She had a half-brother, but he lived in France with his mother, so I had never even met him. It was hard to remember that Willow wasn't technically an only child, even though she was treated that way.

Willow had texted again as my mother's heels faintly clicked in the background through the balcony window.

Willow: Bently is asking where you are. I told him you were sneaking out. I swear I saw the excitement in his eyes at the thought of you being a little rule-breaker.

I smothered another laugh, hearing voices getting louder. The bird had finally gotten the courage to fly, and I did a silent clap when it didn't fall straight to the ground below. My parents *loathed* the fact that I loved animals and wanted to work with them one day, so it felt even better to be out on the balcony having just saved one. It was like a little *F you* to them. *'How does loving an animal relate to politics, Sloane? It doesn't. Grow up.'*

I sighed again but held my breath to strain my ear as I heard faint yelling. *Wait. Is that Willow's dad?*

Me: I'm still stranded on the balcony. It sounds like your parents are here, too. Distract Bently for me! Tonight might be the night...

Willow texted back seconds later.

Willow: Like THE night? Ugh, shit. I need to find someone to lose my V to, too. Who can I choose? Drake? He would gladly do the honors.

I gasped.

Me: NO. He would sleep with a pig and then brag about it after. Do not give it up to him.

My hand squeezed my phone tight as I heard my father's voice closer to the balcony door. A rush of heat swept over me as I detected the quiet anger lingering in his words. My father wasn't an irrational man. He wasn't a man who yelled or lashed out. His anger was the looming type. The kind that festered in the back of his mind until he could come up with a way to deal with it. That was why he was elected mayor so easily. He could be ruthless when needed but also sophisticated and professional. I'd once overheard a conversation between two politicians that he was unhinged in ways that could easily be misconstrued as sly. An autocrat disguised as a man with a charming smile and perfect little family. That was why he was going to climb to the top one day—at least, according to my mother.

"We know, Benedict." I slipped my phone into my back pocket and moved closer to the balcony door veiled by the sheer curtains that hung on the inside. The clanking of ice against a tumbler was quiet between my father's calm and slightly terrifying voice. "We know that you know, and we know what you're planning on doing with the information."

"What? What is he talking about, Ben?" That was Willow's mom, her usually light and airy tone brimmed with worry.

There was more clanking of ice, as if someone was swishing around their amber liquid in a glass. My heart began to gallop, and I had no idea why, other than the fact that, deep down, I was pretty sure something was going to happen that would affect my friendship with Willow. *No, nothing could come between us. Not even our families.*

"How'd you find out?" Willow's dad was close to the balcony door—so close I swore I could hear him breathing.

"You think I don't have ties in the government, Benedict? Come on, I thought you knew me better than that. After all, I am running for governor."

There was a sharp laugh that echoed in the foyer. "It suits you, Derek. You're just as corrupt as everyone else who is in office."

"Oh, please." My mother laughed, and my shoulders bunched. *What the hell is going on?* My phone vibrated again, and I knew it was Willow, but I chose to ignore it as I was too invested in what was likely going to determine the rest of our friendship.

"What's going on?" There was an edge to every word that flew out of Willow's mother's mouth. "Benedict?"

"Derek has turned into someone I no longer recognize. That's what's going on." Footsteps sounded, and there was silence for a few seconds before Benedict spoke again. "They've been working with *different* fixers. Ones who are not like us, who are morally just. They're slowly taking everyone off the map that could threaten their *plans*."

"Their plans? What plans?"

"To rule the state, to climb to the top of the fucking corrupted office." Benedict scoffed loud enough for me to hear it even over the pounding of my heart and the light classical music that was *always* present in the background of this house. A slight gust of wind blew around me. "You'll fit right in. Tell me, Derek. How many?"

"How many what?"

"How many people have you killed to secure your spot? How many deals have you made to protect relationships in the office? You'll surely be elected governor now, yeah?"

"You sound jealous."

"Jealous that you kill people for sport? Derek, what are you doing? This wasn't part of the plan. This was never part of the plan."

Wait, what? Kill people?

"The plan cannot move forward unless certain people are taken care of. I will never become more than what I am now if I don't take out those who are amoral and against everything this government stands for."

"Amoral?" Benedict yelled, and I jumped, hitting my head off the side of the house. My shaky hand slapped over my mouth, and I was thankful when I heard Benedict again, knowing that no one had heard me. "You're the fucking amoral one! You're killing people!"

"Correction." My father was calm and collected, yet I was shaking. "I do not kill people."

"No, you just hire others to do it."

My mother stepped in, and I could tell by the very first word that she was trying to alleviate the tension. "Benedict, it's not like the government doesn't know. They have private, black-market agencies that handle these types of things. You are the type of political fixer that the world needs to see, that the press can deal with. The others are... well..."

"So that makes it okay, Beatrice? Tell me, what would you say if Sloane knew what you two were up to? Would you look her in the eye right now and tell her it's okay to take an innocent life just so you can rise to the top? Would you tell her it's okay because *the government already knows?* The government has fixers for PR problems, yes. But killing people?"

"This is futile." There was a pause, and the only thing I could hear was my heavy breathing. My mind was going as fast as a train, hitting every last bump along the tracks. "Just be done with it, Derek."

"Just be done with it?"

There was a slight pause, and then the door to the sitting room swung open. I knew it because of the heavy sound of the lock hitting the thick wood—it carried all the way to the balcony. I tried to get a glimpse of what was going on, but the curtain was a cloak to me *and* what was going on inside. A cold chill flew through the air as silence filled the space. A moment later, I leaned against the iron rod, hoping it would hold me up.

"You're going to stoop this low, Derek?" There was no longer anger and resentment following closely behind Willow's father's words. Instead, there was defeat there, as if he knew what was coming, and he knew there was no way out.

"I know you won't believe it, but I am sorry. You can no longer be trusted in this incorporation."

"Der—"

There was a faint clicking sound that traveled through the open air around me, and then it felt as if a hand was locked on the top of my head, pushing me into ice-cold water and keeping me there to drown. Something heavy had landed on the floor, the thud traveling all the way through the cracks of the balcony door. Then came Willow's mom's shrill shriek, and the same faint clicking noise, and another heavy thud.

Oh my God. Oh my God. Oh my God.

My phone vibrated in my back pocket, and it was then that my entire body grew hot. A bead of sweat tickled my back as it fell to the edge of my jeans, and there was a split right down the center of my chest.

It was too terrible to be real. These things didn't happen. My head shook back and forth so quickly that my hair fell all the way out of my bun. The pulsing in my fingers itched my hands, and needles pricked the back of my neck.

No.

How could I ever look Willow in the eye again? Did my parents just kill hers? *Are...are my parents killers?*

My stomach charged with nausea as I took a step forward and gripped the door handle. Another gust of wind wafted around me, and that was when I realized there were tears covering my cheeks.

This wasn't real.

They were alive. My parents knocked them out so they could have a calmer conversation with them when they woke up. People didn't just *kill* their best friends. That wasn't a thing.

My hand shook against the doorknob, and when I flung

the door open and rushed into the sitting area, I stared directly at my parents, who were huddled together, talking. There was a sudden cloud of surprise painted along their faces, their expressions forever embedded into my brain.

"How could you?!" I screamed, startling myself with how loud I was. My head turned as I heard the door open again, and my feet quickly propelled me to chase after the dark figure that had slipped a gun into the back of his pants before disappearing through the opening. "You...you...killer!' I yelled again, too afraid to look at Willow's parents. I knew they were there. The smell of metal floated underneath my nose, and my stomach dropped down to the red-stained floor.

"Sloane, no!" My father's strong hands were around my waist, and I wanted *nothing* to do with his touch. I gasped, trying to claw toward the door to...what? Chase after someone with a gun?

"I hate you!" I screamed, spinning around in my father's grip and staring into his fearful eyes. *I see you. I see you now.* "I hate you so much! I hate you both!" I scrambled to my feet and backed myself up against the door, trying to get as far away from them as I possibly could. My mother's jaw was still slacked, face pale even with a pound of blush on the arches of her cheeks. "I will tell everyone what you did!"

Willow. Willow and I would just run away. Yes, that was what we would do. We would run away together and make it work. Her half-brother would help us. We could go to France, and get jobs...and...and—

My father's shadow came over me, and I refused to look up at him. My chest was rising as if I had just played a game of tennis with Willow, chasing after every last stupid ball. "You won't tell anyone, Sloane. Not if you want to keep your best friend alive."

The second I heard his words was the moment I knew

that my friendship was over with Willow and that my future would never look the same again.

"I hate you," I whispered, sinking down to land on my butt. The pain in my chest was nothing compared to looking at my best friend's parents as they lay in a pool of their own blood. I shut my eyes, salty tears falling over my cheeks, as I tried to keep my stomach steady. My heart hurt, the pain so tangible I was afraid it was bleeding right there along with the two lifeless bodies at my feet.

CHAPTER ONE

TOBIAS

I WAS COVERED IN SWEAT. A bead of salty moisture rolled down my chest and in between my abs, landing right above my boxers. My hands dug into my dark hair, the strands damp between my fingers.

Damn, again?

There was anger feasting on my nightmares like a hungry rat in an abandoned alleyway, digging for the smallest scrap of food. Anger wasn't privy to me, but each morning, I woke with another nightmare, as if I were a child afraid of the metaphorical monster underneath my bed. It infuriated me beyond belief.

It wasn't as if I was new to monsters. In fact, most would say I was one.

I'd been kept underground in an elusive, dark breeding area for most of my childhood, beaten by men who were worse than what you thought lived in your closet on Halloween night as a child. I was starved, *brainwashed*—even though I hated admitting that last one—and yet, here I was, eighteen years old, having nightmares in my room, alone, covered in fucking sweat.

"Fuck," I mumbled, sitting up in my bed. I glanced around my new room at St. Mary's Boarding School, having zero emotion besides the fact that I was closer to Gemma, my twin sister. She was one hall over, and this was the closest we'd been, physically, in years. There was a single nerve ending that prickled inside my chest when I thought of her, but that was it. Journey was here, too, and I guess you could say that I felt a little better with her being closer again, considering for the last six months, we'd spent many darkened nights together underneath the Covenant Psychiatric Hospital's main floor, coming up with a way to leave that shitty fucking place behind.

Journey had been a patient at the hospital, driven mad by the fact that she was placed there under false pretenses, and I had been a member of the lowest floor, the one that was hidden from all—against my will. I was just as angry as she was. Together, we made it out alive, but to say we were unscathed would be a bald-faced lie.

Looking in the mirror, my jaw flexed as I fiddled with the tie that my *father*—Headmaster Ellison—taught me to knot the evening before. Tate was the father I'd always hoped for, but now that I had him, nothing but indecisiveness came with every conversation we shared.

Who even was Tate Ellison? Fuck, who was I?

It was a bitter feeling to look in the mirror, even dressed in a new, prestigious, boarding-school uniform with a tie hanging from your neck, making you seem less tainted than you truly were. All the boys at this school held secrets and sin beneath their pressed uniforms, so I knew I would fit right in.

The last several years of my life had done nothing but taken my thoughts and twisted them like an old, wet rag and allowed them to drip to the floor and disappear indefinitely. My sister was worried. My father was hesitant. And the girls in this school saw me as the damaged, bad boy with the thin scar on his eyebrow that they *knew* could give them a thrill.

And me? I saw myself as nothing.

Nothing but a monster.

When I stepped into the hallway, it was mostly quiet. The red carpet beneath my feet made my stomach shrink as it looked every bit the same color as blood, which seemed to permanently cover my hands anytime I closed my eyes.

Red. Red. Red.

Gone were the days of looking at ketchup as a side for my food.

The girls' hall was loud as hell, chatty conversations and high-pitched squeals. The occasional hiss of some hair product caught my ear as I jogged down the steps, keeping my face even and my stride easy.

"What's up, man?" I paused for a single second, tipping my head at Shiner, one of the guys who seemed to command the student hierarchy of this school. It seemed frivolous and unimportant to have power over a group of students that was pathetically centered on academics and gossip that ran through the halls like a fucking sandstorm, but who was I to judge? Maybe if I hadn't been thrown into a basement for years and brainwashed to bow to those who commanded me in the way that the Rebels commanded the students of this school, I'd be the same.

Shiner continued walking past me to catch up to a girl in a short skirt, her long legs catching my attention for a brief second before I realized that it wasn't who I thought it was.

Students whizzed behind me, and although this wasn't my first day attending St. Mary's, it felt like it was all over again.

There were no nerves, but there were reservations that hinted along the lines of anger and skepticism. I leaned back on my shoes, placing my hands in my pockets, and tipped my head up to look at the expansive ceiling of golden figures of famous people that I knew absolutely nothing about.

I had gotten some form of an education at the Covens, but it was all your basic shit, not the kind of education you needed to succeed at a school like St. Mary's—not unless you counted learning several ways of offing a person without being caught. In that case, I could give Einstein a run for his money.

"Tobias." My newly discovered father poked his head out of his office. "Good, you're here. Come on in."

I shuffled the rest of the way down the hall, the sounds of the dining hall disappearing at my back. I followed the man that I shared DNA with, realizing that I got my height and broad shoulders from him.

He was disheveled, in an overworked, exhausted way, whereas I was lazily put together because I didn't give many fucks—a product of my upbringing, I was sure.

"Now, listen, for just a second." My father turned around with worry lines carved into his forehead. "I need you to know that I am on your side, okay? Always."

What the fuck does that mean?

"Alright..." I said, raising an eyebrow.

"But the SMC kind of has my hands tied at this point." He rubbed a hand over the back of his neck, likely working out the kinks that I also had the pleasure of having. "Too much stuff has happened. With your sister, and Journey..."

"I'm tracking," I confirmed, sitting in the chair in front of his desk as he rounded the heavy piece of wood.

"You failed your entrance exam."

My face stayed calm and steady, but it wasn't to be a dick, even if that was always my go-to. It was because I wasn't sure what that meant.

My father pinched the bridge of his nose. "That means

you aren't at the level you should be, and given the fact that you've been kept..." He shook his head with unfinished words trapped inside his mouth. "I've made a counter-offer to the SMC. If they allow you to have a tutor—"

"A tutor?" I interrupted. *You've got to be fucking kidding me.*

"Well..." He choked down some air, and I couldn't read him as well as I could read others. Was he afraid to tell me more? Angry for some reason? Both? "More like an aide. I know you had some education at the Covens, but it's just not up to par with St. Mary's."

"What does that mean?" I asked, voice still lazy and unbothered, even though I was annoyed beyond fucking belief. *You bring me into this school, and now I have to have an aide?*

"I've arranged for you to take all the same classes as another student so they are able to help you if you're stuck, need some extra help, are confused..."

"You make it sound like I'm a fucking idiot." I ground my teeth, knuckles white as I gripped onto the arm rails of the chair. *Am I an idiot?* I was smart but probably not in the way that most eighteen-year-olds were in their senior year of high school.

My father's green eyes—the same damn green eyes that he shared with my sister—widened, and there was a truth burning inside that I could see clearly. "You are not an idiot, Tobias. You just haven't had the education over the last several years that St. Mary's demands."

I laughed, a sarcastic, throaty chuckle floating from my mouth. "Would have been a little difficult to teach me algebra while I was sent to kill people, huh?"

It wasn't funny.

I knew it wasn't.

And by the look on my father's face—the pure torment and guilt—I should have felt bad, but I didn't because I was me, and emotions did not exist.

His mouth opened, and then he shut it again. There was a faint grinding noise, and I knew he was wiggling his teeth back and forth, just like I did when I felt the anger brewing, too.

"So, what," I started, huffing, "I'll have an aide, then? Someone to follow me around like a babysitter?"

"She isn't a babysitter, Tobias." His face softened, and he looked like he felt bad for me, and he probably did. If he knew everything that I truly went through and had to do, he would likely just lock me back up in the psych ward—if it hadn't been shut down and burnt to a crisp.

I replayed his words for a moment and sliced my narrowed eyes to him. "She?"

As soon the word left my mouth, a knock on the door came next, and in some strange and unexplained way, I knew who my new aide was without even looking back.

Sloane.

Sloane *fucking* White.

CHAPTER TWO

SLOANE

My phone was burning a hole in my palm as I held it tightly in my hand, irritated that my mother had called more than five times this morning.

Sure, it was three hours later in New York, so she had been up and likely chugged three espressos and already attended her hot yoga class with a male instructor half her age who she desperately tried to get to pay attention to her, but *still*. Each year, on this exact date, she did this. Called me over and over again to *check in,* but really, it was to make sure she could remind me to keep my mouth shut and to not reach out to Willow.

The guilt was always there when I thought of Willow, and it was tenfold on the date of her parents' deaths. My nostrils flared as I stood outside of Headmaster Ellison's office, trying to reel my thoughts in from that night that crept around the hidden cracks of my intentional walls, seeping in when I least expected.

The lies were difficult to keep straight, which was why I

avoided the spotlight most of the time. It honestly wasn't hard, considering both of my best friends had their own shit to deal with. There wasn't much room for my baggage when theirs was just as heavy, if not heavier.

My phone began buzzing again as I raised my hand to knock on the headmaster's office door, and the vibrating coursed down my spine and into my legs. *Why am I nervous?*

I couldn't remember the last time I'd had butterflies in my stomach at St. Mary's Boarding School. The first day I began attending? Sure. The time I lost my virginity to one of the seniors during a claiming party? Definitely.

But now that I was a senior, accepting my status in the school, comfortable in my short skirt and maroon blazer, I hadn't been nervous in years.

Except for right now.

My tender knuckles rapped against the hardwood as I silenced my phone once more, and took a step into the warm office of Headmaster Ellison, my best friend's father.

My gaze briefly paused on a head of inky hair sitting in the chair in front of the desk before I forced a smile at the headmaster.

"Good morning, Sloane. Please come in and shut the door."

I jumped when the latch of the door clicked and was thankful that Tobias wasn't facing me. *Why the hell am I so nervous?* A hot slash of embarrassment blasted my cheeks as I crept closer to him, feeling an indescribable pull that I'd felt since the second I watched him step into the dining hall a week prior.

He made me nervous.

And I didn't like it.

I managed to force a, "Good morning," out of my mouth, keeping my attention on Headmaster Ellison instead of the slightly intimidating guy beside me. I was annoyed and infuriated with myself that I felt so unsteady around him. It wasn't often that I let a guy affect me, but *apparently,* I didn't have a choice when it came to him.

My phone rested in my lap as I crossed my legs, hooking the right over the left, with my shoulders straight and my silky dark hair laying over my shoulders. *Play it cool, Sloane.*

"This is your new aide, Tobias. Her name is Sl—"

"Sloane White." Tobias' smooth, rich voice commanded the room, and I bit down on my tongue, tasting the blood almost immediately. My chest began to heave as I leveled my chin, avoiding him completely. *Play. It. Cool.*

Was this a mistake? Should I have told Headmaster Ellison no when he'd asked this favor of me?

Gemma's soft and pleading eyes full of relief moved in front of me like a movie playing on the big screen. There was no way I could have said no. And then to pair that with Headmaster Ellison's sincere request, nearly begging me to do this because 'he knew I'd understand', considering I was aware of Gemma and Tobias' upbringing and wasn't as fazed by it as most students would be. How could I deny them? Friendship meant more to me than anything else. I was doing this for Gemma. Plus, it was *just* a guy. A normal guy with a wicked past. I should have understood that more than anyone.

"Yes," the headmaster's voice broke me out of my argument that held absolutely no weight because there was no going back now. I'd already agreed, and Gemma had pulled my hands into hers and thanked me for being such a good friend and helping her brother so he could stay at St. Mary's with her. "Sloane White. Have you already met? That makes sense. She is your sister's roommate."

"No," I answered quickly. Tobias and I hadn't said a single word to each other. The most we had shared was a long, intimidating look that he gave me the day he stepped foot into the dining hall. It chilled me to the bone but left a trail of heat behind, like a fever. I could still feel it. It was like the heat radiated off his body and wafted over to mine.

"Nope." The P sound popped from Tobias' lips, and that was when I peeked over at him. My grip on my phone tightened, and a breath got lodged in my throat as I locked onto his sharp, dangerous features.

Eyes blue as the sea, depths of aqua and navy filled to the top with something quietly heavy. Cut cheek bones, a tiny scar gracing his eyebrow, making him appear wild and appealing all in one. My stomach did a flip, and I cursed myself. *Shit, stop being so stupid.* "Hi," I said, voice croaking like a frog. *Oh my God, what the fuck.*

He snickered before running his large hand through his rich hair. He *actually* snickered under his breath, and my cheeks flamed for the second time in ten seconds.

This motherfu—

"This is stupid." Tobias' long legs stretched out in front of him as I clenched mine together. I was embarrassed and frustrated that he had such an effect on me, and part of me wanted to throw my phone at his head for making me feel two things I hadn't felt with another guy in what seemed like...ever.

The boys at St. Mary's got old after a while. I'd been attending this school since the day my parents decided to ship me off halfway across the United States so they could be sure that I wouldn't ruin '*all their hard work*'. And to be honest, I'd grown bored.

I didn't fight it when they said I was moving to Washington, three years ago, without them. In fact, I stayed silent for days after I had found Willow's parents murdered in cold blood. The frozen look on my mother's face when I had walked in from that balcony that night was the last time I looked her in the eye.

That didn't stop her from calling me every five seconds, though.

I silenced the vibrating again as the headmaster cleared his throat, pulling his attention from my phone back to his son.

"Tobias, this is not a big deal. No one even has to know that she's your aide."

Tobias laughed, a throaty chuckle rubbing over my skin as if he were crowding my space instead of sitting three feet away from me in his own chair. "No one has to know? She'll be following me around like a little lost puppy. I don't need an aide. So what? I failed the fucking entrance exam. That doesn't mean anything."

Headmaster Ellison pinched the bridge of his nose as I sat quietly beside Tobias, swimming in my annoyance from his backlash of me being his aide and the fact that I felt too many uncalled-for emotions in my lower belly regarding his presence. Part of me hoped that Headmaster Ellison would take into consideration that maybe Tobias didn't really need an aide, but nonetheless...

"I won't be following you around," I interjected, hearing the annoyance that I was trying to hide creeping through the empty spaces in between my words. "I'll just be there if you need anything, like if you have a question or need help with homework."

"And studying," Headmaster Ellison said, throwing his hands up in the most exasperated way I'd ever seen. "Tobias, this isn't negotiable. If you want to stay at St. Mary's, this is the deal. This isn't coming from me. This is coming from the SMC. They're aware that you've failed. If you agree to an aide and use Sloane to help you through some of the workload that you are not used to, then they're fine with you staying here. Given you have no educational background that is documented, I'm pulling all my strings for you."

"No one asked you to do that," Tobias bit back, exuding a large dose of confidence.

This boy is a whole new breed.

"Your sister did," I whispered, looking away.

Silence filled the office, and the only thing that did was make my heart beat harder. The thumping hurt my chest, the small muscle tucked behind my ribs, bouncing off it like it were a trampoline instead of hard bones.

I swore that several minutes had passed before we were broken out of our thoughts. My phone vibrated again, and I forcefully declined the call, ready to chuck the device across the room at the bookshelves lining the headmaster's office.

"Fine." Tobias shot up from the chair, and I craned my head up to see his looming height towering over the headmaster's desk. He quickly spun around, taking his unnerving presence with him, and walked out of the headmaster's office, letting the door swing open to hit the bookshelf with force.

The headmaster sighed loudly, and it was obvious he was completely defeated. I shot him a tender smile and shrugged. "He'll come around." I paused. "If not for himself or you, then for Gemma."

Headmaster Ellison's eyes crinkled with hope. His smile was warm and inviting, and for a brief second, I wished he was my dad, too. Gemma and Tobias deserved a dad like Headmaster Ellison, given the fact that they had been raised by their psychotic uncle who was now locked away in prison, but it made my situation sting that much more.

Everyone thought my parents were war heroes—*literally.* The story was that they were military members who deployed so often they decided to send me to St. Mary's so I was taken care of, but that couldn't have been further from the truth.

"I appreciate what you're doing for him, Sloane." Headmaster Ellison smiled again. "For me and Gemma. You're a good friend. I'm thankful that you took Gem under your wing months ago. She wouldn't be where she is without you."

I blinked away the moisture in my eyes, looking down and forcing a smile on my lips. *A good friend?* There was a knife in my back from his compliment. A good friend wouldn't completely fall off the face of the earth after her best friends' parents were murdered and disappear so quickly she couldn't even attend the funeral.

"Car crash. My parents got in a car crash, Sloane. They're gone. Please call me back. My brother is missing, too. I can't get ahold of him. The police can't find him."

I jumped in my seat when my phone started to vibrate again, and I quickly silenced it. Headmaster Ellison glanced down at the screen, and I hoped it went black before he saw that my mother was calling and how I ignored it.

"Okay, well..." he started, giving me an incredulous look, as if he were trying to figure me out. "If you could just make sure Tobias gets this..." He pulled out a piece of paper, and I grabbed it, realizing it was his new schedule that matched mine. "And maybe give me an update every once and a while? Let me know if you need anything or if he doesn't end up coming around?"

I smiled. "Sure. Don't worry, I can get the job done. He'll be fine."

Headmaster Ellison laughed. "I like your determination. That's part of the reason why I picked you."

I laughed under my breath as I stood up from the chair and began walking out of his office. It was nearing first period, breakfast almost over and done with. I quickly sent Gemma a text, pushing aside the missed call notifications and asked her to snag me a bagel that I could scarf down before Mrs. Porter even realized I'd brought food into her class.

Tobias' schedule crumpled in my hand as I walked farther down the silent hall, my boots quietly moving over the glossy black-and-white-tiled floor as I kept my head down and shoulders relaxed. Willow continued to creep in, just like she did every year on this day, but she quickly vanished when a strong hand clamped onto my arm and pulled me through a door.

The bright lights were the first thing I saw when I craned my head back, but then I was quickly met with two blue eyes and an angry browline. "What the fuck, Tobias?" I bit out, snatching my arm out of his strong grasp.

Tobias was tall. *Really* tall. My heart flipped as I took a step away and turned all the way around to peer up at him. His lip twitched as he pushed a dark strand of hair off his forehead. Without even meaning to, my eyes dipped down past his face, and I zeroed in on his neck, watching his pulse beat angrily behind his skin. His tie was looser than most of the guys', and a twisted part of me wanted to grab onto it and pull him in closer. *Why did I just picture that?*

Tobias was my best friend's brother and damaged beyond belief. The scowl on his face and cold glint in his eye told me I needed to stay the hell away from him. *Oh, but he's damaged, and you know how you like to save damaged things, Sloane.*

"There she is. The *real* Sloane."

I took a step back, putting much-needed distance in between us. Tobias rested against the sink, and that was when I realized we were in the girls' bathroom. Thankfully, no one was in here because everyone was at breakfast or still in their rooms, getting ready for the day.

"What does that mean?" I asked, gripping my phone tightly.

A coarse chuckle left his throat, and my mouth dried up. I swallowed, trying to ignore how my mouth was the equivalent of the desert. I wanted to peel my eyes away in the worst way, but that felt like a submission. The dark and dangerous boy standing mere feet away was challenging me, and he had me *all* wrong if he thought I'd back down from his brooding attitude and sharp glare. Sure, he was hot. Hotter than anyone in the school. Hotter than anyone at my last school—even Bently, the star of the football team. But he was my best friend's brother and had an untraditional upbringing—to put it mildly—so letting him intimidate me wasn't in the cards, and allowing his bad-boy persona to make my thighs clench wasn't either.

"You acted all serious and like a good girl in my father's office, pretending to do this..."—he wafted his large hand in between the empty space that separated us before placing it back on the sink behind him—"out of the goodness of your heart. But that's not true, is it?"

I pulled back, instantly offended. "Why else would I be doing it?" I crossed my arms over my chest, holding my phone so tightly I thought it might break. His schedule was in my other hand, and part of me wanted to rip it up and flush it down the toilet.

He laughed. His head swung backward, and his Adam's apple bobbed against his strong neck. "I've got a hunch that you're a little slut, like the rest of the girls here, and you're only doing this to get me in your pants."

My jaw dropped, and a gasp flew out, hitting him square in the face. I was stunned, unable to form words. *A little slut?* Who the hell did Tobias think he was? Best friend's brother or not, I was going to take my Doc Marten and stomp on his annoyingly large foot.

The vibrating in my hand caused me to snap out of my stupor and slam my lips shut. Words were slow to my mouth, but I was seconds from lashing out and putting Tobias in his place, but he quickly pushed off the sink and strode toward me with so much authority that a fine line of fear zipped through me. My back was against a stall door as his hand came up and locked it into place so I didn't fall backward.

His breath was minty as he peered down at me, my chin tipped so high that my head hit the stall door. "You can't help me, Snow White." My eyes flew to his lips, and I swallowed loudly, hating myself for making it seem like I *was* a slut trying to get him into my pants. That wasn't true at all.

I was doing this for Gemma.

I was trying to be a good friend because Lord knew I had room for improvement.

"So..." Tobias let go of the stall door, and I stumbled backward, holding my phone in one hand and his schedule in the other. "Don't even fucking try."

His dark browline evened out as he plucked his schedule from my hand. He scanned it quickly, and I jumped when his sharp gaze fell to my phone. It was vibrating—*again*—and before I could react, his hand swept over my skin, causing goosebumps to fly to my arms as he had the tiny device resting in his palm.

It was still vibrating when we locked eyes, and his smirk did something to me. My stomach fell to the floor, and it felt as if I were trapped in a box. I was banging on the sides, trying to get myself to do something other than stand there like an idiot. *Grab the phone back. Stomp on his foot. Tell him you're not a slut!*

I gasped again when his finger swiped over the screen, and I heard my mother's voice float into the empty bathroom.

"Stop ignoring your mom," he gritted. "At least you fucking have one."

I grunted as he pushed the phone into my chest and turned around, leaving me in the bathroom with my mother's voice breaking through the rushing of blood inside my ears.

CHAPTER THREE

TOBIAS

MY NECK ITCHED WITH IRRITATION. It was red and splotchy —I knew this without even looking. Sweat coated my hands, but I refused to wipe it on my pants. Mr. Cunningham's monotone voice did absolutely nothing to ease the throbbing of my temples, and last night's trip down memory lane—when I finally fell asleep—continued to scrape over every empty space inside my brain.

I glanced down to the pencil in my hand, hearing the wood split in between my tight grip, and half-expected it to morph into a gun right before my eyes. My heart thumped, and I breathed through my nose, vibrating with anger and anxiety. *What the fuck is wrong with me?*

I'd been through hell and back.

I'd been in some truly fucked-up situations.

I'd seen blood and knew the smell of it like a shark in the ocean.

But I couldn't sit in a classroom with other students my

age and pay attention to whatever the hell this pathetic man was going on about?

I swallowed, trying to rid myself of the fresh visual from my nightmare, and moved my gaze to the girl sitting beside me, giving all her attention to the front of the classroom.

Sloane.

It had been over a week since she started as my aide. I ignored her every chance I could. The only time I played nice was when Gemma was around, and that was because if I cared about anyone in the world, it was her. She was the only reason I was here at St. Mary's, but she didn't need me like I needed her.

It wasn't that way when we were younger. When we were young, Gemma needed me to be the strong twin. She was scared all the time. Richard, our fucked-up *uncle* who had custody of us, punished her in ways that were much different than the way he punished me. She knew she wasn't safe with him even from a young age. The only time she did feel safe was when we'd creep into each other's rooms before the morning light and share the space like it was our own personal safe haven. It wasn't, though. He still came for her, and he still punished her. He tried to corrupt her in the most manipulative way possible. And me? He didn't even attempt to manipulate me and make it seem like he cared. Richard hated me from the beginning, which was why I was sent away and treated like a tool.

We weren't blood related, even though he told everyone he was our uncle. If we had been blood related, would he have thrown me into the most aristocratic underground black market for worldwide killers? I think not.

I was just a pawn in his game, and my twin sister was his prize.

The snapping of my pencil made me pause, and Sloane's

fiery gaze whipped over to me within a flash. The spark that punched my chest only made me angrier. *How does she do that?*

"Pay attention!" she whisper-seethed, completely unfazed by my constant state of annoyance with her. I'd been ignoring her since the second I pushed her against a stall in the girls' bathroom. The feeling it gave me to have her in my grasp and at my mercy was unhealthy at best.

"Fuck off," I said back, not even bothering to lower my voice.

There was a faint snicker coming from my left, and Sloane's dark hair fell behind her shoulder as she leaned forward, shooting someone an even dirtier look than she was giving me.

"Something funny?" she asked, glaring.

There I was, in the middle of two girls fighting. Over what? I wasn't sure. Me, maybe?

"You're trying so hard, Sloane. I give ya props."

The girl beside me giggled again, pushing her strawberry-blonde hair behind her ear. She was no match to Sloane, but —*wait, what?* A burning fire of anger started to fester inside my chest again at the thought of thinking Sloane was attractive. Her sleek, dark hair and smooth, pale cheeks painted with a tinge of pink made her look like Snow White. All she needed was a little bird perched on her shoulder, and she could be thrown into a fucking fairy tale, which I had no business being in—unless, of course, I was the villain.

"She is trying so hard, right? But she's no match to you." My words fell effortlessly from my mouth, a trick I'd learned from being locked in a psych ward for years with nothing to do but seduce the female nurses and manipulate them, just like I was taught to do by Richard. I knew how to talk to a woman, and I knew how to make them fall to their knees for me, too.

What I didn't know how to do was deal with Sloane and the way she dug under my skin.

I hated her, but I didn't know why.

I wanted her eyes on me, but I wanted to scratch them out, too.

Fuck.

Mr. Cunningham began walking down the aisles of desks, handing out our graded tests from a few days ago. I spread my legs out long and pushed them under the desk in front of me. Sloane was now ignoring me, and the girl beside me was pretty much purring to get my attention.

She wasn't cute.

I wasn't into her.

Even if I was, I wouldn't subject her to *me*. Not a single girl here was going to get me to bend for them. I wasn't what they were used to, and I was done with the games I had played while locked away.

"Tobias." Mr. Cunningham laid my test face down on top of my desk. "Please look over your mistakes, and let me know if you have any questions. I wrote a note in the top corner for you."

Well, that sounded good.

I kept the piece of paper facedown, making no move to see my grade. Sloane was staring at me. I could have felt her from a mile away, so even more so from just a few feet. My nostrils flared as she grew closer, her perfume something I'd grown accustomed to in the last several days.

"Let me see."

"No," I snapped, crossing my arms over my chest and feeling my muscles flick with annoyance.

"Tobias, stop being such a fucking dick."

I laughed, a true sinister smile carving on my cheeks at her attitude. She was just as annoyed with me as I was with her. *Good, hate me.*

Her hazel eyes flared with something that I ran with. We were chock-full of determination, unwilling to look away from one another as chatter began to start up around us. "I told you to leave me alone, Sloane. I wasn't kidding."

She narrowed her eyes even further. "And I said no."

"You think one tiny little word coming from your mouth is going to change things? I don't want your help."

"Take a hint, Sloane."

I snapped my head to the girl that was now on my last fucking nerve. A feeling came over me that almost had my feet moving to the blackboard so I could punch the shit out of it. "That's enough from you."

The girl's mouth dropped, and she gasped with hurt. I gave her a look that I hoped made her feel stupid and put my attention back on Sloane, who was still glaring at me with those hazel eyes that I found myself diving straight into. "Again, I don't want your help."

Sloane's lips, the color of raspberries, flattened in defeat. *Already tapping out?* A sense of disappointment went through me, and I felt like pouting, as if I were five again. But then, surprise took over as the bell rang, and she quickly shot up out of her seat, the lift of her skirt catching my attention and the snatching of my paper nearly going unnoticed.

Fuck.

"Tobias," she faltered, eyes widening at all the red on my paper. "You *need* my help."

Obviously.

I gritted my teeth, reaching down to take the paper out of her hand, but she was quick and put her back to me, showing off her shiny dark hair that I wanted to wrap around my hand and pull. I stood, unmoving, too concerned with the thoughts of wanting to push her to her knees like she was some rag doll instead of my twin sister's best friend, along with Journey's old roommate, who she had nothing but good things to say about.

Sloane packed up her things as I stood behind her, fuming with anger. Anger over what? Her taking my test? Making me feel things that I shouldn't have been feeling? Making me hate her because of those things? I was so fucked up, which, sadly, made me feel right at home.

"Give it to me now." The five little words skimmed through my teeth like I was in physical pain, and I was.

Sloane said nothing as she stormed out of the classroom, leaving me to follow her like I was on some sort of leash. *Absolutely not.* I didn't give a flying fuck if we were in a crowded hallway with everyone dismissing for the day. Who did Sloane White think she was?

My hand gripped her waist, and the tips of my fingers burned with heat. I spun her around, her plaid skirt flying around her smooth legs as I caged her against the wall, right beside a portrait of some president. "Give it back." My breath wafted in her face, and her small nostrils flared with the minty smell separating us. I was tempted to spit my gum out onto the hallway floor because she seemed like she enjoyed the scent.

"We need to study this weekend. Before next week's test."

My brows furrowed. "I am not fucking studying with you."

Why can't she just leave it be? Why isn't she intimidated by me?

Her hips bucked under my grip on her waist, and my dick twitched. *Jesus. No.* "You are if you want to stay at this school, Tobias. I'm supposed to be your aide and help you study, and that's what I'm going to do despite your bitch attitude."

Did she just call me a bitch? My lips almost twitched with humor, but I quickly stopped myself and dug my fingers into her soft skin, making her shift beneath me. "Who said I wanted to stay at this school, Sloane? You and I both know I don't belong here."

I didn't. I didn't belong here at all. For the longest time, at the Covens, when I was trapped in the bottom of the Covenant Psychiatric Hospital without a single decent soul knowing where I was, all I wanted was to get out. I needed to get back to my sister, and I needed to put Richard-fucking-Stallard in a shallow grave. But now that I was out and had done things that would make everyone in this school shiver with fear, I knew that being locked away was the best thing for me, and maybe that was Richard's plan all along. Fuck me up so badly that I knew I was no good for anyone except the people that tasked me to do their dirty work.

Sloane's dainty little chin tipped, her smooth cheeks hollowing out as her eyes scanned the hall behind me. "Maybe not, but your sister is here, and we both know you'll stay because of her. Now, let me go because she's walking down the hall right now with Isaiah, and I'm assuming you don't want her to see you in this state."

My hand flew off her waist at the same time a rumbled growl climbed from the bottom of my stomach. Sloane's eyes were hazel—a dark green with too many tones to describe and a reddish-brown ring around the pupil that, I swore, burned with intensity when I let her go, as if she had won.

Didn't she know who I was? Didn't she know that I had *literally* killed people? Sure, they were mostly bad and corrupted, but so was I. Being neglected had only made it worse. Heartless didn't even come close to what I was, and with the blood on my hands? I was destined for hell, and if I wasn't careful, I'd take everyone down with me.

"You're playing with the devil, Sloane. You have no idea what I'm capable of." I shot her a glare, and the anger boiled within my veins, feasting on the triumphant glint in her eye. "Leave me be, or you'll fucking regret it."

A small laugh left her pretty lips, and I bit my tongue to keep from slamming her against the wall again, because my sister had walked up. But as much as I hated to admit it, Sloane was right. I would stay at St. Mary's because Gemma was here. Journey was, too. Obviously, I would be staying.

"Hey, you two." Gemma's soft voice, just like our mother's, cooled the heated moment between Sloane and me instantly. "*Howwwww's* it going?" Her words were like a melody, cautious and curious.

"It's going great," Sloane answered without so much as a twitch of her eye. Though, I detected the sarcasm immediately. "Tobias and I were just discussing how we were going to study in the library this evening for our test next week."

My nostrils flared, and my hand flexed as I gripped my book tightly. *This sneaky little bitch.*

"Really?" Gemma's smile punched me in the stomach, and I remained still without an ounce of anger on my face, but I hoped that Sloane could feel the heat radiating from my skin. "Isaiah and I will be in the library, too, for a little bit. What time are you guys going up there?"

"Oh, I don't know." Sloane's stare was on me. I could feel it touching me like a cool winter breeze. "Probably after dinner. Right, Tobias? Say 5:45?"

"Perfect," Gemma said, grabbing onto Isaiah's hand, who was talking to one of his haughty friends beside him. It wasn't that I didn't like Isaiah. I was thankful he was there for my sister, and I knew she was happy with him, but I didn't really like anyone, so I wasn't going to go out of my way to be friends with him or his little wolf pack. "We will be there, too. Right, Isaiah?"

He turned and looked at my sister. "What? Yeah, sure. Whatever you say, baby."

She smiled playfully and rolled her eyes.

"I'll see you for dinner, Tobias? And we can walk to the library together?"

My teeth should have been shattered with how hard I was grinding them.

"Yeah."

She nodded, still half-hesitant with me, even though I was her twin brother. As soon as she and Isaiah had turned and walked away, I whipped my head over to Sloane, who grinned like the coy thing that she was.

You just wait, Sloane. You just fucking wait.

I didn't say a single word as I turned on my heel and headed for the dorms. Sloane had no idea what she was getting herself into. If she thought she could outsmart me and help me with studying while watching my every move, she was mistaken. Sure, I hadn't had much of an education, but I didn't need her help. What I needed was to be left the fuck alone so I could sort through the shit I'd been through and figure things out on my own.

I'd had a babysitter my entire life, whispering in my ear how to think, act, *kill*. The last thing I needed was for a girl like her to be whispering in my ear the questions to a stupid test on the early 1900s.

History was redundant. War repeated itself over and over again.

I should know, I'd been living in one for my entire life.

But I guess one more war with Sloane wouldn't hurt.

<hr>

CHAPTER FOUR

<hr>

SLOANE

THE LIBRARY WAS STILL, in its natural, calm state, and I blended in well. I sat at one of the tables near the back, isolating myself and keeping quiet, but I felt anything but quiet on the inside. My heart thumped with each tick of the clock overhead. My eyes were glued to the doors that I knew Tobias would be walking through any second with his sister. Journey was tucked back in one of the aisles, reading like usual, and I was sure Cade was creeping around here somewhere, trying to get her alone to *talk*.

Thump. Thump. Thump.

I was anticipating Tobias—eager with hidden excitement but cautious with the reality of the situation. Admittedly, I enjoyed making him angry, and I had no idea why. Was I bored? In need of a distraction because my life was chaotic on the other side—the side no one saw? I really wasn't sure, but what I was sure of was that I needed to keep my distance from him. Tobias was lethal earlier. Anger had radiated off him like the vibrations of a guitar string when I had conned him into tutoring. He knew I was right. He would be staying at St. Mary's because his sister was here, and we both knew they'd been separated for far too long, destroyed by the pesky little bitch we all liked to call fate. But I also had to remember that Tobias wasn't one of my wounded little animals that I'd always been drawn to.

It wasn't my responsibility to fix him. Because even if I did, I was certain fate would come swooping in again to ruin something of mine.

Fate had come swooping into my life before and turned it upside down—even worse for Willow. Although, sometimes, I had a mere thought that she may have had it better than me. What would be worse? Having murderers for parents, or having them *die* unexpectedly but still thinking they were good people?

The truth hurt, but it always came out eventually.

"Earth to Sloane." I jumped in my seat, my phone flying out of my hand. It was still on Willow's social media profile that I rarely allowed myself to check. I quickly scrambled, feeling my face grow hot, as I shut my screen down and smiled at Gemma.

"Hey, sorry. I was zoned out." Isaiah, in all his alpha glory, wrapped his hand around Gemma's waist and began pulling her away from my study table, leaving Tobias lurking in the background like a nightmare.

"Enjoy studying, you two." Isaiah's smirk was full of knowing humor, sensing the tension between us almost immediately.

"Where are you two going?" I asked, cocking an eyebrow.

"To study, obviously," Isaiah said, turning away and dragging Gemma down an empty aisle. When I turned back to Tobias, his temples were rocking back and forth, and he appeared so much more intimidating than earlier. *Oh, he is already pissed. Goody.*

"Stop brooding and sit down," I ordered, opening up my book to the pages I knew he needed to reread before we began studying.

His dark chuckle was gasoline to my already hot skin. His tall shadow fell over the study table, and I craned my neck up slowly, facing him as if he didn't scare me at all. He did, in a way, but not in the way he thought. *Why is this so exciting to me? Why do I feel something when his eyes are on me?*

"What?" I snapped, annoyed at how my body was betraying me. *Stop it, Sloane.* I scanned the library behind him, trying to find someone else to put my attention on. *The guy with the glasses who is hot in a nerdy type of way?* He was likely an underclassman, since I didn't know his name, but maybe...

Tobias pulled his chair out slowly, completely obliterating my plan of distracting myself with someone else. His long legs disappeared underneath our table as he leaned back in his chair with his strong arms over his chest like a shield. He was still wearing his uniform, but his tie was gone, and his white shirt was unbuttoned at the top, showing off his tan skin and Adam's apple.

The Rebels—Isaiah, Cade, Brantley, and Shiner—were the rulers of this school, but they were truly no match for Tobias. He was far beyond his years. My eyes fell to his hands when he uncrossed his arms and placed them on the table in front of us. Scars littered his knuckles as he tapped his fingers against the wood, causing blood to fill his veins like he was going to ram his fist into something at any given second.

I cleared my throat, suddenly feeling more nervous than before. "Are you ready? I want you to read these two pages, and then we will discuss, and I'll quiz you." I swallowed, unable to look him in the eye even though I could feel his stare driving into my cheek. "I can make you note cards, too —if you want. Are you struggling in any other classes?"

"No."

I snapped my head over to him, his voice licking over parts of me that had never seen the light of day. *It's fine.* "Tobias," I warned, fighting back on the things going haywire inside my stomach. "Let me help you. Don't be too stubborn to accept it."

"Stubborn? You're one to fucking talk, Snow White."

I tucked my dark hair behind my ear, and Tobias' eyes followed my every move. "Snow White?"

A sarcastic laugh fell from his lips that could likely make every girl in this school lose their minds. His hand reached up, and my mouth clamped shut as he gently placed a strand of my hair in between his fingers, rolling the piece between them.

"Dark hair," he whispered like a feral animal, almost growling, like he was affected in some way.

His eyes traveled from my hair to my face, and I was in a chokehold, unable to breathe, as he scanned my features slowly, like he was memorizing every last curve. "Pale, porcelain-like skin, as if you're easily breakable."

"I'm not easily breakable," I whispered, instantly infuriated that my voice was breathy and sounded exactly like I *was* breakable.

"Too stupid to see that you're in danger, just like Snow White."

Offended didn't even come close to what I felt. Infuriated was more like it. Sparking, fiery-hot anger that made me want to punch him right in the face. As soon as my mouth opened to bite back an insult at him, he pulled my hair between his fingers, and my head jerked toward him. My hands landed on his lap, and I quickly raised my chin and leveled him with a look. *Is he fucking serious? Did he just pull my hair?*

He leaned in close, with my hands on his strong thighs, right beside his dick that I should have elbowed. *"See?"* His *once-again* minty breath wafted over my face and cooled my mouth all the way down to my throat. He moved his attention to my hands as he flexed beneath me. "Stupid. You're just like the rest of these girls. Excited by the mere look of the heartless, damaged new guy of this school."

"I am the furthest thing from excited when it comes to you, Tobias. You're my best friend's brother." I quickly removed my hands from his lap and crossed them over my chest. "And that's exactly why I'm trying to help you! It'll destroy her if you leave again."

His face twitched—barely, but I noticed it. My words had dug into him, and I was glad. "And I'll destroy you if you don't leave me be, Snow."

I rolled my eyes, ignoring the hints of fear lingering in the back of my mind. "Whatever you say. Now fucking read the book so I can quiz you, and we can be done with this session."

Tobias huffed, and it was hard to know if he was amused by my demands or angrier than before. His emotions were difficult to read, and he seemed completely unsteady at times.

"And meet me here tomorrow night, too. I'm sure you're failing all of your classes."

I knew my words were harsh, but fuck him. My nerves were slowly morphing into irritation. Tobias thought he could intimidate me, and maybe on the inside, he did. But I would rather suck off that nerdy guy in the corner of the library *right* in front of the entire school than let his words and minty breath affect me into following his demands.

Sure, Tobias was dangerous and unnerving, but I wasn't as breakable and innocent as he thought I was.

CHAPTER FIVE

Two weeks.

It had been fourteen agonizing days of pretending that Tobias Richardson was a saint and not at all the devil he claimed to be.

When I shut my eyes at night, I saw his cold, blue eyes glaring at me from across the study table. When I heard the heat kick on through the creaky old vents of this school, I pictured his long fingers flipping the pages of the book I dropped in his lap. When I was sitting in the dining hall, trying to convince Journey to come sit at our table or fiddling with my food on my plate, I felt his eyes on me like I was his next target.

I didn't let it deter me, though.

This started off as me wanting to be a good friend to Gemma, helping her brother with his grades so the SMC didn't boot him from our *prestigious* boarding school. I was doing a favor for her father, the headmaster, and unknowingly helping Journey while I was at it because Tobias meant something to her, too. But now? Now this was a challenge. A game between Tobias and me.

Who would break first? Who would throw up the white flag and say, '*Fine, you win,*'?

I tapped my fingers on the book in front of me, crossing my legs again. *Not me. I would not be losing this stupid little game with him.* The library doors swung open, and I popped my head up, seeing Gemma walk in. My gaze moved around her tiny frame and saw only Isaiah.

Her smile was bright as she walked toward me, holding her boyfriend's hand with flushed cheeks. "Hey, where's Tobias?"

I sighed. "He said he was coming with you."

The disappointment fell off her in waves, and Isaiah was quick to pick it up. "He'll be here. He's probably still working out in the weight room."

Unlikely. I knew it would happen eventually. I knew there would be one session where Tobias didn't show up, and he probably did it just to piss me off. Anytime I tried to discuss *anything* with him during class about tutoring, his test scores, or his homework, he brushed me off and went as far as starting a conversation with any willing girl as I stood beside him, demanding he stop being such a dick. It was maddening. Yet, I found myself looking forward to our quarrels.

Thrilling anger began to brew like a witch's spell, bubbling and steaming until I shot up from the library table and grabbed my book and phone.

"I'll go find him," I said, smiling at Gemma. "I'll see you later."

Before walking out the library door, Gemma called back. "I'll talk to him, Sloane." The defeat was there, and in a sense, I felt it, too. I knew Tobias was damaged and angry at the world, but didn't he realize how good he had it here? A sister who loved him, peers who accepted him...kind of...and a father who was trying his hardest to make amends?

I spun around and grinned. "Don't you know me?" I asked. "If you think your brother ditching me for a tutoring session is going to do anything other than make me push harder, you don't know me at all." I laughed, and she smiled.

"Love you," she said, and I blew her a kiss before pushing the library doors open and letting my smile fall from my face.

The hallway was dark and quiet, much like every other hallway of this school, unless you were in the girls' dorm twenty minutes before breakfast started each morning. Some of the sconces screwed into the walls were burnt out, and others were flickering. Chills raced against my bare legs, and I wished I would have changed into jeans before heading to the library, but there was no time to change now.

I was heading straight for Tobias' room, even though we weren't *technically* allowed in the opposite sex's dorms. The boys' hall smelled of cologne and aftershave, and it was doing nothing but irking me.

A breath left me and landed right on his door. It was the very last one, tucked all the way in the pits of the hallway without a single light to lead the way. Seemed fitting, honestly. My fist banged against the wood, one sharp knock that sounded a lot angrier and edgier than I had meant.

I stood. Shifted on my feet. Tucked my hair behind my ear. Glanced down at my phone. And let out a tiny huff.

I knocked again, fuming. *Nothing.*

"Tobias, open the fucking door."

Is he still in the weight room?

I put my ear up against the door, listening for any type of movement. I knocked once more and stomped my foot in frustration. *Couldn't I just break in?*

An evil plan began to form, and I smiled like a sneaky cat. *I will break in, and if he's not in there, I'll wait.* Right before I turned around to head to my room for a bobby pin to pick the lock, with my ear still against his door, it flung open, and I flew forward. My books flew out of my grasp, and the floor was suddenly three inches from my face.

Two strong hands grabbed my waist, and I swallowed my own tongue, immersed in the delicious twisting of my stomach from his grip on me. "What the hell do you want?" The question was a bite to my excitement. He whooshed me up so quickly my hair flew out of my face like I was in front of a fan.

I was plopped on my feet like a child, and Tobias stood over me like a cold shadow on a winter night. He was shirtless, and his dark hair was even darker than usual with damp ends and beads of sweat rolling down the cut curves of his cheek.

Gorgeous.

He was dark, broody, intimidating, and absolutely perfect. My mouth opened, but nothing came out. Tobias' hands were still on my hips, gripping me tightly and grounding me to the floor. My chest rose, and the second I let myself think, my cheeks blasted with heat, and I was mortified. *He was right. I do get excited with his hands on me*.

"You're late," I croaked as I tried to breathe through my nose to make it less noticeable that I was having an actual heart attack. *Shit. Shit. Shit.* "And let go of me."

His hands flew from my waist, and he took a step back, almost as if he were as appalled as I was that his hands were still there. There was a minor dip in his glare that had the sharp curves of his face softening, but the edges of his jaw quickly tightened right back up. "Leave."

My books were still on his floor, along with a bundled-up black t-shirt. I gripped my phone tightly in my hand and crossed my arms, popping my hip out to spit out some insult, but I quickly shut up when I let my eyes dip. My mouth dried, and I cursed myself when I counted the stupid, defined ab muscles taunting me with every labored breath he gulped down. *One, two, three...*

"Leave my room."

"You didn't show." I cleared my throat before biting my tongue and swallowing the metallic taste. "You have a test on Monday. You're supposed to be—" I shifted my attention because there was no way I could look at him after counting his abs in my head like one of the groupies of this school that hoped Tobias would show up at the secret parties we had in the basement to fuck them.

I glanced at his bed. His covers were messy. The dark-navy blanket was a bundle of cotton on one side of his bed, with his pillows on the floor. I flicked my attention back to him, and his temples were teetering, and his inky hair was slightly damp against his forehead. "Were...were you sleeping?"

That's weird.

"Were you taking a nap? At 6 pm? On a Friday?"

His chest was still heaving, and a bead of sweat, hardly noticeable, slowly fell between his pecs. *Why is he sweaty?* The realization came at me like a swarm of bees, and I couldn't stop myself from asking my next question.

"Did you have a nightmare?"

Tobias snapped his attention to me, his full lips flattened with anger. "Why can't you fucking leave me alone?"

Rolling my eyes, I took a step toward him. "You know why. You're nearly failing your classes, and if it wasn't for me helping you study, you'd probably fail them all."

I jerked in my spot when Tobias ran his hands through his damp hair, showing off his defined stomach even more. He stood near his bed, his gray sweats the only article of clothing on him.

"Gemma has them, too," I whispered, trying to extend an olive branch.

I also had nightmares, but there was no way I was telling Tobias that. He'd use it against me—I knew it. Although the room wasn't as icy as it usually was with him and I crammed inside a space together, I knew that he could quickly turn and be a complete asshole and stare at me so blankly that I began to wonder if he had a heart at all.

Silence filled the room, like we were stuck in an elevator together with tension filling every last empty crevice. His chest still rushed, his lungs gulping for air as he swallowed oxygen. "Are you okay?" I asked, treading lightly. Nerves jittered my words, and they came out shaky, which was *so* unlike me. I took a step forward, stepping over my books like they were bombs, and stopped when I was a single foot away from him.

My gaze followed a salty droplet of sweat as it landed against his flushed chest. The beating in my ears propelled me to raise a shaky hand.

"What are you doing?" Tobias hesitantly asked, and for the first time ever, he didn't seem angry.

Our eyes clashed, his deep blue appearing vulnerable and shocking me into disbelief. "Tobias, did you have a nightmare?" I whispered, too afraid to penetrate whatever was going on.

The very second my hand landed on his warm chest, he hissed and moved his head to the side, as if he didn't want me to see him. But I did. I saw him. *I truly saw him.* Maybe for the first time since meeting weeks ago.

"Tobias," I whispered again, my breath knowingly hitting him against his skin. *What is happening?* Our hearts beat wildly together, mine ricocheting off my rib cage and his pounding against the palm of my hand. "Do you want to talk about it? It helps Gemma to get them out. She paints them."

His head snapped back to mine, and I froze. The breath was stolen from my body, and my blood rushed with something too hot to describe. My phone vibrated in my other hand, and his eyes fell to it quickly. "Better get that," he snapped, gripping my wrist and shoving my hand away from his chest.

Embarrassment flooded me, and then came the blinding, white anger. I sighed angrily and put my attention on my phone, frustrated with whatever just happened. *He is such a jerk.*

I glanced down to my phone as I took another step back, nearly falling over my books that were splayed all over the floor, and that was when my heart fell to the ground in one single thud.

Unknown: Bently is asking where you are. I told him you were sneaking out. I swear I saw the excitement in his eyes at the thought of you being a little rule-breaker.

The room was spinning as I zeroed in on the words, quickly snapping my head up and locking onto Tobias. He turned and crept toward his bed, putting his bare back to me, which only sent me into another panic. *The scars.* Everything shook around me. My vision blurred, my phone felt like a burning piece of metal in my palm, and Tobias' red, bumpy, slash-like scars on his back sent me into a complete panic.

My phone vibrated again, and rational thinking outweighed the climbing hysteria.

Unknown: Like THE night? Ugh, shit. I need to find someone to lose my V to, too. Who can I choose? Drake? He would gladly do the honors.

If anyone else were to read these random messages from an unknown number, they'd be completely confused, but that night was forever branded into my brain. The last texts between Willow and me were a reel that I visited over and over again the first year I was sent to St. Mary's.

My mouth opened as I gripped my phone so tightly my

fingers ached and curled with pain. I kept my gaze on Tobias' back, too stunned to stay anything about the earth-shattering pain he'd had to go through to get the scars. I yelped when my back hit his door, banging into the wood harshly. Tobias turned around quickly, his dark brows a shadow over his eyes.

The shakiness of my free palm slapped over my mouth as I began pulling in my panic with a thick rope, and I saw the way Tobias' mouth moved to say my name, but I couldn't hear anything but Willow's voice.

Run.

And that was what I did. Tobias' door flung open, hitting the other side of the wall so loudly that it sliced the blood rushing through my ears, and I ran all the way to my room before colliding with the floor in a heaping mess of panic.

CHAPTER SIX

TOBIAS

Chatter.

All I heard was fucking chatter and the clanking of silver-ware as I sat unmoving in one of the chairs at my father's dinner table.

My father, the headmaster who was *not the headmaster in this house*—his words, not mine—sat at the end of his table with a glass of water in one hand and the other resting on top of the wood, with his fingers tapping aggressively against it. It was after school hours, so he didn't wear his typical dress shirt and loose tie but instead a plain t-shirt and jeans, and it made him look less like a worn-out headmaster with a newfound fatherly twist and more like a normal man that was sitting with a bunch of teens at his table—if that were normal.

"I swear. Why don't you believe me?" I shifted my attention to Shiner, who was sitting *right* next to the girl I couldn't get out of my fucking head.

"Because you're you, Shiner," she said, rolling her pretty hazel eyes that irked me anytime they landed on me, which was completely fucked up because it irked me when they *weren't* on me.

I hated her.

I did.

Something twisted on the inside when I thought of her, and annoyance fluttered through me like I was being summoned from hell. The not-so-distant memory of her standing in my bedroom with her hand on my chest and then the horror along her face after she saw my back, painted with horrific reminders that were now souvenirs from my time at the Covens, did nothing but fuel my hate.

There was pity that was quickly replaced with shock. It was so shocking that she *literally* ran out of my room, leaving her books on my floor like she was afraid of me.

I mean, she should be, but that wasn't the point.

"Ask her yourself, Sloane!" Shiner bellowed, flinging his fork down onto his plate. "That's what she said."

"Scout's honor?" Mercedes, my sister's other best friend, asked.

Shiner's brow hitched, and he grinned at Mercedes. "You know I don't lie, Mer."

"Fuc—"

"Hey!" My father put his hands on his forehead and was likely trying to block out their annoying voices like I was. "Enough. No cussing in front of Jack."

We all turned to Isaiah's little brother, the same kid that my father had adopted through some twisted, fake-family, bullshit story that I didn't care to know about but listened to anyway because Gemma took the time to thoroughly explain everything to me that had happened during my...'leave of absence' from her life.

"You cuss in front of me, Uncle Tate."

He sighed. "Not the point. I'm an adult."

"Most of us are eighteen," Isaiah mumbled, grabbing onto my sister's hand.

"And, not to mention, we've been through some shit."

That came from Cade, one of the other Rebels who I originally didn't like, but now I had to store that hatred away because he and Journey were back together.

"Can we not revisit what happened just a couple weeks ago?" Journey whispered, putting her head down for a brief second. Silence tumbled through the room like a tornado, and I watched as they all shut their mouths one by one until I landed back on her.

Sloane.

Tension between us had risen to an all-time high, but not a single word was spoken about the moment in my bedroom. I simmered, and she pretended like nothing had happened. Except, something *did* happen.

She was on edge.

We hadn't studied much, but every time a test or home-work assignment was laid on my desk, she snatched it up before I even had a chance to do so, and the next day, she'd hand me flashcards or a study guide.

Which I'd rip up in front of her, forcing her to put them in the trash.

It was a fun little system we had.

There wasn't much I enjoyed, but seeing her little temples flick with annoyance made me smirk every single time.

"So, how is studying going, you two?"

I slowly moved my attention to my father, leaning back in my chair and crossing my arms over my tight chest. Something burned, like a hot metal stick branding my chest, as I lazily looked over at Sloane, trying to gauge if she was going to fuck me over or not.

She should. If there was one girl at this school that was determined to get under my skin, it was her.

The very second her eyes twinkled with mischief, I knew I was fucked.

"Terribly, actually," she started, scraping the knife over my skin a little more. "Tobias, why don't you tell them how studying is going?"

This fucking brat.

"Tobias!" Gemma said. "You said you'd try."

Fuck.

"I am trying."

"You are not." Sloane's argument was valid. I mean, I physically ripped up each study guide she gave me and then winked afterward, enjoying the red splotches on her pretty skin. "You haven't studied with me in weeks, and every time I try to help you, you blow me off."

"It's not my fault your services suck."

"There's a whole lotta blowing and sucking going on around here," Shiner joked. Each guy snickered, except for me, and Sloane's jaw unhinged.

"Shut up, Nash."

"You know I hate being called that," he snapped, stabbing his fork into his chicken.

Sloane ignored him and leveled me with her best glare, which I chewed up and spit right the fuck out.

"Tobias," my father started, pushing me clear over the edge of annoyance and anger. "You *have* to study. I don't care if you guys spend the evenings in the library, your room, or in the goddamn courtyard during a blizzard, or even here. But you need to show your teachers you're putting in effort and at least *trying* to get decent grades."

"Tobias, please," Gemma said, causing the table to grow quiet.

I shifted my attention to Sloane, and I hoped she could read my glare for what it was worth. She had thrown me under the bus, and okay, fine, I deserved it in a way, but now I hated her even more, and she didn't know what that meant coming from a guy like me.

A dark chuckle left me as I pushed from the table. "Yeah, fine," I gritted. "We can study on Monday, after the weekend." And then I walked out the front door and into the fucking blistering-cold winter air to cool my heated skin and level my erratic thinking.

EVERYONE WAS HYPED UP. Sweat coated my back, and I was debating stripping down in front of the lacrosse team to shower, even though they'd all take a step back once they saw the angry red lines that covered my skin.

"I'm ready, bro." That came from Shiner—*again*. I swore, he didn't stop fucking talking. He reminded me of Gage, another poor soul that was trained at the Covens. There was a mix of us at the Covens. Some of us, like myself, were thrown into the confidential program that housed the dark web for killers because someone wanted rid of us. Gage was there because he was a thief and was destined for several years in prison.

That was Richard's main doing. Being the top judge in the country and ruling most of the state, he was able to pull strings like the world was his own little puppet show, throwing men who broke the rules into hell and turning them into his own personal hound dogs, making him money from other criminals.

It was a vicious cycle. One bad man threw another bad man into a shithole, brainwashed them, and then other bad men hired those fucked-up little pea-brains, and therefore, you had yourself a circle of fuckery.

"We can tell," I said to no one in particular, standing back against the lockers, waiting for everyone to get their shit and go so I could rinse off.

Shiner, Isaiah, Cade, and Brantley were all on the lacrosse team, and although their season was taking a break, they, too, were working out in the school's small workout area to stay in shape. I, on the other hand, was working out so I didn't kill anyone or, better yet, grab Sloane White by the waist and push her against the library shelves and either one: push her to her knees so I could fuck her mouth, or two: fuck her so hard she would never be the same.

My heart started to race at the thought, and I quickly turned around and leveled my breathing. What was wrong with me? Not a single person had ever gotten under my skin like her, but all I kept thinking about was how she had thrown me under the bus last night at dinner with my father.

Regardless, if she was my sister's best friend, I had a plan that would quickly erase her from my thoughts and make her hate me so much she'd leave me alone. It was pretty juvenile compared to the way my brain was wired, but I knew it would work because it was a plan I'd fleshed out before.

"You going to the party tonight?"

Turning my attention to Isaiah, I shrugged, knowing that I *was* going to the party.

"You should," Isaiah said, throwing his shirt over his head. "It would make Gem happy."

"And I can assure you, you'd have the first pick of any girl there." That came from Shiner again, and Brantley, who was more like me than any of the guys with his brooding silence, snickered.

"Why do you say that?" I asked, lifting my shirt a little and wiping sweat off my forehead.

"Because you're fucking damaged, bro, and girls *love* a damaged bad boy."

Did he just call me a...bad boy? That, too, seemed pretty sophomoric compared to what I'd done.

"I think it's more so because they're sick of you, Shiner." Cade chuckled.

"That's not what Journey said the last time I had her underneath me."

Cade and I both snapped our attention to Shiner, and together, we bonded over the protectiveness we currently shared.

"Jesus, fuck!" Shiner said, throwing his hands up, which made his towel fall to the ground. He was completely naked. "I'm kidding, you psychos."

Damn straight, I'm a psycho.

A few other guys walked through the locker room after their shower and fist bumped Shiner even though he was purely nude. One of them turned to Isaiah. "Will there be any alcohol tonight?"

"Yeah," he answered, getting dressed. "Shots."

"I'm not getting too drunk tonight," the other guy said to his friend. He was on the short and skinny side, looking more like he'd enjoy clicking the keyboard all night rather than partying with the Rebels.

"What? Why?"

The Rebels and I stayed silent as their conversation continued. A few others had walked through the locker room, one of them being Bain, who had just recently gotten on good terms with Isaiah. He was on okay terms with me, too, if there were even terms to begin with. He was fucked up, but so was I. He had helped Journey and my sister so that meant he was okay in my book.

"Because Sloane White has been flirting with me all week. I'm gonna find her tonight and fuck her. After all, isn't that what the claiming parties are all about? Fucking? They're like real live pornos."

Snap.

"No." The word climbed from my mouth with so much

aggression the room began to turn red.

Every single set of eyes was on me, and I ate it up like it was a normal day.

"What?" the guy said, treading lightly. He only kept his eyes on me for a moment before shifting his attention to the Rebels.

"Sounded like he said no," Shiner clarified, shrugging.

"Do you have some claim on her or something?" he asked, raising an eyebrow at me that would have looked a lot better split open with blood from my fist.

I didn't answer him, but instead, I just stood and glared. I did have a claim on Sloane tonight, but it was for all the wrong reasons. If I were a good guy, then I would say fuck it and just do what I needed to do to make it through the school year and get away from everyone that looked at me like I was a ticking time bomb, but I wasn't a good guy.

And the more I was pushed into spending time with Sloane, the more I rebelled because that girl did something to me, and I didn't fucking like it.

"Well?" the guy prodded. His face annoyed me merely for the fact that it screwed up like he thought I wasn't seconds from snapping him in half.

"I said no," I repeated, pulling off my shirt. I didn't care anymore that every guy in this room was going to get a glimpse of my backside. I could picture the red marks and felt each whip of pain like it was yesterday.

"Well, sorry. But you don't really make the rules." The guy laughed and fist bumped his friend, and I pictured myself walking over to him and grabbing him by the throat and pushing him up against the metal lockers so he knew that I *did* make the rules when it came to her.

A wicked surge of possessiveness came over me like a goddamn tidal wave, and I almost stumbled on my steady feet.

Shiner laughed, breaking me out of the stupor that I was in. "Looks to me like he does, bud. I would stay away from Sloane."

That was when I chose to turn my back to them and strip the rest of the way down. Silence stretched as far as it would go as I stepped into the showers, letting the steam cover me like a dooming fog.

Sloane was mine tonight.

She would hate me even more after it was all said and done, but that was exactly what we both needed.

CHAPTER SEVEN

SLOANE

I KEPT SEEING HER.

My best friend that I hadn't spoken to in years. Willow didn't even look like the girl I had known anymore, at least according to her social media, but I kept picturing her around every dark corner of this school. Every time I shut my eyes at night, her face would wander in, along with the texts that were still on my phone from a number that was subsequently no longer in service.

I rubbed my hands over my goosebump-covered arms as I walked down the empty hall with Gemma, Journey, and Mercedes. They were whispering about something, but I was too in my head to participate, which was no doubt a red flag to them if they were to pay attention.

"You okay?" Gemma asked, bumping her bare shoulder with mine.

It was winter, nearing spring, but when it came to the secret parties in the basement that we all attended on the weekends, you would have thought it was summer. I wore a tight black miniskirt and my Doc Martens, and Gemma did the same. The only difference between our outfits was that Gemma paired hers with a loose, long-sleeve, see-through shirt, and I wore a tight, lacy tank top that made my boobs look great.

"Me? I'm fine," I answered, scanning the hallway as if Willow was going to be standing there, waiting for me to explain what had happened that night several years ago.

"Is it Tobias? I'm sorry he's being such a jerk."

Mercedes and Journey were up ahead of Gemma and me, laughing about something, which was nice to hear after Journey had been so quiet since coming back to St. Mary's.

"He is a jerk." Journey glanced back and smiled. "Don't give up on him, though. He's been through a lot."

I knew he'd been through a lot, but so had I. So had Gemma and Journey, too. That didn't give him the right to be a dick to me, did it? *Why* was he such an ass to me? I mean, sure, he was pissed at me now because I had called him out at dinner with his father, but even before then, he hated me.

"It's fine." I grabbed onto Gemma's hand, reassuring her. "Your brother doesn't affect me like he thinks he does. I don't care if he hates me."

Oh, but he sure does affect me in other ways.

"He doesn't hate you," Gemma whispered as we grew closer to the door of the party. Water splashed beneath our feet as we traveled the dark, tunnel-like hallway of the basement.

"I'm pretty sure he hates me," I laughed. "Especially after last night."

Gemma squeezed my hand and tried her hardest at being optimistic. "He doesn't, but even if he did, I'm thankful that you're willing to help him. If anyone can get through to him, it's you."

A tight laugh left me before stopping in my tracks as the

party's chaos erupted around us. The door shut, and music bumped in the background. No one came dressed in their usual uniform or even their 'weekend' clothes. The girls looked like sluts, and the guys were drooling—it was just the way these claiming parties worked. When the lights went down, that was when the true *claiming* started, and at that point, it didn't really matter what you wore.

And wouldn't you know, Tobias found me instantly. Just like I'd done with him.

"What is he doing here?" I asked, panic rising up my throat and threatening to choke me.

Is he here for some girl?

I gasped on the inside when I felt the surge of burning jealousy creep along my bare skin. *Um, why do I care?* More power to her if she's going to be alone with him.

"I have no idea." Gemma was excited. I could hear it in her voice, and although I wasn't the least bit excited, I understood why she was. Her antisocial, mentally unstable brother who rarely broke into a smile was at a party, socializing with *her* friends. Something didn't seem right, though. I could see right through Tobias and his lazy half-smirk in my direction.

I rolled my eyes, annoyed that he was ruining my night and making my body twist and feel things that I shouldn't have been feeling for someone like him.

"Let the party begin," Isaiah said as he walked up to Gemma and planted a kiss on her mouth.

"Yeah," I said, pulling myself from Tobias' dangerous smirk. I began searching the crowd for someone else so I could ignore the way I was drawn to him like he was a wounded animal that needed my gentle touch to bring him back to life. "Let the party begin."

———

THIS WAS the best part of the claiming party. The lights were off, and blood rushed through my body so quickly it heated every part of my exposed skin. Gemma and Isaiah had already run off together, and I was certain Journey and Cade had, too. I had no idea where Mercedes was, or *who* she was with, but I stood in the same spot that I had been in earlier when I'd caught Alex's eye from across the party.

He was coming for me, and that was exactly what I wanted: some guy who knew nothing about me to distract me so I didn't have to think about Willow, my parents, the prank text messages, *or* Tobias and his unexplained smirks in my direction. I was on edge, and I needed someone to dull the thoughts.

Noises began to filter through my ears, and I shifted on my feet, feeling a bundle of nerves twist in my belly. Whooshes of air were ringing throughout the room along with low sucking noises. A giggle to my left. A belt buckle to my right.

My fingers began to tingle, and the longer I waited, the more worked up I became, and with that, Tobias started to poke through my brain. Why was he smirking at me? I knew he was angry with me from last night, so why? And who was he with? Why did I care? His hands were so large, and I kept picturing them gripping some girl's waist like he did to me when I nearly fell flat onto my face in his room the other night.

An angry bubble began to climb from my belly, but I jumped when I felt a presence behind me.

"There you are," I whispered, eyes widening in the dark when Alex's hands fell to my waist. They were large. Much larger than I thought. Although, could I really know? It wasn't like I studied his hands or anything.

Alex said nothing as he crept closer. His front pressed to

my back, and a hiccup of surprise washed over me. *Okay, getting right to it. Fine by me.*

I was no saint. When my parents had sent me to St. Mary's in the middle of my freshman year, I rebelled. I rebelled hard and fast. The seniors all wanted a taste of the new girl who wore a short skirt and painted red lipstick on her mouth to pretend she was something she wasn't. I tried to hide from the hurt and confusion by distracting myself with anything I could, and the claiming parties were definitely a good outlet.

The distractions came to an end, but every once in a while, I liked to divulge in them again. Like right now, with Alex. Some would call it an unhealthy coping mechanism, but I didn't care what people thought of me.

My head fell back onto his chest, and part of me wanted to go to one of the secret rooms that some of the couples like to use during the claiming part of the party, but it was also exciting to be here, tucked away in a corner with a guy I had hardly spoken to. His hands traveled from my waist, up my sides, and when his warm fingers brushed over my collarbone, I felt the heat pool between my legs.

Whoa. Alex was surprising me. He was a little nerdy, although he did play lacrosse with the Rebels, but I didn't expect him to be so *confident.* His hands were steady, his feet planted on the ground, one knee going between mine and separating my legs.

"Do you have a lot of experience, Alex? Because you seem to know what you're doing."

He didn't answer me, and although this was exactly what I wanted—to be distracted—I found it weird that he wasn't talking. His hands skimmed the hem of my skirt, and his teeth bit onto my ear lobe. I gasped and almost turned around, but when his fingers crept up the inner side of my thigh and rubbed over my wet panties, my mouth stayed closed, and I allowed myself to enjoy what I was feeling.

A faint moan left my mouth, and his breathy chuckle was warm and minty as it washed over my cheek. *Wait.* I stiffened, my back going ramrod straight against his chest.

"Relax."

Tobias?! Ice-cold water rained down over my skin as I stood eerily still with his hands on me. My nipples tightened against the lacy material of my shirt, and my legs trembled. I refused to believe that knowing that it was Tobias behind me instead of the poor underclassman that I had flirted with all week turned me on even more.

Was it the danger that got me excited? The surprise?

"Where's Alex?" I hissed, shaking in his grasp. Tobias' hand moved out from under my skirt, and he skimmed my collarbone as his other hand stayed steady on my hip, keeping me in place against him.

His lips brushed over my ear, and my stomach bottomed out. *Oh, God. This is bad. This is really bad.* "Who cares?" His skilled palm traveled farther down, dipping in between my perky nipples, brushing a finger over both before gripping my thigh again.

"I—I do," I said, leaning back into him like I was in a daze of some sort. My eyes still hadn't adjusted to the darkness of the room, but everything else was enhanced—the sounds, the subtle touches, the way my blood sparked with anticipation.

We need to stop.

"You don't care," Tobias argued, inhaling deeply in the crook of my neck. His hair tickled my cheek, and I turned my head, allowing him more access. *What am I doing?!*

"Why..." My eyes fluttered when his hand crept higher up my leg, causing tingles to fly to my skin. "Why?"

"Why, what?" he whispered, pausing all of his movement. My

eyes flew open, and I wiggled in front of him, pushing my butt against his hard length. *Shit.* I turned around in his grip, wishing I could see his face in the dark. *I should move away from him.*

"Why are you here? Why are you touching me? I thought you hated me."

"I do hate you." His tone was both menacing and dangerous. "But I need to get you out of my head." His grip turned rougher, and he spun me back around, putting my back to his front once again.

My back arched as his fingers began moving again, slowly creeping up my leg and spreading me wide. I gasped, euphoria settling in my core and putting some wicked spell over me that begged for him to make it stop. I burned in all the right spots, craving his touch like no other. *What is wrong with me?*

"And touching me will get me out of your head?" I whispered, in some sort of trance.

"Haven't you heard of a little hate-fuck, Sloane? They're the best kind."

I whimpered, and it blended in with the other erotic sounds of the room. *It's been too long since I've done this.* There. That was it. That was why I was so turned on I couldn't think straight. That mixed with the sounds of others? Yeah, that was it. That was why I was so twisted.

"Tobias, we should stop."

His teeth grazed over my skin, and his long finger teased me over my panties. "Tell me again how we should stop, because your body defies you, Sloane." He chuckled, and it was rough against my back, vibrating me as he pinned me closer to his body. I leaned forward, gripping his arm that was locked over my belly, and felt the pulse between my legs. *Oh my God, why can't I stop?*

"We shouldn't," I whispered, sagging into him. *Please touch me.* I would regret this. I knew it.

His lips sucked on the tender spot on my neck at the

same time his finger entered me. *Holy shit.* My eyes shut, and I breathed in the immense pleasure he was giving.

"Tell me what you want. Tell me what you want from your best friend's brother, Sloane."

Fuck, this is so bad. I shouldn't be doing this. I hadn't had a drop of alcohol, but I felt like I was drunk.

I craned my head back, angling my lips up to his. My eyes had adjusted a little, and I could see the outline of his strong jaw and thick hair. His finger was slow, lazy, and teasing, which wasn't what I was used to. Most of the guys I'd been with were too excited to take their time. They were too eager and hungry by the time the lights shut down. But Tobias was taking his time, and it was driving me crazy.

Tobias drove me crazy.

But this felt so good. *Too good.*

"Kiss me," I begged, wanting his tongue in my mouth like some type of wild animal. My hips moved with his finger inside me, wanting more and hating myself for it.

His lips brushed over my ear when he added another finger. "Heartless boys don't kiss, Sloane. And after tonight, you'll see just how heartless I am."

CHAPTER EIGHT

TOBIAS

I was enjoying this way too much. I knew it, yet I couldn't stop. I wasn't enjoying this because I knew my wicked plan was working just as I'd hoped, but rather because her body was responding to me, and she wanted more.

She felt like heaven. My hands roamed over her like I was trying to find some way to ground myself, and each touch of her curves was a punch to my chest. My dick strained, and it wasn't like it was difficult to get hard for someone, but it throbbed in ways that I felt all the way to my throat, my lips, my tongue.

This wasn't like before.

I'd been in this exact situation: seducing a girl, touching her and feeding her dirty words to make her fall to her knees for me so I could use her to my own benefit. The nurses at the psych ward weren't hard to crack, and they weren't difficult to mend into a simple tool when it was all said and done—leaving my door unlocked, feeding me intel from the top floor. One went as far as drawing me a map of the entire building before Journey and I escaped unexpectedly one night, causing chaos. But this? This was different.

I was hungry for Sloane White in ways that I'd never been hungry before.

And with that, I grew angry.

"Wh–what?" Her breath was sweet and intoxicating, and I turned my head, confused by the fact that although I had *never* ever kissed a girl before—*I know, it is difficult to grasp, even for me*—I *wanted* to taste her lips. I wanted her sharp yet sweet tongue inside my mouth, making me drunk with something that would take it all away.

"I don't kiss. It's my only rule." My thumb brushed over her sensitive clit, and I *almost* bit the gasp right off her mouth. "Now tell me what else you want."

Moving back a little, I glanced down at my pocket, straining my vision to see if my phone was still sticking halfway out of my jeans. *Good, now get to fucking work, Tobias.*

Her hot whimper caused my arm to tighten against her. I dug my fingers into her skin and kept her propped up. "Tell me what you want."

"We should stop," she whispered, the words hardly making it out of her mouth.

"Why?" I teased, dipping my finger in slower and slower, even though it was killing me and twisting me in ways that were completely unknown to me. *I could fuck her right now. I* wanted to fuck her. I wanted to fuck her, but not for my own sake, but because I wanted to own her body and make *her* come.

Fuck, what?

"Huh?"

I smirked against her skin, flicking my tongue over the spot I had sucked on a few moments ago. She was in over her head and could hardly form sentences.

"Why should we stop, Sloane? Is it because I'm your best

friend's fucked-up brother that you *know* you shouldn't be messing around with? I'm dangerous. But maybe you like that."

There was a hint of disgust lingering in the back of my head at my words and eagerness to fulfill my plan. *What am I feeling? Guilt?*

"Tell me, baby," I coaxed, feeling her body twist around my finger. *Fuck, that's so goddamn hot.* "Tell me how you've dreamt of me touching you since the moment you laid eyes on me in the dining hall on that first day." *Did she feel it, too? The heavy connection that was unexplainable?* I blamed it on attraction, but late at night, when I was seconds from sleep and at my most vulnerable, I knew it was something more.

My finger stopped moving *right* when she was about to tip over the edge. Her ass pressed against me, and every other sound of girls moaning was drowned out by what Sloane was doing to me and how she was destroying my denial of wanting her more in this moment than I could admit. *Say it so I can make you come around my finger. Fucking say it.*

"I..."

"Say my name, and tell me you want me to make you come so hard you'll never be able to replace the feeling. Tell me how you don't care that I'm your best friend's brother and that you want me to put you out of your misery, Sloane."

"No."

I smirked, and the little war we had brewing got me all sorts of excited. I slowly began taking my finger out of her, ignoring my hard cock pressed against her tight little ass. I waited patiently as her breathing picked up, panic coursing through her veins as I robbed her of the one thing she wanted.

My eyes rolled in the back of my head when her shaky fingers clamped onto my wrist between her deliciously soft legs, keeping me there for her own taking.

"Say my name, and tell me what you want," I whispered, letting her think she was in charge, and honestly, if I weren't in the business of lying to myself, I'd admit that she *was* in charge.

"Fi–fine," she barked, pushing my hand higher to her soaked panties. My stomach hollowed out, and I bit onto her neck, savoring her little cry. "Make me come, Tobias."

"And tell me you don't care that I'm your best friend's brother."

"I do care," she said, pumping her hips back and forth. My nostrils flared, and my jaw flexed, wanting nothing more than to taste the sweet wetness between her legs. *Fuck, what is she doing to me?*

"If you did, then you'd walk away." I chuckled, knowing as soon as I was finished with her, I was turning right the fuck around, stomping through this sex party that my peers called a 'claiming', and heading to my room to beat myself off until I truly did get this girl out of my fucking head.

Her breaths had picked up, and her hips moved quicker. My finger pressed inside of her pussy, and she whimpered, gripping onto my other hand that was holding her in place. I brought it up to her mouth and smiled deviously.

"Suck on my fingers while you come," I demanded. "Because I'll rip out every man's eardrums in this room if they get to hear you break for me." *And that is the goddamn truth.*

I plunged my fingers into her mouth and felt my teeth shift with the grinding of my jaw. Her warm, wet mouth coated me and sucked so hard I saw stars. Between her mouth and her responsive pussy, I was a fucking goner, and that scared me so badly that anger cut through me like a bullet.

The second she hit her climax, I ripped my fingers away from both sets of lips. She stumbled forward, and I didn't even have the ability to catch her before she fell to her knees.

I left quickly, ripping the door to the party open with aggression, and jogged to my room, kicking the door shut with my foot.

I paced back and forth before walking in my bathroom and turning the shower to ice cold.

No, no, no, no.

My chest was expanding, and it grew heavier the more I thought about Sloane. The fear in her eyes when she came to my room and saw my scars hit me like a ton of bricks, and I shut my eyes, bringing my closed fist up to my mouth. My teeth scraped over my knuckles, and I cursed myself further because I could smell her on my hand. I quickly pulled my phone out of my pocket and stared at the device that would likely hurt Sloane more than I intended.

"What the fuck is wrong with you?" I mumbled, pacing back and forth again. The shower was running, and if I wanted to keep up with my facade of not feeling anything and pushing the past several years of my life out the fucking door, I needed to dive into that cold water and let it numb me the rest of the way.

I quickly placed my phone on the bathroom counter, ignoring the shaking of my finger, and pressed play on the video. I saw nothing but a black screen, but the second I heard her voice, I dropped my head, feeling my sweaty hair flop on my forehead. My knuckles were white as they gripped the bathroom counter, and they only grew whiter when I heard her sweet voice clear as day.

"Why are you touching me? I thought you hated me."

The feel of her skin against my less-than-worthy hands filled my head, and I listened more, hearing her hot little gasps and quiet whimpers. *Her lips.* I wanted to kiss her.

"Fuck," I gritted, gripping the counter so hard my fingers ached. I swallowed and pushed myself back, pacing again until I couldn't take it anymore. I hissed when my hand gripped the base of my hard cock. *Sloane, Sloane, Sloane.*

I wanted to punish myself. I didn't deserve to get myself off to a girl like her, especially not after making her come and having her surrender to me only so I could use it against her. She was going to be furious. She was going to fucking hate me —more than she already did.

Sparks went straight to the tip of my dick as my hand moved faster, listening to her on my phone. *Fuck.* Her body was warm and soft and all things that I had no business feeling. Her cunt was like a piece of heaven, and her smell made my mouth water. One hand gripped the edge of the counter again as I yelled out, feeling a rush of all things Sloane, as I came harder than I had *ever in my life.* My head dropped, and my eyes squeezed tightly, listening to the sound of the water hitting the tiles of my shower behind me instead of the sounds of Sloane that were now a constant in my head.

I took one long look at my red face in the mirror and took a step back so I didn't punch the glass and cut my hand. I stepped in the shower a moment later, and the cold water against my skin did *nothing* to cool me down, and I was afraid I'd never cool down again when it came to her.

Sloane White was a package full of snarky remarks and hot demands, and she had a grip on me so tight that I would rather die than let it take me under. Because the truth was, if I went down, she was coming with me.

CHAPTER NINE

SLOANE

ALL MY LIFE, I'd been ambitious. A doer. Someone who got what they wanted because they were determined and never shied away from a challenge. That was not to say I wasn't spoiled as a child, because my parents absolutely spoiled me —up until they sent me away to St. Mary's, which was the complete *opposite* of spoiling. They had groomed me with the best of the best.

Elite prep schools.

Social circles that had the net income of millions.

The best clothes.

The best shoes.

Piano lessons.

But with determination came courage, and at the current moment, I wasn't feeling very courageous.

I wiggled in my seat in the quiet library, waiting for him. The second Gemma's alarm went off this morning, which typically nudged me into a light sleep for a few seconds before rolling back over for another hour, considering she woke much earlier than me, I felt the dread slithering up my body like a vine ready to trap me onto the bed until I repented for my sins.

My eyes burned all day with my lack of sleep, and although I kept my chin held high and my legs crossed beneath my skirt during class, I could feel Tobias' body heat from a mile away.

That wasn't to say he wasn't as cold as a blizzard, though. The frostiness in his blue eyes skimmed over me every time he glanced at me, and I felt a coldness settle into my bones that not even the chilly, wintery breeze outside this fortifying school could top.

My pencil moved over my paper with ease, falling into the routine of schoolwork that had always come so easily to me. Thanks to my *murdering* parents, I had been at the top of my class since I entered pre-school. Not to mention, my pre-school was an aristocracy compared to most, teaching young four-year-olds Latin, as if we were going to use that language at some point in our adolescent lives.

A quiet laugh flew from my mouth as I accidentally wrote a sentence down in Latin instead of English.

My phone vibrated in front of me, ricocheting off the library table as I sat alone, waiting for Tobias to show up—which, to be honest, I wasn't sure if he was going to come.

We had this study date—*whoa, not date*—session planned since Friday when I threw him under the bus in front of his father, but that was before our little...*thing*...on Saturday.

What was I thinking?

In fact, why couldn't I stop thinking about it?

The dread was there, but so was the excitement. Tobias was like a drug, smothering me into submission, even now, days later.

I could hardly look Gemma in the eye the next morning, too guilty with thoughts of her brother's hands on my body, whispering dirty words into my ear. Heat rushed to my skin, and I wiggled in my library seat again, hearing the door open.

Another student had left for the evening, so I was all alone. Not even Journey, who often liked to hide in the library aisles with Cade, was in here.

When I glanced back up to the door again, wondering if I should just pack up and head to my room, I felt the dooming pit forming in my lower belly. *Disappointment.* It was there, and it irritated me. *He* irritated me.

My phone went off again, and I grabbed it, gripping the sides tightly with my red-painted nails before dropping it to the table and sitting up straighter at the sound of the door.

In walked Tobias, his haughty, dangerous attitude following him like a shadow.

My gaze went straight to his hands that were more talented than I could have ever imagined, and I bit the inside of my cheek, hating that I let him touch me the other night. *It was a mistake.*

His long strides were stealthy and domineering as he prowled toward the table, not holding a single book for studying. He commanded the room like some wicked nightmare, sucking up all the air in it and making it nearly impossible to breathe. Dark hair, intense bone structure with a jaw so cut it would make someone bleed if they dared punch him.

"Enjoying the show?" I jumped, my knees banging together as my phone vibrated again. *Who the hell is messaging me? Don't they know I'm fantasizing about my best friend's brother at the moment?*

My hands dropped to my lap, and I pinched the inside of my thigh, bringing myself back to the present. "You're late."

His smirk was annoying, and what was even more annoying was that he walked right past the table, not bothering to pull out a chair at all.

I spun around in my seat with my mouth slightly gaped. "What are you doing?"

"Follow me, and you'll see."

The invitation was nothing more than a sentence with words strung together, but it went straight to my wobbly legs, pushing me up from the table as I ran straight into a deadly nightmare that I'd hoped to have a happily ever after.

The aisles of the library were quiet, with nothing more than books breathing their dusty scent throughout the air. A floorboard creaked when Tobias stepped over it, bending it to its worth and then stepping further into the dark. I did the same, nerves spiking with adrenaline as I continued staring at his tall frame and broad shoulders.

"Tobias, the library closes soon and curfew starts. If you want to study for the test on Wednesday, we need to get started." I stopped a few feet behind him, staring a hole in between his shoulder blades. I half-expected a fire to start brewing right there through his black t-shirt. "Oh," I said, shifting on my feet. "And I'd appreciate it if you didn't rip up my notecards that I made for you. *Again.*"

Tobias spun around slowly, the smirk still on his face. My heart jumped to my throat as I dropped my gaze to his skilled lips, watching his tongue dip out for a second to wet them. Hunger flared in his cool eyes, and confusion hit me like a bookshelf had fallen on top of me.

Words were nonexistent when his hands cupped my waist, and my brain went offline for a few seconds as he pushed me against the spines of the books, making dust fly off to rain between us.

"You annoy me," he admitted, tilting his head in a predatory way, completely turning the evening's events upside down.

The word was no more than a whisper diving through the air. "Likewise."

His chin tipped, his messy dark hair begging me to run my hands through it. He towered over me, and he was the only thing I could see. "I bet you can't stop thinking about Saturday, yeah?"

Not even for a second.

"Saturday? Not sure what you're referring to."

He tsked, flicking his tongue over his white teeth. My heart hammered inside my chest, and it only worked harder when one of his hands left my waist and crept up past my navel and rested right between my breasts that ached in ways that they never had before. *Oh no.*

I felt my heart ramming against his palm, embarrassed that I couldn't hide my reaction from him. I'd always been a decent liar, able to hide my emotions well. It was how I always got away with playing doctor with the animals behind my family's manor. *Of course I wasn't dislodging the rabbit traps the groundskeeper set up. I was taking a walk before I began studying again.*

"You lie," Tobias said, rubbing his thumb over my bottom lip and jolting me back to the present. "You haven't stopped thinking about me."

"That's...that's not true. I regret what we did. If Gemma knew..."

He laughed, his rough chuckle more of a rasp than anything. "What? You don't think she'd be happy with you fucking around with her brother?"

Honestly, I wasn't sure. But I wasn't willing to find out. Friendship meant the most to me. With no family—that I claimed, at least—friendship was the closest thing I had to stability. I was certain Gemma didn't realize how deeply rooted I was to this school and the people I surrounded myself with daily, because I played it off well, always talking shit about St. Mary's as if it were a prison, angry that my parents sent me here, but it wasn't necessarily true.

Was I angry that they sent me here? Yes, but only under the circumstances was I angry. St. Mary's was much more than an old, decaying bundle of bricks and stones. It was comfort and safety and *home*.

"And what about you?" I asked, deflecting the attention he was putting on me. "Have you stopped thinking of me?"

His chuckle rang through my body again, making me squirm in his grasp. His hand had moved from my chest, and he cupped the side of my face, his long fingers weaving through my dark hair.

"No."

Butterflies flew to my lower belly, and the air around us stiffened. One wrong move and I would be at his mercy again, allowing Tobias Richardson to make me crumble beneath his feet.

"No?" I asked, trying my hardest to stay present. If Gemma walked into the library and saw this, what would she say? What would she say if I told her that I wasn't who she thought I was and that I knew more about keeping secrets than she ever could have guessed?

And it was true. I could keep a secret. It was what St. Mary's was made of: secrets, danger, and more fucking secrets. And this? Right here? Whatever was brewing between me and Tobias was a secret I wasn't willing to tell.

"No, Sloane," Tobias said, pulling his hand away from my face and taking a step away, taking my bearings with him.

My brows fell in one single swoosh, and my lip jutted out in confusion. Out of the two of us, I was the one with more morals. But was he the one stepping away, and that had me second-guessing everything.

"Do you want to know why I haven't been able to stop thinking about you?" Tobias didn't let me answer as a sick smile slid onto his face. His white teeth were blinding, and his lips twitched as he pulled his phone out and held it out in between us.

"What's this?" I asked with a snap in my tone. Whatever he was about to do was going to send me into a spiral. I knew it.

"You at my mercy, baby. That's what this is."

The second I heard my voice on his phone, the library began to cave in on me. The pressure of the air drew the breath straight from my lungs, and black spots began to dance in my vision as his hot tone filled my ears. *"Tell me what you want from your best friend's brother, Sloane."*

Moisture gathered behind my eyes as I snapped my head up from his phone. Mortification was a knife lodged into my chest, and part of me wanted to fall to my knees in front of him. *How dare he?*

I reached forward quickly, trying to swipe his phone, but he held it up above my head, and I bounced off his hard chest, banging my lip off his sternum. "Nice try, shrimp." He laughed, shooting me a wink as he kept the device high in the air.

Hot, angry breaths left my mouth as I peered up at him, wanting to smack him clear across the face. "What is this?" I demanded, confused and angry all in one.

"Hmm," he said, taking a step away and pushing his phone back into his pocket in the most arrogant, lazy way possible. "I think they call it blackmail?"

I crossed my arms and put as much distance between us as possible. *He tricked me, and I fell for it. Fuck.* "Blackmail for what? What do you want?"

The humor quickly faded from his features and was replaced with something much darker. "For you to leave me the *fuck* alone." Hurt itched somewhere on my back that I ignored. "And if you tell my father, or Gemma, that I'm not studying with you and allowing you to be my fucking babysitter like I'm a child instead of a man who has done unspeakable things that would make you recoil..." I gulped when he paused, remembering the severity of Tobias Richardson and everything he had been through in the last several years of his life. "Then I'll fucking broadcast this shit over the intercom."

Lies formed on my tongue as I spat my response back. "And why should I care? I don't care if the school knows you and I messed around. So what? We're teenagers, and teenagers fuck, Tobias. That's what the claiming parties are all about."

He rolled his blue eyes, chuckling. "You think you can lie to me, Sloane?" He crowded my space quickly, placing his finger under my chin in a soft, tender way that confused me. "Do you know what I've been doing these last few weeks?"

"Avoiding me?" I answered, knowing he had been at every turn.

"Observing. Watching. Learning."

I said nothing as his finger stayed pressed against my chin, tilting my face up to his as his other finger traced my bottom lip. "And you, my little Snow White, value friendship over everything." His brows dropped in confusion. "It makes me wonder why someone like you is so focused on the protection of your friends and the worthiness of their trust, but the truth still remains. You value Gemma, Journey, Mercedes, and even those boys who call themselves the Rebels, more than you do yourself. You care. You care deeply." Before he twisted his gaze away, I saw something flicker across his features. Something that I couldn't pinpoint. "So, don't lie to me, Sloane. If Gemma knew that you had begged for my touch the other night, without even so much as telling her you have this little crush on me, she'd be hurt, especially given the fact that one wrong move and you might just propel me away from her again."

My mouth opened, but he continued.

"Oh, how easy it would be to say that you broke my heart and that was why I had to leave. That I couldn't stand to be here because I was too fucked up over it. I mean, she already knows I'm unstable." He laughed, and I felt the tears pricking my eyes. "Gem would blame you, sweetheart."

"So, what, then?" I rasped. "You want me to leave you alone and let you fail? Even though your father and sister are both relying on me to help you through this year of school so you somehow graduate?" I pushed his hand off my face, angry that he was winning and angry that my feelings were hurt. I was wounded. Wounded that I fell for his touch. Wounded that I thought he was having the same pesky little thoughts about me that I was having for him. Guilt lingered there, too. *I am so stupid!*

Tobias shrugged, placing his hands in his pockets and leaning against the bookshelf across from me, putting much-needed space between us. "If I need you, I know where to find you."

A sarcastic noise left me as I threw my hands in the air. "You do need me!"

His nostrils flared at the same time his temples flicked. A thought crossed behind his blue eyes that I craved to hear. *What is it like in his head? Who is Tobias Richardson?*

He was much more than just a few mixed signals. Tobias was a bundle of harsh behavior, fleeting hot glances, deep thoughts, and caressing touches.

"Leave me alone, Sloane," he said, pushing off from the shelf, crowding my space yet again, and blurring every line I just drew between us. His warm, minty, dark whisper floated down from his lips and hit me in the face. "Or I promise you, you'll regret it."

"What am I supposed to do?" I seethed, peering up at him. "You want me to lie to your sister and father? Act like everything is fine between us, and you're studying with me and using the stupid fucking notecards I keep making you?"

His lips twitched. "Sure."

"How is that fair?" My voice grew with volume, but I heard the wobbling in my tone. "I'm damned if I do, and I'm damned if I don't!"

The haughty attitude flew off him in waves as he slowly backed away from me, leaving me in the dark aisle of the library. Before he got too far, he said, "Welcome to my fucking life, Sloane. Always faced with another wrong decision that's worse than the last. Pick the lesser of two evils, baby."

I stood there, with my hands by my sides, for far too long, staring at the empty aisle that Tobias had disappeared down. Dread slithered up my back like a slippery snake and threatened to squeeze the life out of me as I weighed my options.

This is such a fucking mess.

I knew what Tobias and I did the other night was wrong. I felt dirty in a way, and untrustworthy as a friend. Guilt stayed perched on my shoulder like a black crow as I grabbed my books and phone and began walking back to my room, half-expecting Tobias to pop out to play the dirty recording he had on his phone of me again.

The girls' hallway seemed quieter than normal and more ominous, leaving me alone with my thoughts. Dark nooks appeared creepier, and every time I turned a corner, I felt as if someone was going to pop out and scare me. My hand shook against the iron knob as I pushed my dorm door open, half-hoping that Gemma was in Isaiah's room instead of ours so I could digest her brother's words, but to my surprise, she was sitting on her bed, cross-legged, sketching in the sketchpad that her father had given her.

"Hey." She smiled, peeking up for a second. "How was studying with Tobias?"

My mouth opened as my stomach thumped straight to the floor. I quickly walked over to my desk opposite of hers, and placed my books on it, unable to look her in the eye. *Shit. Shit. Shit.* How dare he put me in this position? It was like he *knew* the secrets that were trapped inside my chest. It was like he *knew* that Willow was always in the back of my mind, covered with a thick blanket of guilt.

I heard the scratching of Gemma's pencil against the paper and peered back at her, pushing thoughts of Willow and our broken friendship away. My parents and their excuses followed by demands burned my chest so quickly I winced.

"I know he can be tough," Gemma started, not bothering to glance up from her art. Her brown hair was in a high bun on the top of her head, making her look that much more innocent. "Tat—I mean, my father and I have been chatting about him and learning more and more of what he had to do while in the Covens."

The Covens.

I knew all about the psych ward that Journey was kept at with false information, but I knew very little about the covert program on the bottom floor that Tobias was a part of. All I knew was that it was like a prison that housed black-market killers, but the scars on Tobias' back were like little windows showing just how horrifying it was.

Gemma continued on with her quiet thoughts, making me falter over the line of truths and lies. "He's stubborn," she admitted. "And he pretends like he is okay, but I know he's not." She sighed. "I mean, after all, we're twins. We're connected in a way."

"Yeah," I croaked, gripping my phone in my hand and replaying the last twenty minutes I had spent with him in the library, him all but threatening me. "He's definitely stubborn."

"You'd tell me if he wasn't okay, right? Like, truly not okay? Not just his broody self who likes to insult you because you're trying to get closer to him to help. But I mean, like, *truly* not okay. He doesn't talk to me like he used to. There's just this...wall."

I was stuck, feet cemented onto the hard floor beneath me, weighing me down like a ton of bricks. The truth was there, pressing at my lips and wanting to come out, but then my phone vibrated in my hand, and I quickly glanced down at it, reminding me that I had gotten several texts while Tobias had me trapped.

Blood drained from my face and gathered in a pool beneath my feet. It was as if I could smell the icy, metallic, vital fluid that flowed from my best friend's parents. The reminder of the pungent scent did nothing but cause panic to propel more lies from my mouth.

"Yeah, I'd tell you, Gem. He's fine."

I quickly turned around and put my back to her, staring down at my phone like it was a gun pointing in my direction.

Unknown: Bently is asking where you are. I told him you were sneaking out. I swear I saw the excitement in his eyes at the thought of you being a little rule-breaker.

Unknown: You are a little rule-breaker, aren't you?

Unknown: You've hidden a murder from the authorities. Ran away. Left me in the dust without parents.

My heart beat wildly, and sweat coated my back. *Willow?* It couldn't have been Willow. There was no way. How would she have gotten my new number? How would she have known what had happened?

Water pooled in my eyes as I stared down at my phone, gripping the edges like I was ready to snap it in half. A tremor went through my limbs, and I quickly swallowed the lump knotting in my throat.

It's someone messing with you.

I shut my eyes for a brief second and deleted the messages

quickly. I powered down my phone and threw it onto my desk before shooting Gemma a brief smile and storming into our bathroom.

The door shutting her out was just as isolating as I felt holding onto a secret that I was demanded to keep for my parents. The more secrets you kept, the more weighed down you were, and I *hated* Tobias Richardson for making me keep one more.

CHAPTER TEN

TOBIAS

"You do need me!"

My teeth rubbed together, my jaw hinging with pain each time I caught her pretty skin in my peripheral vision during class—and during lunch because God forbid I go back to my room to be alone while everyone ate. Journey made that impossible by literally dragging me out of my room by my ear while Cade smirked in the background.

It didn't matter where Sloane White was. If we were in the same room, the space around us felt tighter than my shoulder muscles. I could sense her, like some electromagnetic pull or something inhumane. I half-expected my twin sister to come knocking on my door with her mighty self to yell at me for blackmailing Sloane, but to my surprise, Sloane kept her snarky little lips shut, and for that, I was thankful.

I still despised her, though.

The weight slammed as I dropped it back to the padded mat below my feet. Irrational anger heated me, and I cracked my neck, reeling myself in.

"Just take deep breaths, bro." I snapped my attention to Shiner as he lifted a few dumbbells in the mirror, keeping his back to me. The Rebels annoyed me more than ever because they were so pompous, and everyone in the hallways parted when they walked through. My sister was the sweet one of their group, and if it weren't for her and Journey dating two of them, I'd probably punch their lights out, but for the only two people in my life that I may have had a caring notion for, I allowed them to breathe the same air as me.

"What?" I asked, wiping sweat from my forehead as it dripped into my eyes, burning them so much I actually relished the pain.

Shiner breathed through his nose, muscles flowing with adrenaline as he lifted the weights higher. It was just him and me in the weight room. Everyone else was with their significant other for the rest of the evening or holed up in their room, hating their life like the rest of us.

"Something on your mind, yeah? I'm sensing anger." Shiner chuckled as he jogged in place after dropping his dumbbells. His damp hair flopped onto his forehead with every other jump. "I mean, there's always something a bit angry about you, but I can tell something is eating you up more than usual."

What was he? Some fucking mind reader?

He threw his hands up as I glared at him. "Oh, now. Come on. Don't direct your anger toward me. I get it, bro. I get it more than you know."

Yeah fucking right.

"Let me guess, you want everyone to leave you alone. You want the staring to stop. You want to stop being featured on St. Mary's Murmurs. You want the girls to shut their mouths and suck your cock so you don't have to feel anything other than a release of pent-up aggression and a second of peace." He paused as he took his wet shirt off and wrapped it around his neck, pulling both ends with his hands and letting the damp material hang down onto his swollen chest. "You may have a lot of shit locked in here..." He tapped his temple and laughed sarcastically. "But you aren't *that* hard to read, my man."

I stared at him for far too long, perturbed that he wasn't as stupid as he acted most of the time. "What's Mary's Murmurs?"

Shiner threw his head back and laughed, walking away with his head shaking. "Well, as of late, it's a gossip blog that revolves around the bad boy of St. Mary's and his *delectable* lips and *strong* hands."

I snapped my head over to him. "What did you just say?"

"Don't look at me like that!" he said, not fazed by my unhinged expression. "I'm not the one who wrote the blog. It's the chicks. They're obsessed with the mysterious Tobias Richardson." He laughed again and left the weight room, leaving me alone with my thoughts that somehow circled back to *her*.

There was an ache present, thumping between my temples and making my blood rush faster. I was perturbed over the smallest, tiniest fucking thought that entered my head, wondering if Sloane was the one who wrote the blog.

"What the fuck," I mumbled, placing my hands on my hips and pacing the gym. *Do I want her to be the one to write it?*

Thoughts came at me in waves, and I was well aware of the panic present. I was infuriated that I was allowing her to infiltrate all my thoughts. It was becoming harder and harder to hide from them.

I grunted, bending down and picking up the weight again. I huffed as I lifted, watching myself in the mirror as I tried to distract myself with pain. The muscles along my forearms screamed in agony, and I shut my eyes at the view of my veins filling with blood in my forearms. *One, two, three, fou—*

"You fucking asshole!" There was a thump on my back from a small fist. I grunted in surprise and dropped the dumbbell onto the mat, opening my eyes. My instincts took over too quickly for me to stop them. They had been drilled into my head since I was too young to understand what I was being trained to do, and some habits didn't die off as quickly as I'd hoped. My hand was around her small neck, and she was pinned against the mirror with enough force to make her panic.

"You *never* sneak up on someone like me, Snow White." *What was she fucking thinking?*

I lessened my grip around her neck and kept my glowering gaze locked on her watery eyes. Sweat dripped onto my eyelashes, but I kept my eyes peeled, refusing to back down from her little bitch fit.

"You're a fucking asshole," she spat, clearly not caring about her own well-being. Either that, or she wasn't as afraid of me as she should have been. My eyebrow slowly arched upward as my fingers heated with her pulse ramming against them. Sloane's jaw was edged with anger, her chin resting on my hand as she swallowed.

Time had passed, but her pulse never died down. It continued to beat against my fingers as a nice reminder that she was a living, breathing being that drove me absolutely fucking crazy. The warm, hazel color of her eyes was muddied with something I'd only ever felt a few times in my entire life. *Fear.*

"You sure do talk a big game for someone that is afraid, Sloane."

The urge to glance at her lips was threatening to kill me right on the spot. My hand tightened on her neck, and she lifted her head higher, trying to scoot away from me. I snatched my attention away, looking at myself in the mirror behind her.

I look like a fucking monster. My arched cheeks were red from my workout. The tiny scar on my eyebrow was as clear as it always was, except sweat droplets traveled down beside it, magnifying it to an extreme. The curve of my jaw was wound as tight as I felt on the inside, and my heart was beating so quickly that I swore I could see it beating against my chest.

"I am not afraid!" There was the slightest wobble in her voice, and she jumped back toward the mirror, banging against it, as I sliced my attention back to hers. Her face was red too, and...wet?

I dropped my gaze to her lips, and every thought inside my head died right there on the spot. "Why are you bleeding?"

An animalistic urge cut through me, claws puncturing my back, rooting me for what I was feeling in the moment. *Panic. Anger.* Who had the courage to hurt her? And why did I want to kill them for it?

I crowded her space in an instant, grabbed onto her wrists, and slammed them up above her head onto the mirror, not going for the kill this time with my hand around her neck. "I'll ask you again, Sloane. Why the fuck is your mouth stained with blood?"

CHAPTER ELEVEN

SLOANE

I WASN'T afraid at the moment. Fear was a vanishing thought that left as soon as I found him in the weight room. Anger and hostility took over, and my fist collided with his wet back, punching him from behind.

Gemma's brother or not, I was full of hot rage.

But that was not to say I wasn't afraid moments ago, locked in a closet, *alone*.

Tobias was sweaty and flushed as he leaned down into my space again, causing my head to tilt. Our lips were close—so close I felt the heat from his breath. "What happened?"

"Don't play stupid with me!" I screeched, stomping my heel onto his foot. His head twisted as he sucked in a breath, but he didn't leave my space. In fact, he got closer, completely ignoring that I just placed all my weight on his shoe. "You... you already know what happened! It wasn't enough to black- mail me, threatening to destroy my friendship with your sister, but you had to push it even further?"

God, I am so angry.

Tobias' hand slapped against the mirror after letting one of my wrists fall from his tight grip. His head fell in defeat before he popped back up and stared at my mouth. My lip felt puffy as I ran my tongue over it. "I don't know what you're talking about. So quit fucking around, and tell me why you're in here ruining my workout."

I glanced down at his shirt and saw that it was heavy with sweat. His arms glistened, and the ends of his hair were darker than usual. *Wait, so it wasn't him?* I jolted my tongue out and licked my lip again, tasting the bitter metallic from the dried blood.

"I'm waiting," he barked, lasering onto my fat lip. There was a rush of something behind his blue eyes, and it was surprising because I didn't see many emotions from Tobias. No, actually. I didn't see anything but anger from him, but even so, his anger and annoyance toward me seemed like a ploy, to an extent.

"Have you been here the whole time?" I questioned, feeling the dread grow stronger the longer I tried to make sense of what had happened.

"Yes," he answered, frustrated. "Did someone make you bleed?"

Does he care?

I tried to wrap my head around the last hour and how I started off in my room, alone, checking on my college applications and dreaming about the future, and then how the hell I ended up here, in the weight room, with a guy who very obviously hated my presence but was locked onto my bloody lip with murder in his eyes.

"It's..." I pulled at the one wrist he still had pinned against the mirror, trying to free it. "Just...never mind. I thought it was you who did it."

"Did what?" he asked, gripping me even harder. I angled my head up, locking onto his strong fingers as they enveloped my entire wrist. "You are not getting out of here until you tell me, so give up now."

I huffed, pulling at my wrist again. He moved so slowly to erase the space between us that my body had plenty of time to panic at the warmth filling my chest.

It's because you're all messed up right now. I was *not* feeling relieved at the fact that Tobias seemed to care about me bleeding, because let's face it, he didn't care.

"Let me g—" The words died on my tongue as his thumb touched my fat lip, rubbing the pad of his finger over it gently. Goosebumps rained over me, and I couldn't stop myself from shivering.

"Tell me," he whispered. The quiet coarseness of his tone put some kind of spell on me. "Did someone touch you?"

I swallowed. "No."

His finger stilled, and he breathed in a sigh, his strong jawline untensing for a single second. When his icy eyes flung to mine, an iceberg made itself known in my lower belly.

"I'll stay in here all night with you pinned between my grasp until you tell me what happened, so you might as well start talking, baby. You have no idea the lengths of my patience." He huffed out a laugh. "I was patient for years before I made my escape from the Covens, and I will stay here for years, too, if it means you'll tell me who I need to hurt."

Whoa. What? "I told you—"

He stopped me, gripping my wrist tightly again to gather my attention. "People don't have to touch you to hurt you. I know that better than anyone." His gaze fell to my lip again, and I succumbed to the truth and validity in his words. *Did Tobias Richardson just go soft on me?*

"Fine," I rushed out. "I'll tell you."

His lips twitched with my surrender. "Good girl."

I took a deep breath and glanced away as I relived the

memory from not even an hour ago, knowing it was something that would haunt me for a while.

I should have been studying with Tobias in the library. Well, I mean, I didn't need to study, but he did. Instead, I was sitting on my bed, checking on every college application that I had sent in, hoping I got into at least one of them and could become a veterinarian and displease my parents even more.

It wasn't that I wanted to become a veterinarian just to spite them. It was what I truly wanted. I have always wanted to become one, and they knew it, too. How could they not? Unless they truly never saw me and only saw the little girl they were breeding to follow in their political footsteps, then they'd have no idea.

I clicked on Cornell University, knowing it was one of the best colleges for veterinary medicine but also feeling that it was the most problematic school on my list because it was in New York, and I swore I'd never live there again.

Too close to them.

Too close to Willow.

Just as her heart-shaped face popped into my head, music began to play throughout the room—so softly at first I had hardly noticed it. I slowly closed my laptop, trepidation making me tread lightly. What is that? *I recognized the tune immediately and felt panicky. The temperature of my room kicked up as sweat began to form at my hairline. "Clair de lune." The sounds of the piano in the Debussy piece matched my heart rate as I listened more, looking over at Gemma's side of the room, wondering if she had left something on.* Why would she have Debussy playing? *Gemma didn't even like music. She liked silence. She worked in the art room each morning with nothing but the sound of charcoal rubbing over her canvas as noise.*

I stood in front of my closet with my hands on my hips, noticing the music was a little louder. Something told me not to go in there. Like one of those girls in the horror movie that Gemma and I watched last Sunday with Isaiah as he huffed and acted annoyed.

But regardless, I went in. My hand shook on the knob, and I made a mental note to tell Headmaster Ellison that the closets needed lights installed—not that I planned to go in them chasing after a weird tune again or anything.

The scent of laundry wafted out as I moved my uniforms around, listening for the music to get louder. The smallest flicker of recollection lit up in the back of my head, recalling the last time I'd heard Debussy. Memories of that night began to break through, and my fear kicked up a notch. I quickly spun around, spooking myself, wanting to run out of the door, but as soon as I stepped forward, it slammed shut, and I screamed.

Dizziness took over as I spun around several times, trying to right my vision and find a way out. My face hit the door, and my teeth banged onto my lip, pain immediately following. Sweat trickled against my palms as I felt for the doorknob. The music played in the background, and with each dip of the piano keys, my heart dropped a little further.

Am I locked in here?

I finally found the doorknob, and relief cooled me. My fingers twisted the metal, but the relief was quickly replaced with dread. Locked? The closets didn't lock. There weren't locks on them. My fists ached as I banged on the door several times, the music sounding more like defeat than anything else. I sank to my legs after several good hits against the door and covered my ears with my hands, trying to right my breathing. Snippets of me on the balcony of my parents' home in upstate New York played right along with the melody of the music, and it was as if I were stuck in a vivid nightmare, reliving the horrors of that night that changed me down to my core.

After gulping air and wiping my face, ignoring the blood on my tongue, I stood back up and jiggled the doorknob again. Who the hell locked me in here? *Tobias came to mind. He was the only one at this school who had serious beef with me. I was going to kill him. Sure, he may not have known the trauma in my life that I liked to hide from, but fuck him. This wasn't okay.*

I stared at the bleak darkness that stood between me and the closet door and took a deep breath, pushing away the sound of Debussy, and rammed my shoulder into the wood. I bounced off and whimpered, rubbing my hand over the soreness in my shoulder. I did that several times before I saw the door wiggling a little from the force of my body. I quickly brought my foot up and kicked it, and then I heard a bang, as if something had fallen to the ground. My hand quickly found the doorknob, and I pushed open the door.

I fell to my knees, breathing in the cooler air from our bedroom versus the hot and stuffy air of the closet. Debussy was still playing, and I stared at my hanging clothes as if they were ominous beings instead of plaid cotton. The room was empty and the same as it was moments ago, except my desk chair laid on its side, inches from me. Anger quickly replaced the fear as I pushed away the memories of that night and headed straight for Tobias, bloody lip and all.

"Let's go."

I stumbled forward, catching my breath after I relayed *most* of the information to Tobias. And by most, I meant I left out all the big parts, and the only thing that remained was the fact that I had been locked in my closet. Nothing about what Debussy meant to me or why I panicked like I did. Or the fact that I no longer felt safe knowing that it wasn't a simple prank that Tobias pulled on me.

"You're not lying to me, are you? I don't trust you." *It really wasn't him?*

Tobias stopped walking right before we went through the doorway of the weight room. His back stiffened, and he glared back at me, still holding my wrist tightly. His cool gaze dropped to my lip, and I almost reached up to wipe the dry blood off it.

"You shouldn't trust me," he said quietly. His thick, dark eyelashes crinkled around his blue eyes. "But I'm not lying. I wouldn't lock you in your closet unless I was in there with you."

The smallest smirk appeared before he turned away, and I

stumbled over my thoughts. I felt the slight heating inside my belly as his words fully resonated with me. *Locked in the closet with him?* Why did that sound so...appealing?

Intrigued, I asked, "What is that supposed to mean?"

Instead of him answering, he continued to pull me through the dark hallways of St. Mary's. Most of the students were in their rooms for the evening or finishing up in the dining hall for dinner, so we didn't pass many, except for an underclassman here and there. Silence continued to follow us as I trailed after Tobias with him pulling me like he was saving me from deep water.

When we were outside my door, he dropped my wrist and looked back at me, his tight jaw catching a ray of light from the flickering sconce close by. "Is my sister in there?"

I shook my head slowly. "I doubt it. She's with Isaiah most evenings."

His tight shoulders dropped, and I rolled my eyes. "Didn't want to play the part of the nice brother who isn't black-mailing her best friend?"

"Something like that," he said, pushing my door open and quickly casing the room with his determined eyes. He was back to holding my wrist, as if he thought I was going to dart out of the room and leave him.

"You can let go of my wrist," I whispered, suddenly wanting to fall into myself at the sound of Debussy *still* playing in the background. It was like I was back home all over again. My mother always had some form of classical music playing through the house. Once, I changed it to eighties rock, and before she was...who she was now...she giggled and shot me a playful smile before switching it back to classical.

I sighed, crossing my arms over my uniform. I glanced down to my shoes and righted my vision, ignoring the hurt.

Tobias swiftly walked over to my closet, his shirt damp

from his workout. He was still sweaty, and his muscles were pumped full of blood. The confidence flew off him in waves as he pulled the closet door open with a look of anger in his cool eyes, and the stealth he extracted the second he stepped foot in my room was hard to ignore. The mean, arrogant boy who refused my help and blackmailed me, threatening my friendship with his sister, was no longer in sight. Instead, there was a glimpse of the man who was sent to an elusive underground prison and forced to become something much worse than a damaged little boy ripped away from his mother and twin sister.

I stayed in the middle of my room, chewing on my nail and rubbing my tongue over my lip every so often. I was jittery, and I couldn't decide if it was because Tobias was acting like he cared about my well-being, or if it was because I now knew that someone had come into my room, placed a music-playing device of some sort in my closet, and taunted me with the same song that played the night Willow's parents had died mere feet away from me.

I should tell my parents.

The thought made me sick. I instantly grabbed onto my belly and flipped around, taking even breaths through my mouth. If I were to go to my parents and tell them that not only was I getting anonymous text messages from someone who obviously knew about that night but also that someone had snuck into my room and locked me in a closet, they would rip me away from St. Mary's in a heartbeat, and I would rather be messed with and tormented here than be in their home again.

Home. What a stupid thought.

A second later, Tobias walked out of the closet. His feet shuffled lazily, and when I turned around, he was glaring at a black cassette player that looked small and insignificant in his large hand.

"Where was it?" I whispered. My heart was ramming against my chest, and I felt a dizzy spell approaching.

"Tucked on the top shelf. Out of your reach. What is the significance of this? Was it meant for you or my sister?"

Ah, so that's where the concern is coming from.

"It..." I tried to swallow, but my throat grew tight with emotion. Fear crept around in my head like a ghost, and the reality of the situation struck me like lightning. *Is there someone at this school who knows what happened?* I tried to convince myself that it was some misunderstanding. That no one knew what Debussy meant to me.

My head slowly inched up when I felt a soft finger underneath my chin. Two deep, blue eyes pinned me to the floor, and all thoughts vanished. I somehow found myself swimming in Tobias' eyes, and for once, I didn't feel like I needed a life raft.

"It's meant for you?"

I couldn't speak.

His finger stayed on my chin as he peered down at me, face relaxed and anger gone. *He is beautiful.* My soul shook. Something brewed inside my chest. I was quickly learning that when Tobias Richardson looked at you—and I meant, *really* looked at you—the world stopped spinning.

"What is the significance of this, Sloane?"

I pulled back, taking myself away from his grip because Tobias had a way of making me stupid. Gemma could walk through that door at any moment and see that I was completely and utterly affected by her brother like I'd never been before.

"None. It's just some song that I heard playing and went into my closet."

Tobias laughed, but it was the type that sent shivers down your spine. His long legs took him over to the closet, where he bent down and picked up the fallen chair that was no doubt placed in front of the door so I couldn't get out. "Someone came in here, lured you into the closet with that recording, and then trapped you in there. I know what it's like to be locked in a tiny room with nothing but nightmares attacking you, and don't even get me started on when you fall asleep at night." I quickly remembered when I had gone into his room and saw his bed messy and his damp shirt. *He has nightmares.* "So, I'll ask you again..." Tobias erased the space between us, and I backed up against my bed until my legs hit the soft blankets. "What secrets do you have buried in that wicked little mind of yours, Snow White?"

My chin rose, and I was quick to latch back onto the girl I had become when my parents changed my last name and threw me into this boarding school. Sloane White was back. She was scared, but she was back and determined to be fine. "None of your business, Tobias. You want me to 'leave you the *fuck* alone,' remember?"

He chuckled sarcastically. His hot, seedy breath hit me in the face and made my chest tight. His dark gaze flung to my bed behind me, and I quickly slipped away from him and walked away. My heart rammed inside my chest like a bull trying to escape, and I was suddenly nervous. *I don't like this.* I was never like this when it came to a guy. I was always in control. I was always cool as a cucumber. But being inside my room with Tobias Richardson had my heart beating faster than it did when I was locked inside that damn closet.

Sparking tingles charged down my arms when Tobias' fingers slowly brushed over my jumbled blankets. The cotton bowed under his grip as he bundled the covers in his tight fist before letting go and lowering to his stomach on the floor in one fluid movement. My stomach dropped right along with him.

The agility he possessed was that of a trained warrior. There was no fear or jerky movements. Tobias was determined, and his actions were easy. He first looked under my bed as I stood back and tried to even my breathing, feeling creeped out that someone had been inside my room. *But who?* Confusion lingered, and I would have been stupid not to be concerned.

It had been four years since I'd seen Willow.

Four years since her parents had died by the hands of mine.

The thought crossed my mind that it was some sick form of reverse psychology from my parents. Maybe they were doing this to see if I would tell them. I swallowed the hurtful truth and watched as Tobias quietly moved over to his sister's bed, which was a few feet away from mine. I stood back with my arms crossed over my chest and watched as he scanned the room, searching in all the nooks and crannies as if he wasn't fazed at all.

He walked past me into the bathroom without even glancing in my direction, and I instantly felt stupid. There was something about him being in here, searching my room for...*what—A person? A clue?*—that made me feel insignificant in ways I couldn't explain. Like I was a nuisance to him. Like he had some duty to search my room even when I didn't ask him to.

I mean, he didn't like me. I obviously got under his skin, and he hated me for it. He had touched me in ways that made my heart soar only for it to fall afterward when I realized it was all a stupid trick in the end.

"I think my room is clear. You can leave now." Small bits of anger shone through my sentence, and I hoped he would detect it and get the hint.

My back was turned to him when I heard him close my bathroom door. He was quiet, and I couldn't hear his foot-steps, but I felt him the second he was in my space again, like a black hole threatening to suck me up. My eyes were closed as I took even breaths through my nose, and when his hand landed on my hip, I jumped and quickly spun around, peering up into his determined gaze.

The tight flicker of his jaw matched the tightness in my belly, but when he slowly reached up and placed a cool wet rag against my mouth, my eyes burned slightly. *What is he doing?*

The rag brushed over my lip, and it sent a jolt down my spine, burning a hole right through my bedroom floor.

"I've got it," I whispered, reaching up with a shaky hand and grabbing the rag from him. Tobias didn't even have a flicker of recognition in his eyes that I had even spoken a word. His fingers flicked mine away painfully, and I pulled my hand back, confused. He kept the cool rag pressed against my mouth for a few seconds as he stared at my fat lip, and when he dropped it, he pulled me in closer with his large hand still glued to my hip.

"Is it still puffy?" I whispered, unable to look away. *Is that why he's staring at my mouth?* My ears rang, and I was stuck in his unmoving pandemonium of hot chaos and jittery tingles.

Our chests brushed when he took a hefty breath. "I beg to know the secrets that want to stay locked inside that mouth, Sloane."

Confused didn't even touch what I was feeling. "Wh–what?"

His eyes flung to mine, and I jumped, our chests rubbing again. "Trust me. I'm just as confused by that sentence as you are." The wet rag fell to the floor beside my feet, and his hand gripped my chin. His thumb slowly brushed over my bottom lip, and it did things to my chest that I refused to accept. *He hated me. He tricked me. He blackmailed me and finger-fucked me only to record it and use it against me with his sister.*

"What are you doing?" I asked with anger, my voice no longer a whisper. I grabbed onto his wrist, my nails digging into his skin. "Want to finger me again and then use it against me?"

His lips rose for a single second as a tiny growl left his chest, rumbling against mine. I hoped to God he couldn't feel the tiny pebbles my breasts were currently sporting.

"You know I didn't come to you for help, right?" I said, pushing away the desire that I felt when it came to him. "I thought you were just being your typical asshole self and messing with me even more. Just forget about it."

Tobias quickly moved away at the sound of the door jiggling. Both of our heads turned in that direction, but right before his sister walked through, he cut me with a glare.

"I fucking wish I could forget about you."

And with that, he walked away, placed a soft kiss on his twin sister's head, and left me standing there with my throat closing as if I'd had an allergic reaction. And I did. To *him*.

CHAPTER TWELVE

TOBIAS

I FIDDLED with my phone in my hand, wanting to crack the screen so I could cut all ties with my life from *before*. That was how it felt. There was a before, and there was an after. When I first went to the Covens, I kicked and screamed while my uncle's hand gripped my shirt tightly. I had no idea why he'd taken me there or what I was up against.

Gemma and I were young when our mother 'left'—and I used that word lightly. It was apparent from the second she didn't come home that my uncle—who wasn't even our *real* uncle—had done something with her. That was probably the first of many reasons he sent me away—because he knew that I wasn't as easily manipulated, like Gemma.

Although I wasn't easily manipulated, I wasn't strong or wise enough to break away from the pit of hell he threw me in. I was too broken and confused to fight back when they tormented me and shut me in dark rooms for days until I submitted, and then I forgot all about him. Richard no longer existed. Gemma no longer was a concern in my head. There was a before, where my life was full of anger and confusion, and then the *after*, where I was consistently and excruciatingly trying to forget about my time spent with men as damaged as me.

Except, Sloane-fucking-White just *had* to drag me back to that place that I refused to acknowledge with her panic and clamped lips that shut out secrets I wanted to know. My leg hopped up and down as I was reminded of that time, and those people, and the feeling inside that I'd turned off since walking into St Mary's.

Heartless. I was really fucking good at turning off my emotions. It was how I survived for as long as I did. You couldn't be hurt if you didn't have feelings, yeah? You couldn't feel guilt if you were a vacant human with empty rounds laying beside your feet. I convinced myself long ago that the people I was forced to hunt down like prey in the large cities of this country were bad people. And to be honest, most of them were. But just because bad people were put to their end, that didn't mean good people weren't affected by it.

The second Tony had come back from his job and walked into my room for the first time, thinking it was his own, I knew he wasn't one of the rogue ones. Rogue ones = the ones who got high on death. I'd been there. I was considered a rogue one at times, but once I saw the torment and guilt on Tony's face, it was like a bullet was dislodged from my chest, and I was pulled back to the surface. He was a large guy with broad shoulders, with thick, black ink covering both of his arms, and he looked intimidating, as if he could break a neck in a split second, and he absolutely could.

His face was buried in his hands, and when he looked up and saw me standing against the wall, realizing he was in the wrong room, it was the first of many visits to my room after our 'jobs'.

We'd sit, in silence, just to know we weren't alone,

allowing our vulnerabilities to silently bleed out into the empty room, seeping below our feet and going right down the drain as we waited for our next assignment.

My hand flinched when my phone vibrated, catching the eye of Sloane who sat no more than two feet away from me at her perfectly neat desk. The scribbling of her pencil had stopped for a brief second as she pierced me with a stare only to go back to her work a second later. Her lip was no longer swollen, and the feeling of desperation no longer assaulted me like I was standing in the middle of a fucking gun fight. But the fact that I was holding my phone, ready to read a response from Tony about Sloane, told me that I wasn't in the clear with her yet.

Fuck, why do I even care?

Tony: You only text me when you need something. Typical Tobias bullshit.

I silently snorted. He knew why I was always down to business. We didn't have much of a choice at the Covens, and unfortunately, some of that shit was too embedded inside our bones to let go. He texted back a second later, but before I looked at it, I made sure that Mr. Rake wasn't paying attention.

He wasn't. He was too busy eye-fucking all the girls in the school like the perv that he was.

Tony: I don't know who this chick is, but someone is hiding her.

I slowly turned my head and caught the side view of her face, zeroing in on her soft features that I knew could harden within a second.

Me: Explain.

"What?" Sloane hissed, glancing at me out of the corner of her eye. She had been giving me the cold shoulder since my moment of relapse the other night, when she attacked me in the weight room, and I basically bent over backward to touch her any chance I could get.

There was just something about seeing her with a busted lip and knowing someone had put their hands on her that fucked me up inside.

The girl in front of Sloane's desk turned around and looked at her with caution before looking at me, waiting for my arrogant response back. Instead of saying something, though, I turned back and looked at my phone and waited for Tony to reply.

"Okay, class." Mr. Rake slowly stood up from behind his desk, his pot belly nearly busting out of the buttons along his shirt. "I have your test scores back. I will be coming around and placing them on your desk and then announcing the best grade."

Sloane placed her pencil down and sat up straighter, like the good little student that she was. I rolled my eyes and grunted out a chuckle, catching another sharp glare from her.

My phone vibrated as Mr. Rake began walking around the room, making sure to go extra slow around the girls' desks. My heart began to thump painfully as he rounded our aisle with his eyes set on Sloane like she was his favorite little pet.

His footsteps faltered right beside us, separating us like a boundary that I wanted to knock down.

"*Sloane,*" he cajoled, placing her test on her desk right side up with a big red A+ in a thick circle at the top. She shot him a hesitant smile and looked away, obviously feeling uncomfortable with his penetrating gaze. *He definitely wants to penetrate her. Perv.* He placed my test on my desk next, facedown for obvious reasons. Instead of looking at me, though, he just kept his gaze on her, and I was beginning to see red.

My phone vibrated again, but I ignored it. I wasn't going to do anything, but the provoking snippets of me standing up, walking over to him, and throat punching him were increasingly worrisome inside my head.

Mr. Rake walked back to his desk, and when his back was turned toward us, I quickly glanced at my phone and felt the trickle of confusion going through my veins.

Tony: She doesn't exist in the database. There is no sign or trace of her name anywhere. As if someone had wiped her presence off the earth. And you know what that means.

I clicked my phone off and slid it into my pocket, coming up with too many fucked-up scenarios that likely were too outrageous to be true. One thing was for certain: Sloane was hiding something. But I'd learned that not everyone knew they were hiding something because *they* were the secret the entire time.

My leg bounced up and down after I slid my phone back into my pocket, and I took a peek at my grade.

An F. Surprise, surprise.

Who even came up with the grading system? A, B, C, D, fucking F. It was stupid and unnecessary. Just another way to be judged for something you didn't want to do.

"Okay, class, drumroll please."

Not a single person gave Mr. Rake a drumroll.

"The best grade of the class is our very own Miss Sloane White." There was a nudge present somewhere deep inside my body that bordered along the lines of possessiveness. "Please come get your prize, young lady."

Prize? I snorted, and Sloane paused as she stood up from her desk, showing off her smooth, creamy legs. I peered up at her, feeling my temples click back and forth, and I suddenly saw her in a different light. What was she hiding behind those expansive, hazel eyes?

I watched her the entire time she walked down the aisle to Mr. Rake's desk. My tongue was bleeding by the time she made it, and my lungs burned for oxygen. I glanced around the room, and nearly every guy was staring at her ass in her short, plaid skirt, and I panicked with rising jealousy. *What the fuck?*

This was why I hated her.

She made me feel things, and I didn't like it.

"Congratulations, dear. You are one of the brightest students I have ever had. I bet your parents are proud." Mr. Rake winked at Sloane as he held out some bucket for her to reach into, and I nearly flew from my desk.

"Keep your dick in your pants," I said, gripping my pencil tightly in my hand. His eyes flew to mine, and I stared at him, waiting for him to say something. Either he didn't hear me, or he was too blinded by Sloane saying, 'Thank you,' to say anything to me. Or maybe, he realized that he was showing his obsession and didn't mean to.

When Sloane turned back around, my knuckles grew white as I gripped my pencil even harder. The wrapper of her red sucker crumpled in her free hand, and her lips were wet as she sucked on it.

Jesus Christ. He would give her a fucking sucker. He was probably imagining it like it was her lips on his cock.

Class was almost over by the time Sloane came and sat back down at her desk, with the sucker inside her mouth. She packed up her things and stacked her books on top of one another. I stayed, unmoving, stretching my legs out in front of me as anger still coursed through my veins like a flowing dam.

"So, are you going to the party tonight? It's going to be a fun one." The girl in front of Sloane shot me a flirty look with her question, and I watched her tense out of the corner of my eye.

"Why?" I asked. "Are you?" I grinned, and the girl's cheeks ripened. She was okay looking, but she wasn't currently sucking on a sucker three feet away from me with a rising chest that was impossible not to stare at.

I heard the slurping of Sloane's cherry sucker, and although I begged myself not to look, I turned my gaze and pinned them to her lips, watching her suck and lick the candy in what I was sure was an innocent way, but *fuck*. My eyes squinted, and I tuned out the girl still jabbering to me about the claiming party and reached forward quickly and pulled the sucker from Sloane's mouth.

Her cherry breath hit me in the face. "What the fuck, Tobias?"

Ignoring her, I held the candy in my hand and moved the stick back and forth between my needy fingers that were aching to touch her. Anger and resentment were pulling me in every direction, so I winked at the blonde who was staring at me with her lip pulled between her teeth. I plopped Sloane's sucker into my mouth and grinned at the girl, "I'll be at the claiming. I'll find you."

The bell rang, and I stood up, still relishing the sucker that was tinged with Sloane's taste, and sent her a smirk. "See ya at the claiming," I said, chuckling with her slowly reddening cheeks. *Maybe this time I'd be able to keep my hands off her.*

CHAPTER THIRTEEN

SHINER SLOWLY CREPT DOWN THE GIRLS' hall, and I half-expected him to do a forward roll, like he was a ninja, because that was something he would do to make us laugh. Gemma and I peeked out of our dorm room while Journey and Mercedes continued doing their hair in our mirror, and when he popped up in front of us, he looked down both ends of the hall and slipped inside our room.

"Why are you being so shady? It's not even after curfew yet." Gemma's brow furrowed as she continued to watch Shiner sneak around our room.

"I have the goods," he whispered, winking at Mercedes, which she returned with a dirty look. He rolled his eyes and dug into his pocket, pulling out several markers, holding them in his hands.

I laughed. "Shiner, you're acting like you have drugs." I grabbed the markers from his hand and read the side of them: *Glow-in-the-Dark Paint Marker.* "And it's a freaking marker."

"Hey!" He snatched the marker out of my hand and

placed it to his chest, trying not to smile. "I went through hell to get these for tonight."

Gemma crossed her arms. "How did you get these? Was it your idea to throw a glow-in-the-dark claiming party?"

Shiner shrugged, smiling. "Yeah, you like it, huh?"

Gemma smiled. "It's definitely a change from the usual. Now, seriously..." She reached out and snatched the markers from his hand, throwing two over to Mercedes and Journey and giving one to me. "How did you get these?"

Shiner rolled his lips as he began walking to the door. I stood back and twiddled the marker in my hand, glancing at my phone that I'd had turned off since someone had come into my room and locked me in my closet. *I can't handle the creepy texts, not right now.* Before Shiner left our room, he spun around and winked at us. "I have my ways."

Mercedes grumbled under her breath, making Shiner's eyes flare with something other than his normal humor.

"I have the mailing address for the headmaster and sweet-talked the mail lady when she came earlier today. Mail comes around 3:30. Perfect timing before weight-lifting with the lacrosse team."

Smart. There was a slight thought that ran through me, eating up my anxiety and fear. *If he can get a secret package that easily, can someone else?* The headmaster's assistant, Beth, went through all the mail and made sure students weren't getting anything inappropriate in packages, but was it that easy? What was next? My best friend's parents' fingers in a box on my bed or something?

"You okay?" I jumped as Gemma's hands lightly touched my arm. I whipped my head over to Journey and Mercedes, and they were standing beside our beds, mid-draw with their glow-in-the-dark markers on one another.

"You've been acting weird," Mercedes mentioned, shooting me a look. She pushed her crazy, curly hair over her shoulder, exposing her neck so Journey could write something on it.

"I'm fine." I laughed it off. "I was trying to figure out what I wanted to draw with my marker, and who I wanted to claim me tonight."

Gemma smiled, taking the cap off her marker and walking over to the mirror. The markers went on clear so you couldn't see what anyone was writing or drawing, which was fun in a way. Secrets could be fun—if they were the right kind.

"I think you're the one that does the claiming, Sloane." Gemma reached back and smiled at me, but the only thing I could think of was how her brother had claimed me without me even knowing it at the last party and how much my body *loved* it.

———

"HOLY SHIT," Gemma mused, stepping in line with me and Mercedes. Journey had already slipped out and found Cade somewhere. "Shiner went all out."

Mercedes' arm tightened against mine at the mention of Shiner. "You know Shiner. He lives for these parties. He says they're the only good thing about this boarding school. Which makes sense since he fucks anything that walks."

It was true. Shiner was a total manwhore, and he did go all out for these parties, which was typical Shiner behavior. He had more energy than most.

Glow sticks on strings sat on a table for the taking, and some students already had them tied around their necks, swaying with the music thumping just low enough not to be heard through the thick floors of this school. The basement was always a little tacky and musty smelling, especially with most of the student population thrown down here, but there was a gust of chilly air, too—probably from the lack of insulation from the colder outside air.

The farther Gemma, Mercedes, and I walked into the large space, the more glow-in-the-dark decorations popped out. Someone had painted *Come to get claimed?* in neon-blue paint on the block wall in the back of the room, and there was a beer pong table outlined in glowing yellow paint with the rims of each cup glowing, too. I noticed a few of the lacrosse guys playing beer pong already, and one of them was the nerdy boy who was *supposed* to claim me at the last party.

I wonder what Tobias said to him to steal me. Jerk.

My heart thumped one long, painful beat as I thought of Tobias and how he had told Penelope that he would find her tonight, all while sucking on *my* sucker. I had no idea why it made my legs tingle, knowing he had put my spit inside his mouth, but it did.

No. Ugh.

"What's the plan for tonight?" Gemma asked, squeezing my hand as Mercedes stepped in front of us and headed for the table lined with shots. "Are you gonna get claimed by someone?" Gemma paused, waving at Isaiah, who was telling her to come over to him with a devious look that flashed every time the techno lights swung in his direction. "Wait," Gemma said, turning toward me. "Who did you hook up with at the last claiming?"

"No one." My answer was quick as the lights flashed a new color every other second, and I hoped my red face blended in with them.

Gemma's brows furrowed, and she sighed. She reached up and gave me a quick hug before whispering in my ear, "Mercedes is right. You are being weird. I'm here for you, okay? I won't pressure you to use me as your bestie, but I *am* your bestie. Journey and Mercedes, too. Okay?"

When she pulled back, I squeezed her hands, hating that

my mind instantly went to Willow. "I know. I'm just getting antsy about college applications and my parents breathing down my neck."

She nodded. "Then, let loose tonight. I know that every guy in here, aside from Isaiah and Cade"—she looked over at Cade who was already touching Journey and making her wiggle in her spot—"would die to have you. You're like the untouchable girl of the school. You know that, right?"

Tell that to your brother.

"I am not," I laughed, locking eyes with him immediately. Gemma followed my gaze and pulled back, confused.

"Tobias is here? He didn't tell me he was coming." There was a sliver of hope in her voice, and I hated myself in that instant for lying to her and pretending that Tobias wasn't the actual villain in my nightmares each night.

Gemma spun around, telling Isaiah to hold on by putting her finger up. He rolled his eyes, but she ignored him. "Be honest, Sloane. How is tutoring? Tobias lies to me about it. I can tell." Gemma nibbled on her lip and rubbed her hand over her face, almost swiping off the little neon, glow-in-the-dark heart she drew on her high cheek bone. "He's like a block wall. So cordial with me. So fake. It hurts."

My chest burned as I closed off air. Gemma looked deep into my eyes, and I swore she had a way of reading every last thought inside my head. That was Gemma, though. She was quiet and kind, but she could sense these things. She was the type of person who could look at you and see right through the lies you were about to spew, which made sense since she was the queen of hiding things herself. "I thought so," she finally said, sucking up all the oxygen in the room and looking at her brother. My stomach was in knots by the time I made eye contact with him, and I hated myself for feeling the intense pang of jealousy as he whispered something in Penelope's ear, making her lick her lips like she was a teenage porn star.

I hate him.

He was doing it on purpose. Taunting me. *Just stop caring, Sloane.* I kept going back to the night he stormed in my room like a tornado and bled protection over every inch of the floor.

"I need a shot," I declared, looking at Gemma. Isaiah was coming up behind her.

"It's that bad?" she asked, wincing. "What am I going to do if he gets booted out of St. Mary's, Sloane? Is he studying with you at all? My dad said his grades haven't improved."

My heart sank to the cold floor as Gemma stared at me, all wide-eyed and innocent, waiting for me to answer truthfully. *Shit.* My mouth opened, but nothing came out. I could have caught flies in that very second, but before I could muster up *anything,* Shiner swooped in beside me and Gemma as Isaiah approached and held two shots out. "For my ladies."

I snatched them both, and Gemma sighed, glancing over at her brother once more. He was staring directly at us. He pretended I didn't exist, which made the vodka in my throat burn more than usual, but he sent his sister a slight smile that I was envious of. So, he *can* smile. And wow, that genuine lift of his lip could make a nun sweat.

"I'll be right back," Gemma said, reaching up and kissing Isaiah on the cheek. He grinned down at her and watched her walk to her brother like she was the center of the world. And for him, she was.

"Another shot, my lady?" Shiner asked, looking more ornery than usual.

"Trying to get her drunk, Nash?"

Shiner bared his teeth at Mercedes as she walked up to the group with a guy I had only seen a few times in the halls.

He was an underclassman, and by the fist bump he gave Isaiah, I was pretty sure he played lacrosse with the guys.

Shiner said nothing to Mercedes, but I could feel his body heat kick up a notch, and the devious look in Mercedes' eyes took a hold of his anger and twisted it to her own pleasure.

Secrets. Secrets. Secrets.

"Pour it," I said, trying to break the tension with not only Shiner and Mercedes but inside my own little world that was full of tormenting thoughts and worrisome assumptions that I wasn't as safe at St. Mary's as my parents had thought. And, not to mention, the boy across the party who had a death glare pinning me to my spot and a nice, juicy secret that he could tell his sister and destroy me altogether.

"Yeah?" Shiner asked, pulling back and smiling like it was Christmas morning. His hand went back behind my head, his fingers interweaving in my dark locks. I tipped my head back and opened my mouth.

"Jesus, what is going on over here?" Cade had walked up to the group, and his eyebrows shot to his forehead. Journey laughed as everyone watched Shiner pour the shot of vodka into my mouth from up above. I wanted to wince at the burn in the worst way, but I knew, without even looking, that Tobias was staring in my direction. And if he thought his little glare and threats were going to ruin my night tonight, he was mistaken.

He messed with my head at the last claiming party.

I wouldn't let him do it tonight.

CHAPTER FOURTEEN

TOBIAS

I WATCHED as my sister slowly backed away from me, dropping my thick wrists out of her small hands and sighing with dejection that I felt all the way to my seed of a heart. The sliver of guilt for her disappointment was there, and the only thing it did was spark a multitude of feelings that I had destroyed years ago after living day after day with ridiculing failures that I endured from my fucked-up childhood spent at the Covens.

You dropped your guard.

You aren't holding the knife correctly.

You're getting too involved in their lives. Just kill them and then walk away.

You shouldn't dwell on what they did to deserve death.

You aren't there to judge. You're there to end.

Penelope snuggled up close to me again as soon as Gemma walked away, and I wanted to physically shove her clear across the floor. *Breathe.* Suddenly, the room was full of chaos. Flashing lights mimicked my racing heart, and the crisp air was mutilated by body heat that wafted over my sticky skin. The music thumped and drowned out all the sounds except my pulse thumping angrily. My thoughts stilled as I watched Sloane's head tip backward with Shiner's hand resting in her hair while the other poured a drink down her throat.

Fucking hell.

Her throat was relaxed, and she didn't gag or choke on the burning liquid like most would do. She took the shot like a champ, and her friends cheered for her when she was done. I wanted to break the arm that was touching her and pin her against a wall to taste the potent liquid in her mouth.

I stepped backward as I pictured myself kissing her ruby lips, feeling sickened at the thought. I remembered the exact moment I declared kissing an absolute no for me. It was an unrealistic thought that was so far out of reach I didn't see it in the future—ever. Once, I had watched my mother get kissed by Richard when she didn't want to be kissed. I knew, now that I was older, that there were many more things that he had done to her that she didn't want.

Penelope ran her hand over the waistband of my jeans as I looked away from Sloane and my sister and heard my mother's voice—so faint it was really just my own—and the only motherly advice that I could remember: *"Kissing is intimate, Tobias, and one day, you'll understand that. Never steal a kiss from someone that isn't willing to give it up."*

"Were you willing to give it up to Uncle Richard?"

She looked away, and I saw the tears forming in her eyes. "No. He doesn't deserve my love."

A girly mew interrupted the memory, and I growled, pushing Penelope away for a moment. "I'll be back," I announced.

She called out, "But the claiming is about to start."

I didn't look back as I watched Shiner hop over to the

music to cut it off. "Then wait for me like a good girl," I snapped.

Her pout cut through my hungry anger for a moment until I glanced back to Sloane, who was staring right at me. She turned her head, her dark hair catching a strobe light as it flashed, and pretended like she wasn't watching me with Penelope.

I was trying to disguise my reasons for striding toward her with the conversation I'd just had with Gemma. But truthfully, I just wanted to be near her. I wanted to grip her hips, and trap her against a wall, and breathe down into her face to watch her internal fight of wanting me but hating me at the same time.

I craved it.

Just leave her alone.

I sighed.

I can't.

"Okay, everyone. Get your glowing asses ready to go! Lights fully turn off in 3, 2..." My head turned, and she was staring at me. Those black-winged eyes made her look hotter than everyone in the room combined, and she shot a confused but intrigued glint in my direction. *Yeah, we need to have a little conversation, Sloane.*

As if she heard me, she turned away and began frantically searching the crowd for someone else, and I already wanted to plow his face in. It wasn't that I wanted her...but I also didn't want anyone else to want her either. Which I knew was completely irrational, but let's face it, *I* was irrational.

"1." Shiner's voice faded as the lights turned off, and the room was filled with glow paint and heavy breathing from the anticipation of what was to come. I hoped Gemma and Isaiah ran off so I didn't have to break his arms by watching him grip my sister. I began striding over to Sloane, knowing that she would be in the same spot as she was a moment ago because she was too interested in hearing what I had to say to move.

"Get locked in any closets lately?" I whispered, running my finger down her bare arm slowly. I inhaled and smelled her familiar shampoo and hated that I was beginning to recognize her by a single scent now.

Her chest rose as she tried to turn away. *Not so fast, little one.* I let out a hiss followed by a chuckle and gripped her waist, pulling her toward the back of the room, near the glowing paint on the wall. You likely couldn't see anything unless you were right up against it, but I craved to see her face.

"Fail any tests lately?" she bit back, angling her chin up in my direction. The glow of the paint shined down on her mouth, and I caught a glimpse of her sparkling eyes and plump lips. Her cut cheek bones had some type of shimmer on them, and it did something to my chest.

My hands tightened on her waist, liking that she had some hips, unlike Penelope who was probably standing in the same spot I'd left her. *Desperation doesn't look good on girls.* Sloane's stomach was peeking out from underneath her tank, and it was so soft that a deep-rooted part of me wanted to pinch it between my fingers.

"Get fingered by any guys lately?"

Hot breath hit my face as my words destroyed her facade of acting unaffected by me. Her back straightened, and my hands went with her. "What do you want, Tobias? Are you here to blackmail me again?"

"Now, why would I need to do that? I have it on video, remember?"

The air around us began to stiffen with heat. My back started to sweat, but I wasn't sure if it was because of the sounds and hot tension between Sloane and me, or if it was because I was hardly keeping myself together by touching her. I wasn't sure what it was about her, but I wanted to break her and then piece her back together so I could do it all over again.

Her short, sarcastic laugh bounced off my chest, and I pushed her up against the wall again, hating that I liked the sound of it. Her tone was soft but edgy, and my tongue jolted out of my lips to wet them. "Maybe you just like touching me, but hate yourself for it because you hate me."

I definitely hate myself.

"What did you tell Gemma?"

Sloane's hands gripped my wrists, keeping them in place against her waist. Her eyes flew to mine, and although I couldn't see the muddy hazel mess, I knew they were full of worry and concern. Her gaze left mine as she searched the room, likely for my sister.

"I told her nothing."

"And that was mistake number one."

"Tobias." Worry lingered, but she was quick to hide it. "She said your father mentioned your grades weren't improving. What did you expect? I'm supposed to be tutoring you and helping you during class. They were going to catch on eventually."

My hand left her waist, and I gripped the outside of her bare thigh. My fingers splayed on the smooth skin as I hooked it around my hip. She was a goddamn magnet. I shouldn't have been touching her, and she should have been repelled by me, but just look at us. "So, what did you tell her?" I gritted, nearly drowning at the warmth coming from her pussy. I had a hold on myself, but admittedly, it was slipping.

It felt like I was rewarding us both with my hand on her body. I should have been punishing her for not sticking to the plan.

Yes, the plan that I created by blackmailing her, but it was still the fucking plan.

Her words were breathy, and the noises around us were getting louder. Girls were giggling as the guys were whispering dirty words against their skin. I had to admit, this wasn't what I thought would occur at St. Mary's when I first started attending. But anything was better than where I was before.

"I didn't say a word when she asked me about tutoring."

My fingers trailed up the side of her smooth leg, and her back arched. "Tobias, what are you doing? If you think I'm going to let you touch me again after you fucking blackmailed me, you're out of your mind."

"It's cute when you lie, Snow White. By the heat coming from you, I'd say you *are* going to let me touch you."

My fingers grazed her middle, and I almost stumbled backward when she laughed. The sweet, girly noise went straight to my core, and for the first time in a very long time, I was surprised. "And it's cute when you pretend like I don't affect *you*, Tobias." She pushed her wet pussy up to my hand, and my chest expanded with trapped air. "Now let go of me, and go play with Penelope like you promised her. Or are you going to try and blackmail her, too, for showing you an ounce of decency?"

My eyes narrowed in on the bright-yellow glow stick hanging from a string between her breasts. The clenching of my jaw hurt as I reached up quickly and snatched it from her neck, pulling it quickly and breaking the string in two. A whimper flew from her mouth, and I positioned it between her legs quickly.

She staggered against the wall. "What are you doing?" Her leg clenched around my waist in haste. *She hasn't pushed me away, though.* I smiled to myself, fiddling with the smooth round tip of the glow stick, knowing the thickness of it would get her just needy enough to beg for me to put my fingers inside, too. *Why can't I stop? Will I be able to stop?*

"You might affect me, but I affect you just the same. I think you like the fact that you shouldn't want me but do anyway. Isn't that right?"

The tip of the glow stick touched her softly, just enough to tease her. Her body was tense, and heat flew off her in waves. Her chest rose and fell quickly, and in the dark light, I could see that her lip was pulled into her mouth by her white teeth.

"Do I drive you crazy?" I whispered in her ear, smelling her shampoo and loathing myself for liking it.

"Yes. I...I...st—" Her hips thrusted upward, and her words died on her tongue as I pulled the glow stick out of her wet pussy, feeling my dick pulse inside my jeans.

"Look at you, nearly begging me to touch you." I pushed the glow stick in again, holding her body up with one hand as her warm palms flattened against my chest. I briefly wondered if she could feel the racing of my heart as I pumped the glow stick in and out of her, eating up her whimpers like I'd been starving for days. "And you said you wouldn't let me touch you."

She hummed as she stopped rocking her hips. My fingers dug into the skin of her belly as I pressed her closer to me. "If I'm not mistaken," she panted, "that's not *you* touching me." Shock rendered me speechless. My lips flattened as my dick fought against my zipper, and I was angry. Angry that I'd found myself in this position. Angry that, from the second I had set eyes on Sloane White, my world seemed to shift just a little, enough to put a sliver of light in the dark that consistently followed me around. It was a light that was unparalleled to anything else in my life from the second I was thrown into a prison in my adolescence, ripping me from a childhood that Gemma and I both deserved.

Sloane's leg fell, and she reached down and pushed my hand away. The glow stick was warm and slick from her sweetness. "You want me to leave you alone? Well, you leave me alone, too."

My voice was as strained as my cock, fighting for sanity. "And what if I need a study partner? Huh?"

"Destroy the video, and I'm yours."

My breath followed her as she walked away from me, likely dripping halfway down her legs for another guy to clean up as I stood back against the fucking wall with a wet glow stick in my hand that I wanted to pop in my mouth, just to have a taste.

Why did hearing the words, "I'm yours," make my world shift again?

CHAPTER FIFTEEN

SLOANE

THE MALE SPECIES was easily distracted. Their hate could morph into something else entirely by a warm touch, a sweet smell, or sometimes even a sultry sigh. Tobias wanted nothing to do with me. Anger billowed from his navy-blue eyes every time he sought me in the hallway or across the aisle in class. His refusal of my help, or even my presence, was a rejection that was hard to swallow. But his need to toy with me, on top of blackmailing me and recording something so personal that it made my face burn at the thought, was what had sent me over the edge.

I wasn't sure if we were playing a game or if we were just trying to survive at this point, but after the last few weeks, I had fallen into a pit of my own self-doubt and fear.

This safe, worrisome, and quiet version of myself was a mere reaction to the texts and closet ordeal, and I was finished with it. Tonight, I was the one that was going to be in charge. I was the one that was going to win this battle brewing between my best friend's brother and myself. Tobias may have been a different breed of male that I wasn't used to, but I still stood by my earlier revelation: the male species was easily distracted.

"Need claimed for the night?" I turned at the sound of a familiar voice, pretty sure it was the same guy who was supposed to claim me at the last claiming before Tobias decided to swoop in and throw me off course.

"Tell me," I whispered, reaching for a shot. I paused and turned around, trying to make out the guy's face behind me. We were blanketed in darkness, but tiny glimpses of glowing paint moved around us. The wall that Tobias had me pushed against had bright, neon paint on it that shone down to the floor. "What did he say to you that made you back out last time?"

A smooth chuckle hit my ears as I waited. "Who, the new kid? The headmaster's son?"

I didn't answer as I turned around and grabbed a plastic shot glass, realizing there were only two left on the table, whereas, seconds ago, there were several. I looked behind the table, but it was bleak. The bright glow was too far in the distance. Part of me wondered if Tobias had run over here to take all the shots so I couldn't have any, just to spite me.

When I spun around, the two shots splashed over my skin before I tipped them both back in record time and swallowed the burn in a single gulp.

"Jesus. In a party mood?"

"You kind of owe me now," I said, ignoring his question.

A warmth spread over me, and the wetness between my legs was sticky, reminding me that Tobias had touched something that wasn't necessarily his. Body heat lingered in front of me, and I could finally see him, noting that he wasn't nearly as tall as Tobias. "Oh, I do? Fine by me. What do you want?"

"Go find a friend," I said, feeling bolder than before,

thanks to Tobias setting a new flame inside of me that was burning for destruction. "Meet me on the wall, under the glowing paint. We have a little show to put on."

"A friend?"

I stepped closer to him, trying to remember his name. "A male friend." I grew impatient. "Party for two, but I'm in charge."

"Seriously?" The exhilaration in his tone was followed by a hot kiss to my mouth. His tongue swept in, and it was greedy as it lapped up the extra alcohol lingering against my lips, and then he was gone, probably ready to snag one of his friends who he knew would be more than happy to assist.

I smiled deviously, quickly making my way over to the spot I left Tobias in, hoping he was still standing over there so I could steal back some of my dignity.

Okay, fine. Having a threesome just to make Tobias angry and put him in his place wasn't necessarily dignified, but whatever. My luck, he wouldn't even care, or he'd record it and blast it all over Mary's Murmurs.

As soon as I began second-guessing my plan, my back was pressed against a warm body as *Mr. Assault My Mouth* popped up in front of me like a jack-in-the-box, clearly excited. "You're in charge, right?" he asked, tipping a shot back before handing me another one. *Where did he get that?*

I took it quickly before throwing the neon, plastic shot glass to the floor, turning my head slightly and fighting through the darkness to see if Tobias had left.

"Yes," I whispered, beginning to feel more relaxed the longer I stood against a warm body. My head tipped backward as I made out the other guy's face, trying to recognize him. "What are your names?"

"That's against the rules, babe."

"Oh, right," I answered, relaxing into his grip around my

body. There was a moving shadow in front of me, and I turned my head again, trying to find Tobias.

There.

A tall, brooding, lingering silhouette stood several yards away. Neon streaks of hair moved in front of him, and I knew it was Penelope, as she and all her friends had painted glow-in-the-dark paint in their hair.

Good. Eyes on me. Asshole.

"Turn this way," I said, stumbling over my feet and facing Tobias as Penelope moved in front of him. *What are they doing?*

"Are you good? Is she drunk?" the guy behind me asked the one in front.

"She had a couple shots. Sloane, are you okay?"

"I thought we weren't sharing names," I whispered, pausing at the slowness of my voice. *How drunk am I?* "How many shots did I have?"

My hair was moved off my shoulder, and soft lips graced the skin, making me feel warm and gooey on the inside. "That feels good," I mumbled, giving him more access.

"You had three shots, I think."

"What were in the shots? Gasoline?" I laughed at myself and put my hands on his shoulders, letting the other guy kiss me from behind. "Move me over a little, I want the glowing paint above us to show what you're doing to me."

"I don't know if we're recording a porno, but I'm down."

"Yes, go down," I said, pushing the broad set of shoulders down below my hips. His warm breath wafted over my bare legs, and I took that moment to look up across the darkened room to see a set of glowing eyes set on me with rapt attention. I swallowed my thick spit tinged with my earlier shot as Penelope's back stumbled toward me with his hands set on her hips. Tobias moved her closer, and I smiled on the inside, remembering what I'd put on my stomach with the glow-in-the-dark pens that Shiner had given to me and the girls.

I gasped as something warm touched my center, and my head flew back, confused at the sensation. I looked down, seeing a dark blob of something underneath me, and then my head was pulled back with a single touch to my chin, and lips were on my mouth, causing my stomach to bottom out and my legs to tremble. *Why is this so intense?*

"I bet you taste even better down there," the voice said, barely gracing my ears. I turned back and looked at Tobias and saw that Penelope was on her knees with his hand behind her head. A strike of jealousy moved through me at snail speed, and the room began to spin in what seemed to be the opposite direction. I blinked back as the pleasure between my legs disappeared, and there was a faint conversation happening in front of me as my legs were magically parted.

"How does she taste?"

"Like heaven. She's soaked." The taste that I knew was mine settled on my tongue as someone stole another kiss from me. "Ready for a switch off?"

"Fuck yeah. This is so hot." I was jumbled between the two guys as I kept my eyes on Tobias. I couldn't see his harsh glare in my direction, but I could see the outline of his sharp jawline, and I pictured him hating me a little more after my show. *I'm not as weak as you think, Tobias.*

"Lift my shirt a little."

My back arched as a new set of lips settled on the pulsing between my legs. Sharp teeth nipped me, and I cried out, feeling like my legs were no longer touching the ground.

Warm, musty air hit my belly as the guy behind me lifted it and trailed his fingers up past my ribs and into my bra. I looked down and smirked, wanting to laugh at the perfectly scripted words on my tight belly. They were upside-down as I stared at it, and the letters began to blur together, but I remembered what I'd written in the bathroom as Gemma, Journey, and Mercedes were putting their shoes on to walk down here: *Fuck you.*

Teeth scraped over my neck as two fingers pinched my nipple, bringing me back to reality. There were waves of pleasure coming from all directions, and I would never admit this out loud, but the most pleasurable thing about this moment was that Tobias Richardson had his dark and steady gaze set on me, and the longer I stared at him, the more turned on I became.

"You gonna come for me, baby?"

"Um..." I blinked, forgetting where I was again. But only for a second. I found Tobias' eyes once more after I looked down and realized there was someone under my skirt, licking me. *Why do I keep forgetting where I am?* I was thankful that there was something hard behind me again, because a second ago, I felt like I was floating as I focused on Tobias. I gasped as something plunged inside of me, and that was the moment I began panicking. My eyes grew wide for a brief second before they felt like closing, and I saw Tobias even closer now, with Penelope loitering in front of him. She was no longer on her knees, and he was no longer a safe distance away. His head moved to the side, the dark clouding half of his face. The other side was glowing from the paint of the wall, and my eyes shut as my body weakened. *I don't feel right.*

"Wait, dude." A set of warm fingers pressed against my neck that replaced the wet kiss that was there seconds ago. "Her pulse is really fucking slow. Is she okay?"

Just then, my eyes opened again, and I locked onto Tobias, wondering if I was going to let my own nightmare save me from what seemed like a sick reality.

———

CHAPTER SIXTEEN

———

TOBIAS

THE ONLY REASON I was hard as a rock was from the girl in front of me and not from the one on her knees below me. My eyes drove into Sloane's as she appeared like a fucking angel sent from the devil himself to taunt me. My legs were still unsteady from when I backed away from her with the wet glow stick in my hand, branding my fingers with her scent that I was supposed to despise but didn't.

My resolve wavered as she stood, looking at me from a distance. I knew it was her. My hands had just been on her tiny waist that flitted out into her curved hips, and it wasn't hard to memorize the way she looked, even if I refused to look at her in the halls of this boarding school.

When she was pressed up against someone with her gaze on me, I realized that she wasn't finished with me for the night, even if she had run off moments ago and told me to leave her alone. Was she winning this little spar that we continued to have every time we were alone? Was Sloane yielding a sharper sword? How could that be possible? Why did it feel like my bones were currently breaking in half while watching her across the darkened room with two guys? I wanted to kill them.

My belt being undone and my zipper moving down stole my attention for a moment. Penelope, with her stupid glow-in-the-dark nail polish, began freeing my hard dick. *Yeah, that's not for you.* I was right earlier. I drove Sloane crazy, but she knew how to drive me crazy, too.

"Wow, someone is ready."

I grunted, wanting to shove my cock into Penelope's mouth to shut her up. *Doesn't she know that I am busy watching something?*

I sighed, pushing my hips into her needy little grip, milking myself with anger as I watched one of the guys in front of Sloane disappear, showing her off a little more to me. My eyes fell, and rage simmered below the surface as I thrust my hips again into Penelope's warm hand.

For a split second, I had forgotten all about the fact that I despised Sloane. I had forgotten that she was my twin sister's best friend and that she was disgusted with me and my black-mailing techniques to make her leave me alone. She had a way of making me forget who I was and where I came from.

Pain etched itself on my skin, and it made me angry. I was going to rip those guys to pieces and rip her to pieces, too. How dare she engrave herself into my bones and spin my world when I wanted nothing to do with her. I had tried my hardest to put a wedge between us, but it had somehow slipped in the last twenty minutes.

Ignoring Penelope and her dirty words that weren't even gracing my ears, I pushed her a little closer so I could be a shorter distance from Sloane. I wanted nothing more than her glittering gaze full of defiance and seduction set on me. I was thankful when Penelope dropped to her knees a second later and took me in her mouth so I had a clear view.

I see you.

And I felt her. I felt something, and I didn't know what to do with it. There was a bomb in my hands, and they weren't nearly as steady as they usually were.

My hips thrust back and forth, my hand catching Penelope's head as I watched what was mine being touched and admired by two guys that truly had no idea what they were up against. Just as my muscles twitched and Sloane was passed off between them, I clenched my jaw and began smiling at the glowing paint on her belly that she'd *obviously* wanted to show me.

Fuck you.

She is such a sneaky little brat.

A flake—the smallest fucking flake—of something warm planted itself, and I was interested in what went through her head. I couldn't deny that I was pleased knowing she had thought of me before even coming to the party.

I moved my gaze right back to her and smirked. I hoped I scared her, just a little, but my smirk slowly fell, and everything else blended together as I focused on her face. My racing heart increased with speed. Protectiveness that was disguised as noble but backed with possession flew through my body like I had been struck by a bullet. The sinking feeling wasn't what I had felt for my sister, or even Journey. This was more potent. This wasn't about safety.

I paused when her flirty, knowing gaze vanished. Her head lollygagged to the left, and the guy behind her paused as the other popped out from between her legs, blocking my view. An unsettled worry flew to my fingertips as I pulled my dick out of Penelope's mouth and pushed her to the side. The environment I was in was not controlled like I preferred, and there wasn't a set plan written in stone that I was to follow to "fix" a problem, but none of that mattered as I placed my fiery glare on the two guys pulling Sloane through the party as she hardly stood straight.

I cracked my knuckles and started after them. *I can't kill them. I can't kill them. I can't kill them.*

A knife-like swallow scraped my throat as I felt an animalistic craving fill my senses, and I wouldn't tell a single soul this, but this feeling wasn't one that I was relieved with. Familiarity didn't mean comfort. In my case, it was pure ammunition for the nightmares.

When I reached the curve of the wall and looked down the distance of the long hallway, I drowned the beating in my ears and listened to their worry.

"Is she that drunk?"

"Did you give her something?"

"She's barely conscious."

A light was on, and the door was *almost* shut as I pushed my fingers through, feeling the wood slam onto the throbbing veins in my hand. My eyes landed on her instantly as the door propelled open, and I was choked at the sight.

"What the fuck did you two give her?" The latch clicked as the door slammed behind me. Sloane blinked several times, her face ghastly as her smeared ruby lipstick poked at the intensity I felt boiling my blood.

"Wh—what?" The guy I recognized from the weight room a couple of weeks ago dropped her right in front of me, and I tapped into my skill set for a brief second and pictured myself breaking his arm.

"Tobias..." I was slowly pulled away to the limp girl hardly being held up by the other guy who eyed me very cautiously. "We didn't give her anything." His eyes flicked to his friend, and I wanted to peel his lips away from his face because I knew they'd been on her.

My hand reached out to the piece of shit that nearly let Sloane fall to the floor, and I wrapped my fingers around his neck, pulling him to the wall with the strength that I'd been yielding since I was old enough to know what muscles were. "Why did he just look over at you? Did you give her something?"

I let up on his windpipe a little, and he didn't even try to escape me. It didn't stop me from taking my other hand and snapping his finger back to get him to come to full attention, though. He let out a yelp, and the sound relaxed me for a split second. "She—she took a shot from me, but it wasn't even meant for her. I didn't fucking spike her drink, if that's what you're asking. There aren't drugs at St. Mary's. It's a fucking no-go from the Rebels, and what they say goes." He winced. "Fuck, man. My finger. I think you broke it."

Good.

"How many shots did she have?"

I looked back over at her, and her eyes were droopy, hiding the mischievous little flare in them that I saw on more occasions than one. *Fuck, why is my heart beating out of my chest?* I pulled my gaze away, uncomfortable that there was something messing with my mechanically ticking heart.

"Like, three? Man, I swear. She was fine when we started." *Yeah, when you fucking started touching something that was meant for me.*

"Three shots? That's it?"

"I don—" Her eyes shut, and a droplet of sweat was forming on her hairline. "I don't feel right…"

"Go get one of the Rebels." This was 'their' school after all. I had no fucking idea what went on during these parties. Were drugs a commodity around here?

"Hey." I snapped my fingers before grabbing Sloane out of the other guy's hands. He willingly let her go and backed away, following after his friend with jerky movements that could only be from fear itself. *Good.* "Did you do drugs?"

"What? Drugssss?" I focused on her lips, instantly angered

that her red lipstick was smeared from kissing someone. I wiped the mess away with my thumb.

"Yes, Sloane. Did you do drugs?"

Her eyes popped open, and I felt the oxygen in the room combust. "No. Drugs are...are...aren't..." Her tiny hands landed on my arms, and I flexed beneath her light grip. "Not here."

My brows crowded as I tried to make sense of her slurred words and confusing explanation.

"Don't tell." Her head fell onto my shoulder, and she shuddered, chills breaking out on her bare arms and legs. *Shit.* "Don't call them."

"Don't call who?" It was like trying to read a book in Braille. I could feel Sloane's worry with every slow breath she took, but I had no fucking idea what was going on in her head.

Her lip wobbled, and her eyes shut before her head hit my shoulder again. I looked around the room, staring at the golden light above us, knowing I was seconds from surrendering to the fucking avalanche of feelings that I had buried so far down below the surface that they had no option but to explode when the moment struck. *No one is in here but her.* I searched the corners of the dirty room, seeing nothing but a cobweb hanging innocently from the ceiling. *There are no cameras. You're not under his watch anymore.* It was an abrupt, short rip in my wall that I knew would only last a few seconds. I winced as I felt the hole digging into my back like a shovel on those distant chilly, rainy nights I had spent perfecting my stone-cold exterior. My fingers dug through Sloane's silky dark hair, and I pulled her face from my shoulder and stiffened at the tears on her cheeks. *This hurts me.*

My voice was soft, and judging by her behavior, she wouldn't remember me being worried, but it was evident from my tone. "Look at me. I'll keep your secrets safe. Don't tell who?"

"Your dad," she whimpered as her entire body shook. "My...my... He will tell my..." The words were like tiny ice chips breaking off through her chattering teeth. "My parents. They can't know... They will take me."

Her fists bundled in my shirt, and as soon as the door opened, I pulled her up to her feet and patched the rip in my walls.

"What the fuck is going on?" Shiner asked, coming into the room with a flushed face and no shirt. His eyes fell to Sloane and then flew back to mine.

"Someone drugged her," I explained coolly.

"What?" he exclaimed. He walked over to Sloane as I held her up with my arm cradled around her waist. His finger touched her chin, tipping her blank face up.

"I feel sick, Nash," she whispered, voice still dipping low in spots that it shouldn't have.

"Who the fuck—"

"Don't tell my da—the headmaster," I said, sick of standing there with her in my arms, shivering with sweat dripping down her face. "I've got her. But it seems you've got a little drug problem in the school. Might wanna tell the rest of your pack."

And with that, I scooped Sloane up in my arms and headed straight to my room.

CHAPTER SEVENTEEN

SLOANE

I LIKED HIS SCENT. I wasn't going to tell him that. In fact, I wasn't sure I could even form words. If I could, I would tell him to take me back to my room and leave me alone.

"You already said that."

I peeled an eye open as I saw him standing above me, his dark and demeaning glare peering down at me like I was in trouble for something.

"Said what?" My mouth was as dry as dirt—tasted like dirt, too.

"To take you back to your room and leave you alone."

I said that out loud?

"Yes."

Oh my God.

"My thoughts aren't safe." I shivered as the words left me, and Tobias rolled his eyes, pulling the covers up around me and stalking away.

Thoughts from the party were still a hazy mess in my head, and I wasn't sure how much time had passed. I craned my neck and looked behind me, wondering if it was daylight. Did I sleep? Tobias was still in the same clothes: dark jeans that hung low on his trim waist, a belt, and a black t-shirt that made his blue eyes as sharp as weapons. He was a simple guy on the outside, but I knew he was opposite on the inside.

"You know..." My lips chattered, and I tried clenching my jaw to make it stop. I felt less funny than I had down in the basement with an entire rave-like party going on around me, but I still felt off. I was floating in the middle of the dark ocean, body weightless as waves crashed, but I was heavy seconds later. "It's not fair to blame the victim."

Tobias came and stood over me again, his dark lashes highlighting the cool blue. "Is that what you are, Sloane? A victim?"

My eyes shut as I fell into another pit of darkness. "Why did you even help me?" I wanted him to. I remembered that much. I saw him from across the party as confusion took me under, and I wanted his strong hands to grip me and pull me away from the unimaginable that was happening.

"I'm not a victim like most girls at a party who get drugged." *I'm so fucking cold.* My hand slipped as I tried to grip his blankets, the muscles not working like normal. "It wasn't like I didn't want them to touch me. They weren't the ones who drugged me."

The blankets were ripped off of me, and my eyes flew back open as a chattering breath escaped my chest. I looked down to see if a cloud of cool air had left my mouth. It was so cold in his room. "Move over."

"What?" I asked.

Tobias rolled his eyes again, completely exasperated with me at this point, and it made me sound juvenile, but it truly wasn't fair. It wasn't like I had physically asked him to take me to his room and put me in his bed. *Or did I?*

"Jesus, never mind," he mumbled before sitting down on

the bed. My entire body jostled with his weight making a divot in the thin mattress, and when his shirt was pulled up over his head, my mouth suddenly went dry again.

I smashed my lips together, afraid that I'd let a gasp slip since I was having trouble holding even my thoughts back, and although I'd seen his backside and the fiery, deep scars that covered his toned skin, it was still a shocking revelation each time. Another round of chills flew down my arms as my stomach dipped, making me feel like I was back to being in the ocean as the choppy waves continued to hit me over and over again.

When he turned toward me, flinging his jean-clad legs onto the bed. I stumbled over my words. "What...ar–are you doing? Do you want me to get out of your bed?"

"Take your shirt off." I felt my eyes widen before I slowly blinked. "For fuck's sake, stop looking at me like that." Tobias pushed me over to my back, and I stared at his rocking temples as his fingers slowly dipped underneath my shirt. His skin was warm against mine, and I breathed out a relieved sigh. The feel of cotton wistfully moved against my skin as Tobias hovered over me, pulling it up and over my head, revealing my bra and tight skirt that felt more constricting than before. "Body heat will make you warm. I'm tired of watching you convulse with chills."

I swallowed with a tight throat, keeping my mouth shut as his bare chest touched my back. I faced the wall as he crowded me from behind, draping his arm over the hollowness of my waist. His smell enveloped me, and I tried my hardest not to enjoy it, because tomorrow, when I wasn't in this twisted and confused state, I would remember this moment with shame.

Sleep was beginning to settle in like a dark storm with him nestled up behind me, skin on skin, but his voice broke through my slumber, and I jolted awake. His arm caged me tighter, and my hand gripped his, nails digging into his skin for safety. "Who's been messing with you, Sloane?"

Alarm bells rang, and another chill ransacked me, but I wasn't sure if it was the drugs in my system or the sinking realization that someone was out to get me and I had a feeling why.

"I don't know," I answered truthfully. Because technically, I didn't. But what I did know was that if I told my parents that someone was texting me about Willow, locking me in closets, and drugging me at parties, they'd be here faster than a red-eye and pull me away.

But don't misinterpret that. It wouldn't be because they wanted to protect me. They just wanted to protect themselves and their secret.

"So, you don't know who...but you know *why*." It was a statement, not a question.

His whisper warmed the crook of my neck, and I pushed back against him, trying to get more warmth. "Why do you care?" I asked, feeling bold with his arms around me.

"I don't," he snapped.

"Fine," I snapped back, pushing against him as he pulled me closer.

Time had passed, and every few minutes, he would press his fingers against my pulse and then let up and place his arm back over my hip. Silence stretched around us like an expanding balloon, and I wondered who would be the first one to say something. Was there even anything to say? Would we just go back to hating each other in the morning and act like this night never even happened? I may have been in a hazy state with an empty belly that rolled with unease and feelings that were unsettled, but I couldn't forget that he was Gemma's brother, and I couldn't forget the angry tension that brewed between us on the daily.

And let us not forget the video that he possessed of me whimpering for him to touch me.

"You'll never find it."

Jesus, again?

"How much of that did I just say out loud?"

His breath was warm against my ear, and I shut my eyes, closing out the spinning of the room. I made a noise and clenched my belly, feeling sick.

"There was more? I'd love to be in your head to know what you really think about me, Sloane."

"Tobias." My body tensed, and I shot up out of his bed, trying to crawl over him in haste. I fell over him, hitting my cheek on his bedside table before he caught me by the waist.

"What the fuck, Sloane?"

My hand covered my mouth, and next thing I knew, he was carrying me to his bathroom and placing me on the cold floor. Tears burned my eyes as my stomach convulsed, and my hair was wrapped around his tight fist as I threw up.

Mortification hit me as I slumped down, sweaty and disoriented. My cheek throbbed along with my head, but Tobias was there, with a wet towel, wiping my forehead. Our eyes crashed, and I felt my resolve crash, too. Too much silence had passed as I breathed through my nose, but he stole my attention with his quiet words.

"You asked me why I helped you."

His worry was prominent, but so was his irritation. The little muscles along his temples flickered back and forth as his gaze scanned my face. When I said nothing, he glanced away to the shower.

"My mother was once helpless, and so was my sister."

I nodded slowly, understanding where this was going. His mother was ripped of her rights, just like Tobias and Gemma at one point, too.

Tobias gripped my chin roughly as he stayed crouched

down, shirtless, in front of me, blotting away the trickling sweat over my temples. "But don't, for one second, think I'm your knight in shining armor, Sloane." He stood up quickly, and confusion swept me away. His stormy eyes peered down at me with distaste and something else I couldn't understand, and then he handed me a bottle of mouthwash and stalked out of the bathroom, leaving me with nothing but uncertainty and embarrassment.

CHAPTER EIGHTEEN

TOBIAS

Whip.

Whip.

Whip.

My teeth clenched tightly as I held back a scream. I refused to show even a flicker of pain to him, and he knew it, too. Richard wanted me to beg him to stop. He wanted to feel in control, and he got off on having power over me.

But didn't he have enough? He did away with my mother, and someday, I'd find out exactly how he did so. And then, he pulled me away from my twin sister who relied on me for safety, threw me into the basement of a psych ward, and "trained" me to be a "better man".

A better man who killed others. He fed me lies, told me they were corrupt, and that was why I was on the wet floor, getting my back mutilated over and over again. I confronted him and told him I knew that the people he was forcing me to kill weren't ready to meet their maker.

And who the fuck was I to be their end? I was fifteen years old.

"Enough!" I shouted, standing up and facing him with heat slicing *through my backside like a knife carving pain that would last years. Richard moved in front of me and smirked, and if I weren't chained to the wall behind me, I would wrap my hands around his throat and kill him right now.*

He knew I would, too. Which was why I was chained.

I gritted my teeth again, finding that small inner peace that forced me to hang on to my mantra of "play smarter, not harder." I knew I'd never move to the top if I continued to go up against him. Desperation forced my head to drop, because I knew, even playing this game with him, that it would take years for him to fully believe that I was molded into the monster that he wanted me to be.

It took the other men in this place mere weeks to begin salivating at the thought of exiting the cold, bleak walls of their rooms to enter the world and end whoever they were hired to kill.

Me, though? I wanted to refuse every time. Even if it meant leaving the torture and four walls that had become my home.

"Is it enough, though?" Richard's voice sent a wrecking ball of anger straight through my back, and I inhaled sharply. "I heard you refused one of your training sessions."

Sending a female nurse into my room to practice fucking *so I could use it in the future when I needed to get a woman alone to kill her was merciless. Wasn't it enough to take someone's life? But to trick them beforehand, too? Especially a woman? It wasn't too much for Richard, though. I mean, he used to fuck my mother when she wanted nothing to do with him.*

My sister's fearful face flashed before my burning eyes, and I winced, afraid to even know what he was doing with her while I was stuck in here. Did she know that I was here? Did she know that I was playing the long game so I could get back to her?

The chains around my wrists were heavy as I pulled away from the wall, and next thing I knew, I was slammed against the hard block wall with Richard's hand wrapped around my throat. My vision grew spotty, and the pain from the slashes against my back burned as they scraped along the scratchy surface.

I gasped for air, trying to reach up to pull his thick, disgusting hands off my windpipe but the chains gave no leeway, and I was stuck in the position of wanting to die and wanting to bow down to him so I could kill him when the moment struck.

"You are not in charge, Tobias. How many fucking times do I have to tell you that? I should have killed you instead of bringing you here." I wish he had. *"You've always been a tough little shit, so I thought I would bend and twist that feeling inside of you and turn you into a man, but you bleed defiance, and I'm sick of it."*

My lungs burned, and the entire room closed in on us, pushing at me from every other direction. Panic began to spike my blood, and I fought the urge to shut my eyes to end it all. Gemma. I couldn't leave her. She was all I had left, and I was all she had, too.

"Tobias." My eyes flung open, and I gasped for air, shooting up out of my bed and turning on the voice that came from my right. My hand wrapped around her neck as I hovered over her, breathing like I had been stuck underwater for minutes. Sloane's wide eyes ensnared me, and I was stunned, trying to figure out where I was and what I was doing.

"Fuck." I quickly unlatched my fingers from her delicate neck and stared down at the fear flowing from her eyes. Her hands immediately replaced mine as she rubbed the delicate skin, and I wanted to say sorry in the worst way, but I was too ashamed to open my mouth.

I flew back and landed on my warm sheets and clenched my eyes, shutting the room out. My breathing was labored, and I still felt as if I were being choked by Richard. I cursed myself for falling asleep beside Sloane. I had only lain with her because of how she was shivering from the drugs in her system. I shouldn't have, but I couldn't stand to see her little body wracking with chills.

"Hey, are you okay?"

My chest was moving up and down as quickly as my heart

was beating, and I hated that she had asked if I was okay. I had just choked her because of a fucking nightmare.

Suddenly, I was back to my five-year-old self, having night terrors of the monster in my closet who had a very close resemblance to Richard.

"It's okay, ya know." Sloane's voice was raspy and sleepy, and it was centered in my brain, canceling out the replays of what I'd just endured. Your deepest, darkest memories had a way of attacking you when you were the most vulnerable, and I was definitely the most vulnerable when I was asleep. That was why I didn't sleep a lot. I didn't like to be caught off guard.

My eyes continued to stay closed as she shifted beside me, erasing some of the space I had put between us. The heat of her hand lingered over my chest, and as soon as I allowed the faint glow of the room to force my lids to open, I felt her soft palm rest over my heart.

What is she doing?

My pulse hammered, and the muscle in my chest banged against her hand with thunderous beats. I glanced away, hating that she was witnessing this. "Do you want to talk about it?"

I swallowed, trying to force the lump in my throat to go down. I didn't even shake my head. Instead, I stayed completely still underneath her touch and kept my mouth shut. I didn't want to talk about it, and I didn't want to think about it. I usually didn't even want to breathe after revisiting the past, but for some reason, with her hand on my chest, I wanted to exist right here, in this moment, with her.

It was just a hand. A small, warm hand on my chest. But it felt like a brand. A tattoo etched into my skin. A reminder of something.

Unease must have settled in her head with my lack of response, because she slowly raised her hand from my chest, and

I panicked on the inside, scrambling to put it back. My fingers wrapped around her dainty wrist, and she stiffened as I held it in my grasp and placed it back down onto my sweaty chest.

Relief burned the back of my throat as I felt myself submerge in the feeling of desperation and longing, and although I hated the weakness I was showing, I didn't make any move to push her away or bite out a response that made her cower. I wanted her near. I knew I was being weak, but I made no move to erase the moment.

"Just breathe," she whispered against my skin, moving a little closer to me. Sloane being this close did nothing to slow my heart rate, but at least now it was no longer beating hard from the night terrors but more because she was touching me and seeing me like *this*.

As soon as her fingers started to move gracefully and slowly over my pec, I began to feel a familiar pull in my core. Was it the dropping of my guard, or was it the fact that she wasn't cowering away from me after I'd just turned on her and attacked her? It was probably some sort of trickery from the mess inside my head, but it felt like an acceptance, and that did something other than make my heart beat faster.

I knew without even looking down that my dick was straining behind my gray sweats. I'd changed after she got sick last night, knowing that I was going to have to lie with her again because drugs didn't leave your system that quickly. *What a mistake that was.*

Peeking down and seeing her lying beside me, with her other thumb inside her mouth, nibbling on her nail, I realized she was feeling just as vulnerable as I was in the moment. Did she remember last night? Was she still feeling the remnants of the drugs? She probably wasn't even in her right mind if she was touching me and trying to make *me* feel better.

Get out of the fucking bed, Tobias.

The lace of her pink bra snagged my attention. I'd forgotten that her shirt was off because I had insisted that body heat would help her chills. I dipped my gaze down past the detailed lace and moved it languidly over her soft, curved hip and settled on her short skirt. I had a flashback to last night when I'd slid a glow stick inside of her.

I shifted, whipping my head away and looking at our shirts tangled together on the floor across the room. Sloane's hand began rubbing over my chest tentatively, like a caring gesture that I had only seen her use with my sister and Journey. She was tender when she wanted to be. She just didn't usually want to be with me. And honestly, who could blame her? I was no good for her—or anyone. I knew it. She knew it. Everyone in this school knew it.

"Your heart is still racing," she whispered. The minty mouthwash she had used was lingering on her breath, and I wanted to stick my tongue in her mouth and lap it up. It hurt to want something you knew you couldn't have, but I couldn't find the billowing anger inside to push her away like usual. I was too spent from the night terror. Too exhausted to care that I would regret this as soon as she was out of my sight. I sighed at the twisting of my balls. The need to flip her on her back and fill her up with my possessiveness to make her mine was alarming. I was so sick of giving and not taking, but I wouldn't take from her.

She was drugged.

You hate her.

She hates you.

I almost laughed at my thoughts. I didn't hate her, but I wanted to. When feelings started to show through, even as faint as attraction, I tended to obliterate them, but the warmth of her hand swiping over my skin as it made its way against my flexed abs was nothing more than a welcome mat to the craving. There was a desire burning within, and it was something I had never felt before.

"My heart won't stop racing until you remove your hand." My chest was trapped with air, and it was hard to get the words out. Sloane's palm paused as she crept it up my chest, and her doe-like eyes caught mine with surprise.

She wiggled, stretching her legs before bringing them up to her chest. I wanted her to drape her leg around mine so she could feel what she was doing to me. I didn't understand it. There was something about her that I continued to circle until I was too dizzy to stop.

The rising and dipping of lace against her expanding rib cage caught my eye, and with her fidgeting, I began to worry. "Are you sick again?"

Her answer was swift. "No. I..."

My abs flexed as I gripped the side of my bed. A quiver of a breath left her as she looked to the ceiling before looking at me again. Her dark locks fell behind her ear, and I zeroed in on the bruise right below her thick eyelashes. It settled on her cheek bone that had last night's shimmery makeup still painted on it. I reached up and rubbed my thumb over the small bruise, recalling when she had flipped off my bed and hit it on the table.

"You what?" I asked, shifting my hips and pulling my sweats down a hair against my hard cock. This was torture, and for someone like me—who had been through actual torture—to say that, meant it was true.

"Nothing." Her shaky voice pulled her eyes away from me, and I silently begged for them to come back.

I watched her hand slowly move over my flexing muscles, and heat came down on top of my head and washed away every part of the nightmare that I'd had. The weakness I'd felt with Richard's hands around my throat was no longer there as I fought with myself on what I should do with her hand.

Once it reached my waistband, I clenched my eyes shut and held my breath. The room had just enough light in it that I could see her every movement painted with faint shadows and a warm glow. "No," I bit out, forcing the word between my teeth.

"You're...right. I don't know what I'm doing." She was appalled, but the vulnerability still lingered.

Sloane began to sit up, and I hated to see her insecure. She was tough, but I sensed her disappointment right along with mine. I looked around the room. We were alone. I flicked my gaze to the door, knowing it was locked. I didn't have a roommate. We could do whatever the fuck we wanted and regret it later. Because one of us surely would regret it.

I sat up with her as her hand fell from my body and stared into her somber eyes. Her lips were no longer sporting the red lipstick, but they were plump and glistening, and surprisingly, I wanted them on my lips instead of my cock.

"Lie down."

Her brows bundled. "But..." She scanned the room, and I hoped she wasn't looking for an escape route. I pushed on her delicate shoulder until she lay back in my bed with her silky dark strands of hair wafting out around her. I hated that she was so beautiful. It made this so much worse.

The bruise on her cheek stood out against her creamy skin, and my eye twitched at the thought of someone drugging her last night.

"You were drugged less than twenty-four hours ago," I said, lying back beside her. Our arms were touching, our fingers mere centimeters away from one another, resting over my sheets. "I'm not going to touch you when you could still be under the influence." I turned and looked at her wide eyes. "But that doesn't mean you can't touch yourself."

A short, hot breath left her lips, and I licked mine, breathing in the minty smell. "You said you didn't want me to touch you last night. Do you remember that?"

"Yes." Her response was more of a gush of air, but I heard it. Uncertainty trickled around us like the beating of raindrops outside my window, but I smirked, looking down at my hard length through my sweats. "Don't back down now, Sloane. You played a tough game last night before I had to rescue you. Tell me," I said, putting my hand down over myself, hissing with my firm touch. It was a fucking turn-on with her eyes on me. I was out of control, which was a digression of my normal behavior. "Did you ask them to fuck you? Were you trying to make me angry?"

"You're always angry. I did it to put you in your place."

I took my other hand and slapped it against hers on my bed and gripped it tightly. The room was quiet. The only movements were beating hearts, rushed breaths, and raindrops against the window. I relished in the fact that she allowed me to take her hand and place it on the top of her skirt. The zipper was in the front, and I wanted nothing more than to unzip it with my teeth so I could see her pretty little pussy.

"Finish what you started, then."

My hand left hers, and she paused, peering up at me with the same doe-like expression from moments ago, but there was a hint of excitement in there. I knew she'd take the bait. She didn't back down from a fight. Her naughty glint full of distrust and arousal showed through the dark hints of hazel.

I stared over at her profile, memorizing her high cheekbones and smooth slope of her nose that led to her plump lips that were meant for much more than her sassy words. Her shaky fingers stopped as she fiddled with her zipper, and it was like I was waiting for the grand finale. *Let me see, baby.*

Her head moved all around as she scanned my room, and

the realization hit me like a swift punch to my core. "You think I'm recording this?" I asked, feeling the slightest pang of remorse for blackmailing her. The remorse was gone a second later, but I felt it.

"I wouldn't put it past you," she rushed out, all breathy and high on anticipation.

A swallow worked itself down my throat as I turned away and gripped the waistband of my sweats. I lifted my hips up and pulled them down quickly, releasing my hard cock into the open room.

"There," I said, gripping myself tightly and feeling a rip inside my chest. "Now we're even."

CHAPTER NINETEEN

A SWALLOW CREPT down my dry, sore throat as a blush spread against my skin. I blinked several times as I felt a pull in my stomach so tight that tingles replaced the chills that I'd been blessed with for hours last night. Tobias' hand was large and completely skilled as he gripped himself at the base and worked it up and down.

"Now we're even."

My zipper was like the prequel to the shame I was going to feel when I left the comfort of Tobias' bed with my dignity completely obliterated. But at the moment, there were no second thoughts. Maybe I *was* still under the influence. Maybe I was still drugged and not in my right mind.

"Touch yourself, Sloane." His whisper was as dark as the midnight sky, and the husk in his voice rubbed me raw. I wiggled my hips as I pulled my skirt and panties down. There wasn't too much light in his room, and I had no recollection of what time it was or what happened last night after he had brought me to his room to ride out the effects of the drugs in my system.

Or, better yet, who gave me the drugs.

The only thing I had a recollection of at the moment was how, last night, Tobias Richardson—the heartless boy of St. Mary's—showed me a sliver of himself that wasn't so bad after all.

"Faster," he demanded, catching my gaze from across his bed. I shot my attention down to his hand, and my mouth went dry. He was pumping up and down, and there was a small bead of cum on the tip, and I shut my eyes, wanting to run my tongue over him. *I feel crazed.*

The smallest whimper left me as my body grew hot. Sweat formed in between my breasts as I worked myself over with his dirty words penetrating my ears. My eyes shut as pleasure took hold of my body, and small slivers of the night before started to slip in my mind like a snake. *The glow stick. His warm breath hitting my face. His hard grip on my hips as he pushed me up against the cool wall. His eyes on me from across the room.*

The rest of the night came in choppy fragments, but I remembered the important parts. The part where Tobias crawled into his bed with me, and wrapped me in his strong arms, and held me tight as cold sweats took me under.

"Don't hold back, Sloane. Let me see you. Do what you'd do if I wasn't watching you."

I popped my eyes open and focused on the tightness of his jaw as his hand worked back and forth. He snapped his head to me, and those dangerous blue eyes pulled me further under. "Look at me while you come," he whispered, voice gritty and eyes flinty.

"No," I said, smirking as my toes curled. The girl I was used to being came swooping back in like she held all the power, and I felt bolder than ever with the effect I had on him. He stared at my hand, and his breathing grew raspier. He liked what he saw, and I liked that.

A menacing chuckle climbed from his mouth, and his next words halted me as tingles spread down my body like a wildfire. "This is the only time we will come together, so get ready, baby."

Ah.

There was a soft grunt from him, and I whipped my head to the left and stared in complete and utter shock as thick ropes of creamy liquid sputtered from his cock as his strained neck muscles flickered back and forth. *Oh my God. That's the hottest thing I have ever seen.*

I couldn't have stopped myself from falling over the edge if I wanted to. I felt the free fall as my head flew back onto his pillows, and his powerful amber smell wafted around me as pleasure took me from all angles.

"Fuck." The bed moved beneath me as my eyes clenched shut, falling into a blissful state, lacking the regret I should have felt from letting him watch me come apart like that. *What just happened?* My eyes flickered open as something warm hit my thighs. His hands gripped my ankles, and he positioned himself, sweatpants back to their rightful spot below his muscular belly. His come dripped onto the bed from the dips and valleys of his abs. He looked down to watch it trickle as a wild smirk curved against his mouthy lips. He took his hand away from my ankle and dipped his finger into the liquid.

What—

"Open your mouth."

I obeyed his dirty words with absolutely no objection and opened my lips as he put his finger inside and wiped his salty moisture on my tongue. A satisfied look relaxed his features. "Look at you, being a good, obedient girl."

My eyes grew wide as I swallowed the taste of him, and

when his pleased gaze fell in between my legs, his hands tightened on my ankles. "I'm going to clean you up. No evidence. Because this..." His stare drove into me for a split second. "Never happened. Right?"

His hands left my ankles, and he slapped them against my thighs and pushed them apart, inhaling as he moved closer to the mess between my legs. *Holy. Shit.* Tobias was in an entire league of his own. Broody, mysterious, demanding, but could be attentive in ways that you never knew you needed.

My hips bucked as my hands clenched his covers. His tongue was hot and wet against my middle, and I began sweating again. His hum vibrated me from the inside out. "Tobias," I warned, beginning to feel panicky that he was going to get me off again. *This is so good but so fucking bad.*

"I've been wondering how you tasted since that first time I touched you." *God.*

There was a knock at his door, and I quickly sat up in his bed, completely off track, when his sister's voice sounded on the other side. The sun began to peek through the thick, rainy clouds outside his window, and when our eyes clashed, we both knew the moment was over. His jaw ticked, and my face grew red.

What the hell am I doing? Tobias was poison, yet I kept going back to drink more.

I looked around his room, confused and angry. I just allowed Tobias Richardson to get inside my head and twist me in his blood-stained fingers. Those same fingers that were inside my greedy walls as he recorded me orgasming over his hand and asking him for more, knowing very well that he was my best friend's brother.

He blackmailed me and was forcing me to lie to his sister, which went against all my morals since my parents had turned my life upside down.

"Tobias? Is Sloane awake? Shiner told me what happened. Open up."

Our eyes caught, and I hated us at that moment. The look was mutual. He climbed off the bed with his mouth wet and his stomach sticky. Pushing myself up, I pulled my skirt and panties back on. My legs were wet, but at least I wasn't dripping. *Thanks to his mouth.*

"Never. Happened," I whispered, jumping off his bed on less-than-sturdy feet. The room spun slightly, and I righted myself by grabbing onto his arm, feeling the muscle flick beneath my palm.

"Oh, it happened," he said, bending down and grabbing both of our shirts. Gemma knocked again, and just as I reached out to grab my shirt, Tobias smirked before yelling, "One second, Gem." The cotton of my shirt was bundled in his hand before he wiped his stomach off, rubbing his wet cum on it.

"Are you fucking kidding me?" I seethed, ripping it from his grasp. The lightest chuckle rumbled out of his chest, and the evil smirk was a coil inside my belly as I threw my shirt on, trying to rub in his cum so it wasn't noticeable.

"Better hurry and clean yourself up." He walked backward, keeping his hot gaze on me as he pulled on his shirt with one hand, covering up his tight stomach.

I refused to sit on his bed as his hand landed on the doorknob. I quickly pulled his covers up and hid the wet spot on the dark-blue sheets, hiding all evidence of what we'd just done. The night's events began to hit me head on, and I crossed my arms over the cum stain on my shirt and stood on shaky legs, too worked up to even focus on Gemma rushing inside the room to stand in front of me. Her head moved in front of mine as she grabbed my cheeks, mere seconds from being wet from my unshed tears.

"Sloane," she repeated, finally coming into my line of

sight. My mouth opened, and panic erased the words on my tongue. I peeked up at Tobias, and his smirk was gone and replaced with that same attentiveness he gave me last night. A mere sliver, but it was there, and although his navy-blue eyes held a wealth of mystery in them, I saw the boy he was moments ago. The boy that still lived and breathed inside of him, hindered by trauma and fear and anger. *Do not go easy on him, Sloane. He just rubbed his cum on your shirt.*

"She's fine," he said, keeping his eyes on me as Gemma ran her hand over my bruised cheek. "She got sick a couple of times last night, but I think maybe only one shot had something in it. Otherwise, she would have been completely knocked out."

"Who the hell would do this?" She spun around and stared at her brother while keeping her hand on my wrist. "Thank God you saw her. Shiner said you saw some guys taking her into a room, and you followed them. Cade and Isaiah got their story, and it checked out. Jameson had some in his system, too. But who the hell would do this?"

Gemma spun around once more and put her hands on my shoulders. "Are you okay? What happened to your cheek?"

"She fell trying to get to the bathroom," Tobias answered for me, and I was thankful. He was putting on a good front with his sister throwing out questions left and right. Another bout of chills ran down my arms, but it had nothing to do with feeling sick from last night and everything to do with the fact that the truth still remained. *Someone drugged me.*

"Hey." Gemma's bright-green eyes locked onto mine, and I knew she could see right through me. This was the first time she had seen me truly afraid. "What's going on with you?"

My teeth clenched as my eyes welled. My lip quivered, and there was an ongoing war happening all around me, rooting me in the center of the battlefield.

Gemma's hands stayed on my shoulders as she looked over at her brother. "Why did you tell Shiner not to tell Dad?"

Tobias' head turned away at the sound of the word *Dad*, and a sense of protectiveness flew up my throat. My words passed by the quivering of my lips to save him. "I asked him not to tell the headmaster."

Gemma's hair swayed in front of her face as she ping-ponged her attention back to me. "Why? I think you should be checked by a doctor, Sloane. This is serious."

"He will tell my parents, and they will rip me out of this school faster than you can blink. You, of all people, should know the fear of being taken by someone who pretends they're good on the outside but isn't on the inside." I sniffed up the last bit of my revelation and sighed. "I'm fine. Don't tell him. Please."

"Your parents? I thought…" Her brows dipped, and her worry lines softened. Her forehead came and rested against mine, and she nodded. "Are you sure you're okay? You've got the Rebels in a tizzy."

A tight laugh left me, and Gemma smiled as she stared into my eyes. As soon as she left my space and grabbed onto my hand, she walked over to her brother and reached up onto her tiptoes and gave him a quick kiss to his cheek. "Thanks for taking care of my best friend. That's the Tobias I miss. Always there to save someone."

He swallowed and raised his chin, not looking at either one of us.

When we walked out into the hall and his door shut behind us, I felt like I could breathe again.

"Jesus, woman." Shiner rushed at us and broke the last bit of tension that I felt. "Caveman Tobias had you locked in his room all night. I was beginning to get worried."

Gemma slapped Shiner's stomach as he backed away from

his hug. "Stop it. He took care of her. He isn't as bad as you guys make him out to be."

"He makes himself out to be that way," Brantley said. "He's an ass. Even more than I am."

Gemma rolled her eyes as Isaiah grabbed onto her hand and kissed her knuckles. He leaned down and looked me dead in the face. "I'm gonna figure out who drugged you, okay? It won't happen again." I nodded and smiled up at him. The Rebels and I had come a long way since the beginning of the year. After Journey was forced away from St. Mary's from what I thought was because of Cade, I hated them all. They were righteous and dangerous when it came to girls' hearts around here, but deep down, they weren't as bad as I made them out to be.

I was beginning to think that Tobias wasn't either. Damaged, yes. But not everything broken stays that way.

Shiner wrapped his arm around my shoulder as we all began walking down the hallway. No surprise that they thought Gem and I needed an escort with random drugs showing up in the school that I knew, for certain, were for me and no one else.

We met Journey, Cade, and, to my surprise, Bain, in the break of the hallways as they held a bundle of food and drinks in their hands. "We brought food," Journey said, smiling at me with a genuine smile. She stood in between Cade and her newfound brother, Bain, who looked less than thrilled to be included in our group.

"Stop looking at me like that," Bain gritted, staring at me. "I'm only helping because Journey asked me to."

Journey grinned. I was pretty certain she and Bain had even more baggage than Gemma and Tobias, who had both been tortured by the hands of their nonbiological uncle. To be honest, I might have been the only one here that had a simple past. Simple but not easy.

"You *should* do anything she asks," Cade said nonchalantly. "If you want to be on my good side at least."

"I don't give a fuck about your side," Bain said, keeping a hold of the four cups in his hands.

"Guys," Journey warned, elbowing them both. "Stop."

Shiner laughed as he began walking me past them to my room. I could hear the bickering back and forth between everyone and Isaiah's booming voice, trying to overpower them and question who brought drugs into the school.

Isaiah wouldn't let it go. He was missing a few pieces of the story, though, and those pieces were going to stay locked away until I knew more of what was going on with Willow. It wasn't my life that I was worried about. It was hers.

"So," Shiner's voice tickled the side of my ear as he passed by Mercedes' room, acting like he wasn't burning a hole through the wood with his gaze. "Tobias took care of you last night?"

I paused, my spine going straight.

"Yeah." My answer was hesitant, and I glanced back to see how close everyone else was.

Shiner's hand grabbed onto my forearms that were crossed in front of my shirt, and he pulled them down, staring right at the wet smears. He smirked and shook his head.

"Better burn that shirt, girl." I quickly put my arms back up, and he opened my door, following me inside to look around my room—probably for anything suspicious. "Don't worry. I'm good at keeping secrets." He plopped on my bed and threw my phone at me. I caught it quickly, and my stomach rolled just at the thought of the texts that were waiting for me. "They call me the secret keeper. Now, go shower and get the stench of cum off you."

As soon as I hurried into the bathroom and heard the rest of our friends enter my room, I placed my back on the bathroom door and sank down to the tile floor, looking at my phone and seeing that all my messages were read and no longer on the home screen. *Fucking Shiner.*

My chest hurt, and dread was in every corner of my brain. I placed my phone on the floor and shoved it away, letting it slide against the tile until it hit the bathtub. I stood up, undressed, and let the cold water pelt me from above, hoping to rid the sneaking worry that I knew was going to follow me everywhere I went.

CHAPTER TWENTY

TOBIAS

It smelled like stale coffee and aftershave in my father's office. The dark, orange glow reminded me of my room each morning as I lay awake with sweat drying on my skin from the things that lurked in the back of my head when sleep came. I'd stare up at my ceiling, trying to level my breathing and reel in the uncertainties over the list of names hung with a piece of fragile tape in the back of my closet.

I glanced down at my phone again, rereading the texts from Tony.

Still at large.

Still no word on target 3.

Did you still want me to look into your girl?

I sighed, pushing my phone into my pocket. Sloane wasn't my girl, but Tony liked to fuck with me, and I didn't have it in me to joke with him like we were old friends instead of two fucked-up humans that found themselves in a shitty situation together.

My father's office door opened, and I pushed myself away

from the bookshelf that I was resting on. The last time I was in his office was weeks ago when he told me that Sloane was going to be my babysitter and help me with my grades.

I wondered what today's meeting was about.

There were no nerves involved, but my resolve fell quickly when my sister followed our father and shot me a hesitant smile. *Here we go.* My confidence wavered. I knew her better than I knew myself, which wasn't saying much because, lately, I didn't feel like myself at all. But, unfortunately, Gemma didn't know *me* anymore. Or maybe she was fortunate not to know me.

"Tobias." My father was on edge. I knew this because we did the same thing with our face when something was chewing at us. He and I looked a lot alike, as much as I refused to admit that out loud.

I turned my attention away from him, ignoring my sister who was standing with her back to his desk with her arms crossed over her chest. She was in a paint-stained shirt, which was also another clue that something was going on, because she always turned to art when she was upset about something.

That something was probably me.

"Tobias." This time, Gemma was the one to speak. My eyes flew to her, and Sloane popped into my head at the very last second, like the flashing of a camera. *Wait, is this about her?*

"What?" I asked, fully invested now and hating myself for feeling that way. I refused to look at Sloane in any of our shared classes and tried my very hardest to light up that anger inside when it came to her. I could fake it on the outside. My pencil snapped in class when I heard her talking to Shiner and joking around with him, and I knew she probably thought I was being my typical brooding self because I continued to pull her in and then push her away, but to be honest, I was angry because it was like the other night didn't exist or affect her when I know it did. Not to mention, who the hell had drugged her? Wasn't she the least bit concerned about that?

I knew Gemma and Journey were. They chatted in front of me like I didn't exist most of the time, and they were both trying to piece together things that wouldn't make sense unless they had the truth, and I had a pretty good hunch that Sloane was keeping that shit on lockdown.

"Tobias." I snapped my head up to my sister and felt the room rock slightly. *Sloane won't get the fuck out of my head.* "Did you hear me?"

"No." I crossed my arms over my chest, feeling my heart drum against them.

Gemma's shoulders fell in defeat, and more worry ate her up as she rubbed her charcoal-stained hands down her legs. "We know you and Sloane aren't studying together."

My teeth clanged together, and a hard pop sounded in my ears.

"Okay, so?" I bit out, instantly angered that this was some sort of an intervention. Did my father, who I had literally just met a month ago, think that throwing me into a boarding school with kids my age was going to change who I was? An education seemed so obsolete compared to everything I'd learned thus far in my life. "Do you both really think that knowing algebra is going to help me in the long run?" *I may not know what x + y equals, but I know twenty-seven different ways to hide a body.*

"That's not why you're at St. Mary's." My father stood up from behind his desk and came to stand beside my sister. Their arms were touching, and a pang of jealousy went through me over the fact that they had a relationship. Would I ever be able to have a relationship someday? With anyone? With Gemma?

The truth was, there wasn't a bone in my body that thought I would be able to truly love someone, and that was a truth so bitter it hurt to swallow.

"You're here because I want you here." That came from my father, and Gemma eagerly nodded. "But in order to stay and have the future that you deserve, you have to put forth effort."

"What if I don't want to be here?" My question was the key to their silence. It was the unlodging of the pin that was holding the bomb steady. An erupting of something ripped through my chest, and the trigger was pulled. "I don't belong here." I stared into my father's eyes, watching the dominance inside of him come to life. His eyes narrowed, and his arm muscles flicked.

"I'm trying to help you, Tobias."

"Why?" I shouted. The lack of sleep, remnants of nightmares, and aches in my hands that I felt every morning from the overuse of them when Richard had tasked his employees at the Covens to give me their worst came at me at once. The phantom pain of holding a heavy gun in my hand for hours upon hours and wasting bullet after bullet until the sun came up so I could *always remember what it felt like to shoot something* pelted me in the back. The burning feeling of guilt I felt on more than one occasion of how often I would think of how easy it would be to shoot myself was centered in my head.

I sliced my gaze to Gemma and squeezed my eyes shut just like I used to do when I was alone and had those twisted thoughts late at night. *If I died now, I wouldn't get back to her. My mother would have died for nothing. And I wouldn't get to kill Richard-fucking-Stallard with my bare hands one day.*

Revenge was the best motivation that I had.

"Do you know what I've done?" I asked, pacing the room back and forth as the pressure of the world was on my shoulders.

"Yes."

"No!" I barked, making my sister jump in her spot. I shut my eyes, knowing I needed to calm down. This was what it was like to have dark secrets dripping with blood trapped inside. Anger found its way out one way or another. "You don't!"

I peeled my eyes back open, seeing my sister and my father give each other worrisome looks. "Did you tell her where I was after Journey and I left the psych hospital?" *Left* equaled *escaped*, but that was up for interpretation depending on who you talked to.

Gemma's face fell as she tucked her hair behind her ear. She looked so much like how I remembered our mother, and there was the smallest tick in my chest at the sight. She looked sad, and that was, unfortunately, my mother's go-to.

"What is he talking about?"

My explanation had an outcome that I wasn't sure I was ready for, but I let the truth spew effortlessly from my mouth as if I were talking about the weather. "I wasn't 'working on myself' like he told you. Or taking time to 'adjust'." I flicked my head to my father, and he sent me a look that was very similar to the one I was giving him. "I was hunting down the rest of my targets. The ones that got away."

Gemma's mouth opened, but then she shut it again, looking between us in confusion and shock. "What?"

"You think a life like the one I lived just disappears because Richard is gone? I've killed people." My voice boomed with anger. *Breathe. Stay in control.* My tone evened out, but even so, it was as sharp as a piece of glass. "There are people who know who I am and what I've done. There are people, still out there, plotting my death because they know I've plotted theirs."

Gemma blinked back the tears that were forming, and I knew she didn't have it easy when I was gone. I knew that our presumed uncle didn't just break me. He broke her too. But fuck, she and I were not the same. Gemma's plan was to run. Mine was to kill.

Twins could be the same, but we could be different, too.

"I still love you," she said, taking a step toward me. I took a step back and nearly combusted when my father nodded. "As do I."

"You don't even know me!" I barked at my father, annoyed that he was telling me something I couldn't even begin to understand.

"It seems I don't either. But I still love you." There was a gaping hole in my chest at Gemma's soft voice. *Why can't they just leave me be?*

I quickly spun around, frustrated and confused. My fist hit the shelf, and a few books fell to the ground before I stepped over them and flung the door open and stalked away. Tony's gruff words hit the back of my head as my phone vibrated, reminding me that he was still a present person in my life even if he was hiding out in some basement somewhere in the US, hunting down names for me like we were still at the Covens.

"Find an outlet, Tobias. Don't let it take you under."

An outlet was exactly what I needed.

$$\overline{}$$

CHAPTER TWENTY-ONE

SLOANE

My pencil tapped back and forth against the table in the library. Willow's face appeared on my screen, and although I never settled for long on her social media profile, I did today.

She posted less than fifty minutes ago, which meant it was nearing night for her, if she was still in New York, halfway across the United States. I wondered if my parents ever saw her, or if she ever came to the house asking for me or wondering why I was sent away without a single explanation right after her parents had died. I didn't even go to their funeral. *Some friend I was.*

When I finally turned my phone back on a couple of nights ago, my parents' texts and voicemails flooded in. My phone vibrated for what seemed like an eternity until I silenced it and read through their messages, ignoring the ones from *Unknown*. Thankfully, my parents hadn't called Headmaster Ellison yet, which I knew was their next step. If I got too sloppy and didn't check in with them occasionally, they usually went to the extreme, and I didn't want any part of that, so I made a mental note to text them tomorrow.

My fingers hovered over my laptop as I clicked through some of Willow's photos. She still looked the same—pretty, auburn hair with a slight wave in it and dark-green eyes. She attended a public high school now instead of the prestigious private school that made us wear matching uniforms, much like St. Mary's. Her hair wasn't as glossy, and her smile wasn't as joyful, but she still looked the same overall. She had friends, and there was even a photo of her with her grandmother, who she had lived with up until a year ago when she'd passed away. Now, she lived with a foster family, which just so happened to be one of her friends' parents.

She seemed fine.

So, what does this mean? I wrote the words over and over again inside my journal that was supposed to hold all my notes from class but, instead, held all my worries and continued stress from the last few weeks.

There were only a couple texts from the unknown number, and the drug incident had been covered up by the Rebels, but I couldn't help the peeving thoughts of someone watching me from afar. Coincidences happened all the time. Maybe the texts were a test from my parents, and I had failed. Maybe the drugs from the claiming weren't meant for me. *But what about the closet thing with the recording?*

"Sloane." I quickly shut my laptop, looking as suspicious as if I had just robbed a bank, when Journey and Gemma rounded my table in the library.

"What's wrong?" I asked, sensing the worry. Slowly, I closed my journal and placed my pencil down. *Did something happen? Do they know? Did Shiner tell them what he saw on my phone?*

I trusted Shiner more than the rest of the Rebels, but with everything that had happened over the last year with

Gemma and Journey, I was pretty sure we were all a little jaded now.

"I need your help." Gemma sat down beside me, and her makeup was a little smeared.

"Have you been crying? What's going on?" I asked, turning fully toward her and grabbing her paint-stained hands in mine.

"It's Tobias."

My heart sank to the floor, and I had a feeling that if it had legs, it would be running toward him at his very second despite my denial that there was a really small part of me that wanted to fix him. Because Tobias definitely needed some TLC. He was hot but cold. Callous but compassionate. Actions spoke louder than words, and his fiery words were often followed by subtle touches and fleeting glances.

I grew tense as Journey's head dropped. "He's failing most of his classes."

My mouth stayed shut, but my mind was racing. I knew he was failing, but Tobias had me by the throat. What would Gemma say if she knew I had messed around with him? Not once but twice. I was supposed to be helping him —for *her*. Pressure fell to my chest, and I gripped my notebook.

"I...know. What do you want me to do? I can't force him to study. I've made notecards for him, and he throws them away in front of me."

Journey rolled her eyes. "He's so stubborn."

"Maybe you should be the one to help him study," I said, trying to pass off my duties. Maybe then, I wouldn't feel *as* guilty.

"I can't," Journey said. "I'm behind, too. I missed out on too many classes while in the psych ward." Her head dropped in defeat, and it was like seeing the old Journey, before she had been taken from our school last year in an ambulance.

"And it won't work if I do it. He won't listen to me. I just tried to talk with him, and—"

I paused. "And what?"

"And he flew off the handle. My dad said to give him some time. That he probably felt attacked because we tried to talk to him together, but maybe you could talk to him?"

"Me?" A hot slash hit my back as I thought of being alone with Tobias again. "Why me? He doesn't listen to me, Gem. I've tried."

"He will listen to you," Journey whispered, pushing her light hair behind her ears. Her eyes pleaded with mine, and I gulped, trying to read her. *Does she know that we did something?* She and Tobias were close. Did he tell her?

I was sorting through every avenue of escape when it came to being connected to Tobias somehow, but then the thought of looking suspicious crept in, and if anything, I owed Gemma this, considering I was failing miserably at being a good friend.

"Have you tried talking to him?" I asked Journey.

She huffed. "Yeah. He blows me off." She shrugged. "I love Tobias, but he keeps things to himself. Even in the Covens, we usually just sat in silence. He's...complicated."

Dammit.

I breathed out a shaky sigh and straightened my shoulders. I was wearing my joggers and a loose, off-the-shoulder shirt because my only plans were to silently uncover my old best friend's life to make sure she was still alive and then go to bed and pretend like there wasn't anything unusual going on, but here I was, ready to go spar with Tobias—again.

"Alright. I'll talk to him. Where is he?"

Gemma and Journey shared looks, and just then, Isaiah and Cade walked through the library doors with their sights set on their girls. "Did you find him?" Gemma asked, standing up and walking over to Isaiah.

He nodded before rubbing his palm down his face in defeat. "He's in the weight room."

"Alone." Cade glanced at me after grabbing onto Journey's hand. "He's losing it."

Gemma stiffened. "What do you mean, 'he's losing it'?"

Cade chuckled, but it wasn't full of humor. It was a dark laugh full of trouble. "He's beating the shit out of a punching bag. He wouldn't even look at us when we entered. I think we should all just give him some space."

My throat swelled as I remembered his nightmare from the other night. The way his heart thumped and screamed in silent agony. The sweat that glistened on his chest and the damp ends of his hair.

Gemma and Isaiah were arguing in the background as she pleaded with him that he'd listen to her if she went and calmed him down.

"I can calm him down."

"No, you can't. He is unstable. Even your dad thinks so."

"He's my brother."

"Baby, you don't even know him anymore. He's been—"

"I'll go get him." I sighed, pushing my notebook and laptop into my bag and silencing them.

"Are you sure?" Gemma's eyes were wide with fear, but the smallest glimmer of hope sparkled. "Do you think he'll listen to you? I was kind of hoping you two had formed a little friendship the other night after he helped you at the claiming."

I laughed, trying to remain calm on the outside. "Friends? Not so much. But I'll try."

Gemma's slender arms wrapped around me, and I winced at the guilt that followed closely behind. "I love you."

"I love you, too. Don't worry." I winked at her, now determined to fix Tobias. "He'll come around. I'll start slipping notecards under his bedroom door if that's what it takes."

Tears filled her eyes. "I hate that Richard did this to him."

I reached down and grabbed her wrists, eyeing the scars that she hid from me for so long. "And he hates what Richard did to you. We all do."

Isaiah tugged her in close and kissed her temple as I pulled my bag over my head and headed for the weight room.

———

THE SILENCE in the hall was piercing as I crept my way toward where Tobias was. The dark wasn't helping much because I still felt seen. My emotions were on lockdown, but the flipping of my stomach was near paralyzing as I heard the sudden jolts of thumping from Tobias hitting something over and over again. I could see him through the small glass window in the door, and I chewed on my lip as I let every smack of his fist against the punching bag hit me without force.

The angry scars against his back were rippling right along with the defined lines of his muscles, and the sweat dripping off him accentuated them like warning signs. One of his legs came up, and he swung around, giving me a full view of his sharp jaw and midnight glare. His dark lashes surrounded red-rimmed eyes, and my throat tightened.

Before I could take a step back and turn around, I opened the door and dropped my bag to the ground with a loud thump.

"Leave." He was out of breath and didn't turn around when the word flew from his mouth. "Get out."

"No," I said, taking another step toward him onto the mat.

Tobias paused, and his head fell onto the swinging punching bag as his hands came up and held it in place. My lips parted at the redness on his fists and the already forming bruises. "You are the last person that should be in here right now."

I gulp, moving closer. *You can do this, Sloane.* "Why?"

"Because I'm fucking dangerous like this, and you're an easy target."

I dodged the obvious blow that he used to wound me and crept forward until I was mere inches away. Heat surrounded us like we were in a steam room. "You think I haven't been around danger before?"

My hand was shaky as I covered one of his fists. It was burning beneath my touch, and he spun around quickly, yanking it from my grasp. His fingers pushed his inky, wet hair off his forehead, and his eyes drove into mine, stunning me for a moment. "Do you know that my hands have literally been covered in blood before, Sloane?"

I blinked, trying to hide from the memory of my best friend's parents. "Are you just trying to scare me to make me go away? Because I've seen blood before, Tobias. You don't know the things I've seen. I've been around dangerous people before."

He threw his head back and laughed, the sarcastic sound hitting me right in between my legs. *Why do I love the sound of his hoarse laughter so much?* It was dark and dangerous, and it swam inside my head, making me think things I shouldn't have been thinking. "Are you talking about the Rebels?" He suddenly grew serious again. The tiny, thin scar through his eyebrow disappeared for a moment before he smoothed his expression, appearing lethal. "Their hands are sprinkled with blood, Sloane. We are not the same. Mine are permanently stained. I don't know why you, along with my sister and my father, can't fucking understand that."

I blinked with each biting word that flew from his mouth. Visuals of the blood beneath my feet several years ago when I was more naive than ever began striking me like I was in the middle of a thunderstorm. The way Willow's mother was surrounded by a pool of blood, hunched over her husband who had a seeping hole in his head, popped into my brain, and then came the screams that I later realized had come from me. I could nearly feel that same breeze from the open balcony door inside this weight room when I saw them both fall to the ground. The stomping of someone's feet with their back turned toward me as they placed their gun back in their pants pulled me in a different direction, and suddenly, I felt like I couldn't breathe.

My back was pressed against the punching bag a moment later, and I gasped for air, shaking the memories away. Tobias' eyes bounced back and forth between mine, and he licked his lips, appearing angrier than before. "Did I just scare you? Good. Now you're finally understanding that you need to stay the fuck away from me."

His hands on my hips were a brand that I would hide for the rest of forever. My skin itched to be touched underneath my shirt. "That's...that's not what I meant," I whispered, flicking my eyes to the door to make sure no one was watching. Why was it like this with us? We were so quick to be angry with one another and try to hide our thoughts and desperation, but he could see right through me, and I could see right through him.

"What?"

"I'm not talking about the Rebels, Tobias." My breath caught, and my stomach rolled with nausea. There was a need woven inside that I was pretty sure only he could douse. It was the protection in his gaze that I could see, even though he tried his hardest to pretend it wasn't there. "I've seen blood. I've watched a murder happen right in front of my eyes, so no, I'm not afraid of you. I'm not afraid of you because I've seen who you really are." His brows crowded, and confusion swept up the anger and threw it right to the floor. "I've seen *you*." My finger poked his bare chest, and he looked down at it slowly, dropping his gaze and staring at my red-painted fingernail.

Suddenly, his hands were under my butt, and my legs were wrapped around his hips. He carried me to the mirror, pinned my back to it, and stared at my lips like he wanted to kiss me. The hope inside burned like a cigarette pressed against my skin. I felt my legs slither down his hips before he took a step away.

"You need to stay away from me, Sloane."

For once, there wasn't anger in his voice but defeat. His head fell, and his hands came up and rubbed roughly at his damp hair before he walked to the opposite end of the gym, past all the workout equipment, and put his back to the wall and sank to the ground with his eyes shut. "Please, just fucking leave."

I should have. I should have because this moment was different. He was wounded, and he was showing me that he was. He wasn't hiding behind his anger or biting out a cruel remark to make me leave. This felt different in the way that he was no longer protecting himself from me, but the other way around.

So, instead of leaving, I crouched down in front of him and gave him a simple answer. "No."

CHAPTER TWENTY-TWO

TOBIAS

*FOR FUCK'S SAKE, **this girl is relentless.***

She was bent down, crouched right in front of me as I pulled my legs up and rested my sweaty forearms on them. My heart continued to thump hard, but it was no longer because of my workout and more so because of her presence and how I began to grow nervous at the fact that I no longer could deny that she was the balm to my cuts.

Before she walked in here, I completely obliterated every thought that entered my head with a swift punch to the bag that hung in the distance. I thought of my sister, my father, my mother, Richard, and the fucked-up reminder hanging in my closet that held a list of names that loomed over me and everyone close to me like a tombstone after death. Then, she came in here, showing off her warm eyes and flushed cheeks, touching me with her soft skin, giving me a piece of truth that I was pretty certain had never left her mouth before.

Why she would tell *me,* of all people, something that was

so traumatic it seemed to steal her away for a moment, was too much to wrap my head around.

My arms were blanketed in chills as my sweat began to dry, and before Sloane could sink back onto her heels in defeat at my silence, I pounced on her like an animal in the wild.

Her back hit the mat with a thud, and my hand quickly fell to the base of her head so it didn't hurt. I breathed down into her face, hating myself for wanting to caress her in ways that had to have been rooted down into the human psyche, because it was an instinct that seemed to be triggered by whatever I had felt with her eyes on me. "You are like a bad habit I can't quit," I bit out, trying to hold myself back from making this more than it ever could be. I wanted to see her smile. I wanted to make her feel something with my lips on hers to show her what I felt instead of telling her, because I never would.

Sloane's back arched beneath me, and she inhaled a breath so big that her soft breasts rubbed against my bare chest. I felt the tight pebbles beneath the thin cotton and clenched my jaw.

"Ditto," she whispered. "Why do you think I've been trying to avoid you?"

"I was hoping it was because you regretted the other night."

"I do," she whispered, licking her pretty lips and making my head fall to her collarbone. *Fuck.* This moment with her was heavy, and my chest screamed with agony because, for the first time since I was a young boy, I felt a sliver of contentment and comfort with her beneath me. I shook with the realization that I would never feel this way again. Because the truth was, I was afraid that I would never be able to live up to the standard that she deserved.

"I hope you regret this, too, then," I whispered, sitting up and peering down at her hooded eyes with too much emotion in them. My hand was near shaking as I pushed the thin cotton up past her belly button and watched her tiny belly muscles tighten with my eyes on her.

My mouth hovered over her body, and my pulse was exploding in my ears. The second I pressed my lips to her skin, I shut my eyes, relishing in the feel of her warmth flowing into my veins. *My God.*

Blood rushed to my fingertips as I dipped them below her pants, pulling at the waistband of her sweats and revealing her perfect body in simple black panties that would be burned into my brain until the moment I died. She lay still beneath me, with only her chest moving, and when I hooked my thumbs under the thin straps of her panties, I slowly slid them down her smooth legs. My mouth watered as I pulled her shirt over her head. *No bra.* I stared down at her, memorizing her curves and running my finger over the enclave of her cheek as she turned her head into my hand, closing her eyes for a moment and breathing out a shaky breath.

She is nervous.

I am, too.

The nerves were terrifying. The way I was taking my time with her was making me both mad and satisfied.

"What are you doing?" she whispered, glancing up at me.

"Pretending to be something I'm not," I answered truthfully, allowing myself to feel every bit of her swarm my head and fill my veins. I stood up with her naked below me and glanced at the door.

My back was to her as I slowly prowled over to the gym door, and the clicking of the lock echoed like a bomb throughout the quiet room. I flipped the light switch off, allowing only a sliver of light from the locker room to showcase her lying perfectly still where I left her.

She didn't say a single word as I stared at her from above,

weighing my options. *I should make her leave.* I was arguing with myself because I knew I would destroy her heart. Sloane was tough, but I was fucked up. I couldn't care for someone. Didn't she understand that?

Her chin tipped as we locked eyes, and a shaky breath left her split lips. She was waiting. She was lying there, ready for me to use her at my own disposal, and I was going to because something tore through my chest, and there was a need so toxic I almost buckled at the knees.

My pants fell to the floor in a single swish, and my boxers were next. I was hard, and although she'd already seen me like this, her eyes flared, and her lips begged to be kissed. The cool mat hit my knees as I crowded her space, bringing my hands to cage her head and pulling on her dark strands a little.

The room was cast in a faint glow, but I swore I saw her eyes shine with something that tried to burrow inside my skin. There was nothing spoken out loud, but there was a magnitude of words flowing between us in silence. Like a deal sealed in lust and high emotions.

I ran my nose over the side of her delicate cheek, feeling my balls tighten between my legs. She smelled so damn good, like honey and the warmth of a sunny day that I'd craved while locked underground at the Covens.

Anger slashed at my back like I was being whipped again. My brain unknowingly reprimanded me for wanting to put my lips against hers, for wanting more than just this one moment of indulgence. I deserved retribution, and maybe after this, that was exactly what I'd get.

My teeth nipped at her ear, and her back arched again as her sweet little legs parted for access. I licked the spot I'd grazed with my teeth, and I could literally smell her arousal. My dick touched her pussy, and I almost buried myself inside her at that moment, but her perky, perfectly sized mounds were begging for my touch, and that was one thing I wouldn't deprive my mouth of.

"These are perfect," I whispered, blowing on her nipple and watching in awe as it tightened. I jolted my tongue out and circled each one like it was the forgiveness I needed to move on with my life, and before I knew it, I was positioned between her legs and locking eyes with her from above, silently asking for her permission. If she was hesitant, I'd stand up, using every bit of will power that I had, and walk away.

I was used to giving, not taking. I could handle it if she didn't want this. But I really wanted to take from a girl like her.

The silent parting of her legs and wistful look on her face was the unlocking of chains around my restraint. My hands slapped the mat beside her head, and I rocked my hips forward, hissing between my teeth.

She was tight, warm, and wet, and I wanted to die in that position, buried inside of her. Everything disappeared. St. Mary's, the weight room, our hatred for one another, the blackmailing shit I'd pulled with her, the pressure to be something I wasn't and excel in school as if I hadn't physically choked people in my past... It was gone. All I saw was her.

Sloane's hands gripped my tight shoulders, and her nails dug into the skin. I craved the pain, wanting more of it. "More," I bit out, staring down at her with a bead of sweat falling from my forehead like a teardrop and landing on her lips. Her tongue shot out, and she licked at the same time her nails drove in even more.

My body moved back and forth as I rammed in and out of her, filling her up completely. She withered beneath me, and I couldn't help but move my mouth to her neck, sucking on her delicate skin and needing to feel her against my lips. Kissing her on the mouth would be a sin. It was a red flag to me. It scared me. Although, I wouldn't admit that out loud. Things with Sloane were different, and I didn't just mean this moment.

A sweet whimper left her mouth, and I quickly pulled myself up, eager to watch her break around me. Her head flew back, and her delicate chin pointed to the ceiling as a stream of light from the locker room graced her soft skin. I wanted to freeze the moment. *Fucking hell.* Her pussy tightened around me, and her legs spread even further. I moved in and out of her again and again, slowing myself down to enjoy watching her succumb to me. My hand gripped her chin, and I brought her face back down so we could lock eyes.

"Look at me," I demanded, gritting my teeth at the feel of her milking my cock. *Sex has never been like this. Ever.* My sister could have been knocking on the weight room door, and I still wouldn't stop fucking her best friend. Sloane's hooded eyes opened, and the lustful, dopey look in them gripped my entire soul. My thumb rubbed over her wet lip, and I pressed down, wanting nothing more than to seal my mouth over hers and suck in every last secret and hidden thought that laid deep inside her head.

"Fuck," I whispered, staring into her eyes. This was too intimate. I was seen. My guard was down, and Sloane watched as I nearly broke in front of her, pulling out quickly and coming on the mat beside her. My head came down on hers, and I shut my eyes, hating myself for feeling a small connection, even if for a single second. *No.*

There was agony inside my chest, beating me up like I'd just done to the punching bag, but instead of making me angry, it made me worry.

I quickly pulled myself up, leaving her naked on the mat, and went to the locker room and grabbed some clean towels, wetting one for her. *Am I taking care of her now?* My hand was shaking, and I flexed my jaw as I met her halfway and handed it to her. She was holding her clothes in one hand and wouldn't meet my eye. Her hand brushed mine as she swiped it from my grip, and tingles charged all the way up to my neck.

After cleaning myself and the mat, I threw my shorts on and waited for her to come out of the locker room. She didn't take long. Her cute jogger sweatpants were back on her hips, and her shirt was pulled over her head and smoothed out. Her silky hair was pushed behind her ears, and she took one look at me before inhaling and walking past, to the door.

Panic rose to my throat, and I pushed off the wall, wanting to do something like storm over to her and flip her around to show her that what just happened wasn't a mistake. Except, it was.

"Sloane," I rushed out, taking one step toward her.

She spun around, confusion sweeping her features. "Yeah?"

I looked away as insecurities flooded from every direction. I was just inside her, yet I had a hard time looking her in the eye when I felt like this. "Fine."

"Fine?" She was hesitant but stayed rooted in her spot.

It killed me to ask for help. Physically made me sick. "Will..." I cleared my throat, still not meeting her eye. "Will you help me study?"

When I peeked back up at her, there was the smallest flicker of resolution covering her features. "We start tomorrow." Then, she whipped around and left me in the weight room, fumbling with the thing inside my chest that was beating wildly for someone for the first time in my entire life.

CHAPTER TWENTY-THREE

"You seriously got him to agree?" Gemma's hands planted themselves on my shoulders as I nodded with feigned happiness.

It wasn't that I wasn't happy that Tobias was finally accepting some help and letting me tutor him, but the guilt was eating me up like a million mosquitoes on a summer night. Not to mention, we had sex.

We. Had. Sex.

And it wasn't the normal, *take-take-take* kind of sex that I would expect from Tobias. Not that I would admit thinking about him and sex in the same sentence to anyone, but I'd imagined it to be rougher and faster. I imagined around fifty different verbal insults he'd shoot me after it was done, but that was not what happened.

He was raw. The blue in his eyes that resembled a storm cloud was more like pure sea glass. There were vulnerabilities that hung loosely around him as he moved in and out of me.

There was a softness to his rough hands that touched my body, and an intimacy that I'd never experienced lingered between us.

"Sloane?" Gemma nudged my shoulder with hers and glanced at my phone vibrating on the table that sat in front of us.

I quickly snapped out of my thoughts and darted my hand out, feeling the blood drain from my face. Silencing it quickly, I shot her a half-smile and shrugged. "Parents."

Her eyes swept down to my phone as she stood up from the library chair and pushed it in slowly. "Why do they keep calling?"

"Well, I keep ignoring them, so..." I shrugged again, beginning to sweat. It wasn't my parents calling, and I knew that without even looking down at my phone.

"Why do they call in the middle of the night? I thought they were super strict about you getting good grades. Hence, why you're at the top of the class, little miss *valedictorian*."

Ugh, how did she know that? "Did your dad tell you that?" I put my phone in my lap, afraid it would ring again.

Gemma smiled. "There are perks to having your father as the headmaster."

I laughed and rolled my eyes. "Must be nice."

Silence fell between us along with an awkwardness that made me cringe on the inside. It hadn't been this awkward between us since she had first come to St. Mary's and was hiding much more than a few prank calls here and there like I was currently doing.

"Hey." Her voice was much softer, and I peeked up at her worried, emerald eyes that she shared with her father. "Are you okay, Sloane? Like, for real? What's going on with you?"

"Noth—"

Gemma gave me a look that bordered on anger, but she

was too nice to truly look angry. "I didn't forget what you said the other day. About your parents and how they aren't who I think they are. So, why do they keep calling?"

Remember the story. Remember the story. Remember the story. I went over it all in my head. Parents are in the military. I lived with Granny until she passed. Parents weren't home much, so they sent me to a boarding school.

"They're just strict—"

"Sloane." Gemma's eyes flared with unease, and I was sure it was like looking in a mirror with her. In fact, there were numerous times I had tried to pry information out of her about her Uncle Richard that she wasn't willing to give up, and I pleaded, just like she was doing with me.

The doors to the library swung open as my phone began vibrating in my lap again. Tobias appeared in the doorway, wearing a plain black tee and dark jeans that made him look even taller than he already appeared. I never thought I'd be thankful to see him, but here I was, feeling thankful that he just saved me from a lengthy conversation with his sister.

I shook my phone in front of her, knowing Tobias would distract her enough that she wouldn't press me on the lie coming from my mouth. "I'll go see what my parents want, okay? Will that make you happy?"

Her shoulders dropped as I turned around and headed for the aisle.

The number on the screen said the same as it always had: *Unknown.*

"Hello?" I forced out, putting the phone up to my ear. It was the first time I'd answered the phone, and when I heard heavy breathing through the speaker, a chill raced down my spine.

"Who is this?" I asked, lowering my voice so no one would hear. I knew that sometimes Journey and Cade liked to frequent these aisles, so I moved into the next one over, hoping there wasn't anyone listening.

"It's Willow." The air was snatched from my lungs as I heard the one name I didn't want to hear, even though I knew it wasn't her.

My nostrils flared, and as I glanced behind me, I saw Tobias standing over our study table, like a statue, staring in my direction. I turned my back to him, hoping the color would come back to my face so I didn't seem afraid of him when that wasn't the case at all. "This isn't Willow," I seethed. "Not unless she turned into a guy."

"So...you do remember her? Your old best friend?"

I panicked.

"Who is this?" I asked again, beginning to feel light-headed. My parents needed to know about this. I knew it deep down, but I was too selfish to tell them, knowing they'd fly off the handle and make rash decisions. They could go after Willow and end the problem that way. Or they could pull me from St. Mary's and make me ride out my senior year of high school through an online school, or worse, a school that wasn't even in the United States. I mean, shit. I was pretty much in Canada as it was.

The line went dead, and I dropped my phone to the library floor, grabbing onto the edge of the bookshelf to keep myself propped up straight. I wanted to bend over and clutch my stomach to stop the rising nausea, but I knew that Tobias had his eyes set on me. I could feel the way they burned the back of my skull. So, instead of reacting to the call, I bent down and swiped my phone and gripped it so tightly I thought the screen might be cracked when I finally walked over to him.

"Did you finally stop ignoring your mother?" he asked nonchalantly, as if he hadn't been inside me the night before.

He didn't spare me a single glance in any of our classes today, and I was going to repay him with the same coldness he showed me, even if, deep down, we both knew things were *different*. We totally crossed a line.

A line that we *kept* crossing.

"My words must have stuck with you," he said coolly, taking the seat in front of me, resting his elbows on the table, and drumming his fingers against my notebook.

"What words?" I asked, pulling out my own seat.

"The first day we met." A dark chuckle left him, and it raced over my skin. "I followed you into the bathroom and—"

"I remember," I mumbled. "You called me a slut and then told me to stop ignoring my mom." My belly bottomed out as guilt itched at the surface. *Am I slut? For sleeping with him?* I think I may have been a slut for him—and only him.

Silence stretched between us, and when I looked up and saw him staring at my hand still gripping my phone so tightly my knuckles were white, I quickly let go, allowing it to clamor to the wooden table. The scar embedded into his eyebrow disappeared as he furrowed his forehead, but he smoothed his face and pierced me with a lazy look. "So, should we start studying?"

Smoothing out my own features and pulling my phone over to my side of the table, I cleared my throat and straightened my shoulders. "Sure, after you delete the video."

The smallest flicker of his mouth made me grind my teeth. A piece of his thick hair fell onto his forehead before he whipped his head to the left and flung it back on top. My mouth stayed shut as I forced myself to stay still on the chair beneath me, locking onto his stupid, sexy smirk.

"Oh, are we bargaining now?" he asked, tsking his lips and leaning back in his chair to show off his broad chest. "I thought we made great progress last night."

"Do we really want to talk about last night, Tobias? Because you and I both know that it was something much more than a quick *fuck* in the weight room." I hissed the last part between my teeth, leaning across the table and reminding him of what last night really was. He could sit here and pretend like last night was *nothing,* but we both knew that wasn't true. As much as I'd like to pretend it didn't happen and ignore the way my insides did a little flip when he was near, I couldn't.

Tobias' chin tipped, and he showed off his angled jaw. His minty breath flew from his mouth as he sighed agitatedly and quickly stood up. "Fine. Let's go get it. We can study in my room."

I hurriedly put the brakes on, standing up with panic. "That's not a good idea."

Tobias smirked over his shoulder. "Why? Afraid to be alone with me, Sloane?"

Yes. "No." I crossed my arms over my chest. "It's just...not allowed."

Tobias laughed. He actually laughed, and I was pretty sure the entire library had paused to take in the sound. "So, what? You no longer break rules? That doesn't sound like the Sloane I know."

"You don't know me." I pouted, crossing my arms over my chest like a child. I almost stomped my foot, too, before I realized that Tobias had probably seen the real me more than his sister, who was my roommate *and* best friend.

His eyebrow raised, and he gave me a look that had me scrambling to pick up my books to follow him out of the library and down the boys' hall to his room. We said absolutely nothing the entire time, and the only thing I could hear was my heart beating in my ears and the chant of *turn back, turn back, turn back* in my head.

When we stepped into his room, I immediately glanced at his bed, remembering the hazy memory of what we had done in here several mornings ago before his sister came knocking on his door. I *am* a slut for him. My face was red at the thought.

I kept my distance, walking over to his desk and putting my books down before turning and crossing my arms over my chest. Tobias was looking out the window with his hands in his pockets, standing there like he owned me and the room.

"Well?" I said, sighing. "Where is it?"

His sharp gaze cut me from across the room, and I bit my tongue. *Why is he so hot?* His Adam's apple bobbed as he swallowed and turned on his heel and stalked over to me before pulling out his phone and putting it in between us.

"You mean this recording?" he asked slyly, obviously toying with me.

I popped my hip out. "*Tobias.*"

Innocence covered his face, and his dark eyes held a wealth of playfulness in them. "Yes, Snow White?" My lips wanted to curve in the worst way, but as soon as the recording started to play, embarrassment burned me like a hot strike on my skin.

My hand reached out as anger took over, and I tried ripping the phone from his hand. A smile so beautiful covered his mouth, and I paused, surprised by what his face was doing. His arm shot up, and he held his phone above my head, pausing the recording. "Why are your cheeks red?"

He was still smiling, and I was acting like a girl with her first crush, unable to say anything. That smile could end century-long wars. Did he use that smile as a weapon when he hunted people down for his uncle?

"Don't be embarrassed," he teased, getting closer to me. "I like the sound."

"Delete it, Tobias. Or I won't help you study."

He chuckled again, the laughter rumbling out of his chest and making my cheeks burn even hotter. He and his sister shared the same smile, probably from their mother.

"Please," I whispered, feeling my phone vibrate in my back pocket.

"Fine." He sighed, flopping back on his bed like he was totally relaxed around me, unlike I was with him. "But what will I listen to while beating off?"

"Oh my God! Stop it," I hissed, silencing my phone.

He laughed again, and my heart fell to the floor. *What is going on?* I wasn't sure if I saw him in a different light after last night, or if last night meant more to him than I thought. Regardless, things weren't nearly as tense between us as usual.

"Okay, okay," he rushed out, sitting up on his bed effortlessly. His phone came between his long legs, and his finger hovered over the screen. "Let's make a deal."

I leaned back against his wall, beside the desk that held all our study materials. "A deal? This is the deal. You delete the recording, and I help you pass all your classes so your father and sister will stop worrying that you'll be kicked out of St. Mary's without a high school diploma."

His head tilted, and he shrugged. "The deal is I'll delete the recording *if* I graduate. Who's to say that you tutoring me will actually work? I'm not sure I trust you. You might give me all the wrong answers and have me studying shit that isn't even on the test."

"Why would I do that?" I asked, confused.

"Payback." His blue eyes flung to mine and...was that fear I saw in them?

"Or..."

Suddenly, this side of the room felt like the wrong side to be on. "Or what?"

"Or I'll delete it if you tell me who is calling you right this second."

I froze, dropping my hands to my sides as my phone vibrated again in my back pocket. I looked at the window, avoiding him. *That isn't obvious at all.* "It's my parents."

"Don't lie to me. Not after last night."

My eyes narrowed as I stooped to his level and let my anger do the talking for me. "So you're admitting that last night was more than a quick fuck out of desperation? Who knew you could have feelings."

Tobias flew up from his bed, and I pushed myself back against his wall again. "Oh, last night was definitely out of desperation, Sloane. And it won't happen again."

"You're right about that," I spat back, frustrated and confused and tired of feeling this way when it came to him. I wanted to pull him in but push him away, too. "I only let you fuck me to bring you back to reality. Your sister came to me and begged me to help you and said you were losing it in the weight room."

Tobias snapped his fingers as he rounded his desk and stood in front of me, towering over me with his height. "Another lie. You're two for two, baby."

My jaw hurt from clenching it so many times in the last twenty minutes. "How is this fair?" I asked, annoyed that he was wanting to play another game with me.

"Life isn't fair," he whispered, looking into my eyes with that soul-crushing stare.

"Who is calling you? An ex-boyfriend? From before you started here?" He took a step toward me, but I kept my face even and unbothered.

"Who said it isn't an ex-boyfriend from St. Mary's?"

He looked at me like I was stupid. "Because I would have done away with him weeks ago." He must have sensed the confusion on my face, because he followed up with, "I asked.

There aren't any broken-hearted boys here at St. Mary's because of you. In fact, I heard you haven't dated *anyone* since attending St. Mary's."

He asked about me?

"So, someone from before?"

"It's my parents," I lied again.

His eyebrow raised, and my gaze dropped to his lips as they moved again. "So, your parents came here and pushed you into a closet and locked it? *And* they drugged you at a party?" He blew that minty breath into my face, and I inhaled like I was starving for oxygen. "And here I thought I had it bad with my non-biological uncle throwing me into a psych ward and abusing me until I was turned into his own personal hitman."

"I hate you," I said matter-of-factly.

"Good." He quickly took a step away from me, and I felt a rush of cool air separate us. "So, that's the deal. Take it or leave it. Tell me who's calling you and fucking with you, and I'll delete the recording. *Or* you can just wait until I have my diploma in hand. Both are great options."

My phone vibrated again, and I whipped it out of my pocket in frustration and pressed on the off button until the screen went black and threw it across the room, almost hitting him in the head. "Fine. Now sit down and shut up so we can go over this week's assignments. You will not leave this school with that recording, Tobias. You will graduate."

He smiled again. "I think I can manage with a tutor like you."

I spun around and busied myself with opening my books, but the truth was, there was a really small part of me that liked him holding something over me. It bound me to him, making it seem like I didn't have a choice *but* to spend time with him.

And I liked that he had asked about me and tried to figure out if I had an ex-boyfriend.

I liked that there was a brief sliver of possession in his tone, too, even if I knew that a guy like him would never be capable of being more than what he was now—which was *nothing*.

CHAPTER TWENTY-FOUR

TOBIAS

"Let's play a game."

Sloane shot me the most exasperated look I'd seen so far, and I had to look away so I wouldn't laugh.

This was night four of studying with her, and every night that she left my room, my face would ache from holding back a smile. It was becoming tiresome, pretending that she annoyed me just as much as I annoyed her. What annoyed me was when she tucked her hair behind her ear to show off her pretty, creamy skin. Or how she would make me sit in the chair across the room while she splayed out on my bed, kicking her legs up behind her as she put those perky little breasts on my covers, making my entire bed smell like her. Or that I felt like a small piece of me left with her as she stalked out of my room without even saying goodnight. I looked forward to our study sessions, too, and I fucking hated myself for it.

"We are not playing a game. We're studying."

My brows furrowed. "I need motivation."

The golden flecks in her eyes twinkled from across the room, but her scowl deepened. "We are definitely not playing that kind of game."

I chuckled, pleased that she picked up on the sexual innuendo. "I didn't mean that kind of game, but I'm glad to know where your mind is during our study times."

Her cheeks ripened with a blush that I wanted to touch with my fingers, but I focused back onto the flashcards that she was scribbling on for me to use before the test in English Lit tomorrow.

"I ask you a question, and then you can ask me a question, and I'll be serious and answer it correctly." I wouldn't be me if I wasn't still acting pompous and indolent when we studied, but I would be lying if I said studying with her hadn't helped me in class this week. I still liked to get a rise out of her, though. I enjoyed her reactions as much as I enjoyed having the freedom from Richard.

"Um, no."

"Okay, *fine*. You ask me a question, and if I get it right, I can ask you a question."

Sloane didn't even look up from the flashcards. She used a pink pen. I think she did that on purpose to annoy me. *Pink*. "I don't need help studying. I know all the answers."

"Oh, you're so cock..." Her eyes flared as she peeked up from the bed. "Cocky. I'm sorry. I meant to say cocky."

"Why are you only this annoying to me? You don't talk when we're in our group of friends. You're so grumpy."

I corrected her. "*Your*. Your group of friends."

She sighed. "I forgot. You're incapable of friendship. I'm almost done with these, and then we can review them."

"And if I get them right, I get to ask you questions."

"What kind of questions?" she asked without looking up

at me. I kept feeling something unfamiliar when I was alone with her. I wasn't me when I was with her.

"Simple ones. Come on. I thought tutors were supposed to reward their students."

"Your reward is me not killing you, Tobias."

I laughed loudly, which surprised her. "What a thing to say to someone who has been trained to kill."

"I—" she stumbled over her words.

"It's easy to forget what I did before coming here, huh?" She looked down at my hands, and her face softened.

Silence stretched around us before I broke it with the truth. "I didn't say that for you to feel bad for me. Pity is the last thing someone like me wants, Sloane."

"Fine. I'll play," she rushed out, sitting up on the bed, cross-legged, wearing the same jogger pants that I tore off her legs the other night in the weight room. Flashes of her naked body came to mind, and I hummed on the inside.

"Yeah?" I asked, teetering over the edge of no control in the situation. Sloane had me by the balls, and she had no fucking idea.

She shuffled the notecards, positioning them straight in her hands. "If I don't want to answer the question, I'm not going to answer."

"Fair enough," I said before standing up and leaning against the wall. Sloane's eyes trailed me from my shoes all the way to my eyes before realizing that I caught her. "Go on," I urged, moving past the ever-present buzzing between us.

There wasn't a single female at the Covens that I had ever felt anything for. I mean, the nurses could get me up. It's not hard—no pun intended—to get a boner and fuck. But with Sloane, it was persistent. Even looking at her hands holding the flashcards made my blood run hot. I wanted her hands on me. I also wanted to pin them above her head and make her wither beneath me as I rammed into her with everything I had held inside from the second I saw her touching herself on my bed. *That was out-of-this-fucking-world hot.*

"What are the three major idealizations of the Romantic period?"

I pushed off the wall and paced the room, taking long strides, keeping myself busy so I didn't climb on top of her. "Freedom..." Not the hardest word to remember. It was the one thing I'd craved from the moment I was left in the care of Richard. "Imagination...and emotion."

"Good jo—"

"My turn," I interrupted her. Her mouth shut, and her back straightened, preparing herself for the worst. "What is your favorite color?"

She began pulling her hair up into a high pony, showing off more of her slender neck that I'd licked the other night. There were tiny hoops in her ears, catching the stream of light from the lamp beside her. *She's cute.* I paused, wondering if I had ever called something cute in my entire fucking life. "My favorite color? That's the question?"

I shrugged. "I'm curious."

"When I was younger, it was turquoise. But now, it's black."

"Black?" I stopped right in front of her and paused. "Makes sense."

"Why is that?" Her question was hesitant as she stared at me from down below.

"Only people who hide things are drawn to the color black."

Her cheeks relaxed, and there was a slight look of wonder there. "Is that true? Do you know the meanings of colors, or are you just making that up?

"I do. One night, when I'd had a nightmare at the Covens..." My voice dropped slightly as I put my back to her, slowly pacing again. "Journey was there. She would sneak into my room, and we'd just lie on opposite sides of the bed in silence."

"Yeah." Sloane's voice was soft, and I clung to it. "She told me that."

"Anyway, I was pretty much like I was the other night with you—messed up, heart beating quickly, sweating. And she broke the silence by asking me what colors were in my nightmare." I grinned, shaking my head. "I had no idea why, but I told her, and then she began telling me the meaning behind every color. She said one of the patients of the psych ward claimed to know magic. I guess she read palms and shit, so she could decipher dreams, colors, futures, all of it."

Sloane laughed lightly, and I shot my attention to her. "Athena. Journey told us about her. We had a girls' night after everything had happened, and Journey tried to read our palms."

I smiled at the look on her face, wanting that to be the last thing I saw before I fell asleep at night so maybe I wouldn't wake up sweating and disoriented. "Yeah, Athena. Anyway, that's how I learned the meaning of colors."

"So, what does black mean, then? Why does it make sense that it's my favorite color?"

I shrugged. "It means a lot of things. For you, mystery, hence why I said only someone who likes to hide things would choose it." She glanced away, knowing it was the truth. "But it can also mean death, evil, power, control."

Her brows dipped, as if she were in deep thought, before she grabbed another notecard. "What's your favorite color?"

"Black. But not for the same reason it is for you."

We locked eyes for a moment before her phone began vibrating, halting everything. "Another call from your parents?" I asked, knowing damn well it wasn't her parents. Before our first session, when Sloane had wandered off through the library after talking with my sister, Gemma looked up at me and said, "Something is going on with her." But what my sister didn't know was that there was *a lot* going on with Sloane. And some of it had to do with me.

Sloane ignored me *and* her phone and read the next note-card. We played our game for almost an hour before she decided she wanted to wash her hands after eating my small bag of Cheetos—one of life's greater gifts that I discovered after leaving the Covens where I had nothing but scraps of cafeteria food. As soon as the bathroom door shut, I heard the lock, as if she didn't trust me, which was accurate considering the second she was out of sight, I reached down to the bed and grabbed her phone that she had silenced three separate times since sitting in my room. As soon as I held the phone and turned it in my hand, I swiped up and began trying to enter the password.

The thing about me was that I was observant as hell, and most of the time, you couldn't even tell that I was memorizing shit. I went over the way she moved her fingers to unlock the screen when she didn't use face recognition. It wasn't often, but there were a few times that she didn't, and a few times was more than enough for me to guess the number combo.

Up, down, up, left-down.

0, 2, 0, 7. Incorrect.

8, 2, 0, 7. Incorrect.

8, 2, 8, 7. Incorrect.

"Fuck."

I tried one last time, cataloging what I had already done in case this didn't work before she got out of the bathroom. This was absolutely crossing a line, but that was what I did. I crossed lines and didn't usually feel bad about it afterward.

8, 2, 8, 4.

The background of Sloane and Gemma popped up, and I

felt a jolt in my chest. Sloane's arm was around my sister's neck, and their faces were smooshed together. They were mid-laughter, and the pang in my chest grew to a punch. I paused, looking over at the bathroom door as the water ran in the background. I quickly went to her missed calls and furrowed my brow as it said *Unknown*. I swiped up, and sweat began to form on my neck. *Jesus*. The number had called her over and over again. At least twenty times a day for the last several days, and the times that the person called were interesting, too. I hurriedly took my phone out and took a few pictures of the missed calls and went to her texts, where Unknown had texted her, too. I took pictures of that and then typed my number in and called myself before clicking her phone off and walking away to stare down into the courtyard from the window.

The wind blew in the distance, the trees swinging their bare branches through the darkness. Small buds of leaves and flowers were on the ends, a rebirth of spring, which was how I was able to tell that years had passed while I was in the Covens. Each time Richard let me out to go on a 'job', I would bask in the outside air and realize that another season had passed.

Time was a slippery fuck. I was locked away for so long, but standing here, looking out the window, with my back to a girl who was quickly becoming the center of all my thoughts, it felt like not much time had passed at all. Maybe it had to do with what you did with your time to make it move slowly or quickly. What I did know was that I found myself wanting time to go slow when I was with Sloane, and that was unnerving.

"It's getting late," I said, closing my eyes at the sound of the bathroom door opening. "You should probably go."

"Yeah, I was going to say the same thing." I noticed the dip in her voice but continued to keep my back to her. See what I meant about time? It was finicky. We'd spent one minute apart, with her in the bathroom and me in my room, and the little safety net that surrounded us was ripped wide open, and we were backtracking the easygoing hang-out session that just occurred between us.

It was hard to remember who I was when I was with her. It was hard to remember that I was incapable of being someone she needed or wanted in life.

As soon as Sloane had left my room, without saying so much as a goodnight *again,* I pulled my phone out and flopped onto my bed that was still warm from her body. Her feminine, honey smell wafted up and covered me like a blanket as I read the texts that were on her phone. They didn't make much sense and were confusing, to say the least. They were like pieces of an already present conversation via text, but Sloane's responses weren't there. After flipping through them a few more times, unable to make sense of them, I went to her phone number and copied and pasted it to a text to Tony.

Me: See what you can get from this number.

He texted back within seconds, and I half-imagined him to be sitting in some weird, damp basement with a headset on and a growing beer belly, as he sat in front of several computer monitors. We had to stay fit at the Covens, but Tony was always on the larger side.

Tony: Big doggggg. She gave you her number? Solid.

Me: I stole it.

Tony: Can you picture my unsurprised face?

Me: Yes. I do not need another unsolicited pic from you. Let me know what you find out.

Tony: I'm on it.

I clicked my phone shut and tore my shirt off before lying back on my bed and staring at my ceiling. Although I was out of the Covens and there was no longer a padlock on my door, part of me still felt trapped. Sloane had a way of making me want to be something more than what I was. I wasn't sure what, but there was a bomb that ticked when she was near me, and I knew that bomb would destroy us both.

CHAPTER TWENTY-FIVE

SLOANE

How did he manage to do that?

I stared at Tobias on the other end of the bleacher, sitting completely by himself. There weren't many of us students out at the lacrosse field today because we were in that weird in-between season of winter and spring. The breeze felt like small icicles landing on my cheeks, and I knew they were likely as pink as Gemma's, Mercedes', and Journey's.

"Why are you sitting down there?" Gemma bent forward to ask Tobias.

"Studying," he said, flicking his eyes to me for the briefest of seconds. There was a gush of something warm on the inside, and I looked away, pretending to be unfazed. My phone was burning a hole in my hand as I reread the texts from a random number, not the *Unknown* that I'd been getting for weeks, but a number that I now knew to be his.

Tobias: Ask me an English Lit question and we can continue our game.

Me: Tobias? What the fuck. How do you have my number?

Tobias: I'm waiting, Snow White.

Me: Not until you tell me how you got my number.

Tobias: Journey gave it to me.

Me: You're lying. She wouldn't give you my number unless she asked me first. She, unlike you, understands privacy.

Tobias: I've been inside you. But I can't have your number?

My fingers hung over my phone in defeat as I peeked over at him again. Gemma, Journey, and Mercedes were saying something in the background, but I was too busy trying to figure out how Tobias could look so innocent and relaxed with the notecards I had made him while texting me that. Part of me wondered if it was a trap, more ammunition to use against me for blackmail.

Tobias: Your cheeks are red.

This asshole.

My fingers pounded against my screen with force.

Me: It's cold! So are yours.

I glanced over at him again, even though I told myself not to, and he was staring directly at me with his stupid black beanie pulled down over his hair. His cheeks were hardly pink. Was he immune to the cold now? He had the perfect skin tone. Not too pale, but not super tan either. His face was smooth except for a little scruff visible late at night, and there was a defined muscle that popped out every once in a while when he was angry and grinding his teeth.

Our eyes locked and stayed for far too long before he tilted his head to his sister, and I snapped out of it.

"What was that?" she asked, laughing while looking skeptical.

I shrugged, clicking my phone off. "Just making sure he was actually studying instead of pretending."

"He's stubborn." Journey placed her back on the bleacher that I was sitting on.

Gemma nodded, pulling her beanie down on her head a little lower. Her shiny hair was a mess over her shoulders. "He gets that from our mother."

"Makes sense. The headmaster isn't stubborn. He's pretty easygoing."

I nodded, agreeing. "He is. Can he be my dad, too?"

We all laughed, but the laugh lines around Gemma's eyes softened as she snagged my gaze for a split second. I glanced away, feeling my phone vibrate again.

"Woooooo!" Gemma yelled after Isaiah made a lacrosse goal. They had taken a few months off during the winter, but usually St. Mary's played lacrosse year-round.

"Hey." Bain popped up out of nowhere—as usual—and sat beside Journey. He only hung around his recently discovered sister when she wasn't with Cade or the rest of the Rebels. There was a whole history there that would take years to uncover, so I busied myself with my phone again after Bain and Journey dove into a conversation.

Tobias: It would be weird if my dad was your dad too, Sloane. That would make us siblings, and...I've been inside you.

It took everything in me to not glare at him.

Me: Stop eavesdropping on my conversations. Aren't you supposed to be studying, or are you just sitting over there like a hermit to annoy me?

Tobias: I told you to ask me a question. I'm waiting.

I watched as his long fingers flipped through the note-cards over and over again as his phone rested on his lap. He only picked it up to text me and then went back to studying.

I sighed, leaning back like Journey as I watched the boys run down the field with their lacrosse sticks in hand.

Me: What are three recurring themes in Sylvia Plath's work?

I shot my attention over to him as he sat up and paused for a moment. Those ever-present jaw muscles tensed for a moment, and then he bent his head and moved his fingers effortlessly over his phone.

Tobias: Death, isolation, loneliness.

Tobias: Did you ask that on purpose? Do you think I'm lonely sitting over here?

I didn't have a chance to answer when another text came in. I ignored it for a moment, chatting with Gemma about college applications.

Tobias: What do you want to be when you grow up? What are you going to college for?

Me: Listening to our conversation again, I see. God forbid your sister starts talking about sex with Isaiah.

I laughed under my breath when Tobias' entire body shuddered.

Me: I want to be a veterinarian.

His head tilted, and it was obvious that I'd surprised him. That was something no one knew except Willow. My parents pretended like it was a far-fetched dream. They bought me a cat to "curb the desire" when I was six, and I almost brought him when I came to St. Mary's.

Tobias: Didn't I just hear you say that you were going for political science? Whatever the fuck that is.

He heard right, and my stomach clenched, causing a breath to leave my tightly wound chest.

Me: My parents don't approve of my career choices.

Tobias: And you're going to let them decide for you? Doesn't sound like you.

I was in the middle of typing, "You don't know me." When another incoming text came in.

Tobias: Let me guess. You're typing: "You don't know me." Which just proves that I do.

Feeling defeated, I put my phone into my coat pocket and looked over at him briefly to see him smirk. Sitting up quickly, I turned away and joined in the conversation, pretending like I didn't know deep down that he was right.

"OKAY, CLASS. DRUMROLL PLEASE!" Mr. Rake stood in front of his desk, like he did a few days after each test to announce the best grade, with his eyes set on me. Tobias shifted in his seat, and I swore I could feel his body heat from a mile away.

Not a single person did a drumroll, per usual, and when my name left Mr. Rake's mouth, no one was surprised.

"Come get your prize, love." My face scrunched. *Love?* That was a new one. I stood up, passing by Tobias who was holding the sides of his desk like he was going to snap it in half. *Did he not do well on the test?* I'd forgotten all about Mr. Rake and his little nickname that was borderline inappropriate and started to worry that the studying Tobias and I had been doing all week wasn't paying off.

It should have surprised me that I was more worried about him not passing than I was worried about him having that video of me moaning his name and giving it to his sister, but I wasn't. Tobias had officially taken up residence in my brain, and it was a bone-crushing feeling knowing that I was beginning to care about someone who claimed not to have a heart.

"Thank you, Mr. Rake," I said, reaching my hand into the bucket full of suckers, pulling out my favorite kind—cherry. It was like this every week, and I always chose cherry.

No one was paying attention as I walked back to my desk. They were either half-asleep or packing up their things, stuffing their tests into their folders and waiting for the bell to ring. I almost stopped in the aisle when I saw Tobias glaring at Mr. Rake from his desk. His knuckles were as white as the test paper on his desk as he continued to grip it.

"Did you get a bad grade?" I asked hesitantly. Worry gnawed at me as I unwrapped my sucker and popped it into my mouth.

"Can I break his neck?"

"What?" I asked, pulling the sucker out and leaning in closer to him. "Did you get that bad of a grade? There is no way."

Confusion replaced my worry, but when Tobias whipped his head to me, I saw the angry lines on his forehead and wanted to smooth them out in the worst way.

"Tobias, what's wrong?"

"I am certain he only calls you up there to stare at your ass."

My shoulders dropped. "Oh my God. Stop." The words squeezed out of my mouth with anger. "I thought you got a bad grade. Did you pass?"

"Who cares?" He stared at me in disbelief. "I'm seconds from breaking his neck, and you're worried about my grade?"

The bell rang, but Tobias made no move to get up from his seat. His head slowly craned to the left as he stared at Mr. Rake, who had settled behind his desk. Tobias' knuckles were still white, and the light blue in his eyes that I saw in the late evenings tucked away in his room were shadowed by a dark, angry, midnight color.

I stood up quickly and snatched his test, along with my stuff from my desk, and grabbed onto his forearm. His eyes dropped to my fingernails digging into his skin, and I pulled him up. "Follow me."

Surprisingly, Tobias allowed me to pull him through the class without any protests. Mr. Rake flicked his attention to us for a moment before busying himself again with more tests to grade, and I rounded the busy hallway, hoping to avoid too many lingering eyes. A few seconds later, I pushed him underneath the main stairwell until we were tucked in the back underneath them.

"Get a grip," I reprimanded him as he pushed back onto the wall and loosened his tie around his neck. A deep breath flew from his mouth, and he looked anywhere but at my face. His jaw clenched, and a part of me wanted to massage it with my fingers because that had to hurt eventually, right?

"Is it him?"

I blinked, wondering what he was talking about. His dark gaze flashed to mine, and I froze. Why did I suddenly feel like I was in trouble, and why did that bother me?

"Huh?" I clenched my toes and sucked on my sucker harder than before. *I am the one who needs to get a grip.* A few nights spent with him in his room studying and I was feeling things that I absolutely refused to admit.

"Did you two have a fling or something? Is he the one calling you thirty-plus times a day, after school hours? That makes sense. How could he call you during class hours?" He rolled his eyes and pushed off the wall, stomping back and forth as students stomped up and down the staircase above our heads. Small dust flakes flew from above and rained down on us like we were in the middle of a snowfall.

"They're all after school hours?" *Why didn't I realize that before?* "Wait. How do you know that?"

"Because I'm fucking observant."

On cue, my phone began vibrating in my bag, and his eyes flared. "See." The scar embedded in his eyebrow that I was certain people saw as an imperfection moved upward, and I swallowed the words lingering on my tongue. "Give it to me."

My hand fell over the pocket on the side of my backpack to silence the noise. "No."

His head fell, and his dark hair bounced for a moment before he reached out quickly and spun me as he pulled my backpack off my shoulders. His test flew to the floor beneath us but I made no move to grab it. "Stop it," I whisper-yelled. "It is not Mr. Rake."

"It's not?"

My phone was in his hand a second later, and he put it up to his ear. "Hello?"

Silence filled the tiny area as I stared at him with skepticism. The sternness in his features didn't let up, even when he pulled the phone from his ear and pushed it against my chest. A trapped breath left me, and his gaze dropped right down to my lips.

"They never say anything," I admitted, knowing very well he knew that I was getting calls and that they weren't from my parents. I rolled my eyes, snatching my phone from him and putting it back in my backpack that was now on the dusty floor. A cobweb hung in the corner with a spider resting on it, and I kind of wanted it to fall on Tobias' head. "And it isn't Mr. Rake! Why would you ever think that I would be with a teacher? Especially one that's old and gross?"

"Well, he wants to fuck you, and I don't like it."

My jaw dropped. "He does not! How would you even know that?"

His hand shot out quickly again, like a reflex that only someone as dark and dangerous as Tobias could have. He turned me around so I was the one pressed against the stone wall instead of him. Another bundle of dust and dirt rained down from the stampede of feet above us. "I know that because he looks at you the way I look at you when no one is watching."

My lips smashed together, and every warning that I'd

hastily thrown up the second I grabbed onto his arm disappeared altogether.

"Tobias," I warned, feeling the beating of my heart increase with him moving closer to me. A shiver rushed through me as his fingers splayed out against my back, and when he bent below me, I froze, peering down at his full head of hair. The memory of his mouth in between my legs came rushing back in, and I started to sweat before he slowly exhaled. His warm breath hit my bare thighs, ruffling the end of my skirt, as he stood with his test firmly in his grasp.

"Here." His voice was seductive at the very least and sinful at best. I scanned my gaze above our heads as I heard Gemma's laugh, knowing his sister was likely rounding the stairs in search of me. Isaiah was chuckling, and Shiner was talking about something that I couldn't focus on because I was dying by the hands of Tobias Richardson.

His palms left me, and he took a step back before reaching up and ripping the sucker out of my mouth that was resting inside my cheek. My hands crushed the paper he forced onto my chest before I gaped.

"Tobias!" A feeling that I hadn't felt since everything started with Willow over the last month surprised me. Our eyes met, and there was the *smallest* flicker of pride in there that I wanted to reach inside and touch. "You did it!"

He shrugged, pretending to be his hard, callous self.

I gaped in awe. "This is amazing!"

He smirked but tried to hide it. He looked away, and something propelled me to reach forward and grab onto my sucker that he was holding between his fingers. I took it, put it back in my mouth for a quick second, and then popped it into his.

"You deserve this. Not me."

A tiny smile played at my lips until the moment between us suddenly felt less playful and more serious. A wild hunger gnawed in the center of his pupils as he took the sucker from his mouth, slowly licking the end of the sticky red candy. His hand went to my lower back again as he pulled me onto his hard chest, and then he slowly pushed the sucker past my lips. A loud swallow hit my ears, and there was heat coming from between my legs that I could no longer ignore.

The cherry flavor was tinged with his taste, and I wanted him to kiss me. I didn't care if it was wrong. I wanted his mouth on mine, and I wanted to kiss him back.

"How do I taste?" he asked, bringing me even closer to him. Tobias was tall, so I hit him mid-chest, and that was when I realized his heart was racing as fast as mine. The nook we were in seemed to spin around us, and I had a hard time standing upright.

"Like I want more," I admitted quietly. I knew I shouldn't have said it, but it was there in the open, echoing around the small alcove.

Tobias' free hand moved in between us as he grabbed onto the end of the stick and pulled the sucker from my mouth. The sticky, cherry-flavored candy was a barrier holding us apart, and when Tobias' tongue darted out to lick it, I felt my stomach bottom out like I was on a thrill ride. My nipples hardened, and my blood ran hot.

Kiss me.

"Where is Sloane?" Journey's voice pelted through my foggy brain, and I choked on air. Tobias and I immediately stopped staring at each other's mouths, and our gazes collided. His hand left my back, and the air turned to ice. I stepped away, and mortification stunned me. *What am I doing?*

Shiner's voice was even louder than Journey's, and I slowly craned my head up to the smallest crack in the staircase, and the blood drained from my face. Shiner was looking right at me, and even though I couldn't see his mouth, I knew he was grinning. "Oh, who knows where she is, but we need to find her because she will be all about the senior movie night."

I quickly bent down and grabbed my backpack and draped it over my shoulders before walking past Tobias, who was standing with his test crumpled in his hand. He made no attempt to move or look me in the face.

My steps were quick as I basically ran away from him and rounded the stairwell to see everyone standing on the lower landing. Isaiah was leaning against the glossy wooden rail with Gemma's back pressed against his front. His arms were draped around her shoulders, and Cade and Journey were opposite of them. Shiner stood in the middle with his tie long gone and his uniform shirt halfway open in the front. Mercedes nibbled on her nail, and Brantley paid no attention to anything that Shiner was saying.

"Speak of the sexy little thang, there she is."

My cheeks burned, but it had nothing to do with Shiner and his greeting. It was because he knew very well that I was just underneath each and every one of my friends, skirting the lines with Gemma's off-limits brother that I had no business having feelings for.

Wait, is my heart invested now? The amount of pride that had filled me when he'd shown me his test had red flags popping up everywhere. I wasn't proud because *I* helped him get there... I was genuinely happy to see him happy and to watch him succeed.

"What's up?" My voice was shaky, and Gemma definitely noticed.

"Movie night in the quad. For the seniors." Shiner gave me a pointed look, and I knew he was throwing me a lifeline. Shiner was a good guy. He always was my favorite of the Rebels. I'd never tell him that, though. His head was already big enough.

"Ooh, when?" I asked playfully, shifting on my feet and

begging myself not to look down through the same crack that Shiner was looking down a moment ago.

"Tomorrow night. Be there or be a loser." Shiner bumped his shoulder into mine and whispered when no one was looking, "Incoming."

"Hu—"

Just then, my heart seized. Tobias jogged up the stairs with minimal effort. His cheeks were flushed, and his tie was even looser than moments ago. "Tobias, you're coming!"

"What?" he asked, keeping his attention away from me on purpose. I knew it was better that he didn't look at me, but I craved his blue eyes like I craved oxygen.

"Senior movie night," Gemma answered, backing Journey and her request. "You're definitely coming."

"It'll be outside. You can sit with the wolves if you want. I know you prefer them to us." Journey grinned, and Tobias rolled his eyes.

"You two are kind of annoying together."

"They absolutely are," Cade agreed. "They're two peas in a pod. It's scary."

"It's scary when they team up." Isaiah innocently threw his hands up after Gemma elbowed him.

"What else will you be doing?" Shiner prodded from beside me. "*Studyingggg?*"

"Sloane is coming, too. Right?" Gemma looked over at me, and I nodded with a big ol' fake smile on my face.

"Yeah!" Journey was totally on board with this idea, which surprised me. She knew what it was like to feel like an outsider and to have someone push you into doing something you didn't want to do. "Unless you are studying alone, what else will you be doing? Holing up in your room like a hermit?"

Tobias quickly flashed his gaze to me, and it was like a lightning strike came directly from his toes to mine.

He took his attention away, and I breathed out a held

breath, leaning into Shiner for moral support. "Naughty, naughty," he whispered, pretending to cough.

"Do not start," I hissed, watching as Tobias was dragged by his sister and Journey, who interlocked their arms in his.

"I have a headache," I announced to no one in particular. "I'm going back to my room."

"Want me to walk you?" Mercedes was concerned as she popped up in front of me. Her wild, curly hair blocked Tobias' easy strides down the stairs.

"Sure." I smiled, turning with her and leaving the rest of our group to follow after their girlfriends.

Mercedes was a good distraction as she droned on about how much she hated Shiner and his incessant girl addiction. We usually took turns talking shit, me with Tobias and her with Shiner, but this time, I let her distract me until we got to my room. I gave her a quick hug and thanked her for walking with me, and the second I was in my room, with the door shut and the lock secure, I slid down to my butt and put my head against my knees.

Several deep breaths later, and a good distance between me and Tobias, and I was already beginning to feel better, before my phone started to vibrate again. Anger came in like a tidal wave, and I ripped the zipper of my bag open and put the phone up to my ear.

"What do you want?!" I yelled, voice going hoarse by the last word of my sentence.

"Excuse me?" Shock rendered me speechless at the sound of my mom on the other end of the phone. *Could this day get any worse?* "Sloane Michele McCann!"

I knew it was serious when my mom used our *actual* last name instead of the one generated for me by one of their many "fixers". "I'm sorry, Mom. I didn't realize it was you calling."

There was a long beat of silence, and I wanted to back-track in the worst way.

"Who else would be calling you? Has someone been bothering you?"

"No!" My answer came too fast, and I banged my head off the back of my door in defeat. "Just some four-year colleges that I had applied to on a whim in case I didn't get into the top-tier ones. They keep calling me."

"Why wouldn't you get into the top tier?" Her voice was echoey, and I knew she had put me on speaker. My dad was probably listening now, too. There was the smallest part of me that missed my parents when I talked with them, but I knew better than to miss someone that no longer existed.

It was a traumatic feeling to see who your parents were when they were no longer obstructed by your immature, fairy-tale eyes. It was painful and lonely.

"That's what the guidance counselor told us to do." There was no longer a guidance counselor at St. Mary's, but my parents didn't need to know that.

I imagined my father nodding at my mother in agreement with my excuse, which was what caused her to say, "Oh, well... okay, then." A pause. "Are you sure no one has been calling you, Sloane? That was still a pretty aggressive way to answer the phone."

"Yeah, I'm sure. Who else would be calling me?" A wicked smile curved on my face. I bet they were regretting getting me this *fancy* untraceable phone that they couldn't hack into. Anything to protect our conversations and keep me from the outside world as much as possible.

Change my name.

My school.

My phone number.

All of it.

"Are you sure?" my father's voice, one made for politics,

boomed on the other end of the phone with his casual aggression.

I began to second-guess myself. What if it was them? What if they were behind it all, and they were testing me? I started to get sweaty, and my stomach suddenly had a million snakes inside of it, coiling and uncoiling every three seconds. "Yes, I'm sure. Why? Is something going on with Willow?"

"Sloane," my mother warned, like she did every time I brought up the one thing in our life that destroyed our family —their words, not mine. "You need to let it go. Every time I think you're over it, you bring her up again."

I need to let it go? I wondered how many other innocent people she and my father had had murdered to rise to the top of the political hierarchy. The thought made me sick.

"Are you sure nothing is going on?" My father's voice was distant, and I knew he was in his classy office, perched behind his mahogany desk with his hand on his expensive pen, refusing to look up from whatever he was reading.

"I'm sure. I gotta go. My roommate is due back any second now."

"You'll tell us if something is going on, right?"

No.

"Is there something *you* need to tell *me*?" My question wavered with worry, and I was beginning to think that they knew more than they were letting on. They checked in often and usually gave me a few quick reminders to study hard and all that parent bullshit that was required of them, but they typically steered clear of showing any type of worry. We had a system now, and they were veering from it.

"No." My mother's quick answer was sketchy. My heart slowly sank down to the pit of my belly when I looked over at my closet, remembering that there *was* something going on.

"Okay, well...I'm going to go study, then. Bye."

"We love you."

I shut my eyes after hanging up. Moisture crept out of the corners as my throat clogged with emotion. It was like this every time we got off the phone. Nine times out of ten, I didn't say the three little words back to them. Because how could you love someone you didn't even know?

CHAPTER TWENTY-SIX

TOBIAS

GEMMA AND JOURNEY thought they were fucking hilarious, and if I wasn't such a brooding, stereotypical teen with baggage so heavy it would weigh down the entire student body of St. Mary's, I would have laughed. I sat down beside the cardboard cutout of wolves sitting on the blanket they "reserved" for me and scoffed.

"You two think you are funny, don't you?" I asked, bending my knees and resting my arms over them. There was a bite in the air, and with the wind blowing, I could see why my sister was wearing her beanie with a blanket draped over her shoulders. Isaiah shook his head as she buried hers in his shoulder, hiding her laughter from me.

My lips curved—barely, but they did.

Shiner shrieked like a girl, and we all turned toward him. His apology was legitimate before he said, "I just didn't know he could smile."

Everyone laughed, including Sloane, who I was well aware of from the moment she sat down beside Journey and

Mercedes. We didn't study last night. I hoped she would tap on my door at seven, like usual, but I wasn't surprised when she didn't.

My father appeared at the front of the lawn with a giant white projector behind him. It was hard to see him because of the time of night, but his presence was one that I could sense anywhere because a restlessness usually followed.

"Thank you all for coming tonight," he started, voice echoing around us. I looked away, feeling the pressure like I did every time he spoke. I didn't want to hate him, but my chest grew heavy, and anger brimmed the surface each and every time I looked at him. "The SMC and I decided to reward you for all your hard work. We have had so many of you reach your academic goals while attending St. Mary's, even while jumping over personal hurdles. College acceptance letters are coming in left and right, and I am so proud of you. Nash Miller—er, Shiner has decided to pick out the movie for tonight, so I hope you all enjoy it, and please do not tell your parents that I'm allowing you to watch something that is not technically appropriate in a school setting."

The senior class all yelled and whooped, and Shiner stood up and bowed like the class clown that he was. I trailed my father as he hurried off to the side and headed straight for me. *Fuck.*

The beginning sounds of the movie started up ahead, and everyone was glowing with the bluish light from the projector as they settled onto their blankets on the grass with their popcorn and sodas from the cafeteria. Gemma threw a piece of popcorn into Shiner's mouth, and her laugh numbed the rising anxiety of my father coming to stand beside me. She peeked back and shot him a warm smile. *How? How can she just be okay?*

I knew it wasn't his fault that he wasn't there for us as children. He didn't know we existed, but I still held a relentless grudge against him. It wasn't fair to him, but the nagging feeling was out of reach and out of my control.

"Can we talk?" he asked, bending down beside me. I knew he was staring at my face, and my gaze moved over to Sloane. She peered back, and just one simple warm glance from her calmed me enough to give him a subtle nod. I stood up with ease and placed my hands in my front pockets after flipping my hood on top of my head. I followed him toward the back of the forest, away from any prying ears.

"How is studying going?" My father was looking at the ground, and I cursed under my breath when I realized we were both taking our right foot and digging the toe of our shoe into the dirt at the exact same time.

I gritted my teeth and peered at the starry sky. "It's fine."

"Mr. Rake came to my office yesterday evening." I paused before staring at him in the face. Mr. Rake's name surely got my attention. My father's brows dipped for a split second. "He said your grades are improving drastically. Like something has clicked."

What clicked was Sloane, but I kept that to myself.

"Not what you expected me to say?" he asked, eyeing me with skepticism.

I shrugged. "I thought he might tell you that I mentioned breaking his neck."

Surprisingly, he didn't look fazed in the slightest with what had just come out of my mouth. "What did he do?"

I chuckled. "What makes you think he did something to make me want to break his neck?"

His sigh was loud as it mingled with the breeze in the air. "Just intuition. We *are* related, you know."

"He wants to fuck every girl with a tight ass. He stares at them. It annoys me."

"Every girl? Or one in particular?"

I felt the anger flare, and I didn't enjoy the way he was

pretending to know me. Silence stretched between us, and if someone were to walk in between us, they'd bounce right back from the tightness in the air.

"I just wanted to tell you I was proud of you and to keep up the good work. We're gonna get you that diploma and continue to work on...things."

The thick cement wall that I had built around my feelings cracked before I quickly patched it back up and said, "Is that all you needed?"

His chuckle was coarse as he dropped his head in defeat. "Yeah, go back to the movie. Glad to see your sister talked you into going. You deserve to be content and to have some fun."

My chest was tight when I turned around and stalked back up to the movie playing. The dirt and dead grass from past winter days crunched beneath my feet, and I swore the earth shifted below me when I realized that Sloane wasn't in her normal spot beside Shiner.

Everyone was quiet as the movie played. I saw a few students secretly passing around a flask in their social circle. I scanned the crowd, looking directly for the two fucks that had Sloane in the back room at the last party. I recognized one of them by the splint on his finger, and I didn't feel bad about breaking his finger at all.

Shiner leaned back in a stretch, and when he met my eye, he casually tilted his head to the right and did a little flip of his chin. I looked over to the darkened end of the forest, and he nodded before sitting forward again in between Mercedes and Brantley, who was buried in his phone.

Solid. If I chose to be friends with any of the Rebels, I'd be friends with Shiner. Maybe in another life, when I wasn't a walking grenade. But not this life.

My steps were quiet and stealthy as I walked down the path near the side of St. Mary's. Some of the windows were glowing faintly from the underclassman being in their rooms for the rest of the night. My ears were on high alert as I listened for footsteps or any indication that Sloane was sitting out here by herself. *Why would she go by herself?* I wanted to reprimand her and remind her that she had been drugged not too long ago and seemed to have a little stalker problem. *Is she crazy?*

I stopped in my tracks as the wind blew her perfume in my direction. I inhaled and turned toward the scent of pine and warm honey and spotted her right away. My breath moved right along with the breeze, and there was a pain deep inside my lungs as I stared at her delicate profile, hardly visible through the night. She was on her knees, with her hands placed on them as she looked into the forest with full intent on something. She was beautiful. Something as pretty as her shouldn't be alone in the forest like this. Nightmares lurked in the dark. Didn't she know that?

"Do I need to remind you that you have a stalker problem?" I asked, moving closer to the delectable scent of her shampoo. I stood above her, looking out into the wooded area in the same direction she was.

A fearful gasp rushed out of her before she realized it was me. Then, she turned away and shushed me before whispering, "I'm well aware. I have a weapon."

"A weapon?" I whispered back, not sure why we were whispering in the first place. I looked around, wondering if anything was off around us, but not a single thing was moving except the bare limbs of the trees.

Just then, Sloane hit my shin with a large branch, and I pulled back quickly. Surprise flickered down my body to the spot she had hit, and this time, I couldn't help but smile. "Really?" I asked, pretending to be unfazed. "A stick?"

"Shut up and sit down."

If I were a fish, I'd be hooked on that bait. Curiosity gave me no choice but to bend down beside her. Our arms touched, and even through the thickness of my hoodie, I felt the buzz. "What are we doing?" I asked, whispering close to her ear.

She looked at me out of her peripheral vision, and I wondered if the blush on her cheeks was from me or from the cool air. "*We?*" She scoffed quietly. "*I* am watching a bunny."

"We're sitting here because of a bunny?" I feigned annoyance, but I liked being this close to her. It was self-indulgence, but I didn't even attempt to stop myself.

"No one asked you to follow me out here."

My lips ached to turn upward again, which was what I found myself doing every single time we were alone together. I turned my head to the side but paused, lips falling back to their normal position. I suddenly clicked back into the person I was pretending I wasn't when I was with her. "Sloane." My voice was lethal, and she noticed it when she turned toward me. The playfulness we were just experiencing was gone. "Did someone tell you to meet them out here?"

"No..." She turned away from me. "I actually wanted to be alone. So, you can leave now."

I sighed with irritation and grabbed onto her hand, pulling her to her feet. The small animal up ahead paused and stared at us and then moved its head in the direction that I was looking a moment ago. "Go back."

"What? Why?"

"Someone is out here."

Sloane's phone started to vibrate in her pocket. She hesitantly pulled it from her jeans, and when the screen illuminated her face, her resolve wavered. The word *Unknown* flashed on it, and I suddenly felt like a predator.

"You have a stalker, Sloane. You shouldn't be out here alone. Why aren't you more afraid?" Every word that left my mouth was followed by anger.

"There's no way the person who is calling me over and over again is out here in the forest right now. That's just not possi—"

"Go back right now."

Her eyes were glossy, and her mouth opened before her phone started to vibrate again. She wasn't far from the rest of the students, so I was seconds from pushing her in that direction so I could go the opposite way when her shaking hand grabbed onto mine. "I am afraid," she admitted.

"The truth. For once." Our fingers intertwined, and hers were freezing. I brought our clasped hands up to my mouth and blew my warm breath on them, and the sweet gesture surprised me. "Give me your phone. I'm going to text Shiner and tell him to come get you."

Her fingers clenched over mine. "No."

"Yes."

Her phone started to vibrate again, and she dropped it to the ground. I wanted to take my shoe and stomp on the device, but instead, I swooped down, tucked it inside my pocket and rushed us both to the only place in plain sight.

"*Fine.*" I opened the creaking door of the toolshed and pushed her inside the dark room that held the stench of mildew and dirt. The windows were so filthy you could hardly see the glow of stars. "Then stay here."

My hand left hers as I gripped her lightly around her hips, pushing her toward the way back. Panic flew from her fingers as she wrapped them around my wrists. "Where are you going?"

"To end this. Someone is fucking with you and obviously watching you. It's juvenile shit, and it needs to end."

"Don't go out there, Tobias."

My head ticked to the side. "If you're worried about me, I can assure you that I am the very last person you need to be worried about." *Doesn't she know what I was?*

"I..." Her head dropped, but her hands stayed on my wrists, burning the skin underneath hers. "Please don't leave me alone here."

Her breathing began to pick up speed as I whipped my wrists from her tight grip. My hands flew to her cold cheeks, my fingers diving into her silky strands of hair. "Calm down."

"I'm calm. I just don't want to be alone." Her foot stomped, and she bit out her next response. "That's not true. I just don't want you to go out there."

"Why?" I prodded.

"Because...there *is* someone messing with me, and–and I don't know what they're capable of."

I laughed. "Sweetheart, you don't know what *I'm* capable of."

"Yes, I do. Which is another reason I don't want you to go out there."

I was instantly agitated with her worry. "Stop worrying about me. I don't like it. It's nothing I haven't done before. I was literally trained for this type of shit. Stay in here so I don't have to worry about you getting yourself into something that I need to save you from...*again.*"

I took a step away from her, and she sighed loudly. "So, you can worry about me, but I can't worry about you?"

"Catch," I said, throwing my sheathed knife at her. She caught it quickly, surprise flickering across her features. "I'll be back. Scream if you need me." I winked and turned around, knowing she wouldn't have to scream because if there was someone out there, they'd be the one screaming. It had nothing to do with the fact that I was used to being a hunter, either. This was purely because I didn't like that someone was hunting what was mine. I was the predator here, not them.

CHAPTER TWENTY-SEVEN

SLOANE

I PULLED the knife out of the leather sheath and ran my
finger over the sharp edge as my heart beat in triple speed.
Tobias took my phone with him, so even if someone did
come after me, I would have no choice but to stab them.
Could I stab someone? What would it be like? I've stabbed a
piece of food before... Did that count as practice? I rested
my back against a bumpy wall that I was pretty sure had mold
covering it. My eyes had adjusted to the little building he'd
pushed me in, and I realized it was the St. Mary's toolshed.

It wasn't the worst place to be if someone came to attack
me. Any tool could be a weapon—even words, if I was being
honest.

Chills still covered every inch of my body as I pushed off
the moldy wall, waiting for Tobias to come back. I went over
the texts, the phone calls, the closet incident, and then the
drugging, and nothing was making sense. No one at St.
Mary's knew who I was. There was no way anyone could have
found out—not with the measures my parents had taken to

shield me. I wondered if Willow had somehow found out the truth, but if she knew the truth, my parents would have taken care of her, too. Right? And would she really torment me like this? The Willow I knew would never do such a thing, but then again, I didn't know my old best friend anymore.

I shut my eyes, blocking out the confusion. The conversation with my parents last night burned a hole in my guilty conscience, and I briefly considered calling them this morning to tell them that someone had been pranking me and that there were texts from an unknown number that were an exact replica of texts between Willow and me on the night her parents died. But what would that mean for Willow? What would that mean for me?

"Dammit." A sob tried to race up my throat from my chest, but I gripped the knife in my hand, letting the burn of the cut distract me. The knife clamored to the ground with a loud clatter as I clutched my injured hand to my stomach, making a fist to keep the bleeding to a minimum. My head whipped to the left as I heard something swipe at the tool-shed, and a shrill was locked behind my lips. I quickly bent down and grabbed onto the knife that Tobias threw to me, and I held it out with my wounded hand, rethinking the fact that I had just cut the hand that I needed to use to stab someone.

Stupid.

A breath whooshed out of my mouth as I braced myself for a battle I wanted nothing to do with. I wanted nothing to do with anything regarding that night with Willow's parents. If she knew the truth, what would she say? Would she hate me just as much as I hated them, or would she understand that I had to disappear from her life for them to spare her?

The door swung open, and I jutted the knife forward, shutting my eyes and shrieking. My entire body flew forward, and the person I was aiming for was now behind me with their arm wrapped tightly around my waist. Their other hand gripped onto my wrist, and the knife fell to the floor with another loud clatter.

"You suck at protecting yourself," Tobias grunted, pulling me further into his chest. "Wait..." I was suddenly whipped around, and the room spun around me like I was on a roller-coaster. My back hit something hard. A table maybe? A work-bench? Tobias' chilled fingers pulled mine open, and the hard lines around his eyes softened. "Sloane, what the hell? I left you alone for a minute, and you end up bleeding?" He turned his head and looked at every corner of the room, as if he could see anything in the dark.

I took a breath, trying to say something snarky to him out of defense, but nothing came out. My throat closed like I was having an anaphylactic reaction to something in the air. *Again, probably him.*

"Take a breath, Sloane. You're fine."

I tried, and little glowing dots formed in my vision. My head shook, and Tobias cursed. He gripped me tightly around my waist and sat me on top of whatever I was resting on so we were face to face. The glow of his eyes bounced all over my face. What he did next surprised me so much I forgot I couldn't breathe.

He buried my face in his broad shoulder and placed my arms around his neck. His went around my body, and he crushed me in a hug. His warm body heat enveloped me like a cozy blanket, and everything else seemed to fade away—even the burning of my hand.

"I hate animals."

I stiffened with my nose rubbing against the cotton of his hoodie. I sniffed, realizing that tears had fallen from my eyes at some point. "You what?" I croaked, refusing to look him in the eye.

"I hate animals. Isn't it funny that you love them and I hate them? We couldn't be more opposite if we tried."

Tobias' hands went around my cheeks, and he pulled my face from his shoulder, all while taking his thumbs and wiping my wet cheeks. "It makes me uncomfortable when you cry. I don't like it."

A choked laugh left me with too much emotion. "A month ago, you would have loved it."

His lips twitched as he wiped my cheeks again. "Is that why you want to be a veterinarian? Because you love animals?"

I nodded, staying silent. The wind howled outside the shed, and I jerked when I heard the swiping noise again. Tobias brought my gaze back to his, making me focus on his face. He appeared more relaxed than usual. Maybe it was because we were in the dark, tucked away from everyone. Our barriers still felt wobbly, though, and things were definitely unsettled between us.

"How can you hate animals?" I wanted to roll my eyes at the timidness in my voice. Fear was there, but with Tobias distracting me, it was slowly dissolving.

Tobias' rough swallow was the one sound that cut through the choppy breeze outside, and when he took a step away from me, I suddenly felt jittery and cold. His tall, shadowed body was shielded away as he began to talk. "Richard," he answered. "He had a way of making me hate a lot of things."

I'd said it before, and I'd say it again: Richard Stallard was the worst kind of human being, and he deserved the prison cell that he was forced into after Gemma was taken months ago.

"He's the epitome of evil," I whispered, crossing my arms over my chest as a chill racked my body. Tobias stalked over to me and pulled his hoodie off, showing off his defined stomach when his black tee moved upward with it.

"Here." He held out the bundle of cotton, and my chest melted with something unfamiliar.

I took it hesitantly with my hurt hand and pulled it over my head with my legs swinging down below. The panic I was drowning in moments ago was gone, and it seemed the center of my attention had switched to the boy I promised myself I wouldn't be alone with again, especially not in a dark room, hidden away from the rest of the school. Everything was muted when he reached out and pulled my hand toward him, bringing it up to his face. The gentle swipe of his finger near the small cut made me wiggle, and when he noticed, he slowly put it back in my lap and took a step away.

"He used to make us practice on the animals."

Wait. "Practice...what?"

I could see the whites of his eyes as he moved his attention to me. "Killing."

A rushed breath left me as my mouth gaped. *What?*

His back was to me again, and the blood drained from my face. My heart skipped a beat, and there was an ache nestled deep inside my chest that resembled a swift punch. "I don't know what it was about killing an animal in the way that he made me do it, but it sent me over the edge." His hands went into his pockets, and my lip trembled at the sudden change in the small toolshed. There was a bone-chilling sadness to him, and it bothered me more than it should have.

"What did he make you do?" I proceeded with hesitancy, wondering if I was taking it too far. Tobias was hard to read. He was a bomb, and you never knew when it was going to explode.

My ears strained to hear his next words. They were low, but instead of them being grumbly and coarse, they were soft and resolute. "The first one, he made me choke with my bare hands." A sarcastic huff left him, and I found myself sliding off the workbench he had placed me on. My feet hit the floor at the same time my heart did. "And that was after I'd refused and had been punished."

I knew that he had been through a lot. But saying that was an understatement.

"Then, he let me use a knife." His hand came up to his mouth, and I watched as he chewed on the end of his thumb. *Is he nervous?* His head turned more toward me as I crept over to him. "But at least it was fast, you know? I preferred that over choking."

I moved another few steps toward him, and he stood like a statue, unmoving, as he stared at me. "What are you doing?"

My arms went around his tense torso, and his muscles rippled with tension. I pulled him in close and placed my head over his chest, wincing at the pummeling beat of his heart. "I'm sorry he made you do that," I whispered. "I'm sorry he made you do more, because I know that's not even the tip of the iceberg."

Tobias remained unmoving under my hug, but he didn't fool me. His heart slowed, and his lungs deflated as he breathed in and out of his nose.

"I've met him. Did you know that?"

Just like that, his heart was jumping with speed again. "No. When?"

I nodded against his chest, still trapping him under my arms. "When he came to get Gemma. I walked into our room, and he was there, hurting her." I shut my eyes, remembering how fearful I was at that moment. After things were okay and Gemma was safe, I kept revisiting that moment and wondering if Willow's parents had felt that same fear I did when Richard dangled my life in front of my face. "He pointed a gun at me."

"I wish I could kill him over and over again."

I nodded, understanding. Only a sick man like Richard could do all that he had done, and it made me want to double over, knowing that Tobias had suffered at his hand for so long. It was a miracle that he had turned out the way that he had.

Sure, he had anger, and he pushed everyone away most of the time, but I saw the softer parts of him. The ones that were hidden beneath cold stares and rapid insults. The flare of protection he had inside that burned bright when provoked. He wasn't all bad. Did he know that? Had anyone told him that?

Pulling back slightly, Tobias stared into my eyes, and even through the bleak darkness, there were silent words spoken. There was a thick wall that separated us. It was full of uncertainties, guilt, insecurities. And together, we were both vulnerable. When I was alone with Tobias, I felt seen. I didn't usually wear my emotions on my sleeve, but when I was with him, it was like they were stitched in bright-red thread.

"I want you to kiss me," I whispered, taking his hands and moving them to my hips. My wounded palm was burning, and he must have noticed the sticky feeling against his skin because he took it and looked at it immediately.

He didn't take his attention off the cut when he said, "I know you do." Then, he sighed, looking to the dark ceiling, and cursed under his breath. His thick neck bobbed with a swallow, and I realized that I wanted him to do much more than kiss me. I wanted him to take me in his hands and silence my worries, because Tobias had a way of making my world revolve around him. That was the only explanation. Because why else would I continue to crave his attention when I knew I shouldn't?

"No one has ever come as close to me as you have." I was handing Tobias all the ammunition it took to destroy me altogether. I wasn't only referring to my friendship with Gemma, because he could easily end it in a heartbeat, depending on what he told her, but my heart, too. I was invested in Tobias, and I didn't realize how much until this moment with him, opening up to me and me silently bleeding from the hurt that he rendered. I wanted to fix him. I wanted to be the one to help him heal.

"Why do you think I try to keep my distance from you?" There was a pinch against my skin as Tobias picked me up by my butt and forcefully put me on the workbench again. He nestled himself in between my legs and placed his hands beside them, caging me so I wasn't able to move. "Why do you think I try to push you away and lash out?" My head moved back, and my hair cascaded down my back as his lips touched my neck. *I want him to kiss me so bad I am ready to beg.* "Why do you think I won't kiss you, Sloane? Do you think it's because I don't want to?"

"Yes." I assumed it was because I didn't mean to him what he secretly meant to me. There were so many parts of Tobias that I didn't know. He buried things so deeply I wasn't sure he'd ever be able to dig them up, but the vulnerable girl inside of me, the one who wanted to save everyone because she was trying to rid herself of the guilt, begged to be let inside. I used to think I had this burning desire to help Tobias because of Gemma, and maybe it started out like that, but that wasn't the reason anymore.

My palms were sweaty. My heart reached for him as it beat with anticipation. The butterflies in my stomach were heavy and dragged their wings around with fear but still tried to find him in the midst of heavy emotions.

His thumb gently brushed my bottom lip. "I've never craved someone's attention as much as I crave yours." There was defeat in his tone mixed with melancholy, and it pierced my skin. "I've never wanted to kiss someone before until I looked at your lips." His steady fingers moved to my jeans, and he slowly moved the zipper down. "I'm not worthy of you, Sloane. That's why I won't kiss you. That's why it frustrates me that I keep finding myself in this position where I can't keep my hands off you. I *will* ruin you. It's what I do."

"Then, ruin me," I whispered, lifting up and letting him take my jeans from my legs. He wiggled the denim over my hips, and a relieved breath cascaded from his lips when I grabbed onto his hand and pushed it between my legs.

"Sloane. Fuck. Why can't I resist you?"

He was a poison. The type of poison that you didn't care if you died from it because it tasted so good to begin with.

"I ask myself the same." My heart climbed to the very top of the cliff I was dangling over when he spread my legs and traced his finger up the inside of my thigh. He crowded my space and gripped the back of my head and forced me to look at him.

"Why do I want to know everything about you?" He somehow moved in even closer to me, and I swore he was sucking my breath from my lungs and into his own. "Why do I like watching you smile when I text you a stupid question?" His finger stopped right outside the brim of my panties, and I gripped onto his shoulders and silently begged him to break for me like I was breaking for him. "Why do I want to kill whoever is calling you? It makes me jealous that they get to hear your voice on the other end of the phone thirty times a day."

In between puffs of air, I forced my next words out. "I hardly ever answer the phone when they call."

Tobias' free hand, the one that was woven in between the strands of my hair, cupped the side of my cheek, and his finger brushed over my cheek bone. "I'm going to answer the phone from here on out." I wiggled as he slowly swiped over my wet panties before he moved them aside and pushed his finger inside. A hiss left his mouth before he said, "You make me wish I wasn't me." His admittance was as if he took the knife and sliced a piece of my heart away. The sorrow that lingered within his honesty was truly sad. I bled for him because I knew, even if it was a fraction of what he carried, how it felt to hold trauma inside.

My head dove onto his shoulder as he continued touching me and breathing just as fast as I was. "I can't even look at you without wanting to tell you my deepest, darkest secrets. Why is that? Why do I want to believe the truth in your eyes when you look at me like you do?"

"How do I look at you?" I asked, pushing my hips to meet him. A whimper left me, and I was thankful that it blended in with the wind howling outside this little toolshed.

"Like you think there is still some good left in me."

I stopped moving my hips. He had me in a tight grip, and his finger stilled inside me. I felt my body react, wanting more, but I refused because this moment between us felt like the heaviest one yet. "There is," I whispered, placing my hand over his chest. "And I want to be the one to find it."

His teeth gritted, and I watched as his vulnerabilities turned to stone. "There isn't," he bit back, flicking his thumb over my sensitive clit and making me throw my head back. His hand was a quick barrier between the window and my skull, and my hips thrust on their own.

"If I had any decency left, I wouldn't be locked away in this fucking toolshed, touching something as delicate as you."

"I am not delicate." I bit down on my lip as he pushed another finger inside, all while rubbing my clit over and over again. *It feels so good.* "I can list all the times you have shown decency, and even though those moments are few and far between, together they're huge."

"Come for me."

"Don't change the subject by bossing me around." I grabbed onto his wrist and tried to pause his hand moving in and out of me. "Admit it, Tobias," I said between tight teeth, trying not to focus on the messy parts of my body and brain that were trying to sync up to follow his command. If there was one thing I knew for certain about Tobias, it was that his gruff, mysteriously sexy voice could actually make you come on command.

"No," he whispered, jolting his eyes to my lips for a moment. "I don't know what decency you're referring to, but it is nonexistent. Look at what I'm doing to you," he rushed, tipping my head and making me look at his finger moving in and out of me. It was hot and forbidden, and it sent me over the edge with his dirty words. "Look at me making you come all around my finger even though we both know I don't deserve it. Because this is as much for me as it is for you."

I flew over the edge, crushing my lips together so I didn't yell his name and alert everyone who was watching the movie in the quad. *My God.*

My body was still riding the high when he stepped away. I was cold a second later when he handed me my jeans without sparing me a single glance. His back was to me, and I hastily took off his hoodie after I pushed the button of my jeans back into its rightful hole. "You make me lose control, Sloane." He snatched his hoodie out of my grasp, and I jumped with his eyes on me. "It makes me crazy. *You* drive me crazy."

Just then, there was a twig breaking in the quiet night. The trees were unmoving when we both peered out the cloudy window, and reality swooped in and turned our moment to mush. My phone vibrated, and Tobias didn't even blink when he pulled it out of his pocket and silenced it.

"Let's go," he intoned, annoyed with something. Me? The situation? My...stalker? Is that what I had? A stalker?

A chill hit my skin, and it had nothing to do with the fact that I'd given Tobias back his hoodie. My mind was pulled in a million different directions as we walked side by side to the back doors of St. Mary's, in the opposite direction of the movie. I was pretty sure it was almost over. Time had a way of flying when I was with Tobias.

My phone vibrated again when we made it to the girls' hallway. The entire floor was quiet. All the seniors were in the quad, enjoying their night of bliss with innocence and without concern. Not that some of my friends—like Gemma and Journey—didn't deserve it. They did.

But now it was my turn to sink in a pit of secrets and worry. Now it was my turn to round every bend in the hallway with unease and skepticism.

"Hello?" Tobias' voice echoed throughout the empty hall as we stood in front of my door with my small phone up to his ear. His jaw moved back and forth with anger as I peered up at him with my heart in my throat. The scar in his eyebrow moved down as his brows crinkled, and I froze, wondering if it was my parents that had called. *God, I hoped not.*

He shut the screen off, and a second later, he handed it back to me, taking his long fingers and opening mine before closing them around the device. "Don't answer when they call again."

Silence was my response, and I suddenly wanted to go back to the toolshed, when he was opening up to me, even if it was just a sliver. Defeat sucked up all the progress we'd made when I opened my door and stepped inside my room. I immediately glanced at Gemma's bed and knew, deep down to the very darkest parts of my heart, that Tobias was right.

He was no good for me.

I put my back to him even though it made my bones ache to see the regret on his face that he pretended wasn't there. I stared at my shoes and sighed when I heard my door shut, and the cool air from my room hit my flushed face, and I wanted to throw my phone across the room when it vibrated again.

"Are you fucking kidding me?"

I glared at the screen, and my fingers shook with anger. When I glanced away, ready to throw my phone onto my bed, I froze in my spot. A scream tore out of my chest like I was in a slasher movie, and my entire body turned to ice. *Oh my God. Oh my God. Oh my God.*

My eyes clenched shut immediately, but I still saw it. Blood stained my pillow like it had fallen in a puddle of it. Dark-red pools of the metallic scent made me double over as my scream echoed throughout the room. I flew back onto my door as my eyes bounced to every corner of my room, expecting to see a man standing there in a dark hoodie with the same gun pointed at me that had been pointed at Willow's parents.

I flew forward as my door swung open, and if it had been Gemma, I would've shoved her out until I could clean the mess. Except, instead of two almond-shaped eyes full of life, it was two blue eyes full of concern. Tobias' thick lashes hooded the midnight color, and he stalked in my room like he was ready to tear something apart. His hands immediately grasped onto my forearms, and he swung me around, putting his body in front of mine.

Everything was happening so fast, and I couldn't breathe.

"My bed," I croaked, staying completely still against his back.

His head snapped to the right, and he jerked as he saw what was on my bed.

"The smell." I gasped, covering my mouth. It wasn't just that the smell had sent a distinctively chilling scent into the room. It was the fact that I'd smelled this before, and the memories were flying at me. Tobias turned around, putting his back to the dead rabbit on my pillow, and gripped my cheeks, making me look at him instead of the blood. "It smells like that night." I was frantic. My shaking hands grabbed onto his arms, and my vision grew dark.

"What night?" he questioned. His fingers against my cheek spread out wide as he kept me in place, not allowing me to look over his shoulder.

"They were in a pool of blood, Tobias!" I yelled, trying to force the words back down to where I'd had them trapped, but the smell was egging me on, and every few seconds, my eyes would scan past Tobias', and I'd see drips of blood on my pretty, furry rug. "There was so much," I whispered, feeling my legs shake beneath me. My eyes closed, but I saw them. I felt the pain of losing my parents, seeing them in a different light that was warped and disgruntled, like a car that had been wrapped around a tree on a rainy night.

"Sloane, you're not making sense. Look at me."

I pressed against something hard, and I opened my eyes again, darting past Tobias' face and seeing the red all over the floor and my blankets. "I watched them die." My chest ached as the emotions came spilling out, as if Tobias was plucking them out one by one. "And then I had to lie about it. They threatened me. They threatened her if I told anyone." I knew my words were fast and jumbled, but I couldn't stop them. "I haven't told anyone!"

"That's it." The words were final as they left his mouth. His hands around my face tightened, and when I felt his mouth on mine, I was *back*.

CHAPTER TWENTY-EIGHT

TOBIAS

KISSING her was like seeing the sun for the first time. I was surrounded by darkness, but her lips against mine were as if I'd found the light. I latched onto it, and I swore it lit a path right down to the very bottom of my soul. Our tongues tangled together, and the kiss was long, deep, and intimate. Something vibrated in my chest, and a noise came from my throat as I took her hands and pinned them up above her head, banging her small wrists against the wood.

The taste of her could bring me back from the dead. The feel of her soft lips would keep me up at night for the rest of my life. The burning desire that swam in my veins drove away every bad thought and intention I had ever had, and the only thing left waiting for me was her.

I pulled away at the last second, and we both gasped for air, racing to the top of the water to make sure we were still alive. Our eyes crashed, and I knew, in that moment, I would never be the same.

"Go," I rushed out, opening the door and pushing her into

the hallway. Her door slammed behind me, and she jumped, gripping onto my hand a second later. My phone was already pressed to my ear before we made it to the end of the hallway, and I was thankful I'd snagged Shiner's number after Sloane was drugged.

"Hello?"

"I need you to go to Sloane and Gemma's room and clean it before my sister makes her way up there."

There was a ruffling on the other end, and I pushed Sloane inside my room, where she stayed by my side with my hand in hers. I glanced at her lips and almost forgot where I was and what was happening around me.

"Why? If I have to clean up your jizz or something, I will kill you in your sleep." There was a hint of cynicism in his voice, and I would bet my left nut that he was smiling coyly.

"Sloane has a stalker. They left her a gift on her pillow."

Her hand jerked in mine, and I felt the anger spark in my blood. I was willing to let it go for a while longer, but I was done with this shit. This was taking it too fucking far. What if that had been her on that pillow instead of the fucking rabbit? What if my sister had walked in the room when this person was in there, delivering that?

"A stalker? For fuck's sake. Why is it always something?" Shiner mumbled the last words through the phone, and I hung up after reminding him to keep it quiet for now and to make sure that Gemma stayed with Isaiah.

I pulled my hand from Sloane's a moment later and took a step away, knowing I didn't trust myself to touch her. My arms crossed, and I could see the blood pumping up my veins when I said, "What the fuck was that?"

Her bottom lip popped out from behind her white teeth, and I shifted on my feet, feeling slightly unhinged after kissing her. *Fuck. This changed everything.* I still wasn't worthy of her, but now my heart wouldn't stop beating like it was more than just a simple muscle keeping me alive.

"A dead rabbit on my bed," she answered solemnly, looking down at her feet like she was in trouble. Her dark hair was shiny and silky, and I wanted to run my fingers through it.

I snapped my head to the side, watching the trees sway through the window. "No, I meant you freaking out. What were you going on about?"

Her eyes widened. I could see them grow big, even though she wasn't looking directly at me. I bet if I were to run my finger over her spine, it would be ramrod straight, too. It was hard to know what she was thinking, but her body language was tense and defensive—two things I'd learned were a sure tell to a lie.

"Don't do it," I warned, locking onto her sharp gaze as she whipped those hazel eyes back to me. "The hiding shit stops right here. Right now. Who is stalking you?"

Her head shook, and the gloss that glazed over her eyes was a hand around my throat. "I really don't know."

Anger won out as I stormed over to her and gripped her chin. I gave her silent props in my head that she didn't take a single step away. "Start from the beginning, or I swear to God, I will give my sister that video of you begging me to make you come." *Fuck.* I hated that I was pulling that card, but it needed to be said.

"Blackmail, seriously? Again?"

"I play dirty, even with you." My finger brushed her bottom lip, the one that she had been biting into. It was hot and plump, and I continued to stare at her mouth when she gave in and started to tell me everything.

"My parents aren't in the military," she started, staying completely unmoving in front of me with my finger tracing the curve of her lips. *I can't believe I kissed her.* Sloane had me breaking every single one of my rules. Sloane had me pretending to be someone I wasn't. "My father is in politics. My parents sent me here so I wouldn't ruin their campaign." A sarcastic little noise left her mouth. "More like their lives."

"Go on," I coaxed, moving in a little closer to her and peering down at the empty space between us. Her pretty eyes were full of so much verity that it stunned me for words.

"I know a secret. A *big* one. I told them I was going to tell everyone, so they..." She took a big gulp full of air as I waited with bated breath. "They threatened me and sent me here to make sure I couldn't go back on my promise."

"What secret? And what did they threaten you with?" The choices were endless when it came to my wicked mind. I was putting puzzle pieces together—the snippets of words from earlier as she freaked out, the fact that her phone was a burner, and how she didn't exist in the database that Tony searched daily.

Her quiet swallow silenced my thoughts, and my breathing ceased altogether when a single teardrop escaped from her eye and fell over my finger. It cascaded down her cheek, and I almost choked. "They killed my best friend's parents."

My surprise lasted a split second before I asked, "In front of you?"

She blinked, and another tear fell from her eye, and it alarmed me that I felt a rip inside my chest. *Why does that hurt so much?* "No. Well..." She looked away for a second. "They didn't know I was there. I saw it through the balcony window. It wasn't just my best friend's parents. They were their friends. They were political partners."

"People have a way of having no remorse when it gets them what they want. Trust me." I thought of Richard and everyone that he killed or had ordered me to kill. Even the dirty men he "lended" me to all seemed so *normal*. Just a normal, reads-the-newspaper-with-his-morning-breakfast guy ordering a kill on someone. It was like natural selection to them.

"I told my parents I was going to tell my best friend what they had done." Another tear fell, but I quickly swiped it away. "I told them I was going to tell everyone and that they were going to go to prison." A disgruntled sound left her, and she tried to shy away from me at the last second, looking to the floor before I tilted her chin back up. My eyes bounced back and forth between hers, and the tears welling up had me wanting to switch places with her on a moment's notice.

I wanted to do nothing but kiss her and steal her pain and confusion. I wanted to silence whatever was going through her mind because that was what her kiss did to me. But instead, I continued pushing on, knowing I needed to know everything so I could find a solution. "And this has something to do with someone stalking you? How is this connected?"

Sloane shrugged. "I don't know. It started with text messages that were an exact replica of the texts between Willow and me." She sniffled. "That's my best friend—the one whose parents were murdered by mine. It was the same conversation that we had the night they were murdered. The last time I talked to her."

"And you don't think she's the one stalking you?" It seemed obvious, but something wasn't adding up.

Her eyes flashed to fear for a moment before she shook her head. "No. I really don't. She's in New York. I just checked the other day."

"What is her name?"

"How could it be her? Whoever is doing all of this has to be here at St. Mary's, right? It's not just the prank calls. It's the closet incident, the drugs, and the animal on my bed. Is someone sneaking into the school to do these things? How does anyone even know? No one is supposed to know what happened!" Her words were becoming more frantic, and there was a sudden panic that I felt right along with her.

I watched as she changed in front of my eyes. She was no longer my sister's best friend. She was no longer the girl who was tutoring me that I felt guilty for touching in the dark and blackmailing. She was everything I wanted in my future and everything I needed in my past.

"Sloane," I whispered, bringing her face to mine. Her short breaths hit my lips, and I inhaled, wanting to silence the words spewing from her mouth. "What's her name, baby?"

She slammed her lips together, pausing for a second. "Willow."

"Good. What's her last name?"

She hesitated, and I backtracked, running my fingers over her cheeks slowly, soothing her to calm down in the same way that I used to do to my mother when I would find her crying in her bed late at night after Richard would go back to his room. "Johnson." *Of course, it just had to be a common last name.*

Her skin was a hot brand against mine, but I still felt chilled to the bone. My thoughts latched onto the name, and I repeated it over and over again. *I have a starting point.*

"Tobias?" Her soft whisper brought me back down to level ground, and I nodded, putting a quick end to the conversation. Her head was crushed against my chest, and the feel of her in my arms was more for me at that moment than it was for her.

"I'll figure out what's going on."

"They will kill Willow if she knows the truth. They only spared her because I promised I wouldn't tell her what happened—ever. She doesn't know her parents were murdered. She thinks they died in a car crash. My parents aren't who I thought they were. They're dangerous."

So am I.

"That's why I didn't want you to tell your dad about me being drugged. If they suspect anything is off, they'll take me away and put me somewhere else where no one knows me. It cannot get out. No one can know. I shouldn't even be telling *you* this."

"Stop panicking. I've got you. Don't underestimate my ability to keep someone alive even though I've done nothing but kill."

I waited to see the fear. I waited for her to push me away and flee at the truth to my words, but the only thing I witnessed was acceptance. Her eyes had dried up, and her ruby lips stopped trembling. She was a blank canvas standing in front of me, spent from spilling a heavy secret. An unsettling urge to make her happy pressed on my refusal, and I simply gave in.

"I'm going to kiss you again," I warned, unable to stop myself.

I stole the breath off her lips, and everything in my body jolted when she let me steal her innocence. Warmth covered us as she reached up and wrapped her hands around my neck, kissing me back with just as much emotion as I was giving her. My entire being shook with need when I lifted her up, wrapping her legs around my waist. I laid her back on my bed, and it hurt to pull my mouth away to stare down at her. Those deep, hazel eyes locked onto me, as if she was waiting for something that I would probably never be able to give her.

"I thought you didn't kiss girls," she whispered as I continued to peer down at her, weighing my options. I knew I needed to leave her and walk away. I fucking knew it like I knew that I would never be the type of guy she needed. I wasn't the guy that had family dinners like my father was forcing me into to pretend like everything was normal. I was the type of guy you visited in prison, which was exactly where

I deserved to be—whether or not I'd had a choice in the shit that Richard made me do.

"You're different," I admitted. My arms began to shake as I kept myself propped up above her. "But I'm different, too," I said. "I am not a guy you should let kiss you. You understand that, don't you? I'm not goo—"

Her fingers gripped the back of my neck, and she pulled my mouth to hers again. The sensation was enough to take away every restraint I had left, and I kissed her like my life depended on it.

Actually, I kissed her like *her* life depended on it, because moving above her and touching her and feeling her tongue move against mine was the reminder I needed that she was worth far more than I was.

"I'm not going to stop if you don't push me away," I rushed out the words before I fell into a pit of intimacy that I would never feel again with anyone else. "Push me away, Sloane," I demanded, wanting to stop because I knew this would be too much for me to handle in the end.

I had been through a lot of shit. I had lost my sister for years—and my mother. But Sloane pulled at different heart strings. The protectiveness I felt for her ran through my limbs with an intense shock. I would break every bone in my own body when it came to her, and I hadn't been able to admit that until this moment with her. There was so much vulnerability in her gaze, and it was a mirror of my own.

"Don't make me push you away," she whispered, diving her fingers underneath my shirt and pushing it up over my head. Her eyes cascaded down past my face, and she traced every curve and dip over my stomach until she sat up and pushed me back onto my bed. I kept my mouth shut as I watched her crawl over me. Her knees were on both sides of my hips, and when she lifted her shirt, I was ravenous.

"I feel dangerous looking at you like this," I confessed. *I want to brand myself to her.*

"This isn't the first time you've seen me in a compromising position," she reminded me, putting her hands on my shoulders as she dipped down low, whispering over my lips.

I took my hand from her hip, and I rested it over her heart, feeling the tiny muscle beating hard. The lace of her bra scratched my palm as I spread my fingers. "But now, I see this. Your heart is pure, Sloane." I grabbed her wrist gently and moved her hand from my shoulder and put it over my chest. "And now *this* is invested."

The quietness of the room fed into the silence shared between us. Something quietly intimate was bonding us together, and the determination I felt to be better, for her, drove me to kiss her again.

It was a high that I couldn't stop chasing. I would make any deal I could if it meant I got to keep her. If she always looked at me like this, with admiration and acceptance and like I had the ability to put the sun in the sky, I would do anything.

Sloane's hips began to move over me the longer we kissed. I touched every part of her body, memorizing the soft touch of skin and the curves of her hips. I unclasped her bra and felt the thin material fall in between us as we continued to tangle our tongues together. She lifted up a second later as I fiddled with her jeans and pushed the button through the hole. I wiggled the denim down her legs, only breaking our kiss for a second before she began kissing me again and taking my jeans off.

Her hair was like a halo around her head as I flipped her around and dropped her onto my bed. We both gasped for air as I grabbed her thigh, loving the softness of her skin. I pushed her leg up and cursed the thin material that separated us before she lifted her hips up and quickly pushed the silk down her legs. I ripped her panties off the rest of the way and pushed my boxers off a moment later. I settled between her thighs, and we locked eyes before her back arched, and I pushed into her, cursing at how wet she already was. *Perfect.* I wanted her forever. I wanted to feel this way every single day with her eyes on me like I was more worthy than I actually was.

"This is so goddamn dangerous," I said, moving in and out of her achingly slow. Her hips spread wide, and our hands clasped together as I drove them into my pillow with her dark hair spread all around like she was a goddess. "You'll be broken by the end of this, and I don't mean your body."

"Sometimes, the pain is worth it."

Our mouths sealed together again, and I died with every swipe of her tongue against mine. We moved in sync, like we were meant for each other, which was complete and utter bullshit. How could a girl like her be meant for a guy like me?

My muscles tightened when she hit the brim of the surface, and I quickly took my mouth from hers and watched her fall off the edge, taking my soul with her. Her body took me to heaven and back, and a second later, I pulled out of her and came on her belly before collapsing and rolling on my back. *That was...fuck.* Our heavy breathing filled the air, and a few minutes later, I climbed off my bed, took a towel, and cleaned her up before covering her tired body up with my blanket, turning my light off, and sitting on the edge of my bed, in defeat, with her even breathing filling the room.

I wasn't sure how much time had passed, but I was certain she was sleeping as my thoughts circled the night's events and everything we both shared with one another under the guise of intimacy. I stayed still on the end of my bed, but when her sleepy voice rocked the room, my ears perked, and I was suddenly alive again.

"Do you regret what just happened?"

She has it all wrong.

I looked back at her, cuddled on her side with my blanket pulled up to her chin. It was dark in my room, but I still latched onto her tired, glassy eyes. "I wish."

"You *wish?*"

I nodded, putting my back to her again and exhaling.

"I will never be the guy you think I am."

I put my fist up to my mouth like I was hoping for something major to happen, like a blast to the past, where I hadn't been subjected to the things I did and saw in my childhood that made me into this cold person who was unstable and unworthy of a girl like her.

I mean, what were we doing? It wasn't like we were going to leave St. Mary's and have a grand life together. We were living in the current moment. We weren't thinking of the future, which was something I *always* thought about. Gemma kept hoping I would heal, and I was pretty certain that Sloane thought she knew me just because I'd given her small glimpses of the guy she wanted me to be, but I wasn't that person.

I wanted to be. But I wasn't.

"There is going to come a time when you have to stop pushing everyone away, Tobias. There's going to come a time when you have to see yourself the way we see you." Her next sentence was muffled by the blankets, but I heard it. "I'm going to make it my mission to get you to see the good in yourself."

I wasn't sure when, but eventually, Sloane was going to see that I wasn't good. Especially not when it came to her.

CHAPTER TWENTY-NINE

THE SCENT of cleaning supplies and freshly laundered blankets hit me when I opened my door the next morning. Tobias and I remained quiet as he walked me to my room before anyone was awake, and I was pretty sure he hadn't slept at all. We caught eyes as we passed by Isaiah's room, knowing Gemma was likely inside, and the thought occurred to me, *again,* that what we were doing behind her back was a shitty thing to do. I imagined what I would tell her if given the chance, and every scenario I'd come up with was total and utter mayhem: *I've been sleeping with your brother since we started tutoring. I've lied to you on numerous occasions and pretended to hate him when I didn't.*

I bristled at the thought before pushing it away as I scanned my room. Everything was in its place. My bed was made with freshly washed blankets, and Gemma's was neat, too. I turned back and looked at Tobias and questioned him silently. He shrugged, leaning against my door frame with his shoulders slightly slacked and relaxed. "Shiner can clean well, I guess."

I wanted to laugh in the worst way when I saw a mint perched on my pillow, but things felt too edgy. Everything was unsettled between Tobias and me. There wasn't a brewing fight that was brimming underneath the surface of our skin any longer, but there was something tense lingering. Like an unknown force pulling us together. Although, I could feel him pushing us apart, too.

"Gemma doesn't know about the...dead animal, right?" I asked hesitantly, not wanting her in the equation. Just talking about her was making me queasy, and it had nothing to do with the fact that I'd lied to her and everything to do with the fact that I *might* have been falling for Tobias, despite his refusal to allow it.

"Right," he answered, pushing off the door frame but staying in the threshold of my room. He stared at me, and I stared at him. The way his eyes stayed clear and far away from any kind of emotion told me that he was feeling *something*. He just didn't want to show it.

"Okay, well..." I stepped farther away from him as hurt settled on my tired shoulders. Last night wasn't something I could forget. The way I twisted for him as he claimed my mouth was something I'd never experienced before, and even though I knew it was coming, it still hurt to watch him shut down. I was suddenly like one of those girls who acted as if they'd lost a limb when a boyfriend broke up with them. *This isn't me.*

"I have someone looking into Willow. Just to make sure she isn't involved." Tobias' back was to me a moment later, and I held my breath. My throat grew tight. Disappointment bled from my pores, and I clenched my teeth to keep myself from saying anything that made me sound irrationally crushed.

He had warned me.

I'll never be the guy you think I am.

That was as good as him saying, *We're nothing.*

"Don't answer the phone if it's unknown, and don't go far without someone with you." His head lifted, as if he was looking at the ceiling. His shoulders tensed, and his chest expanded like he was sucking all the air in the room into his lungs. In fact, I was having trouble breathing, too. "They're trying to get a reaction out of you by scaring you. I don't think they will hurt you. They want something. I just don't know what."

That didn't make me feel better, but I didn't say that.

"Okay." The word was clipped with hurt that I disguised as anger. My lip trembled, and the night's events were catching up to me along with Tobias' refusal to look me in the eye.

I spun around and put my back to him, like he was doing to me. The sun was hardly peeking through the forest, and a cool draft from the window cooled my warm skin. I tucked my hair behind my ear as I waited for the door to shut so I could be alone and have my thoughts back, but I stilled when I heard a low growl and the slapping of something. I peeked over my shoulder and saw Tobias' fingers gripping the door frame above his head so tightly the tips of his fingers were white. When he spun around and stalked toward me, I met him halfway. His hands cupped my cheeks, and his fingers found their way into my hair.

The kiss was powerful, and my thoughts spun with each hungry stroke of his tongue. I was left breathless when he stepped away, staring at my mouth like it was going to save him from himself. He shook his head in defeat, but something soft lingered in his dark gaze. He gently brushed a finger over my cheekbone before turning around and walking out my door, shutting it a moment later.

Even in the midst of everything, a small smile still found its way onto my mouth, and the butterflies were flying quickly in my belly. Tobias said that he wasn't the guy I made him out to be, but he was wrong.

———

THE LAST TWO DAYS, I'd avoided Gemma as much as I could, which was hard, considering we were roommates. Thankfully, Isaiah had a way of keeping her busy, and she was working endlessly on her art portfolio that was due when she visited the fanciest art schools around and conducted interviews with them. More often than not, she was covered in paint or charcoal, and she stayed in Isaiah's room most nights—unless we had a girls' night planned. But she was starting to catch on whenever I'd avoid her stare or walk with Journey or Mercedes if there was a chance that she and I could be left alone together.

I had considered them *fibs* when Tobias and I were first thrown together and skirting over the lines of *something*, but now I was fully invested in him, and those small indiscretions were deep-rooted lies. If Gemma looked closely enough, I could guarantee that she would notice something was going on. Anytime Tobias would catch my eye in the dining hall, my cheeks would flush, and I would stumble over my words, causing everyone to eye me suspiciously. In class, the only thing I could focus on was his breathing as he sat mere feet away from me. He dropped his pencil in the aisle at one point, and when we both bent down to grab it, his fingers brushed my hand, and his eyes flared just as brightly as mine.

My phone vibrated in my cardigan pocket as I walked beside Mercedes to the girls' hall, and I was hoping it was Tobias confirming tonight's tutoring session that he had postponed the night before. I tried not to read too much into that, but my little ol' heart most definitely did.

"I'll see you later," I said to Mercedes as she departed to her room to work on her paper. "Good luck on your paper. Bullshit it if need be." I winked, trying to act like myself as much as possible, and she laughed before shutting her door.

I quickly pulled my phone out like it was a bomb, and my stomach did a somersault when I saw it was Tobias.

Tobias: Check your bag.

I rushed to my dorm door and opened it quickly, peeking down both ends of the hall to make sure there wasn't anyone following me. I hadn't had an unknown call since the movie night in the quad, but I knew the dead animal on my bed wasn't the last of whoever was trying to get a reaction out of me. Tobias said they were just trying to scare me, and I had to admit, they were doing a good job of it.

My foot closed the door as I walked into my room, silently laughing that it still smelled like a freshly cleaned hotel room, and opened my bag while holding my phone. I pulled my books out, wondering what Tobias had put in there. My hand brushed over something soft, and I gasped when I pulled out a tiny, stuffed bunny with fur the color of stone. It was just like the one we saw during the movie, which was the same one that ended up slaughtered on my bed.

I crushed the stuffed animal to my chest as I slid down the door to sit on the floor. I pulled my knees up and began typing a text.

Me: Did you get me a stuffed bunny?

How did he even manage to do this? Did he order one online and have it delivered?

Tobias: Maybe.

My cheeks hurt from smiling, and I placed my hand up to my mouth to hide it as if it was going to disappear any second.

Me: Why?

His text was almost immediate, and I wondered where he was at the moment. In his room? Alone? Texting me?

Tobias: I don't know. I just did. It's not a big deal. Thought it might make you feel better about the other night.

It was hard to believe that he refused to accept that he *was* good. A bad person wouldn't do something this sweet.

Tobias: Well...do you like it?

I smiled again. Why did such a small gesture from him feel like the biggest one ever?

Me: I love it.

Time passed as I kept my back pressed to my door. My fingers rubbed the soft fur of the tiny stuffed rabbit, and I contemplated telling Gemma what was going on. I wasn't just referring to her brother making me fall over my own feet, but everything else, too. My gaze moved to my bed, and as I pictured the dead animal bleeding all over the floor, anxiety clawed at my throat with the thought of what else they would do.

Me: Are we going to study tonight? Don't forget, I'm supposed to be helping you. I caught your grade today. A C is good, but it's not an A. We should work on tightening up your short-answer responses.

Tobias: Come to my room.

I kept a hold of the stuffed animal as I stood up with too much excitement.

Me: Now?

Tobias: Yes, now.

Me: I thought you were avoiding me.

I quickly stuffed my books back in my bag and held onto the stuffed animal before looking at myself in the mirror and cursing at how pink my cheeks were. I silently laughed as I blew air out of my mouth. I wondered if Tobias knew how happy a simple look from him could make me. *When did this happen?* My stomach sank a little as I opened my door, dreading the moment I pulled Gemma aside and told her what was going on.

I tried to look to the future, but my brain wouldn't allow it. I knew deep down that Tobias was right, and I was going to end up hurt, but I couldn't stop myself. It was like I was signing my own death certificate, accepting my fate.

My bag was slung over my shoulder as I walked quickly down the hallway, hoping I didn't run into anyone. I didn't usually walk alone—stalker or not—but now that there was something odd going on, I was more aware of how dark and disturbing St. Mary's could be. When I was a freshman, I started off by referring to it as a ghostly, gothic school, which surprisingly ended up feeling more like home to me than my rich, prestigious townhome in the middle of New York.

"Hey!"

I jumped when I heard Gemma's voice over my shoulder. I spun quickly, putting the stuffed bunny up to my chest while gasping. Gemma's green eyes softened. "Did I scare you? I'm sorry! I was just heading to the art room to finish up one of my portraits from this morning."

I panicked, and my voice broke. "Oh, it's fine." I paused. *Shit, act normal.* "Who is the portrait of?"

"Tobias." My heart lurched, and it was then that I realized that I was in way over my head.

"Does he know you're making a portrait of him?" I laughed while trying to push away the shock of my heart flipping just at the sound of his name. "I feel like he wouldn't be happy with the fact that you're painting him."

Gemma smiled when she looked down the hall to his bedroom. "Don't tell him."

I nodded. "Your secret is safe with me." *Along with all those other secrets bouncing around in my head.*

"What are you doing?" Her perfectly arched eyebrows crowded as she looked at me strangely. "Oh, and where did you end up going during the movie night? I've been meaning to ask you, but you keep disappearing." Her eyes dropped to my hand before she laughed. "Wait, what is that?"

"Oh," I said, holding onto the stuffed animal a little tighter. I glanced down, and for the first time since I began getting phone calls, I was thankful when my phone started to vibrate. I held it out and shrugged. "My parents are non-stop calling me these days. I'm gonna answer before they call your dad or something."

Gemma looked disappointed, but she nodded with a small smile. "I'll see you later then?"

"Yeah!" I tried to act cheery when she walked away, but the word *Unknown* flashing on my screen was a warning sign that I couldn't ignore.

My stomach jolted when my phone was ripped out of my hand a moment later, and a scream was cut off when Tobias pulled me into an empty alcove in the boys' hall and placed a hand over my mouth. He pressed the green button and put the phone up to his ear, and his rough, "Hello," caused me to hold my breath.

"Is the heavy breathing a fear tactic that you were told worked? Or are you beating off to my voice?"

My eyes widened when I moved his hand from my mouth. The line disconnected a moment later, and Tobias slipped my phone back into my bag before dropping his attention to the stuffed bunny I was holding onto with all my might.

I broke the silence and asked, "What are you doing creeping around the boys' hall?" There was dust covering the stone walls, and with my phone tucked away, it was darker than the hallway where there were at least a few sconces with small flames lighting the way.

"I realized I didn't want you walking by yourself, even to

my room, so I was coming to get you when I saw my sister dipping out of Isaiah's room, which is why I slipped in here."

"So, you're avoiding her, too?"

His dark, midnight scent filled my senses, and I took a step closer, blinking through the darkness to see him better. "Why are you avoiding her?"

"Because I'm lying to her, and I think you already know me well enough to know that friendship means a lot to me." I shrugged, even though he probably couldn't see it. "I feel guilty."

"That's my fault," he said, pushing my hair behind my ear and keeping his hand on the side of my face. I turned slightly, letting his long fingers weave through the strands. I loved his touch so much that it physically scared me. My heart flew in my chest, and the desire burned me from the inside out. "I threatened you with ruining your friendship with her."

My stuffed bunny fell in between our feet as I stood there, stunned with his regret. "Are you saying I should tell her?"

"Tell her what exactly?" His question was ice against my hot skin. "That I can't stay away from you even though I need to, and you can't stay away from me even though I keep warning you to? What next? We start dating and you go off to college while I stay behind and contemplate all the shit I did at the Covens that haunts me when I sleep?" The next sentence was mumbled under his breath, but I heard him. "Not to mention everything else."

"Everything else?"

"What will it take for you to walk away from me?"

Nothing.

"Stop it," I whispered, grabbing onto his hands. "Let's just...stop."

His hands left mine, and he wrapped them around my waist, in their rightful spot. "Stop what? Seeing each other? Meeting like this? I agree, we should stop."

The dread wrapped around my neck like his hands were choking me as I stood in front of him. "I was referring to you trying to push me away. Why do you do that?"

"Because I can't fucking stop feeling things when I'm with you and wanting things to be different, but the second you're not with me, I remember that it can't be like that."

"Why can't it?"

"You know why, Sloane."

"Fine." The burn of his words was suffocating, and I couldn't feel my limbs anymore.

He growled and slapped the wall above my head as I stood with my arms crossed over my chest. "I want you even when you're a stubborn brat. You're infuriating."

"You're infuriating," I snapped back. "I even enjoy arguing with you. That's completely demented, right?"

"Almost as demented as me wanting to kiss you every second of the day. Do you know how hard it is to see you sitting in the row beside me in class and not even looking at you? I cannot keep myself from you. It's frustrating. I am known for my control. I controlled myself for years at the Covens until I had the chance to get the fuck out, but one look from you and I want to burn down the entire school so people stop getting in my way of touching you."

"No one but you is in the way."

"I wish that were true."

There was nothing more to say because Tobias was as stubborn as he was mysterious. His sentence was final, and although I wanted to continue to dig underneath his skin until he confided in me like I confided in him the other night, I didn't. Instead, I pulled him in close and kissed him before he could kiss me. He paused at first, but his body relaxed against mine a moment later as he swallowed the breath right out of my mouth. His teeth nipped at mine, and his hands roamed like he was searching for something to ground him.

"I can't stop myself," he whispered as he pulled back, pushing my skirt up so he could grip my bare ass. He squeezed and gritted between his teeth. "I love it. I love touching you. I love what I feel when I'm with you. It's something I've never felt before, and I don't know what to do with it."

"Run with it, and fuck the consequences?" I huffed out a laugh that quickly turned into a gasp when he picked me up and wrapped my legs around his waist.

"That's easy to say, except you're the consequence, baby." His lips were back, and I felt my world spin. "I'm taking you back to my room anyway, though. Let's go."

My feet were planted back on the ground, and his hand fell into mine as he bent down and swooped up the stuffed bunny. I caught his slight smile that sent tingles to my heart as he pulled me into his room, and he shoved me inside, locking the door behind us.

"I'm sorry for what I'm about to do to you."

I paused as he pushed me down to his bed, dropping my backpack onto his desk that held his own books.

"What are you about to do?" I asked, watching him silence my phone as it started to vibrate again.

"I'm going to fuck you and wish I regretted it after."

CHAPTER THIRTY

TOBIAS

MY LEG BOUNCED up and down as Mr. Rake handed out the tests, and I could see Sloane nibbling on her lip, waiting for him to put my test down. I was passing my classes now, thanks to her, but it all seemed so futile with the fact that I was still trying to piece together what was going on with her. Tony had gone offline, which was just another worry added to my back pocket.

When I left the Covens, I knew my job wasn't technically over. Could I ever *really* be free from the past? It followed me like a dark cloud, constantly glooming over anything good that was happening. When I was with Sloane, though, things weren't so dark. I wasn't healed, nor was I the version of myself that she would eventually hope I turned into, but things weren't so bad when I was with her. Though, I was smart enough to know that just because Sloane made me feel something other than anger, that didn't mean I was okay.

The bell rang as soon as Mr. Rake put my test down on my desk, and he whispered over to Sloane. "Sorry, honey. I am no longer able to give out suckers." He glanced at me, and I paused, removing the vision from my brain of grabbing him by the throat and slamming him onto his desk for getting too close to her. *See? Not okay.*

"Oh, that's okay." Sloane smiled up at him and shot me a dirty look, as if she were asking me if I had something to do with the odd exchange.

"You have the headmaster to thank for that, not me," I said, half-laughing. *I guess ol' Daddy wasn't so bad after all.* The reminder of my issues with my father weren't so far off either. Such heavy pockets I had.

She grunted as she packed her things up. The classroom was empty. Even Mr. Rake had left. "Headmaster Ellison doesn't do anything unless there's a reason. I have a feeling you're the reason." Her half eyeroll had me grinning. I eyed my test that was face-down at the same time she did.

Her naughty smile stunned me just long enough for her to snatch it off my desk before I could, and I stood back with my arms crossed, heart thumping with anxiety. I knew why I was nervous, and it had nothing to do with the actual grade but more so because I wanted her to be proud of me.

"Well?" I asked hesitantly. My arms flexed as I waited, hating every last nervous thought going through my head. *Why am I nervous?*

A smile broke out along her face, and she lifted up on her tiptoes with a desk separating us and grabbed onto my face while still holding my test. "You aced it."

"What?" I was stunned at first and even more frozen when she kissed me feverishly, in the middle of a classroom. She pulled back and smiled so brightly that I couldn't think. There was chatter outside the door, and her smile fell instantly as she placed the test against my chest and let go, backing up and packing up her things.

"I'm proud of you." She glanced up at me once to drop her

eyes to my mouth and then shot me one more sad smile before saying, "I'll see you in your room later to study."

I smirked, knowing very well that we were not going to study the entire time. It was our new normal, and I had stopped trying to push her away as much and began pulling her in further. I told myself it was because the closer she was with me, the easier it would be to figure out what was going on with her stalker, but that wasn't entirely true. Things had been pretty quiet since the dead rabbit on her bed, but I knew that meant something else was bound to happen soon. That was how these things worked.

Long-lived infatuations and deep-rooted grudges didn't just die off, and either someone was obsessed with Sloane, or they wanted something from her.

Maybe both.

"Yeah," I said, pushing my test into my backpack before watching her walk away in her plaid skirt that I had lifted up way too many times over the last few days. "I'll see you later."

She turned around at the last second and shot me a flirty smile, and I clung to it as I walked out after her, passing by all our peers who glanced at me fearfully with my grim attitude. They parted the way for me like I was going to reach my hand out and snap their neck for looking at me wrong—except Shiner. Anytime I saw him, he threw a fist and waited for me to pound it, which I reluctantly did because he was as persistent as an annoying fly.

Gemma appeared in front of me just as I was about to climb the stairs to hole up in my room until Sloane came later, and I paused, nearly running over her. "Um, hey," I said. "Do you need something?"

My hardened rock of a heart sank to the bottom of my gut, and I froze when her lips didn't form a smile like usual. "Gem, what's going on?"

"We need to talk."

Ah, shit. I nodded solemnly, following her to the art room where she spent the majority of her time. The door latched, and I locked onto the canvas perched in the middle of the room with open jars of paint and several paintbrushes beneath it.

"So, that's how you view me?" I asked, tipping my chin to the painting, wanting to rip it to shreds.

It was as if she was cutting me with each angle and edge of my jaw on the canvas. She was talented. So fucking talented. Latching onto the piece of art was like looking into a mirror, except the only thing that wasn't right were the hues. I walked over to it slowly, my black shoes shuffling over the worn floor, and stopped right in front of it. I placed my hands around the straps of my backpack and kept my eyes trained to the blue of my eyes that matched our mother's to a T.

"You have the colors wrong."

She huffed. "What?"

"You need to make it darker." I took my thumb and ran the pad of my finger over the edge of the canvas, wondering how she could paint someone so dark but make them look so light.

"Tobias, what the hell is going on with Sloane?"

I turned around and walked over to one of the art tables and sat on top of it, acting casual even though I was uncomfortable as fuck. How could I be so uncomfortable around my twin?

"That's what this is about?" I asked, drumming my fingers over the black-top table. "I thought it was about Richard."

She winced, hating when I brought him up. I hated it, too. "He's still holed up in prison. Last I heard, he was in solitary."

Good. Then, maybe he could contemplate all the times he

had thrown me in a dark room for days without food or water.

"So, no. This isn't about him. It's about Sloane."

I swallowed, clenching my jaw and keeping my gaze set straight on my sister, trying to brace myself for her reaction. What did she know?

"What about her?" I acted unperturbed, but curiosity was overflowing onto the floor between us.

Gemma grabbed onto her phone that was perched on the canvas beside her and threw it at me. I caught it with one hand, and the second I glanced down, my head jerked to the side, and I crushed the device inside my palm. *What the fuck?*

"How long have you two been sleeping together? And why didn't she tell me? I know why you didn't, but why didn't she?"

There was hurt seeping from her but not the kind that made her cry, but more like the kind that made her feel less than what she was. I jumped up from the table and held her phone out for her to grab. "It's not her fault." The words fell from my mouth as I tried to protect both Sloane and my sister. "I told her not to tell you. I threatened her."

"What?" She was baffled. "Tobias, how could you? What did you threaten her with?"

"Do you really want to know?" I asked, shooting her a look that I hoped she would be able to read.

"Yes." My temples ticked, and if I weren't so perturbed by the photo on her phone of Sloane and me, I would have smiled at the attitude coming from her mouth. Gemma had been walking on eggshells with me since coming back. I understood why. She had grown up with Richard, and she knew what he was capable of. She thought I was glass and assumed I would either self-combust and cut everyone around me, or I'd break in half from the trauma, but right now, she was pissed, and I enjoyed it. *Finally, a real fucking emotion.*

"Fine." I sighed, leaning back on the table. The ledge cut into my back, and I latched onto the pain. "I made her come at the claiming party, recorded it, and didn't tell her it was me until the very last second. And then, I told her I'd give you the video and ruin your friendship. That was all for her to leave me alone with tutoring. Then, I asked for her help and threatened her again with it." *I'm an asshole.*

Gemma's gasp flew so quickly from her mouth that her hair ruffled past her face. "Tobias! Are you serious?"

I couldn't help it. I smiled. I put my hands up in defense when she took a step toward me with blinding rage. "I'm not smiling because of what I did. I'm not proud of it."

She paused, mid-step.

"I'm smiling because this is the first time since I've been back that you've shown me the real Gemma. A real emotion. Not the let-me-act-like-everything-is-okay facade you and Tate have been putting on for months." I shrugged. "It's nice to see the real you."

"That isn't true," she whispered. "I just—"

"Don't want to set me off? Yeah, I know. I get it. But I'd much rather you admit that I'm not the same brother you knew as a child."

She rolled her eyes and spun around, picking up a paint brush. She started swiping over parts of the portrait of me, and it was obvious she was angry by the sounds of the brush strokes against the canvas. "Well, I'm not the same sister either."

"I know that." I looked out the window at the swaying trees. "You're better."

We caught eyes, and her paintbrush stopped moving. Her lips flattened, and her tiny chest sucked in air before she exhaled and wiped her hands on a nearby towel. "I'm mad at you," she admitted, crossing her arms and leaning back on the table opposite of me.

"I'm mad at myself." Not necessarily for blackmailing Sloane but for not being able to pull myself away from her. The guilt caught up to me fast, and I stared into my sister's eyes, feeling as if something had healed in the last few minutes of being together. "Don't be upset with her. Once things…changed, she wanted to tell you. I told her not to."

"Changed how?" She looked at the ceiling. "You've made her fall for you, haven't you?"

"Wait." I pushed up from the table, and the realization hit me like a fucking train. "Who sent you that picture of us?"

I was so blinded by the photo in the first place and my sister's anger that I didn't put two and two together.

Gemma pulled her phone over to her and flipped up the screen. "I was trying to figure that out. I'm no—"

Her phone was in my hand mid-sentence, and my world shifted when I read the name at the top of the text: *Unknown.*

"This mother fucker." My teeth ground together, and I put my back to my sister as daunting anger had me stranded with a noose around my neck. *This fucking asshole.* I thought through the reasons why he'd—and I was certain it was a he—would send a photo of Sloane and me in the toolshed to Gemma, and it was obvious. *He's trying to turn her friends against her.* My heart slipped, but the anger was still there, riding in like a black horse. The pieces were scattered like the parts of my soul, and I was determined to make sense of what was going on.

A hand landed on my shoulder, and I spun around quickly, meeting Gemma's worried gaze. "What's going on, Tobias? That's the real reason I wanted to talk to you. I know something isn't right."

The feeling was eerie. It seeped in like fog and took hold of me like I was back at the Covens, shutting down every emotion but anger. That was how I managed to do what I did each time Richard had a 'job' for me. There were no emotions. I was numb to the very bone. I focused on my anger for Richard and everyone who had ties with him and thought of nothing else when I murdered someone.

"Someone is stalking her." My words were like gravel against my tongue.

"Stalking her? What? How? Here at St. Mary's?"

My hands shook as I pulled the phone up to my face again, letting the photo seep into my memories to stay there to feast on anger. Sloane was in a blissful state in the photo, sitting on the workbench with me ripping her jeans off her legs so I could touch her and make her wither in front of me. I could tell the photo had been taken through the window of the toolshed because there were parts of her body hidden from the cloudiness of the glass.

"Yes," I gritted between my teeth.

"Do you know who? Or why?"

I glanced over at her, clicking the phone shut. "I don't know who, and I don't know why. I only know bits and pieces of what she has told me."

Gemma looked away and began chewing on her lip. "Something with her parents, for sure."

"Yes. Don't worry. I'm going to figure it out." I pushed her phone back into her hand after deleting the photo and pulled out my own. "Don't say anything to her. She didn't even want to tell me, but I forced her to."

"No surprise there." She laughed, and it was as sarcastic as it could get. "Should I be worried? I have to tell Isaiah."

"Shiner knows."

"He does?"

I shrugged. "He's not half bad, you know?"

She laughed again, but this time, it reached her eyes. "None of us are. You're just too stubborn to see that."

"I don't think I need to remind you to stay alert, right?"

Suddenly, my sister's face grew serious. Her laugh lines disappeared, and the light in her emerald eyes dimmed. "I've been alert since the moment Richard threw you away and I was alone."

"He's gone," I reminded her, cursing the guilt that swarmed me when I thought of her being alone with him. *Will that ever go away?* "And even if he wasn't, I wouldn't let him touch you. I would kill him and not think twice about it."

Gemma walked over to me and hugged me, and this time, I hugged her back, and I felt it seep into the crack in my chest that Sloane had put there. "I would, too." She pulled back a moment later. "I won't tell Sloane I know about the stalker issue, but I'm totally bringing up the fact that you two are together."

My jaw ached as I squeezed my phone. "This is why I didn't want you to know."

"Why?"

It killed me to say it aloud and to recognize it for what it was, but there was no way around it. "Sloane is going to go off to college after you all graduate, right? Just like you and the rest of your friends."

"After *we* graduate, you mean. You're going to graduate, too. Your grades are improving, Tobias. I might even say they're *good.*"

Sloane's words scratched at my thick skull, and I bristled. *"I'm proud of you."*

"Yeah, well, I'm not going to college with her. She's going to go on and live her life after I take care of whoever the fuck is stalking her, and I won't be going with her. There isn't a future for her and me, and you know it. She knows it, too. I can't be with her."

"You know, Isaiah said the same thing about me and him, and look at us."

"That's different," I shot back, frustrated that she wasn't understanding what I was saying.

"How?"

"Because Isaiah didn't kill people for sport, Gemma!" I walked away and put my back to her, staring out the window again. "There is unfinished business out there. Not only with the people whose lives I ruined, but...I'm not okay, either. Sloane doesn't deserve to carry my baggage. Fuck, it's so heavy I can't even carry it."

A few long seconds passed, and blood filled my mouth as I bit onto my tongue to control the emotions that were erupting out of me like a volcano. Gemma's hand softly landed on my shoulder, and she gave me a light squeeze. She didn't say a word, but I knew it was her way of understanding what I was saying. Maybe she didn't agree with it, but I thought she understood.

Her hand was gone a moment later, and as soon as the door shut, I opened my phone and called Tony again—for the seventh time in the last two days. It didn't even ring. When I heard the automated voicemail, I kicked my foot out, and a chair went flying across the floor, hitting the canvas that my portrait was hanging on. A paint brush fell to the ground, and white paint stained the floor.

Fuck.

CHAPTER THIRTY-ONE

SLOANE

THE 3D PAPER butterflies that I had taped to my ceiling two years ago were like looking into a past memory—one where I was young and dismissive to the real hardships that feelings could cause.

They were white and whimsical and full of innocence. Over the last few months, I'd become the complete opposite of such. Where I was once able to dissociate myself from the havoc that my parents had caused the night they murdered Willow's parents, I now felt like I was the center of it. The phone calls were beginning to catch up to me. The fear of Willow being the one behind it made my skin itch with unease because it was the obvious first thought from Tobias, and it should have been mine, too. But I refused to believe it.

I was afraid.

There.

I said it.

I placed my hands down by my sides, resting over the hem of my plaid skirt, and stared at the butterflies and wished I could go back to a few years ago when I was just happy to be away from my parents and the pain of losing everything I knew.

Now, I was paying for it. It was catching up to me, and apparently, it was bothering someone else, too, if they were tormenting me with it.

My door jingled, and my heart lurched to my throat as I sat up quickly, gripping onto the blankets with my shaky fingers. When Gemma's face appeared in the crack before she pushed the door all the way open, I breathed out a sigh of relief that quickly turned into dread.

Shit.

"Hey." She smiled at me, and I hated myself for being such a shitty friend. "Can we talk?"

Oh no.

"Um..." Tobias came to mind, and I wanted to sink into a hole in the ground so I could avoid this entire conversation. *Here it comes.*

"I know, Sloane."

My knees came up to my chin, and I wrapped my arms around them, feeling tears halt at the backs of my eyes. Words spilled out of my mouth a moment later, and there was no way to stop them from coming out. "I'm sorry. I'm so sorry. I should have told you from the beginning, but I kept trying to pretend like nothing was happening between us, and I tried to avoid him, but he kept popping up out of nowhere, and I couldn't help it and—"

"Sloane!" My bed dipped, and Gemma's warm hands were around my body a second later. "Stop! I'm not mad."

I stilled. *What?* "How are you not mad? I've been lying to you, and that is one thing that friends shouldn't do. This is totally different from me hiding something. I have flat-out lied to you. It's...it's exhausting."

"Tobias told me he blackmailed you. He told me not to be

mad at you because it was his fault." A snicker flew from her mouth when she pulled back and crawled over beside me and lay down. My legs straightened out, and I glanced over at her. "It was honestly kind of funny to watch him squirm to protect you." Gemma's snicker turned into a full-on laugh. "I've never seen him flustered before."

My silence made her look over at me. "I haven't seen many emotions from him, but the second I brought you up was the second he opened up." There was a spark getting brighter and brighter in my chest, knowing that Tobias felt something when it came to me. "I won't lie, though. I'm worried."

For the first time in a long time, I told the truth to my best friend. "I'm worried about him, too."

Her brows fell with confusion. "No. I'm worried about *you.*"

My pulse flew through my skin. "Me?" *What else does she know?*

"Yes, I'm worried he will hurt you." She sighed and looked up at the hanging butterflies over my bed. She had the same ones over her bed that I had put up when she first started attending St. Mary's earlier in the year. So much had changed since that first day. She was the broken, loner girl who hid behind an invisible cloak, whereas I was the one who tried to uncover her quiet scars and protect her, but now the roles were reversed.

"I'll be fine." I grabbed onto her hand and gave it a small squeeze. "I'm just glad you aren't mad at me. I don't even know what your brother and I are. One second, we are arguing and acting like we hate one another, and the next, we're—"

"I'm stopping you right there."

We both laughed. "It's been even more exhausting not

talking to my best friend about guy problems, but *fine*. I won't go there."

She gripped my hand again, and the guilt that felt like a pile of rocks in my belly lightened, and I felt a weight lift off my shoulders. It was a brief moment of normalcy, though, because a moment later, we both sat up on the bed when we heard something against our door. Our easy conversation disappeared, and I didn't miss the way Gemma suddenly became serious.

"Did someone just knock on our door?"

"I'll get it," I said, pushing off the bed before she could. I knew it was probably Isaiah or maybe Mercedes and Journey, but there was an ounce of skepticism that came with every breath I took. I shivered at the thought of opening the door and there being a dead animal on the floor.

I tried to snap out of the apprehensive feeling I'd been succumbing to lately. This wasn't me. *Pull yourself out of it, Sloane!*

I opened the door with my shoulders square. I exhaled when no one was out there. I peeked down both ends of the hall, wondering if Gemma and I had just thought we heard a noise.

"No one is there?" she asked, swinging her legs off the end of my bed and eyeing me closely.

I shook my head and looked for my phone. I hadn't had many calls lately, but I knew there would be one eventually. When I stepped back into my room, there was a crinkling of something under my foot, and my heart skipped when I slowly scanned my gaze down and saw the black-and-white photo that I recognized immediately, even with the giant red X over Willow's face.

The blood slowly drained from my body, leaving an ice-cold emptiness behind. I quickly bent down, scooped up the photo, and spun around to put a normal, unaffected mask on for Gemma.

"What is that?"

"Just a piece of paper that someone must have dropped while walking past. Trash." I walked over to my desk and shoved it in my small, sparkly trash can and smiled, opening my phone to see if there was a missed call.

There wasn't.

But that didn't make me feel any better about what I just found outside my door.

"Oh, okay. Well, what do you say we have a girls' night? I already informed Tobias that you were mine tonight." She shot me a wicked smile and patted the bed beside her.

My heart was still beating hard when I put my phone away. I hoped that my face wasn't as pale as it felt. My stomach rolled, and the thought of eating junk food with Gemma made me want to double over, but instead of refusing, I nodded with enthusiasm. "That sounds perfect." I put my phone on silent and jumped onto my bed beside her, eyeing the trash can one more time, making a mental note to hide the photo better because although I felt guilty for lying to her about her brother, I didn't feel that way about hiding everything else.

The last thing Gemma needed was to be afraid again. I finally felt the weight slide off my shoulders now that she knew about me and Tobias, but this little threat would only serve to complicate things even more. Ignorance was bliss, and I could ignore it—but only for a little while.

CHAPTER THIRTY-TWO

TOBIAS

"I CAN'T BELIEVE you told your sister about blackmailing me with the video."

Sloane had her hands placed on her hips as she paced back and forth, clearly annoyed with me as I lay back on my bed, sprawled out. I was thoroughly enjoying her stomping her way across my floor with my notes resting on my stomach as my hands were perched behind my head.

"She asked, and I didn't want her to be mad at you. Not to mention, we've been over this multiple times." *Every day since my sister confronted her.*

She paused and shot me an exasperated look. I grinned before musing, "I could have told her the truth."

Her shoulders tensed. "That is the truth. You 100% threatened to ruin our friendship. Remember?"

I sat up, letting my notes fall to the floor like my anger the moment I was with her. "I remember." I climbed off my bed and prowled over my floor to where Sloane's resolve wavered. "But I also remember how much you enjoyed my touch at that first claiming, even after knowing it was me."

My hand gripped her chin, and I soaked in the feel of her skin against my palm. No matter how many times I told myself not to touch her and pull her in further, I did it anyway. There was absolutely no use in trying to resist her at this point. We were in too deep. There would come a time where I wouldn't have to resist her because she'd be gone, and I would have her little stalker by the throat, and all would be well.

"Are you mad that she knows about us? I thought you would be happy that you don't have to lie to her anymore."

"There's an us?" she countered, tipping her chin under my grip. Her question stung because I wanted nothing more than for there to be an us, but I knew there would come a time where we wouldn't exist.

Instead of saying that, though, I pushed the future away and gently shoved her over to my desk and lifted her up by her hips and sat her down on the study guide she made me. "There's as much of an us in this moment as there is air in my lungs, Sloane."

Something moved gracefully across her features, and I was pretty certain I just watched her fall for me as hard as I'd been falling for her since the second we touched. I didn't want to think about the future, and I didn't want to think about the fact that someone was fucking with her and driving me to the deep twisted part of myself that I wanted to kill with my bare hands.

"You can't say things like that to me and expect me to go along with this whole spiel that you're a terrible guy with no feelings." The curve of her lips was like stepping into the sun. "You have some good in there, Tobias." Her fingers crawled up my chest and landed over my heart that was no longer mechanically ticking like a robot.

"Only for you." It was the truth.

"Not true. For your sister and Journey, too. You helped her in the psych hospital, didn't you?"

I chuckled. "Journey didn't need my help."

My phone vibrated, and I pulled it out quickly, hoping it was Tony. He still hadn't reached out to me, and there was a slight worry that wasn't just hanging out in the back of my mind but in the forefront, right beside Sloane and her stalker. The list in my closet still had the same four names on it that it had when I came to St. Mary's, and that was concerning. Tony was supposed to keep track, check the database to see if they popped up and were on the move.

Sloane's legs stopped swinging in front of me when I scanned the text. "Did you find anything out about Willow?" Her question was cautious, and it pulled me from my phone.

I flicked my eyes up to her and shook my head. "Not yet." *I need more info.* I needed Willow's entire backstory. I needed her parents' backstory. I needed to know why Sloane's parents murdered them and who else knew. *I need Tony and his counter-intelligence skills.*

"Gemma just texted me. She wanted to know if we needed a break from studying to come hang out in Isaiah's room for a...video game tournament?" *Whatever the fuck that is.*

Sloane sighed wistfully, looking at my hands still wrapped around her hips. She lifted up a little and pulled my study guide from underneath her. "Not much studying going on around here."

I grabbed the paper from her and winked. "This is the best form of studying I've ever done." She playfully slapped my chest, and I backed up, letting her jump down.

"Do you want to go? We don't have to if you don't want to."

"I'll do anything you want to do." I blinked as the words

fell from my mouth. *When did I become this guy?* Instead of it being my goal to push everyone away and stay numb to the circle jerk of feelings that were trying to make sense inside my brain, it was my goal to make her happy.

Sloane sucked her cheeks in a little as a blush spread over them. "I guess we can go for a little while. I've been pretty... distant with everything going on. But I'm bringing the study guide and going over it with you."

"Alright," I said, pushing my phone in my pocket and grabbing onto her hand before spinning her around and kissing her forehead. "Then, let's go."

A warm smile spread across her mouth as if she thought I was going to say no. Before I pulled her through the door, I glanced down at her and said, "Don't think I'm not going to touch you, though."

———

"THIS MOTHERFUCKER! SUCK MY COCK." I craned my neck over to Shiner, who was wearing a headset and pacing back and forth in front of a small TV with a controller in his hand, hitting a button so aggressively that I was wondering if it was going to snap in half soon. Sloane was beside me, and although I told her I was going to touch her, I'd played nice and hadn't done much other than let our legs brush back and forth a few times.

My sister was looking at me from across the room as she sat in between Isaiah's legs. Journey and Cade were on the floor, both reading books, which I found to be perfectly fitting for her. Her head rested on his legs as he propped his back against the wall, both completely unbothered by the profanities coming from Shiner's mouth. Brantley was glued to the TV, giving Shiner commands left and right, and it was all very *normal.*

It irked me that this was what I had missed out on while trapped behind a locked door with a man unworthy of air breathing down my neck, filling my head with insults and lies. I glanced over at my sister again as Sloane read over my answers on the study guide. Her eyes crinkled at the sides, and I paused, locking onto the silent words my sister was trying to pass over to me.

What?

Gem's eyes dropped to my phone that was laying on my stomach. I peeked at Sloane, who was still reading my answers, and then back to her. Isaiah's chin bobbed above her, and he flicked it to his bathroom. I caught on quickly. Prickles shot up from my feet as I swung over the bed and told Sloane I was going to use the bathroom. I casually walked behind Shiner and the many curses from his mouth and opened my phone a moment later.

Gemma: Did Sloane show you the photo?

Me: What photo? No? When?

Gemma: A couple of days ago. There was a knock on our door, and no one was there, but she was acting weird and said she found a piece of trash on the floor, so she threw it away. When I went back to look for it, she had taken it and hid it in between her books.

My heart beat viciously against my chest, and the racing of it made me dizzy. I paced the small bathroom, moving over the tiled floor. When another text came in, I froze, zooming in on the photo my sister was holding.

What the fuck?

I recognized Sloane right away. She was younger in the black-and-white photo, but she still had that pretty smile that rocked my very fucking world. Her arm was wrapped around someone's slender shoulders, but the other person's face was crossed out with a bright-red X. It didn't matter that I couldn't make her face out, though. I knew it was her best friend, Willow. It confirmed my already present suspicion that it wasn't Willow who was stalking and tormenting her.

I tucked my phone back in my pocket and left the bathroom, my eyes directly on Sloane. She was staring at the TV that Shiner was standing directly in front of, and my frustration with her dropped for a moment when she peeked up at me and shot me a tender smile. The apples of her cheeks reddened when she caught me staring, and those hazel eyes flirted with me from across the room. *Fuck, why didn't she tell me about the photo?*

Sitting back on the bed, I pushed away the confusion that came with her hiding the photo from me and did what I did best and constructed a plan. My hand landed on her thigh, and she jerked, flexing the tight little muscle before relaxing again and shifting so she was closer to me. Her hair shielded her face from me as she went back to look at my answers, taking her pen and making small notes in the margins. Shiner threw his headset at the wall a moment later, pausing my thoughts. Sloane's hand stopped moving, and the room fell silent.

"Fucking pieces of shit."

Brantley threw his hands up. "You almost had it, bro."

"It doesn't matter," he said calmly—a little too calmly for how he just threw his headset. I ran my finger over the inside of Sloane's thigh, and I felt her stare penetrate the side of my face, but I kept my eyes trained on Shiner. I didn't trust myself to look at her and keep my emotions in check. I was angry, but mostly frustrated, and there was some other emotion filling the gaps that I couldn't name. Shiner stole the room's attention, but my finger continued to brush over Sloane's soft skin. It burned like she was pouring hot wax over my skin when I felt the goosebumps race to her flesh.

"Forget the game. There is something else we need to discuss."

Shiner quickly spun around and locked onto me and Sloane. "Are we all just going to ignore the huge-ass elephant in the room?!" He placed his hands on his hips before wafting them out with surprise. "Who else is just blown away by the sight of these two? Huh?" He looked at Cade and Journey who had peered up from their books, both hiding smiles. "You? Are you surprised? I know I am! I never would have guessed it. Sloane and Tobias sitting in a tree...k-i-s-s-i—"

Sloane crossed her arms, smashing her lips to hide a smile. "Shiner!"

"I'm just saying..." He shrugged, picking up his controller and putting his back to us. "I never would have guessed it."

I peered down at Sloane, and she caught my eye immediately. We both smiled at the same time, and she snuggled in closer. She moved her leg over to the side so I could touch her more, and I pushed back against the bed, knowing that as soon as we left the comfort of her friends, I was going to have to lure the truth from her lips and then pretend like I regretted it afterward.

CHAPTER THIRTY-THREE

SLOANE

I walked beside Tobias in silence when we left Isaiah's room with my body buzzing like a million firecrackers were lit up on the inside, but he seemed so *calm*. His hand had rested on the side of my thigh the entire time we were with everyone, and it was as if he was tattooing his name on me with his palm. A pull burrowed itself in between my legs as he ran his finger down the seam of my thigh, and I wiggled so many times that I was finally the one who said we needed to head back to his room to go over the study guide.

Right when we got inside his room, I glanced at his bed, and my body jerked with anticipation. I yelped a moment later when he pushed me against his door and caged me in.

"Hey," he whispered against my lips.

"Hi," I breathed out as I moved my body up to meet his. "You can't touch me like that for an hour and then expect me to be able to study with you."

His lips curved, and I couldn't breathe at the sight. I wondered if I would ever not be unsteady by the sight of his smile, no matter how small it was, but a part of me didn't want that feeling to go away. It was warm and soul-crushing all in one.

"Did you like it?" he asked, grazing my neck with his teeth. "Maybe I should check."

"Mmm..." My hips shot forward when he gripped my leg tightly and wrapped it around his hips. His jeans scratched at my inner thigh, and when his fingers brushed over my wet panties, I fell back further onto the door.

"Ah, you *did* like it." His blue eyes snagged mine, and I pushed his dark hair off his forehead so he could clearly see my nod. I felt shy for a second when he pulled his fingers from in between us and licked my wetness off the tips before putting them back down between my legs.

My God. Tobias was skilled. So skilled in everything he did. He was even becoming skilled with his grades. Such little effort and he was climbing to the top. Part of me wondered if he was this dominant in the Covens, too.

I moaned quietly, breathing heavier when I felt his finger tease the brim of my panties. I wasn't sure if he wanted me to beg for it, but I was about to. "Here's the deal." His sentence shot out and gripped me by the throat. "I'll make you come, as long as you tell the truth." *Wait, what?* "Can you do that for me, baby?"

I loved it when he called me that.

"Tell the truth about what?" I asked with hesitation. Everything was so mysterious about Tobias. He always left me guessing.

He pulled back and sent a chilling look in my direction, as if he were reprimanding me. "Nope. Not until you agree. I'll walk you back to your room right now if need be."

Anger skimmed my tone. "Fine, I'll just get myself off."

His dark and dangerous smile jumbled my thoughts as he pushed my hair away from my face gently. His other hand was still under my skirt, and he tapped on the inside of my thigh, and I felt the spark zip all the way to my mouth. "Won't be the same, and you'll be left unsatisfied."

He didn't give me a chance to rebut. "Understand the rules? Perfect. Let's get started." My eyes widened when his finger hooked into my panties. Only, he didn't allow for his finger to actually touch me anywhere else.

What the hell?

"Did you get a little gift a few days ago?"

"What?" I asked, trying to move my hips to meet his finger. His other hand came down, and he gripped my hip tightly, keeping me in place. I pouted as I sliced my gaze to his. His eyebrow, the one with the perfectly imperfect scar slashed through it, raised. Was he...challenging me?

"Did you? Did you get something from your stalker?"

"How d—"

"Answer me," he rasped.

He flicked his finger once, and I gasped, feeling weak in the knees.

"Yes." I sagged with relief when his thumb rubbed over me.

His lips brushed over mine, and it scared me how willing I was to give him anything when he was this close to me. My body and mind were his to toy with, and there was absolutely no refusal from anywhere inside my body.

"Tobias." A breathless whine flew from my mouth when he pulled his finger away.

"Who was in the photo?"

"How did you know about it?"

His teeth bit onto my lip, and my eyes widened. When he pulled back, I felt the pain linger. "You don't get to ask the questions, Sloane." His tongue dipped forward, and he warmed the sting from his teeth. "Answer me."

I'm not sure I like this game. The disappointment that came with hiding it from him was buried deep, and he quickly uncovered it with one glance from his steady gaze.

My answer was quiet, barely considered a whisper. I looked down at his firm grip on my hip, tracing the whites of his knuckles with my eyes. "It was me and Willow when we were younger." I swallowed past the lump of regret. "The picture was tucked away in one of my books. I'm not sure how long it was missing."

Tobias' mouth covered mine, and the deep kiss stunned me. It was passionate and held a wealth of unsaid words that I couldn't read. When he pulled away, he dipped down to a knee and stared up at me from below with a look that I could only describe as wicked. Tobias had a hint of good in him. I'd reminded him of that when he needed to hear it the most, but he had a barrel full of bad in him, too. The bad boy that girls dreamed of having was literally bowing at my feet.

"I'm sorry," I choked out, blinking away the eagerness to please him and make up for not telling him.

He nodded before going under my skirt and placing a tender kiss to my most sensitive spot. I sucked in air when he came out and peered up at me with a look on his face that stumped me.

"Why didn't you tell me?"

He stood a second later, putting both of his hands on my waist softly. My back was pressed against his door again, and my resolve fell when I searched the blue in his eyes, trying to figure out what was going through his mind.

Is he hurt?

A single strand of hair fell onto his smooth forehead, and when he glanced away from me, showing off that ticking jaw muscle, a piece of my heart chipped off. *Oh my God. I hurt him.*

"Does it bother you that I didn't tell you?" I treaded lightly, hoping that he'd actually open up to me and not push me away because things were becoming dicey. The ice around his heart hardly ever thawed, but I felt like I was holding the ice pick.

He swallowed loudly, still flexing his jaw. My hand was shaky as it came up in between us, and I placed it on the side of his face, feeling the slight scruff of his cheek against my palm. "Tell me," I urged, grounding us in the moment that felt more real than ever.

When he looked back at me, the blue pierced me. I froze as we held each other's gazes, and I didn't think either of us had taken a breath until his rasp of a whisper filled the room. "Yes." He looked over my head as he spilled the rest of his secrets. "I shouldn't let it bother me. I know I can't be the guy you tell all your secrets to and pick to protect you for the rest of your life. I know that you probably think I'm too dangerous to tell these things to, and I am." I stayed completely still when his eyes reached me again, peering down at me with an urgency that I felt down to my soul. The room faded, and I wouldn't have been surprised if the lights flickered. "I want to lock you away until I find out who is messing with you and kill them, which just proves, right there, that I am fucked up, Sloane. I get why you didn't tell me, but it bothers me. And I don't know what to do with that because I want to be different for you."

"Stop," I rushed out, grabbing onto his face tightly and bringing his forehead to mine. The second our skin touched, it coaxed me to tell the truth. "That's not why I didn't tell you." I sniffed and sucked in the tears that wanted to spill. "Things were beginning to seem...normal. Gemma knew about us, and it was like a weight had been lifted off my shoulders. If I told you about the photo, then things would get scary again because, despite what you think, I am scared."

"If you think I'm going to let someone hurt you—"

"No." I pulled back. Tobias' brows were crinkled, and the

hooded look he held did nothing but force me to keep going. "That's not what I'm afraid of."

His face softened. "Tell me, then. Tell me your fears so I can make them go away. That's all I want. Is it me? Are you afraid of me?" He looked up and cursed. "Of course you are."

"No!" I rushed out, stomping my foot. "I'm not afraid of you. I'm afraid that once you find out who is stalking me, and I'm safe again, you will stay true to your word. There won't be a reason to walk me back to my room after tutoring or text me to see what I'm doing when we're not together. Soon, school will be over, and we will graduate, and you've told me over and over again that there isn't a future between us. I didn't tell you because I just wanted to be normal with you and my friends. I wanted to see how it felt to not be worried for five fucking seconds."

Surprise took me swiftly when Tobias crushed me to his chest. His racing heart pounded against my ear, and his arms wrapped around me tightly. It was then that I realized that in his arms was where I felt the safest.

"Tobias," I whispered against his chest. His arms didn't let up, but I managed to peer up at him. "I know you'll hate this and try to argue...but I haven't felt safe since the night I found Willow's parents, and the only time I do feel safe is when I'm with you."

His eyes shut, and he breathed in all the oxygen in the room. I knew he'd hate it and want to argue, but instead of doing that, he spun me around and walked us over to his bed. He lifted his shirt up over his head and then caressed the side of my face with his warm palm and placed a soft kiss to my mouth. His tongue dipped inside, and it was a slow kiss, one that sent light to every hidden crook of my body. He kept his lips over mine, moving his mouth achingly slow, as he unzipped the back of my skirt and let it fall to the ground. Our kiss only broke when he lifted my school blouse over my head. My fingers rushed to unzip his jeans, and when they fell to the floor with my skirt, he pushed me back onto the bed.

My heart was through the roof, and my pulse beat just as quickly. With every lingering touch, his lips came next until I was positive he had marked every single inch of my skin. When his finger hooked inside my panties and he slowly moved them down my legs and into the pile beneath his feet, he bent in low, jumbling all my senses with his admittance. "You make me want to be better, Sloane. You make me want to be good."

"You are," I whispered back, bringing his mouth to mine. My bra was pulled off my body, and when he entered me, my hands went to his back, feeling his rugged scars beneath my fingers.

This time wasn't fast and rushed, and it didn't immediately send me over the edge. He took his time with me, like he was trying to memorize everything about the moment. It was slow, sensual, passionate, and full of too many emotions that neither of us could express otherwise. But that was the thing with us—our actions did the talking for us, not our words.

There was pain that followed the feeling, though, because I knew it likely wouldn't change anything between us. But there was hope, because Tobias had said that heartless boys never kissed, and look at him now.

CHAPTER THIRTY-FOUR

TOBIAS

My back was to her as she slept on my bed with the covers wrapped around her like she was the sweetest thing to ever exist. And to me, she was.

Equal parts independent and mouthy as she was compassionate and accepting. Sloane could be a brat and sting you just as sharply as a wasp, but she was always quick to cool the sting moments later with a softhearted look and warm touch.

I didn't want to get my hopes up and think I could change for her, but the thought was there, buried underneath a load of second thoughts. I glanced back at her and traced the simple curve of her cheek with a piece of dark hair laying on top of it. I felt my sham of a heart beat faster with my eyes on her. It sent me into a panicked frenzy, thinking I actually could go on with my life without giving it my all to become a better man for her. I wasn't sure how, or if it was possible, but I had to try. Right?

I quickly looked back at my phone, and my shoulders relaxed when Tony's name popped up at the top. *Finally*.

Tony: I'm here. I have news.

Me: Where the fuck have you been?

Tony: Don't tell me you started to worry about me. That doesn't sound like the Tobias I know.

My thoughts started to spin as I watched the bubble pop up. I looked back at Sloane, and she had started to stir a little, but I quickly put my back to her, anxious to see what Tony had to say.

"Hi." I couldn't help but smile when I heard her sleepy voice.

My phone vibrated again, but I couldn't *not* look back at her. "You're beautiful when you sleep."

Her cheeks brightened, and I felt mine get hot, too. *Where did that come from?* Apparently, I was full of all kinds of truths lately.

"And when I'm awake?" she asked, sitting up and letting her legs dangle. I turned around because she was still naked from whatever you'd call what we did hours ago. It wasn't fucking, that was for certain.

"Depends on if you're sassing me or not."

Her huff made me chuckle as I looked back down at my phone, forgetting that I was texting with Tony.

Tony: I went offline because there was movement, and I was trying to hunt him down.

Me: Who was it? Are they on the list?

"Do you care if I get a shirt?"

My heart was pounding like I was back in the weight room, punching out my frustrations against the black punching bag. "I'd love nothing more than to see you in my shirt. They're in the closet."

Her bare feet slapped against my floor, and I stood up when Tony texted back, too anxious to sit still and pretend I wasn't concerned with Sloane in the room while I texted with my ol' pal from my previous life that was nothing but the complete opposite of normal.

Tony: I got a lead on Silas Laurant. He is going under a new name. William Bowden. I have made a connection, but I don't think you're going to like it, man.

"What..."

I turned around at the sound of a paper being ripped. The crinkling pulled me out of the stupor I was in with Tony's text, and when I saw Sloane standing right outside my closet, wearing one of my black shirts, holding a piece of paper, I froze. The pink hue on her cheeks that was there a moment ago had turned into a grayish color. There were suddenly dark bags under her red-rimmed eyes, and I began to move toward her when she stepped backward.

"Are you... Have you..." She stepped back again, hitting my closet door. I dropped my eyes to her shaking hand and watched as the paper fell from her grip. "You've known about them this whole time?"

"What?" I asked, trying to make sense of the clipped words coming from her mouth. The hazel color of her eyes that usually glittered for me was dull, and they became glossy a moment later.

"Did they hire you to come here and watch me?! Is that why you always push me away? How long have you been working for them?"

"What are you ta—"

My phone vibrated in my hand, and the second I saw the message, I wanted to die right there. Pain like no other slammed into me so hard I lost my breath.

Tony: Willow Johnson? I looked into her, and she is Silas Laurant's half-sister (otherwise known as William Bowden). He's on the move, and that's how I

found the connection. He contacted her two nights ago, and I traced it back.

Oh shit. No. No. No. No.

Sloane's mouth was still moving, but I had turned off every rational sense and stood paralyzed as she came over and hit my chest. *Fuck.* Every last worry and concern I had with Sloane being involved with me came crashing down around us.

"How long have you been working for them?" Her shouts turned to sobs, and it killed me to see her like that. My knees buckled, and I wanted to reach out in the worst way and grab her hands and pull her into my chest. "Why are their names written on this paper above Silas?"

Sloane hastily bent down, her dark hair a wild mess surrounding her panicked face. The paper was thrust into my chest, and I grabbed it before it fell again. I stayed quiet, compartmentalizing everything that just came to light as Sloane yelled at me in between taking gulps of air. I zeroed in on Silas' name and winced internally at the two names above it: *Governor Derek McCann and Beatrice McCann.* Sloane wasn't even upset with me for the truth. Silas' name was under theirs because they had hired me to kill him, and I let him get away.

Fuck.

I laid the paper on my desk and continued to sort through the shitstorm that was occurring around me. I centered on Sloane's broken spirit from across the room. I was right about one thing: my black t-shirt looked damn good on her. It was devastating to know I would never see her in it again.

"You and your parents have different last names," I stated, nearly suffocating on the evenness of my voice when, on the inside, I was completely obliterated.

"Like you don't already know that!" Her sarcastic laugh was cut short by the trembling of her lip, and if I didn't know she would be better off without me—especially now—I would have run over there and scooped her up in my arms.

I hated myself now more than I ever had in the past.

Somehow, hurting Sloane hurt me worse than anything Richard ever made me do.

"They gave you a new last name when they shipped you away."

The pieces were coming together like pen on paper. It wasn't hard to write out the history. Sloane thought I was still working for her parents, but she had it wrong. I'd been trying to clean up their mess from the moment they secured a contract with Richard and ordered me to kill Benedict and Amy Johnson—along with Benedict's son, Silas.

Except, Silas Laurant was after the wrong person.

His target should have been me.

CHAPTER THIRTY-FIVE

SLOANE

Hate was a strong emotion—maybe one of *the* strongest emotions—and that was what I felt while looking at Tobias across the room with his nonchalant, nothing-bothers-me face on.

He shut down. Emotions were void, and if I didn't see the occasional tick in his eye when he watched the tears slip down my cheeks, I would have thought it was all one big lie. One big show to get me closer so he could watch me and report back to my parents.

"Answer me," I demanded, rushing over to my skirt and pulling it on within seconds. I hated that I had his shirt on, but I was too desperate and devastated to take it off and leave it on the floor. My heart was broken. I could feel the jagged pieces cutting me up on the inside, and I wasn't ready to let him go, even though this revelation was making me do it anyway. "Have you known this whole time? Is that why you've been pulling me in and then pushing me away? Are you reporting back to them? Do they know that I'm being stalked?"

Silence exploded around us, and the only thing I could hear was the fast beating of my heart. The quiet was like a bomb of pain going off around me, and I shut my eyes so I didn't have to see the blank stare on his face.

"Go back to your room."

His curt demand was a knife in my back. I was bleeding on the inside. Confusion swept me up in a tornado of emotions, and after taking a step away from him, I felt raw. My phone vibrated in my pocket, and Tobias' eyes flared. I pulled it out and saw that it was my parents calling, and I chucked it over to him with as much force as I could. He caught it with a gruff wince when I said, "They probably want to talk to you anyway."

His door hit the wall as I ripped it open and rushed down the boys' hall. I left everything in his room. My phone, bra, shirt, and, unfortunately, my pride. Another tear escaped my eye. I had told myself that the heartbreak that came with Tobias would be worth it, but now that my heart was bleeding, I wasn't sure it was.

An angry sob crawled out of my chest, and I knew there was no way I could face Gemma. My fast walk turned into a jog, and when I found myself at the library, I slowly opened the door and crept inside, keeping my head down and face shielded.

My back rested against the spines of several books, way back in the corner where the spiders liked to live, and I sank down to my butt, contemplating every decision I had made in the last two months.

What was I thinking? Getting involved with someone like him? He was destined to break my heart the very second our eyes crashed. My soul twisted, my heart jolted, and my blood spiked with something dangerously potent. I should have known better. I did know better. I just didn't fucking care.

"Hey, you okay?"

My head jerked upward, and I caught two brown eyes peering down at me through black-rimmed glasses. I recognized him. He was an underclassman who hung with the nerdy crowd.

"I'm fine."

"You don't look fine. You're crying."

I shot him a dirty look when he sat beside me, putting his hands beside him, mere inches from me. I had my arms crossed over my chest that was sporting tiny wet droplets from my eyes.

"Girls cry," I whispered, turning away. "We usually like to be left alone when doing so."

He chuckled, and it sounded gruffer than he appeared. I peeked over at him, and although he was an underclassman and didn't have those dark features and bad-boy eyes—unlike Tobias—there was something mature about him. Maybe it was the scruff along his edgy jaw or the largeness of his hands.

"Let me guess." He sighed and looked down at me. "He broke your heart." He shrugged. "You just keep getting hurt, huh?"

"What do you mean, 'I just keep getting hurt'?"

His hand landed on my leg, and I jumped, trying to pull away. "Take your hand off me."

The guy ignored me, and instead of moving closer or pulling me to my feet, he lifted up a hip and pulled out a phone that looked like the one my grandmother used to use years ago. I stared at him, and then the phone, and then back to him.

"Call your parents, Sloane."

"Excuse me?"

His stare turned lethal. "I said, call your parents. I've been trying to get you to call your parents for weeks. You're so fucking stubborn. So determined to pretend everything is okay."

I was frozen. My brain was muddled as I tried to make sense of what was happening. His grip on my leg grew firm, and when I tried to pull away, he gripped me even harder.

"I see that you're royally confused, so let me lay it out for you." His back hit the bookshelves, and his next words sent my world into a spiral. "The first thing you need to understand is that I can hurt Willow with a snap of my fingers. All those internet searches you've done on her... Well, newsflash: she's no longer safe with her adorable little foster family. I have someone that can rip her from their home in seconds."

My determination was a wave that came crashing down with every word that came from his mouth. Air was trapped in my lungs, and his hand on my leg burned like a rope pulling me taut.

His whisper coaxed me into submission, and I nodded when he said, "So, don't scream or make a fuss. Hear me out, Sloane. But not here. Let's go."

His fingers dug into my skin so hard I winced. I was on my feet next, trailing behind him through the library until we rushed to the doors. The library was near empty, and I knew that Tobias was still in his room, stewing over our fight. So, I was alone. I was alone with someone who was clearly unstable and got off on scaring vulnerable girls like me.

The cool night air hit my legs when we made it through the double doors on the side of the school without anyone so much as glancing in our direction. This guy had a way of blending in, which was alarming, to say the least. *Has he been watching me this whole time?*

"Who are you?" I finally asked as we headed for the forest. My stomach clenched each time I stepped over a log or stick, and I wanted to peer back and look at the school in the worst way. I hoped that Tobias was looking out his window and could see me being pulled into the dark.

The guy in front of me stopped so abruptly that I ran into his backside, hitting my lip off his hard back. He spun around and looked me dead in the eye. "It makes sense that you wouldn't know what I look like. We've never met."

My eyes squinted, and I ran my tongue over my teeth, tasting the blood from hitting my mouth on his back. The longer I stared at him, the more visible he appeared in the dark. The moon was above our heads, and we were surrounded by the scent of pine and cool spring air.

"Silas?" I questioned, taking a step back when he let go of my hand.

He smiled, and it was charming—too charming. "Bingo, baby. I've been right under your nose the whole time." He shook his head and placed his hands in his pockets. I stepped back, and a twig broke beneath my shoe. His eyebrow raised. "Don't do it. I will chase you, and I'm faster. Then, I'll have to tie you up, and I really don't want to."

"What do you want?" My voice was on the verge of shaking, but I squared my shoulders and crossed my arms over my chest.

"For you to call your parents. That's all I've wanted from the moment I started the calls." He threw his head back and looked up at the stars, chuckling. "You are so determined not to call them. I honestly couldn't believe it. Especially after the dead animal and the photo? Why wouldn't you tell them what's going on?"

"You've been the one tormenting me? Why?"

His laughter faded, and he suddenly grew serious. "Because I can't get them alone without their security. If they come here to get you because of everything that's been going on, they'll be quiet about it and come alone. After all, no one is supposed to know where you are, right? They don't want the press to know anything about you. Isn't that why they sent you here? To make you disappear?"

A chill ransacked my thoughts, and I tried my hardest to ignore the racing of my heart. "You've been trying to get me to break so I would have my parents come get me...so *you* could get to them?"

"Yes." He let out a loud, exasperated sigh, as if I was stupid for not catching on.

"Why do you want them alone?"

He flashed me a pretty smile, and my stomach was riding a wave. I wanted to step back, but I wasn't stupid. Running from a guy like him wouldn't be in my best interest. He'd catch me, and right now, although he was spewing some weird shit, he wasn't hurting me.

"So I can kill them like they killed my father and step-mother. *Obviously*." He shook his head. "I'm not here to hurt you. Although, I have to admit, it irks me that you've kept it a secret for this long."

Fear came in like a rainstorm, and although I'd always thought I'd choose the flight mode when it came to that fight-or-flight instinct, my teeth bared, and I stood my ground. "They threatened Willow," I barked, meeting him halfway. "You think I've been hiding their secret to protect them?"

He paused before taking his glasses off and stomping on them. The crunch was deafening. "Those things have been so fucking annoying since putting them on." The whites of his eyes disappeared as his eyes formed slits. "Anyway, I have to admit, you might have just saved your own life if it came down to it. I appreciate you trying to protect Willow."

"But you're threatening to hurt her if I don't help you?" I countered, trying to get a good read on him.

I knew that Willow had a half-brother, but that was *all* I

knew. In my understanding, he had lived with his mother. Willow hardly spoke to him unless she traveled with her parents to France, where he lived. There was one photo of him in their home, but he was young and had two missing teeth with his backpack slung over his shoulder.

"Just call your fucking parents, Sloane." He held the phone out in between us, but I made no move to take it.

"What are you going to do if they come?" And 'if' was a big component in this entire situation. Who was to say they would even come if I called? I didn't know my parents. I didn't understand their motives or their political agenda. All I knew was that it wasn't too far-fetched to think they wouldn't come, especially if I told them that someone knew their secret.

"Just know that I'll let you go if you do what I say."

That will never fly with Tobias—or the rest of the Rebels.

"Did you drug me at the claiming?"

He sniffed and looked away. "Yes."

"And you put a dead animal on my bed? And you left me a picture of Willow and me in front of my door with her face marked out with a giant red X. Tell me, does she know you're doing this? Does she know that my parents essentially killed her parents?"

"Our," he corrected. "They killed *our* parents. They weren't just hers."

"And you locked me in my closet with Debussy playing on a cassette player. How did you know that song would get to me?"

"Because I know every detail of that night, Sloane. I snuck into your house after I watched someone take my father's and stepmother's bodies out in body bags and stared at the blood on the floor. Then, I disappeared before someone came to kill me, too."

He thrust his phone at me again, and I took a step back. "I don't trust you."

"You don't have to. Call them, tell them to come to the school and pick you up because someone knows their dirty fucking secret and that they're coming after you. They'll come, and I'll take care of them. Then, you and Willow can live happily ever after in your own little lives."

The phone lingered in between us like a lifeline. My conscience was in limbo, and I was teetering on a tightrope, wondering which direction to go that wouldn't kill me in the end. I wanted to hate my parents, and maybe I did a little. But did I want to be held responsible for killing them? Or not stopping it when I knew I could have? That would make me just as bad, and if they had taught me anything, it was how *not* to be by doing the exact opposite of what they'd do.

"Time's ticking. Call them."

My eyes flashed to Silas', and I wished I could have preyed on his vulnerabilities and weaknesses like he had done to me for the last month. Instead, I geared up for a fight and said, "No."

Then, I turned and ran with the hope that he'd follow and end up in the hands of Tobias because wasn't he at St. Mary's to watch me anyway?

CHAPTER THIRTY-SIX

TOBIAS

My room seemed smaller and smaller with each stride I took. My hands ran through my hair, and I gripped the back of my neck. I breathed in and out of my nose, trying to find a way out of the mess I was in. My natural reaction was to hunt Silas down and kill him, but then Sloane popped in my head, and I hesitated.

I wanted to chase after her, but I knew better than to do so. That was an impulsive decision and one that would only make things worse. I could have very easily told her the truth, but would it matter in the end? She still would end up hating me, maybe even more. Sloane was strong, and her heart was big. It may hurt at the moment, but she would eventually get over me and move on with her life. And in the back of her mind, I knew there was a little voice that was telling her she was better off. It was in the back of mine, too.

I gripped my doorknob with Sloane's phone in my hand and ripped open my door. I paused at the sight of my sister coming out of Isaiah's room, and she gave me a strange look before walking over to me. *Fuck. Here it comes.*

"Where's Sloane?"

"In her room probably." I handed her Sloane's phone and kept on walking. "She'll be fine, Gem."

"What do you mean, 'She'll be fine'?"

Sloane would be fine, but would I?

Tony texted as I rounded the stairs and hopped down each one with more effort than I was used to. My feet were heavy, and my legs were Jell-O. The tightness in my chest didn't go unnoticed either.

Tony: Here is his location. He's in your neck of the woods. Better find that gal of yours. He seems to have some sort of infatuation with her.

I tucked my phone in my pocket, already suspecting that Silas was near. Needing to act fast, I walked right to my father's office and put aside my differences and doubts when it came to him and knocked on the thick wood.

"Come in." The door creaked as I pushed it open, and my father's browline deepened when he saw me standing there.

"Tobias?" There was a flicker of surprise in his tone, which made sense, considering I avoided him more times than not. "What's wrong?"

I took a deep breath after shutting the door behind me. The veins on my hands were pumping blood to every outlet they could find, and the anger and resentment caught up to me. My voice was shaky, and for the first time, my father was seeing the real me, instead of the blank, cold front that I put up every time he got close.

"I need your help."

He slowly sat back down at his desk and placed his hands on the dark wood. His worried gaze was set right on me. "I'm here. What can I do?"

"It's catching up to me." It was painful to recognize the

past with him looking at me like that. It was painful to recognize it with anyone, but especially someone that wasn't going to judge me, because that's one thing that my father didn't do. He didn't judge. He listened, and up until now, I resented him for that. I wanted him to hate me as much as I hated myself, but he had proved me wrong time and time again, and now it was the moment of truth. He was about to see who I was and just how fucked up I was from being raised by the man who killed my mother.

"Explain," he urged. "What can I do?"

"You know how I was finishing business before I came here?"

That was another thing about my father: the easygoing headmaster of St. Mary's knew of my past, and he *still* wanted to help me.

"Yes. The people that knew of you and what you did."

"They weren't all taken care of, and one has popped up."

"Okay, well..."

I held up my hand, beginning to pace back and forth. "I'm not done."

"Does this have something to do with Sloane?" I paused and snapped my head over to him. He shrugged. "Your sister told me that someone was stalking her. I've been watching the few cameras the SMC allowed me to put up. I haven't seen anything. So, go on," he urged.

I hesitated, not wanting to say it out loud because fuck, it was bad. It was truly fucking bad. "Sloane's parents ordered a hit on their close friends. Something to do with politics. Or maybe it was just to save their own asses. I'm not sure, and it doesn't matter. But they sent Sloane here because she said she was going to tell the police what had happened. They threatened her and told her that her best friend, Willow—the daughter of the couple—would have to die, too, if she found out. So, in order to protect their secret, they sent Sloane here, changed her last name, and forbade her to talk to Willow."

"And someone is stalking her because of that? Who? The best friend?"

My words came out like sharp pieces of glass, and I choked on every single one. "I was the one to do it. I killed them." I dropped my head when I sat in the seat in front of his desk. My hands came up, and I gripped onto my tight shoulders. I hissed between my teeth. *Shitty decisions had a way of coming around to bite the fuck out of you.*

"*Jesus.* What?"

"It was me." I pushed the confession out like I was in the confession box that Richard used to drag Gemma and me to when we were younger to confess his wicked sins. Gemma and I would run up and down the aisles of the Catholic church, too young to understand what our life was going to turn out like with him as our main proprietor. "I did it. They hired me through Richard. It was one of my first kills. I remember it because there were supposed to be three targets, but there were only two. Richard went with me and waited outside to make sure I went through with it. I remember a scream. It was her. It was Sloane. She was the one screaming as I left the house."

I left out the part where I threw up in the bushes on my way out and was haunted by her scream for many nights afterward. I'm thankful I forced myself to continue moving through the house with ease and that I didn't look back, because if she would have seen my face, then I never would have gotten to experience what it felt like to be truly happy for the first time in my life. I never would have been able to feel my heart stumble like it did when she was in my sight.

"Does she know?"

"No. She found the list in my closet. The one with the names of the people that are still out there. She thinks that her parents hired me to watch over her, and that's why I agreed to come to St. Mary's. I didn't correct her. She ran out of my room, and I'm assuming she and Gemma are planning my death as I speak."

There was a knock on my father's door, and I quickly stood up. My father rounded the desk and opened it, and my sister walked in with her glare on me. "She isn't in our room. She isn't in the library. Cade and Journey said they can't find her either!" She smacked my chest, but I didn't feel it. "What did you do, Tobias?!" Her breath was warm against my chest as she stepped away, placing her hands on her hips while still holding Sloane's phone.

I couldn't face her as my father filled her in, and at some point, Isaiah had walked in, too. My heart pounded, and the titles on the books lining the shelves blurred together as I stood and stared at them. The room faded away as I rested my forehead against the leather spines, going down every route to figure this out and fix it.

Not for me, but for her.

If there was ever a moment where I chose to have morals, it was this one. If I died trying, then at least I did one good thing in my life.

I turned around quickly and held out my hand to my sister. "Give me her phone."

A moment later, the ringing echoed around everyone in my father's office when I put it on speaker. Sloane's mother answered, and there was a sick feeling growing more evident the longer Sloane was missing.

Shiner walked in the office mid-"Sloane?" from her mother and looked directly at the phone in my hand.

"Not Sloane. Try again," I seethed, bypassing a simple hello. There was a loud shuffling on the other end of the line, and I was certain she was signaling to her husband to rush over to the phone.

"Who is this?"

"Do you remember that time you used Richard Stallard's services and hired a hitman to fix your problem with the Johnsons?" The word *problem* left a sour taste in my mouth.

Silence filled the room, and I continued on.

"Sending Sloane away to protect her didn't work. I assume you were protecting her. Or maybe it's true and you were actually just saving your own asses."

"Who is this? Silas?" I expected to hear more panic on their end, but the fact that her mother's voice remained neutral sent me straight to the red.

"It's Tobias, the one who you hired. Shit has caught up to you, I'm afraid. Silas is back, and he wants something. I'm assuming it's you two." Or me. Maybe he'd take me in exchange for Sloane? "He has Sloane. He's been stalking her for months."

"That isn't true. She would have told us that."

"No, she wouldn't. She doesn't trust you," I replied. "And can you blame her? You literally hired someone to kill her best friend's parents and then sent her away to protect yourselves."

Her father's voice cut through, and it was smooth and calm, just like his wife's. "That isn't true. We sent her away to protect her."

I laughed. "Then, I suggest you get here because Silas has her, and if you don't show up to admit to your faults, I'm afraid of what'll happen to your daughter. Have you ever heard of revenge?"

More silence, and I locked onto everyone's faces in the office. My father stood with his hand over his mouth and one arm crossed over his chest. I was absolutely certain he was regretting the moment he had impregnated my mother, because this was likely something he didn't sign up for. My sister was pressed against Isaiah with tears in her eyes, and

Shiner glared at the phone like he wanted to dive inside and strangle Sloane's parents, just like me.

"Silas has her, or you have her? What are you doing at St. Mary's with my daughter's phone?"

"Does it matter?!" Gemma stepped forward, and Isaiah quickly pulled her back, putting his hand over her mouth. He and I locked eyes, and we were on the same page. The more people who knew about Sloane's parents and what they'd done, the more danger everyone was in.

I wasn't the only hitman in the United States. There were plenty of Tobias Richardsons running around gun-happy. Richard made sure of that. I wouldn't be surprised if he wasn't still calling shots from his prison cell.

"I'm not playing games. Get your asses on a plane and get here. Fix your fucking mistake, Governor."

There was faint whispering that I couldn't make out from the phone, and Sloane's mother's voice rubbed me wrong in every way possible when she finally spoke. "You pulled the trigger. You fix *your* mistake."

The line went dead, and everyone in the room was quiet. I blinked once, then twice, and then I took the phone and threw it against the wall, mere inches from Shiner's head. It crashed to the floor, and I turned around and gripped the bookshelf, knowing that I was going to fix this, no matter the cost. As long as Sloane was fine, everything will work out just the way it was meant to.

CHAPTER THIRTY-SEVEN

SLOANE

HOURS AGO, I thought I would die from a broken heart by Tobias, but here I was, tied up with two beady eyes staring at me with sweat dripping from his forehead, likely seconds from killing me.

"It doesn't have to be like this, Sloane."

"Like what?" I asked, spitting out the blood filling my mouth. "You think I'm going to call my parents if you hurt me enough? Why don't you just call them yourself? What do I have to do with any of this?"

He threw his head back and laughed. His broad shoulders shook, and I saw no resemblance to Willow anywhere in his features. Not his eyes, smile, nothing. There were no similarities. I wasn't sure if he took after his mother, but it seemed that my best friend got all the good features, whereas he got...none.

"And have them bring all their shady security with them? They need to come get you without the press on standby and without their right-hand man. I need them alone and unaware of my plans. Otherwise, I would have killed them long ago or taken you and kept you hostage."

"Don't you find it unjust that you're killing my parents because they killed yours? Whatever happened to the saying 'two wrongs don't make a right'?" I swallowed my fear. "You know I was there that night, right?"

"Yes."

"So, you know that I was devastated when I found your parents. Did you know that they locked me in my room afterward because I was threatening to call the police? Did you know that?" I was beginning to grow agitated and beyond frustrated that *I* was being punished for something *they* did.

The sharpness of his tone made the hairs on the back of my neck stand erect. "So you should hate them just as much as I do. They ruined my life! Not only did your parents order the hit on my parents, but they ordered it on me, too."

I ran my tongue over my teeth, cleaning the blood off them from my fall before he caught me. "Why did they order it on you?"

His sharp glare made my stomach feel like a hollow hole. "Because I knew too much. I was present for *many* conversations my father had on the topic, and your parents knew that I was going to be a political fixer, alongside my father. Except, when my father found out just how deep their "upsets" went and how they went about 'fixing' things on their own instead of using the politically correct route— what he and my stepmother were hired to do—they ended up the same way." A chilling feeling hit the air around us. "Dead."

Pressing up against the bark of the tree, I held my breath when Silas moved closer. "I faked my birth certificate and transcripts when I realized you went to school here and that there was no other way to get your parents alone. You were the key, and although it took some time to find you, I eventually did." He shrugged, looking somewhat remorseful as his gaze scanned the trees across from us.

"And what do you plan on doing to them if you get the chance?" My wrists burned with the rope tied around them. My fingers spread, and I winced, making a fist again.

"First, I'm going to figure out if there is still a hit on me." He gave me a side eye. "*Obviously*. And then..." He crowded my space, and I turned my head, trying to get as far away from him as possible. "I'm going to kill them."

What was the end game here? What was I supposed to do? Try to talk him off the ledge and hope that he came to his senses before dawn and realized he had to do something with me before someone came looking? Or did I give in and call my parents? Willow's face crossed my mind, and I had my doubts that he would hurt her. They were related, after all. Would he actually do that? To get me to bend? It was a good tactic, and it was obvious that he liked to prey on my vulnerabilities.

"Do you wanna watch?" Silas' mouth curved, and unsettling thoughts were bullets fired off in the back of my mind. When his finger ran down the side of my face, I *almost* kneed him in the balls, but suddenly, a sound caught my ears from the forest, and we both paused. "Did that brooding ol' boyfriend of yours come to visit?"

I didn't correct him that Tobias wasn't my boyfriend and never was. Instead, I listened to the direction of the ground moving and hoped he *was* here to save me. The last thing I wanted to be was a damsel in distress, but here we were.

"The word 'boyfriend' seems childish for what Sloane means to me." The small hope that lingered before burned so hot that I felt like it would burn the rope right from my wrists. Tobias appeared like a knight in shining armor, and although he had once told me he'd never be such a thing, I begged to differ. Tall, dark, and dangerously handsome, with his shoulders square and his face calm, Tobias crept farther into the open area between the pine trees, and I sagged in relief. I winced at the reminder of earlier and the betrayal I had felt knowing he had lied to me, but that didn't matter now.

"Well, that's sickeningly sweet," Silas said, blocking me from Tobias' line of sight. If Tobias moved to the right, so did Silas. When he stepped to the left, Silas did, too. I finally caught his eye over Silas' head, and the deadliness that covered the curves of his face was evident even from several yards away. The ticking of his jaw told me he was beyond angry.

"Untie her."

Silas looked back at me and winked. "Not until she calls her parents. I have to settle something with them. She's very stubborn." He hitched his thumb back to me, and Tobias shook his head.

"They're not coming. I already called them."

He did?

Tobias crept farther into the open area, his black boots breaking every blade of grass, dead leaf, and twig underneath his weight. "After I informed them who was after their daughter, I told them they needed to come fix their mess." His voice dropped slightly, but I strained my ears to hear. "And they said no. They told *me* to fix it."

My parents said no?

Why did that hurt me so much?

My head drooped, and disappointment slid down my throat and suffocated me until I was brought back to the present with Tobias and Silas' conversation.

"They did, did they? Why would they have *you* fix it? They don't even know you." Silas laughed.

"They do know him," I whispered, feeling a pang of hurt from earlier.

"Oh, that's right. You don't know." Silas was only a few feet away from me as Tobias continued to creep toward him. Or maybe he was creeping toward me. "Sloane's correct. Her parents know me, but not for the reason she thinks."

"What does that mean?" I asked, forgetting that Silas was even a part of this equation until he spoke up.

"Yes, I'd like to know that as well."

"I'm the one you should be hunting, Silas. I'm the one who did it. I pulled the trigger that night."

My entire body went numb. If the rope around my wrists wasn't holding me up, I would have fallen to the ground.

I shut my eyes as my mind traveled back to five years ago. I remember the slippery feel of the blood under my shoes as I dove forward after the killer. A black hood was pulled up over their head as they walked out of the room like nothing had ever happened.

"It was you?" I felt the tears on my cheeks, and my lip trembled as I tried to hide the emotion.

Tobias pulled his attention away from me, but I saw the pure, tangible regret covering his features, and it blinded me so quickly I forgot where I was.

His voice grew more lethal the longer he stood in front of Silas. My back was against the tree, but I could no longer feel the bark scratching me or the ropes burning my wrists.

"It was me, Silas. I'm the one who killed Ben and Amy, and I'm the one who let you get away. You're *very* good at hiding."

Silas' hands bundled at his sides, but Tobias continued to creep toward him. Silas could have had a gun pointed at him, and I don't think he would have stopped.

"When I called Sloane's parents, do you know what they meant by telling me to 'fix' it?" Another step and I shrieked when Tobias darted forward and grabbed Silas by the throat and threw him to the ground without any effort at all. Loose dirt flew up and surrounded them like a cloud, and Silas clawed at Tobias' hand like he was a wild animal let out of the cage for the first time.

My hands were released, and I stumbled forward, looking behind me to see Shiner standing there with his dark gaze set on Silas like he was ready to kill him. "You okay?" he asked, watching Silas struggle underneath Tobias' weight. "Let's go."

"No!" I ripped my hand out of Shiner's and took a step closer to Tobias and Silas. I was panicky, and anxiety made my vision blurry as I tried to lock onto the guy I felt the safest with taking the breath from someone, as he has done so many times. "Tobias!"

"Do you know who I am? Do you understand that I have been trained to kill and hide the body?"

Silas smacked Tobias' arm as he tried to pull it away from his throat. I breathed right along with Silas as he let up a little. Shiner grabbed me around my waist and began pulling me back again, but I pushed him off.

"Take her back to the school." Tobias didn't look at Shiner or me when he gave the demand.

Shiner began tugging at me again as Tobias got off Silas and pulled him to his feet. He took a step away and cracked his neck, preparing for something big. I could feel it in the air. Goosebumps littered my skin, and when Shiner barked at me to stop pushing his hands away, I whipped around and looked him dead in the eye. "I will not let him be that person again. For me or my parents. *No*, Nash."

"So, what'll it be, Silas? Do I need to kill you, too?" Tobias' chuckle was painful, and I hurt knowing that he was trying his hardest to disassociate himself from the person his uncle made him into. I could feel it from several feet away. I felt it in my very core. *He was trying to do the right thing.* "Because I've gotta say, I'm sick and fucking tired of killing people because I'm told to do so, but I will if I have to. I should kill you just for touching her." He lifted his chin and briefly caught my eye, disappointed that I was still standing there. He sliced his attention over to Shiner but quickly went back to Silas.

"Tobias." His name was an unearthing of what I felt down to my soul. "You *are* good," I reminded him. The moment he laid his eyes on me, I watched something flicker in between the depths of his thoughts. I knew that, for the first time since the very second we touched, he believed my words.

CHAPTER THIRTY-EIGHT

TOBIAS

You are good.

You are good.

You are good.

Her voice was on repeat inside my head, and if she weren't standing here, looking at me with glassy eyes and a face so sweet and encouraging, I might not have been willing to do what I was about to do.

"I'm not good," I reminded her. "But I'm trying. For you."

Silas' step backward made a growl tear through my chest. "What'll it be, Silas? Do I have to kill you? It was life or death for me when it came to your parents, but I really don't want to kill you. It's a choice, and it isn't up to me. It's up to you. Do you want to die?"

"Of course I don't want to fucking die."

Good answer.

Taking a step toward him, he took one back. But I continued forward until he fell on his ass. It wasn't that I was much bigger than him, but there was something that made you more lethal when you held the type of baggage that I held. He knew it, too. "Then go." I clenched my teeth, restraining myself from allowing my buried impulse to recklessly lash out and choke him out for all the shit he put Sloane through. On an antagonistic level, I understood his behavior. It wasn't that he was infatuated with Sloane or wanted her romantically in an obsessive way. He was obsessed with revenge, and he thought she was the key to redemption.

"That's...that's it? You're just going to let me go?" he questioned my demand like he rightfully should have, and I smirked, making him think twice. Sloane's sweet voice came in like a tyrant, and although she thought I was good, I wasn't *that* good.

"Of course not," I said matter-of-factly.

Isaiah, Cade, Brantley, and, to my surprise, Bain came out of the forest, and they were on him like I'd personally wielded them as my tools. They held him in place as I shot toward him, blocking out Sloane. I got close and took his fear and threw it over my shoulder. "If you ever so much as look in her direction again, I will pluck your eyeballs out of their sockets. If you see her on the street fifteen years from now, you turn the fuck around because I'll kill you. This is your one-time, get-out-of-jail-free card, Silas. I don't give a flying fuck what you do to her parents, but she will not be part of this. Neither will I." My fist landed in his stomach, and his breath was stolen from his lungs.

He wheezed moments later and nodded. "Fi–fine."

"I don't think he gets it," Bain snickered, twisting one of his fingers and smiling wildly like he was cut from the same cloth that I was—and maybe he was, considering who his father was.

"I don't either," Isaiah joked. "I've gotta give it to you, Tobias. I know Richard, and if I had spent as much time with him as you, I'd burn the whole world down with anger. You have some real fucking restraint."

"I didn't used to," I whispered, bringing my knee up and colliding it with Silas' junk. He yelled out, and the guys dropped him a moment later, stepping away and letting him roll around in the dirt.

"They have a way of changing us for the better, huh?" Isaiah said under his breath. He flicked his chin up to Sloane, and a bullet shot right to my chest, reminding me that although she had grounded me and reminded me that I wasn't the man my uncle created me to be, I still wasn't good enough for her. Not by a long shot.

Before turning around to deal with the hardship that I created for her long before I'd ever dreamt of making her mine, I looked down at Silas still withering below me. I bent down to his level. "If you ever fuck with Willow or Sloane, you're mine, Silas. Don't forget what I am capable of. My skills go way further than yours."

Then, I stood up, turned around, and set my eyes on her. I surrendered to her wistful stare and felt myself long for a future with her that I knew I couldn't have. Not yet, and maybe not ever.

I walked past her, glancing at her once. She followed shortly after, and the dark that surrounded us was welcomed because I didn't want to see the pain on her face. I knew it would rock my world and possibly set me back months of progress that I had made with her by my side.

When I stopped walking, she stopped, too. The air was unmoving around us, and the crickets stopped chirping, as if they were waiting to hear what I had to say. *This is going to hurt.*

"I'm sorry." I didn't recognize my own voice. What was once gruff and coarse was now subtle and restrained. Emotions that typically sent me into a spiral of anger and undoing were now making me feel stranded. There was a pain that I wasn't used to feeling. It was deeply ingrained, and I could feel the slip on myself. "I didn't know they were your parents. I didn't know I was the one who made your life a living hell since that night, Sloane. I never lied to you." I looked up at the dark sky, focusing on the one star that I could latch onto. "I didn't know we were connected. I had no fucking idea."

"Tobias."

"And I'm sorry that I can't be what you need or want. Not yet. But I'm trying."

My teeth may have been broken by the clenching of my jaw, but I wouldn't have noticed because her warm, slender arms wrapped around my waist, and I broke in half, shattering right there in cutting pieces that landed in the dirt below our feet.

"I'm so proud of you."

Emotion hit the backs of my eyes, and it stung. My hands gripped onto her arms, and she held on tighter, burying her face in my chest like she was trying to attach herself to me physically. What she didn't know was that she had already attached herself to my soul, and she was a brand that I would always wear with pride.

"Do you hear me?" The shakiness of her voice made me grip onto her wet cheeks, wiping away the tears that I could feel running down my face, too. *Fuck.* I couldn't breathe, and it truly felt as if my chest was being ripped to shreds.

"I hear you," I forced out, crushing her to my body again. Her arm came up, and she pushed my head down to rest on her shoulder, and I felt the tether snap in half. I was letting her go because I had to. "If I could love anyone, Sloane White, it would be you."

Her chest rocked against mine, and if I didn't have hope that someday I'd be able to be the man she needed and deserved, I would have wished that Silas had killed me moments ago. It was so easy to fall back into the version of myself that didn't feel emotions and that fed off of the angry, debilitating person I once was, but feeling the pain that came with losing her was worth just as much as feeling the warmth I felt with her in my arms. I'd take anything Sloane gave me, and if it was pain, I'd relish in it.

"You say that like you're saying goodbye."

I pulled back and stared down into her face, feeling the ground beneath my feet shake. "I am."

"No."

"I have to."

She was panicky as she buried her face into my chest, crying harder than I'd ever seen before. *Fuck.* "No, you don't!" she yelled and gripped my sides with all her might. "You're good. You are good, Tobias. Stop pretending you're still the same person you were with Richard whispering in your ear!"

"Sloane, baby." I forced out a breath and squeezed my eyes shut before pulling her away and trying to get her to understand what I was saying. "I know I'm not the same person. I know. I just proved that, but..." I looked in the distance, too hurt to look her in the eye. "But I still need to get myself together. I'm not who I want to be yet, and honestly, I didn't even think that there would ever come a moment in my life that I would want to be anything more than what I was months ago."

Her head shook, but I continued on, "You have to let me go, Sloane."

"I won't. What if Silas comes back?"

Even though we were in deep water, and things were messy as fuck, I couldn't help my grin. "Are you trying to make me go back and kill him?"

A hiccup of a half-laugh, half-cry left her. "I'm going to go find another stalker so you have to stay and protect me."

This time, I threw my head back and laughed, but the moment was short-lived. I leveled her with a look. "Sometimes people are only in your life for a short time, to teach you something. Maybe forever isn't in the cards for us."

"What did I teach you?" she asked.

"That, one day, I might be capable of loving someone." *And that someone would be her.*

She dropped her wobbling chin, but I was quick to put my finger underneath it and raise her watery gaze back to mine. I sealed my mouth over hers and kissed her like my life depended on it because, to be honest, it kind of did, which was exactly why I needed to fix myself before ever trying to fix us.

CHAPTER THIRTY-NINE

Two Months Later

SLOANE

The sun was bright when Gemma, Mercedes, Journey, and I walked through the side doors and to the bleachers overlooking the lacrosse field. The Rebels were down below, helping the headmaster and some faculty members set up the chairs for graduation, and even though there was a giddy feeling deep in my belly at the thought of new beginnings at college, away from the drama that followed us everywhere at St. Mary's, there was a nervous feeling, too.

I peeked over my shoulder and scanned the side of the boarding school, peering up at the windows that I knew faced the boys' hall, wondering if he was looking down at me like I was looking up at him. Tobias had remained a constant in my head, even though we hadn't been alone since that moment in the forest where everything came to light.

There was regret, pain, torment, longing, but also pride. So much pride. When we left to go back to the school that night, his father assessed my wounds and acted more like a father than mine had in the last several years. Headmaster Ellison crushed me to his chest and wrapped me in the biggest fatherly hug that made me feel as if I were actually part of his family. Headmaster Ellison was a father figure to so many—me included.

As for my parents? We talked briefly that night, and I laid it all out in the open, holding back my emotions as I scolded them and begged them to leave me out of their lives. There was silence on their end of the line as I broke in two, wondering why they didn't even try to right their wrongs when Silas had me, but the conversation ended quickly after that, when Tobias took the phone, and Gemma pulled me out of the headmaster's office.

I hadn't talked to them since, but turned out, some serious shit got leaked about my parents, completely unrelated to the murders. But their careers were completely destroyed. Their names were smeared all over the news, and to be honest, it had been kind of fun to watch their life implode in on them from the sidelines. I had a nagging feeling that Tobias had something to do with it, or maybe even Silas, but so far, I'd kept my questions to myself because, after that night in the forest, I knew that Tobias and I were over—at least for now. I didn't want to accept his decision, but after learning of his future plans, I knew I had to.

I had to accept it for him, because although he said he wasn't capable of love, I knew it to be incorrect. He *was* capable of love. He was capable of love the night he let Silas go for me. He was capable of love when he decided that he wanted to go into the military after high school to put his skills from the past to better use. He was willing to work on himself, and if Tobias Richardson deserved anything in the world, it was that he was able to make his own decisions and find happiness.

"You okay?" Gemma nudged my shoulder as Journey and Mercedes laughed at the Rebels trying to work with the faculty on how to set up the chairs for graduation.

"I'm good," I said, turning back and facing the sun that was beginning to set in the distance.

Her hand landed on mine, and she gave it a tight squeeze. "I love you," she reminded me, resting her head on my shoulder. "He does, too. He just doesn't know it yet."

I rested my head on hers, nodding. She laughed against my shoulder when Shiner did a cartwheel in the middle of the lacrosse field and looked up at us, perched on the bleachers. Mercedes took out a piece of paper from her backpack and wrote the number 0 on it and held it up. Journey grabbed it out of her hand and wrote a 1 in front of the 0 and held that up.

Shiner whooped and did another, and Journey held it up again. We all laughed, but mine came to an abrupt stop when I heard a familiar voice. Gemma sat up and spun around, but I kept my back to him, soaking in the way my heart came to life at the way my name rolled off his lips.

"Sloane," he said again, and this time, I slowly turned around and prepared myself for the impact of meeting his eyes. It was always a brutal punch to my chest followed by a soothing caress from a million butterflies. He had a way of making me fall to my knees with a simple breath in my direction. "Can we talk?"

I dropped my gaze down to the bag beside him, and the realization came in and swept me off my feet. *He's leaving.*

My legs were wobbly when I stood, and Gem shot me a soft smile. I counted each set of bleachers as I stepped over them, trying to rid myself of the nerves from being alone with him again, and walked around to where he was standing. I followed his tall frame as he walked farther away from where everyone was sitting.

The heat of the sun disappeared on my skin when he stopped and turned around, locking his blue eyes with mine. "Hey," he rushed out, putting his hands in his pockets and leaning against the metal backing of the bleachers.

"Hi," I croaked. I shook my head and cleared my throat. "Sorry. Hi." I peered down at his bag again and then up to his face. He was scanning every inch of mine, and I felt heat rush to my cheeks.

"It's nice to see I can still make you blush."

"Are you going somewhere?" I asked, knowing very well where he was going.

"I leave for boot camp in the morning. I'm staying at my dad's house tonight." He gestured behind us to the field. "It's just a ceremony. I already have my diploma."

I nodded before crossing my arms over my chest. I could feel the beating of my heart against my arm, and I hoped he couldn't see how nervous I was. "I heard you got into UCLA." His hand reached out, and he pushed my shoulder gently, grinning. "Congrats."

He took me by surprise. The withdrawn version of him I'd sensed over the last two months in the halls or in class wasn't present. He seemed relaxed—happy, even. "Thanks," I said timidly.

"Good luck in boot camp." The nerves pushed my words together in one smooshed sentence, and his arms fell in defeat. He gripped the back of his neck tightly, and I stood back, wondering what was happening.

"I couldn't leave without saying goodbye to you, but I didn't realize it would be this difficult."

I blinked. "Why is it difficult? You haven't even looked in my direction for over a month." I wasn't about to tell him that it had been exactly thirty-four days since I met his eye, because that would make me seem desperate.

Tobias let go of his neck, and his long arms fell by his

sides. "I have watched you every single day since that night in the forest, Sloane."

I felt my face fall, and my cheeks burned brightly again.

"The restraint I have had to have was likely enough to get me into heaven despite everything I've done in my past."

I blinked again. My mouth parted, as if my brain was trying to get me to say something, but nothing came out. I took a step back when he pushed off from the bleachers and spun me around by my waist and grabbed my face with his large hand. "It's not fair that I'm about to do this, but this is the last time I'll see you for a while."

His lips landed on mine, and it took not even a second for me to kiss him back. His hand was in my hair as he deepened the kiss, bringing me back to life, as if I were a walking corpse. When he pulled back, the blue in his eyes was bright and healthy and lighter than I had ever seen.

"When I'm ready, I'm coming back for you, Sloane."

He kissed me again, pressing our bodies together so they were flush. When he backed away, I gasped for air. His hands left my face, our bodies were separated, and his last words to me were enough to send me to my grave.

"Live your life. Fall in love, make shitty decisions, drink too much and then regret it the next day, but always remember you're my goddamn sun, and I will fight like hell to find my way back to you. You don't have to wait for me, but I'll always wait for you."

Then, he walked away with my heart in his hands.

EPILOGUE

Three Years Later

SLOANE

Wake up.

Class.

Coffee cart.

Class.

Lunch—aka ramen noodles warmed up in our shitty microwave.

Study.

Class again.

That had been my life every day this semester. There wasn't much time for partying, or girls' nights with my roommates, or even early morning walks of shame that I had given up after my spiral during *the year that must not be named* (freshman year was rough, okay?).

I pushed my hair behind my ear and focused on writing the last few notes down in my notebook that Professor Berkly had rushed out as class ended. There was chatter around me, and Willow's ringtone went off, but I pushed it aside and continued walking while writing—one of my many newfound talents acquired from college.

Yes, you read that correctly: *Willow's* ringtone. Turned out, the stuff that got leaked about my parents three years ago turned into a snowball of gossip, and one of the rumors was about *'numerous murders that Governor McCann and his wife were linked to'*. Of course, there was no concrete evidence, but one year after I left St. Mary's, a random number called me, and I dropped my coffee all over the cobblestone walkway when I heard Willow's voice on the other end. She had put two and two together, and after many conversations and unpacking of our baggage, we were messaging daily, and she was even planning to visit me over spring break.

After sending her a quick voice text that I'd call her later, I tried to recall what Professor Berkly had said when I rushed out of his class. "Wait, what was it again?" I said out loud to myself. Organic Chem was a total mind-fuck, and I kind of hated that St. Mary's was such a breeze to me, because UCLA was not. No one warned you that college was hard, and in order to keep my scholarship, my grades had to be top notch.

"Hey, watch it!" My entire body slammed into something hard, and my notes went flying. I yelped, spinning around quickly and reaching for the stars when I ran into someone else, hitting my face off their hard chest immediately.

"Whoa." A strong hand landed on my bicep, and I looked at my set of notes that was in his other hand. *Thank God.* I breathed out a sigh of relief and pushed my hair the rest of the way out of my face.

"I'm so sorry. Thank you so mu—"

Words died on the end of my tongue, and it had nothing to do with the fact that my notes were saved. I blinked once, and then twice, trying to right my vision and force myself out of the daydream that I had walked right into.

It had been a while since I had imagined Tobias strolling through campus like he was on a mission to find me. But somehow, the more I blinked, the more real he looked.

"To-Tobias?"

His white teeth were visible when he smiled, and if he hadn't been holding onto my arm, I would have fallen down. The chatter of students going to and from classes and the throwing of the football across the courtyard was no longer there. The only two things I could see were the blue sky and the set of eyes that matched it.

"Hey, Snow White. Did you drop this?"

My notes were in his large hand that he put in between us, but I made no move to take them. "How? You're...you're here?" I looked over to the left and saw the UCLA sign along the stone building, yet I was still flustered. *Oh my God.*

"Take your notes before I drop them," he whispered with his other hand still gripping my arm. I quickly took the notes and shoved them into my chem book and followed after him as he pulled me underneath a stone awning. His hand left my arm, and I looked down at it to see if he had somehow left an invisible branding behind. He did three years ago, and no one had been able to erase it since.

"You look different." I was both in awe and surprised. Where he once had longish, inky hair, he now had short, cropped hair that was a little longer on top. The new cut heightened his square jaw, and those ticking muscles were still just as evident as before. His shoulders were somehow broader, and although he had an athletic body our senior year of high school, he was more filled out and defined in places he wasn't before.

After I got a good look in, his hand reached out slowly, hesitantly, as if he were asking for my permission. I gazed up at him with wide eyes, and when his finger lightly touched my cheek and followed a path down to my mouth. "You're more beautiful than I remember."

I bit my tongue to hold back every emotion that was trying to fly out of my soul that I had trapped there years prior. Tobias and I hardly had any contact. I stayed in the loop of his whereabouts from Gem, but I never dared ask too much, too afraid to know anything that would reopen the wounds that were freshly healed.

"Did you get my letter?" he asked, putting his hands in his jean pockets. "And did Willow ever call you?"

I locked onto that tiny scar in his eyebrow and nodded, knowing exactly what letter he was referring to and where it was inside my room. "The one you sent a year ago? Yes, I got it. Wait... Willow? You were the one that gave her my number?"

He smirked. "I'm glad you got my letter. I wasn't sure if you would. I was overseas."

My heart was soaring through my chest so quickly that I wanted to put my hand there to rub the spot. I shifted on my feet, and the excited jitters flowing through my blood made me feel like I had chugged a gallon of vodka before seeing him. "I did."

"This is year three."

I didn't have to ask what he was referring to. I knew exactly how long it had been. We'd spent three years apart, with him in the military, putting better use to the emotions he struggled with in high school. It had been three years of me being at UCLA, working through the trauma that Willow and I endured as my parents drowned in their self-pity.

I remained quiet when Tobias took a step toward me, prowling like he had done so many times in the past. Except, this time, he was different. There wasn't a spark in his eye that was dangerous. Instead, it was hesitant. He was unsure, and so was I.

"Three years away from you, and it's still true, Sloane."

"What is?" I asked, voice no more than a gust of wind traveling through the tight awning, tucked away from everyone else at the college.

When his finger lifted my chin, I peered into his eyes, seeing the past right there in the center. I knew that time had passed—three years, to be exact—but looking into those blue eyes made me feel like no time had passed at all. We were different people now, but so much of my heart was still the same, and it still belonged to him, even now. "Three years apart, and you are still my sun."

"Tobias," I said his name like a shaky leaf ready to fall from a tree branch.

"Let me finish, please."

I nodded, glancing at his mouth for a second before I moved back to his face. "I'm different, and I know you are, too. But I cannot go another moment of my life not being in yours."

My lip wobbled, and I tried to suck it in, pretending that his words didn't send an arrow through my chest. "We don't have to be anything more than friends. We can get to know each other again, but I can't do it anymore. Going away was the best thing for me, but leaving you was the hardest thing I have ever done in my life, and it gets worse with each passing year. You are the first thing I think about when I wake up each morning and the very last thing before I close my eyes at night."

I pressed my head to his chest, surprising him as a huff of air left his mouth. His arms were around me, and the safety net that he secured around my body unknowingly came back down, and I felt complete for the first time since leaving St. Mary's.

"Is that a yes, we can be friends? I only live an hour and a half from here now. I'm stationed in Cali. We don't even have to see each other often, but—"

"Yes," I rushed out, squeezing my arms around his slim torso so tightly I wasn't sure he was able to breathe.

"Yes?" His body sagged with relief, and I smiled against his chest.

I nodded against him, and the tingles from the nerves had long turned into excitement and happiness. Being back in his arms felt like home, and I hadn't realized I'd been homesick until this moment.

I pulled away and peered up at him. His kissable lips lifted, and his grin sent me straight into oblivion. "But you're crazy if you think we can manage being just friends."

Suddenly, his grin dropped, and his tongue darted out to lick his bottom lip. The bad boy inside Tobias Richardson was still in there somewhere, and I couldn't wait to break for him again.

The End

AUTHOR NOTE

Now, listen. Before you get angry with the way I did the ending for this book, hear me out!

Tobias and Sloane aren't your traditional couple. There's baggage—TONS of it. It didn't feel right to end their book with a happily ever after right after every thing came to light. I always try my hardest to stay true to the characters and in my opinion, Tobias really needed to work on himself and his trauma before he could ever truly make things work with Sloane. That's why I put a gap of time in between their relationship at St. Mary's and the future. They get their happily ever after and there is a bonus epilogue available!

You can find it here:
https://dl.bookfunnel.com/gzv6n6p7yx

Make sure to join my newsletter so you don't miss out on SJ Sylvis news and stay tuned for more of our favorite St. Mary's characters!

ALSO BY SJ SYLVIS

English Prep Series

All the Little Lies

All the Little Secrets

All the Little Truths

St. Mary's Series

Good Girls Never Rise

Bad Boys Never Fall

Dead Girls Never Talk

Heartless Boys Never Kiss

Standalones

Three Summers

Yours Truly, Cammie

Chasing Ivy

Falling for Fallon

Truth

You can find all books on Amazon or at sjsylvis.com

ABOUT THE AUTHOR

S.J. Sylvis is an Amazon top 50 and USA Today bestselling author who is best known for her angsty new adult romances. She currently resides in Arizona with her husband, two small kiddos, and dog. She is obsessed with coffee, becomes easily attached to fictional characters, and spends most of her evenings buried in a book!

sjsylvis.com

ACKNOWLEDGMENTS

As always, I have to mention my family first because they are the reason I work so hard and chose to chase my dreams of becoming a full-time author. <3 Thank you for always supporting me and for making me laugh every single day.

To my close author friends (you know who you are), thank you for being the support system I never knew I needed until I had it. You are encouraging, calming (I love our rants), kind, hilarious.. and I could go on forever. I love you all so much and am so thankful I have met you (even if I haven't met all of you in person, ha!)

To my wonderful alpha, Lil. I have no idea where I would be without you! You're not just the best alpha but the best friend, too. I love you and can't wait to leave you ten minute voice messages about my next book.

To my betas (Danah, Emma, & Erica), thank you so much for your speedy reading (I swear I'll give you more time with the next book) and for all your help. My books are so much better with your feedback!

Jenn, my editor— as always, thank you so incredibly much for being an amazing editor! You are so understanding when I give you several "dates" and push my deadline! Thanks for being you!

To my proofer/PA, Mary. Where would I be without you?! Probably somewhere in a messy room, trying to get a schedule organized.... LOL. Thank you so much for being a wonderful friend and for always picking up my slack!

Last but not least—thank you to all the readers, PR companies (wordsmith and give me books!), bloggers, etc., who help spread the word about my books. Whether you picked my book up, wrote a glamorous 5 star review and/or posted it everywhere you could think of, I am thankful for YOU!